THE GIRL IN LIFEBOAT SIX

ELIZA GRAHAM

Storm
PUBLISHING

Ebook ISBN: 978-1-80508-100-5
Paperback ISBN: 978-1-80508-101-2

Cover design: Sarah Whittaker
Cover images: Arcangel, Shutterstock

Published by Storm Publishing.
For further information, visit:
www.stormpublishing.co

For Christina Skarbek McCullagh

PART 1

ONE

An imposter. That's what she was. Walking through *The Lucknow's* foyer was like returning to the lost pre-war world of brightness and comfort. Romilly wanted to laugh: this liner couldn't be real? And if it was real, someone like her certainly didn't belong onboard.

From the foyer, a grand staircase splitting into left and right flights rose to a painted and moulded plaster dome high above Romilly. Galleries on each side opened to what Mrs Dekker called the better class of cabin at the ship's fore. Framed by white pillars, painted murals of palm trees and orchids spread across the walls. The scent of lilies from the huge vases at each side of the grand staircase wafted around the passengers. It was like a film set: audacious, almost tasteless when they were leaving poor smashed-up Liverpool and London. Even the gilt doors of the lift to one side of the staircase looked like something from a different world.

Romilly stretched out a hand to touch the petal of one of the lilies. Mrs Dekker frowned at her. 'You'll get pollen on your clothes.' Her accent was a mixture of American and middle-European. A few heads turned to stare at them.

Romilly drew her hand away but resolved to touch the lilies again when her employer wasn't with her. Comfort and brightness was what she craved in her new life. Romilly Brooks was going to squeeze every moment of material comfort from this voyage. Beside her, eight-year-old Freddie, her charge for the journey to New York, whistled. 'This isn't half-bad.' He sounded almost enthusiastic.

'Probably more comfortable than the place you were living in.' His grandmother pursed her lips. 'Cleaner, too, perhaps.'

Freddie looked away.

'Your luggage will be taken straight to your cabins, madam,' a steward told Mrs Dekker. Like most of the crew, he was a Lascar, an Indian seaman, probably displaced from his usual voyages in balmier parts of the world by war. 'In the meantime, perhaps you would like to go up to the promenade deck to see the casting-off?'

Mrs Dekker shrugged. 'Why not? The fresh air will be pleasant after that abominable train. Smoky would like it.' She glanced down at the small white dog in her arms.

They followed him up the righthand flight of the staircase, through a door off the gallery and out on to the promenade deck. When the Lascar steward left them, Romilly gazed down at the people calling up to their loved ones from the quay. Their party of three had nobody to wave them farewell. No one would watch the ship cast off and feel a pang for Romilly. Neither would anyone be counting the days until she arrived at her destination.

'We're so high up. They look tiny down there.' Freddie hadn't spoken much and Romilly turned to him.

'Do you feel giddy?' she asked. The smile she put on reminded her she was out of practice at smiling.

He sniffed. 'This isn't as good as going up the Monument in London. You can see all the city from there.'

'In New York there are scores of buildings taller than

anything in London,' his grandmother told him. 'I will take you to the Empire State Building, Friedi.' His mouth tightened as she pronounced his name in a middle-European way.

Romilly wasn't paying attention to Mrs Dekker and Freddie anymore. She pushed her way to the railings, counting the seconds until the lines were cast off and the tugs pulled the liner out into the Mersey. She resisted the urge to glance yet again at her wristwatch. They were running late: something about rough seas off the coast of Donegal holding back their departure.

A group of children lined up beside her, carrying small Union flags. Perhaps this meant they were about to cast off. A shiver of anticipation passed down Romilly's spine. She was leaving battered, grimy England behind: the bombs, the ruins, the rations. The shame. Now she could reinvent herself. Her arms prickled with goosebumps. Her cardigan was short sleeved. She'd removed her coat on the train and it would be on its way to the cabin now, along with her suitcase. It was only April: still early in the year for an Atlantic crossing. Romilly probably hadn't packed enough of the right kind of clothes for this voyage, caught up in the rush to meet Mrs Dekker and Freddie at Euston Station, feeling an urgent need to escape. She was nineteen and supposed to be taking care of a child. Time to grow up.

'There you are,' a disapproving voice said. Romilly turned her attention to Mrs Dekker, who'd managed to reach the front of the crowd on the deck, too. Freddie stood beside his grandmother, gazing down at the gangway, an impenetrable expression on his face.

Romilly had tried talking to him on the train, but only received monosyllables in return. As far as Freddie was concerned, she was just one of those wrenching him away from his foster family. Apparently, his real mother, Mrs Dekker's younger daughter, had sent him from Prague to London on a train for Jewish child refugees on Hitler's arrival two years ago.

Freddie's family were Czechoslovakian Jews, but Mrs Dekker herself and her older daughter had lived in New York for some years. From what Romilly had picked up on the train, it seemed Mrs Dekker hadn't even met Freddie until a few days ago.

Poor kid. Romilly would have to find a way of getting through to him. Otherwise, the five days on the ship followed by the rail journey from Montreal to New York would be very tedious for them both. Mrs Dekker had already made it clear that she expected Romilly to supervise her grandson for most of the voyage while she rested in her cabin or, if the weather was warm, sat out on deck. God knows why she'd made the double voyage herself to extract Freddie. She could have paid someone like Romilly to do it all for her and saved herself the effort.

Romilly looked around at the other passengers. A man, late twenties, wide-shouldered, not in uniform, lit a cigarette, gazing thoughtfully at the crowd below on the quay. An older passenger asked for a light and he answered politely in an English accent. Why wasn't he in the services, and what was he going to do in Canada or the United States? As though sensing her questions, he turned towards her. Their eyes met briefly. His expression was hard to read. He nodded and looked away.

'Romilly.' Mrs Dekker's exasperated tone was familiar by now. 'Are we sure those children won't be in cabins near ours?' She'd been demanding on the train, insisting on windows being repeatedly opened and then closed, complaining about the sandwiches from the buffet, telling Freddie off for fidgeting and Romilly for daydreaming. 'They may be rowdy,' she added.

'I think their cabins are further aft, if that's the right term, and the boys are on a lower deck, anyway. That's what I over-heard the steward telling them.' The children themselves, aged from about four to thirteen, looked well behaved: socks pulled up and coats buttoned, hair combed. Some of them had parents waving them off and they waved back, beaming. Romilly swallowed and distracted herself by looking at the children's official escort, a girl of about her own age or possibly a few years older. Her red shoulder-length hair was pinned firmly back against the breeze and she wore spectacles. She was pointing out the elegant white buildings on the waterside: Liverpool's Three Graces, now a little grimier with soot from the fires but still a tribute to the city's maritime history. Romilly pointed them out to Freddie, too. 'That one's the Royal Liver Building and it was the first skyscraper in Europe.'

'What are the other two?' Mrs Dekker asked.

'I don't know,' Romilly admitted. She only knew about the Royal Liver building because she'd overheard someone on the train speculating that the Luftwaffe used it as a landmark for their bombing raids.

Mrs Dekker sighed. Lesson learned, Romilly thought. Only offer information if you know everything on the topic.

Horns blared. The lines were cast. The crowd on the quay burst into the National Anthem. 'Say good-bye to England, everyone.' The redhead had a clear, enunciated voice, earning herself a more approving glance from Mrs Dekker.

'At least that escort is trying to keep them in order.' She clasped her tiny dog closer to her chest. Smoky seemed to be the only living creature with whom Mrs Dekker could relax. Romilly wondered why Freddie couldn't also have joined a children's group for the voyage across the Atlantic – surely it would have been more fun for him?

They appeared to be moving very slowly, the tugs manoeuvring the liner away from the docks seeming too small for the task, but already the people on the quay were growing smaller and smaller, the Three Graces diminishing in size, too. Mrs Dekker's arms were still rigid around the dog, who whined slightly. The tugs pulled them out into the estuary, surprisingly powerful for their small size, before casting them off. The ship's engines rumbled reassuringly somewhere deep below deck as she took command of her own course. A puff of steam blew above their heads. No going back now. The younger children in the escorted group still seemed mostly excited rather than upset at leaving their families. One or two of the older boys and girls stared back towards the receding docks as though imprinting them on their memories. Romilly herself felt an emotion knotting itself up in her stomach that she couldn't define. Perhaps she didn't want to. If you didn't name a feeling maybe it didn't really exist. The trick was to absorb yourself in the details of each moment. Stewards handed out lifeboat and safety instruction cards. Romilly read hers attentively.

The captain had left the bridge to address them and appeared on the deck, clearing his throat. 'Welcome on board, ladies and gentlemen, boys and girls. This evening I'll greet you more hospitably when we dine together. For now, I ask you to read these cards carefully. There will be a drill later on and every day of the five we are on board. Your stewards will tell you your muster points and lifeboat numbers and the route you should take in an emergency. You will see the rest of the convoy members and our naval escort as we convene.'

Some of the audience were already looking around as if anxious to spot the accompanying ships. 'But that will be out in the Irish Sea And finally, you will be expected to carry life-vests with you at all times. At night, you should sleep in them.'

One or two of the adults groaned.

The captain frowned at them. 'No exceptions. It's for your safety and for those of the ship's company who might have to risk their lives for you in the case of an emergency. For the same reasons of safety, we will also be under curfew during the voyage. That's all, thank you.'

Romilly counted the escorted children as they filed away with the redhead and her fellow escorts. There must be a hundred of them. There were also a couple of dozen businessmen, a few with their wives. A handful of passengers spoke in German and what sounded like Dutch – refugees like Freddie, perhaps heading to new homes in Canada and America? All of them would mix for five days in this strange luxurious world. Some of them would be interesting to talk to, if she ever had the chance. Mrs Dekker had made it clear that Freddie would require her attention around the clock. Fair enough, she was paying Romilly what seemed like a generous amount to carry out her duties. All the same, Romilly intended extracting the most from this voyage.

Freddie watched the other children too. 'Can I play with them?'

'You'll be busy with Romilly, catching up on lessons,' his grandmother told him. The boy seemed to slump into himself. 'We should go down to our cabins now,' she added. 'Nothing more to see here.' She looked at the life-vests a steward handed them with distaste. 'And you expect me to sleep wearing that?'

The same Lascar who had shown them up to the deck was waiting for them when they returned to the gallery. He bowed. 'I am Ahmed, madam. Miss. Young sir. I will be looking after you. Please to come this way.' He held open the door leading to the starboard cabins in what must have been the first-class section of the deck under normal circumstances. 'Would you like me to take your little dog down to the kennels, Mrs Dekker?' His voice was mellifluous, his face gentle but he wouldn't miss much, Romilly thought.

'Smoky's staying with me.' Mrs Dekker glared at Ahmed. 'It was all agreed at Liverpool. He couldn't manage a kennels at all.'

The steward nodded, expressionless. 'You have a small balcony, madam, which should assist with the dog's needs.' He led them down the corridor, panelled in wood, its floor carpeted and stopped at a door. 'Your cabin, Mrs Dekker.' He unlocked it and she swept in. Her cases were already laid out for her on the luggage rack. They were expensive looking, initialled *VD*. The double bed was covered in a satin quilt. Ahmed opened the door to the small bathroom. 'And this connects with your room, miss,' he told Romilly, opening another door.

Their cabin was a little smaller than Mrs Dekker's, with twin beds and a handbasin. 'Lavatory and showers are down the corridor that way,' he told them. 'Young sir, there is a playroom on the deck below, just off the foyer. You will find games and a train set.'

Freddie brightened.

'Do you have everything you need, miss?' Ahmed asked.

'Yes, thank you.' Was she supposed to tip the steward? Surely that was for Mrs Dekker to organise. Romilly's purse only contained a few pound notes her uncle had handed to her as a contribution to starting her new life in America, as he'd put it, looking half-relieved and half-guilty.

Ahmed bowed and left them. He'd closed the communicating door between their room and Mrs Dekker's and Romilly felt herself relax. She looked around the cabin, her home for the next few days. It had a proper window, she saw with relief, not just a porthole. She'd had a terror of being shut up in a room below sea level. This cabin didn't have a balcony and was obviously intended for a governess or less fortunate companion to the more important passenger in its connecting cabin.

'No bunks.' Freddie sounded disappointed.

'But look at the little wardrobe. And this desk that pulls out from the wall.' He looked somewhat appeased when she showed him. 'And a new bar of soap, still in its paper.'

He sniffed. Perhaps it was unrealistic to expect a boy of his age to be very excited about soap. She hadn't realised herself how much she took it for granted until it became scarce.

'Which bed would you like?' she asked.

He shrugged.

'Have the one by the window. You'll be able to keep an eye on the naval ships escorting us. Can you still see the docks?' Had the last physical connections with England left them now?

He took a running jump on to the bed. 'Can't see them anymore.'

'Careful.' She gave a warning look at the connecting door. He grimaced. 'And take your shoes off.' With a sigh, he did as she asked, flicking them off so they landed haphazardly between the bed and the desk. Romilly thought of asking him to put them tidily away but decided to leave it, pushing them to one side with her foot instead. 'Shall I unpack your suitcase?' she asked.

'If you want.' There wasn't much in it. A few spare shirts and some underwear. A small flannel bag with his toothbrush and hairbrush in it. A toy rabbit, the fur worn.

'That stays in there,' he said sharply. Romilly nodded. Perhaps the rabbit had come from Prague when he'd left home on the way to the foster family in London. Her own suitcase didn't take long to unpack either. She'd been in a daze when she'd chosen what to take. Her heart sank when she looked at the clothes she'd packed. A velvet dress. A change of skirt. Another day-dress. Two blouses. A pair of slacks. Underwear. Pyjamas and dressing-gown. One spare pair of stockings, darned at the heel by Mama only a few weeks ago, telling her she'd have to make them last – they were becoming impossible to find in the shops. Her dark-green hat. Her navy wool coat, probably too warm for New York in the spring. It looked worn in the light pouring in through the cabin window. She'd worn today's outfit and the coat for her interview with Mrs Dekker in the hotel in Piccadilly.

Her clothes had seemed perfectly adequate that morning when she put them on, but she felt scruffy as soon as she met Mrs Dekker in her tailored oyster cashmere suit and patent leather shoes. Mrs Dekker had silently studied her before firing questions at her about school and her job. 'Will you be able to make the voyage without feeling homesick?' she asked, finally.

'There's nothing for me to feel homesick for,' Romilly said.

'No ties?'

'No ties.' She was still in the stage of numbness where she could say this without feeling emotion.

Mrs Dekker frowned at the letter Romilly had written in response to the advertisement. 'Interesting name, Romilly. I haven't heard it before. Is it English?' Her almond-shaped eyes were sharp.

'It was supposed to be Rose Emily, but the registrar misheard my father when he registered my birth.'

'Your father didn't correct him?'

'He liked Romilly. Even though it's not really a girl's name.'

'Ah.'

Mrs Dekker had asked her if she had any questions.

'What does Freddie like doing?'

'He will do lessons.'

'But when we've finished?'

'That I cannot tell you, Miss Brooks, as I have not yet met him.'

Romilly was convinced she'd failed the interview, but as she stood up to leave, the older woman told her the job was hers. She wasn't sure what it was about her that appealed to Mrs Dekker, who'd already told her that she'd interviewed three other girls that morning. It clearly wasn't just Romilly who was desperate to leave England. Those others probably hadn't the same reasons for wanting to run away as she did, though. They might just be keen to leave the bombs and rations behind.

Romilly had dashed back to the small mews house that she and Mama had shared to pack up their belongings and place them in storage, taking a suitcase of more valued, if not valuable, possessions, down on the train to Uncle Simon's and begging him to look after it for her. Aunt Isobel had sniffed but agreed the case could go in the garage. 'It's some of Mama's clothes and other things of hers,' Romilly told her. 'I haven't had a chance to go through them.' The truth was, she hadn't been able to bring herself to carry out the task. Her uncle and aunt had looked at one another.

'Have you heard from that chap?' he asked, his tone dripping antipathy.

He meant Douglas, Mama's fiancé: if you could be engaged to someone who was still technically married. Romilly shook her head. 'I wrote to him at the last address we had. He'd have had the letter last week, if he's still at the camp.' Perhaps Douglas had been posted somewhere remote: the Highlands, or maybe South Africa or India. The letter telling him Mama was dead might take months to reach him.

'You're doing the right thing,' Uncle Simon said, 'getting away from it all, my dear.'

'There's talk.' Aunt Ursula folded her arms across her beige cardigan. 'People suspect they know what happened to your mother, what she did.' Her lips pursed.

They hadn't told anyone anything more than that Mama's routine operation had caused a fatal infection. But that was probably enough for some of the gossips to piece it together.

Romilly closed the wardrobe door and lay down on her bed. Here she was, sailing away from all the malicious talk. Damn them all. She'd escaped now. If she let herself, she could feel nervous about throwing in her lot with Mrs Dekker, who'd made no promises as to how long she would employ Romilly once they arrived in New York. Her visa allowed for up to four weeks of domestic employment in the USA. Freddie would live with his Aunt Ruth, Mrs Dekker's older daughter, who inhabited an apartment in Mrs Dekker's own block along with her husband and twins. Ruth, Mrs Belman, had her own domestic help and wouldn't need Romilly permanently. So once she'd settled Freddie in, Romilly's work for Mrs Dekker would be over. She'd be on her own in a new city. Her visa couldn't be automatically renewed. She'd have to apply again if she found another job. Blow that, she'd simply stay and find something

humble if she had to, out of view of the authorities. She'd
managed the Blitz, surely a peacetime city couldn't be so impossible a prospect? *Romilly is a dreamer.* The headmistress's
words on her last school report floated unwelcomed through her
mind. *She is highly able, perhaps more so than she believes, but
she needs to focus her attention.*

Well, she certainly intended to do that. She was now a year
older than she had been leaving school and much tougher. On
the train up to Liverpool today a small group of German planes
had latched on to them just north of Crewe, firing on the train,
shattering a window in the carriage behind them. Mrs Dekker
had clutched the dog to herself, muttering in what might have
been German or Czech or perhaps Yiddish – that was what
some Jewish people spoke, wasn't it? Freddie blinked, looking
only slightly perturbed. Mrs Dekker's hand had reached out for
his and he'd let her hold it for a few seconds before snatching it
away. Romilly had felt unmoved by the planes. The RAF had
chased the Germans away.

She knew about bombers and air-raid shelters and rationing
and queues. She knew about sudden death. Now she'd learn
about skyscrapers and smartly dressed people. She could type
and take shorthand and had her bookshop experience. Someone
must need a girl like her to work for them?

Romilly fingered the rings she wore on a chain around her
neck: Mama's wedding ring from her marriage to Romilly's
father and the engagement ring Daddy had given Mama. If she
was desperate for cash in New York, she could probably sell
them, but the idea seemed unbearable. She hadn't known what
to do with the diamond ring Douglas had given Mama when he
asked her to marry him as soon as he was free. The nurse had
handed it to Romilly with a brown paper bag containing
Mama's clothes. In the end, she'd put it back in its box and gone
to the bank where Mama held an account, asking if they had
safe boxes for rent. They'd been kind and it probably wasn't the

first time they'd been asked questions like this by people who'd lost family. If Douglas ever reappeared, she'd direct him to the bank to reclaim the ring. She wasn't sure she could face her mother's lover herself.

Freddie seemed to have dozed off, mouth slightly open, hands still clenched but the fingers looking more relaxed. He looked even smaller in repose, his brown hair falling over his forehead. They'd have to get ready for dinner shortly, but for now she could let herself just lie here, engaging in the daydreaming that had so annoyed schoolteachers. In New York she'd be a changed person: sharp, well-dressed, flitting from taxi to cocktail bar, buying beautiful clothes and books: lots and lots of books. She'd enjoyed her job in the bookshop in Chelsea; leaving it had been one of the few regrets she had. There'd been such pleasure in uniting the right book with the right customer. Not that there had been as many books to sell in the last year, with paper and print rationing. In New York this wouldn't be the case. She could perhaps find a bookshop taking on staff.

She was going to make this work.

TWO

Five days on *The Lucknow*. Then the train journey from Montreal to New York.

Vida Dekker felt herself counting the days on her fingers like a child. This grandson of hers would soon be safely placed in Ruth's apartment, just above her own. Freddie – she forced herself to use this name – would go to school with his twin cousins, a boy and girl just a year older than him. She was more than halfway through her expedition to bring Freddie to safety. She could do this.

Vida knew that anxiety made her dictatorial with people, too defensive, too blunt. If only Jackson was still alive, with her now in this cabin, exclaiming over the neat built-in desk, the little en-suite bathroom, the balcony, telling her it was all going to be just fine. Were all marriages made up of an optimist balanced with a pessimist? She'd helped ground Jackson, he'd told her more than once. Stopped him from pursuing some of his more grandiose business ideas. In turn, he'd helped her see the world as a generous, kindly place.

Without Jackson Dekker, Vida was reverting to the Vida who'd always known danger was right behind you, breathing down your neck, its jaws ready to snap your bones. Did little Freddie understand why it was safer to have the whole of the Atlantic rather than just the narrow English Channel between him and Hitler? Probably not. He was pining for that foster home in Whitechapel in London's East End – a kindly place, for sure, but not safe, not with the bombs, especially as Mrs Cohen had refused to have the children evacuated to the country. Apparently, she'd just taken them to friends in rural Essex when the raids were particularly fierce.

Mrs Cohen had brought Freddie to the hotel herself to hand him over to his grandmother, refusing to let anyone else do this, even though it meant taking a half-day off her factory job. She was a woman in her thirties, but looked older, probably worn down by life. Standing in the doorway, she stared at Vida, hands on hips as though assessing her.

'Freddie likes a story at night. He hates sardines. And liver. And you have to make him drink his milk at bedtime.' Those eyes of hers, blazing, interrogating Vida as though she was Freddie's family and Vida herself wasn't. Mrs Cohen pulled Freddie into a deep embrace, kissing the top of his head and whispering some kind of blessing. She released him and hastened away without another word.

Vida closed the door. Freddie stared at it, silent. He hadn't wept, hadn't complained, hadn't in fact said very much at all to either his grandmother or Romilly. Talking of Romilly, her interactions with Freddie seemed half-hearted, as though she was just coming to after some blow. That was Romilly's business. She'd have to sort herself out. *Go easy on the girl for a bit, honey. She's leaving her home for the first time*, Vida heard Jackson tell her.

Hadn't Vida left her own country, too, ten years ago, when she'd married Jackson and crossed the Atlantic on a liner not too dissimilar to *The Lucknow*? And little Freddie had left his own country, and his mother, Irma, just after Hitler had walked into

Czechoslovakia. *I didn't cry in front of him. I managed that. Hopefully it won't be a long separation*, Irma had written to Vida. *France and Britain and America will kick up a fuss and the Nazis will leave. My boy will come home again.*

But Hitler hadn't left. He showed no sign of leaving anywhere he invaded. Quite the opposite.

Vida smoothed an invisible crease from the bedspread and removed her shoes to lie down. In New York, Irma would once again be part of Freddie's life. Photos of her and Freddie's father, Josef, adorned surfaces in both Vida's and Irma's apartments. *I'll keep you alive in his memory until you can come to the States yourself*, Zeeskeit, Vida promised Irma. *And this time, I'm not letting you go back to Europe. You'll all stay safe in New York. I will have all my family around me.*

Smoky, curled up on the cashmere shawl beside her on the bed, looking the size of a hand muff, emitted a small whine and stretched. Probably needed an outing on the deck, or wherever dogs were exercised onboard. Romilly could take him out. In the meantime, he would have to manage with the balcony. She got up and opened the door for him and he followed her out. It was breezy and cool. He sniffed the railings and looked at her enquiringly. Vida hadn't had the dog long: she'd taken him on unexpectedly in circumstances that would make Ruth roll her eyes when Vida told her. He and she were only just getting to know one another, but Vida had already made more progress with Smoky than she had with her grandson. She made herself stand up. The photograph album that had travelled with her sat on the desk. *I'm mad, aren't I?* she asked Jackson, walking over to sit down at the desk. *Making this voyage when I could have employed someone like Romilly without coming to London myself?* And mad to have taken on a dog? She heard the boom of Jackson's warm laughter so clearly she was surprised the dog didn't startle.

I like you when you're a bit crazy, Vida.

THREE

Few people had expected much of Romilly. She hadn't expected much of herself, to be honest. She knew her dark-blonde locks weren't striking. Her features weren't the kind people sighed over. Her figure was slight and she was neither daintily short or elegantly tall – unremarkable, in fact.

Mama had had expectations of her, but she was one of the few. Perhaps Romilly's father had entertained hopes for his daughter, but he'd died when she was seven. Douglas had become Romilly's champion, though. Her mother's suitor, companion, lover, partner, fiancé? – she never really knew how to think of him – was the kind of person who asks questions and pulls answers out of you that you didn't know you had in you.

'You're going to do well in life, Romilly.' From anyone else the words would have sounded like platitude, but Douglas spoke so quietly and with such intent, Romilly started to believe it. The bookshop job she'd taken on just as the war started became more than something done for pin money. She'd thrown herself into all the aspects, amazing Miss Jones, the owner, with her enthusiasm for dusting shelves, unpacking boxes and getting to know their customers so she could telephone them when a title came in that they might like to read. Miss Jones talked about Romilly becoming a partner in the business. But then the war had come, and paper and print became scarcer and bombs drove a lot of clientele from the Chelsea and West Kensington streets.

The night before Douglas had gone away to wherever it was the army had sent him, he'd come round for a final dinner with Mama. They insisted Romilly eat with the two of them, even though the precious piece of beef could barely stretch to three. Miraculously there hadn't been an air-raid that evening. As Douglas had risen to leave at the end of the night, his cheerful face had grown serious. He took Romilly by the shoulders. 'Althea will tell me your news when she writes to me, Rom. You're going to do great things. Won't it be fun when we're all together again? We'll have so much to talk about.'

Had Mama been looking a bit peaky that evening? Romilly couldn't remember her showing signs of anything other than sadness at Douglas's departure.

'Look after her for me,' Douglas had said as Romilly made her excuses so the two of them could have a final moment together.

But she hadn't looked after her mother, had she? A few weeks later, she'd seen Mama emerge from the door of a small Roman Catholic church, just as the siren began its wail. They were Church of England, not Catholics, and the church wasn't noted for its fine architecture, so she couldn't think of a reason why Mama would visit it. Mama stepped purposefully towards the shelter where they always headed during air-raids. Romilly followed, knowing it would be impossible to ask questions in such a crowded, noisy environment.

Apart from anything else, Romilly's own mind had been full of a secret of her own. The secret's name was Philip. The relationship was very new.

·   ·   ·

Mrs Dekker knocked on the connecting door between the cabins, jolting Romilly out of her reverie. Freddie opened his eyes. 'Your grandmother probably wants me to help with her unpacking,' Romilly told him, rising from the bed. 'Don't move while I'm next door.' He scowled.

'It's boring here.'

'You'll have to help me with your grandmother's unpacking then.'

He sucked in his cheeks and kicked a heel against the bed. At least it was a change from the blank-faced indifference he'd shown up until now.

'Can't I go and play with those children?' He sounded more wistful than naughty. Must be tough for him, stuck with two females.

'If you stay quietly in here, I promise I'll ask your grand-mother.' He blew out his cheeks and nodded, seeming to recognise a good deal when he saw one. He was the first child Romilly had had much to do with and she felt her lack of expe-rience. She went into Mrs Dekker's cabin with a last warning glance at Freddie. Mrs Dekker sat at her desk looking at a small photograph album. She'd taken some of the dresses out of the case and laid them over the foot of the bed. Most of them were silk or fine wool jersey, Romilly noted. One or two full-length. Were they to dine on the captain's table on *The Lucknow*? Romilly prayed not: she'd only packed that one velvet dress that would be suitable.

'If you could put those in the wardrobe for me.' Mrs Dekker nodded at the gowns. Romilly noted how even the rugs under-foot in this cabin were softer and springier than those in the neighbouring one. The walls were covered in what looked like silk-patterned wallpaper. Mrs Dekker's dresses smelled faintly of Mitsouko, which Romilly recognised as her Aunt Ursula's favourite scent.

'I'd do it myself,' Mrs Dekker said, 'but I've been breathless.'

She rubbed the small ring she wore on the little finger of her left hand.

Romilly hung up the dresses. 'Shall I unpack the other things, Mrs Dekker?'

'Yes, do. And put the hatboxes somewhere out of the way.'

'Freddie's settling in nicely,' Romilly offered. 'The cabin's comfortable, thank you.' Keep Mrs Dekker sweet. Perhaps if she was happy with Romilly's services, she'd keep her on for the full four weeks allowed by her visa or help her find a job with one of her acquaintances so she could apply for another work permit. The image of Douglas's kindly face flitted through her mind. How convinced he had been that she'd do something worthwhile. And look at her now, fawning to a rich older American woman so that she could stay in a safe and comfortable world.

So be it. Douglas wasn't going to look after Romilly. He hadn't looked after Mama at her time of crisis, not that he could be blamed for that. The only person who could look after Romilly now was Romilly herself.

Mrs Dekker nodded. 'When you've finished, find that steward and ask about moth balls. I left mine in London.'

'Do they have moths on ships?' Romilly asked idly, as she piled the pair of hatboxes one on top of each other. She was fond of her only hat: the small dark-green felt object she'd only bought last autumn but had probably already suffered too many rainy outings.

'How should I know, Miss Brooks? But why take unnecessary risks?'

They were embarking on a voyage across the North Atlantic in wartime and Mrs Dekker's mind was on eradicating moths. Romilly tried to stop the corners of her mouth turning up into a smirk.

'What about Freddie? I don't want to leave him in the cabin alone.'

'He can go with you. And ask the steward to bring me tea.

Lapsang. Or Darjeeling. Lemon, no milk.' As though they were on a pre-war cruise. Romilly thought of the tea she and Mama would drink each afternoon on her return from the bookshop: thick, brown, served in old green china cups and saucers that, Mama joked, could probably survive a direct hit. It hadn't seemed worth packing up the cups and saucers and putting them into storage. When she shut the front door on their home for the last time, Romilly had left them on the steps for scavengers to help themselves.

'Take Smoky as well.' Mrs Dekker shifted her weight in her chair, resting her elbows on the desk and placing her fingers on her temples. 'He can have a run on the deck. He's had a long day.' The photograph album was open on a page of pictures of what looked like two small girls in white summer dresses. Freddie's mother and aunt, perhaps?

Romilly found Smoky's lead and clipped it to his collar. He hopped down, looking enthusiastic. 'Come on,' she told Freddie, back in their cabin. 'Let's go and explore.' He was sitting on the edge of the bed, a faraway look on his face. Back in Whitechapel? Or with his parents in Prague? 'Let's go.' They went out into the corridor and headed for the gallery. Ahmed was standing at the door. She asked him for the mothballs.

Ahmed turned to a young man, really just a boy, speaking to him in a rapid eastern-sounding language. Perhaps Mrs Dekker was immediately recognisable to the ship's staff as someone who might prove demanding.

Freddie was asking Ahmed about the playroom. 'You like to go down there, young sir? I take you now. Don't worry, Miss. I will bring him back to you shortly.'

She wanted to say yes, longing for time alone, for walking around *The Lucknow*, taking it all in, catching up with herself and with what had happened to her. But she couldn't. 'I'll come too.' She didn't trust Freddie not to hide in a lifeboat or secrete himself in some cubbyhole below deck. He was small for his age, and she'd already noticed how quickly he could move.

Ahmed led them down the grand staircase. 'Before the war, many famous film stars made their entrance down these very stairs to the flash of cameras and the toast of champagne glasses, miss.' He sounded proud. She half-expected someone to stop them and tell Romilly she was in the wrong place. 'And young ladies like you would be on the way to a ball. We have our own ballroom. It's being used as a games room for wet weather now, though.' Perhaps one day, when peace returned, Romilly would buy herself a passage on a liner and embark with a trunkful of evening gowns.

Worried that Smoky would be trodden on by the passengers walking up and down the staircase, she picked him up. He weighed more than she thought he would despite being no bigger than a teddy bear.

Ahmed took them to the room off the foyer. A small girl rocked on a wooden horse. Boys sat on the floor with a large train set. The shelves were full of puzzles and books. 'Let's get the Meccano down,' Freddie said, running forward.

'Later.' She turned to Ahmed. 'We should probably give the dog a quick walk on the deck now. Mrs Dekker will be waiting for us.'

'There is a beauty salon, hairdresser and shops, too, on this part of the deck, miss. You should have a look.' His eyes seemed to express some kind of kinship with her. 'In the meantime, I will take you to the section of the deck where dogs exercise.'

They went back up to the gallery and then up a side-staircase or companionway, as Ahmed described it, leading to the exercise area above the promenade deck. When Ahmed opened the door, they saw a boy throwing a rubber ball for a golden retriever. Smoky whined and she set him down.

'How do I, erm,' she nodded at the dog, 'clear up after him?'

'There is a sand bucket and one of the crew will assist you with any matter needing disposal.'

'I'm sorry.'

He bowed. 'We are here to serve you.' Romilly swallowed. She wasn't the kind of person used to being served or waited on. 'There is lifeboat drill at six,' he went on. 'Do not miss it, very important.'

He left them. Freddie watched the boy throwing the ball. After a while the boy lobbed it at Freddie. He leapt forward and caught it easily, tossing it back to the boy, who returned the throw. The two of them grinned as their throws grew more challenging, sometimes throwing the ball to the retriever, who seemed enthusiastic, too, his tail wagging as he brought it back to the boys. The game continued while Romilly waited for Smoky to finish his business. She dared not let him off the lead: he was small enough to squeeze under the railing. Romilly shuddered at the thought of telling Mrs Dekker he'd gone overboard. She found her cigarettes and lighter. Each puff of smoke seemed to vanish immediately into the salty air.

'Jack.' A woman in a smart mink coat and pillbox hat appeared on the deck. 'Your father wants you to come in now, sweetheart.' She nodded at the deckhand. 'Take Rover back down to the kennels, will you?'

The deckhand bowed. 'Yes, Mrs Franklin.'

Freddie's face fell as Jack ran to join his mother, waving a casual farewell. 'Just when we were having fun.' He kicked the railing.

'I'm sorry.' Romilly meant it, but he turned on her, one side of his mouth tightened in scorn.

'Why do you care? You want to go to America. I don't. I wanted to stay in England. It's where my parents sent me to live.'

There was nothing she could say in reply. Perhaps it was best to say nothing, anyway. Romilly nodded. A young Lascar appeared and threw a bucket of sand over the deposit Smoky had produced and swept it under the railings. What a world, where a boy from Prague went to London and then on to New York City and another boy from India, not so many years older than Freddie, found himself in the North Atlantic. She felt a sudden kinship with them both.

'You will be able to play with the other boys tomorrow, sir?' the deckhand said shyly to Freddie.

'My grandmother won't let me.'

'They eat at the same time as you, even though they sleep on a lower deck,' the deckhand offered, picking up the retriever's lead. 'The captain said it would be better to have one serving as we do not have a full crew. So, you will see them at dinner.'

Romilly and Freddie returned to the cabin. As she unlocked the door, Jack and his mother returned, accompanied by a middle-aged man in a tight mackintosh, stopping at the door next to theirs. 'Oh,' Mrs Franklin said, voice bright. 'Hello again.'

As they went inside, Romilly heard her say to her husband, 'Those Jews were out on the exercise deck with that dog of theirs. But they're keeping it in the cabin, not down in the kennels.' Freddie heard the words too. He shrugged.

'Jack didn't mind me.'

'Probably glad to have someone who can throw a decent ball.' For once, she'd said the right thing. Freddie's shoulders lost their stiffness. The sea air had brought a bit of colour into his cheeks. Romilly knocked on the connecting door and took Smoky through.

'Lifeboat drill's at six,' she told Mrs Dekker.

'You go and report back, dear. Tell me how it works.'

'I think everyone has to go, Mrs Dekker.'

Mrs Dekker pursed her lips. 'I had hoped that some of the more tedious requirements could be dropped, especially for those who have recently sailed. We have a naval escort, after all, for the first half of the voyage, and the German submarines don't have the range to trouble us after that.' Her hand went to that ring on her little finger. She turned it round and round. Romilly watched her, remembering how her mother had run an index finger round and round the face of her wristwatch when the bills came in all at once or the ration books seemed to run out too quickly, seeming to fall into a hypnotic trance that eventually soothed her. Perhaps some of Mrs Dekker's demanding ways were the result of anxiety that needed abating in a similar way. *Watch her closely,* Romilly told herself. *This is how you'll get by from now on, by observing people and using what you learn to your advantage.* Old Romilly had tended to do her own thing, not worrying too much about others.

Freddie came into the cabin and sat down on the end of Mrs Dekker's bed, bouncing up and down. She tutted at him, but as though her heart wasn't in it.

'You'll have plenty of time for high jinks when you're in New York with your cousins.' She looked at the dainty gold watch on her wrist. 'I suppose we should make our way up to the drill.'

'Should we leave Smoky here?' Romilly asked hesitantly.

'Very well. If it's only for a short time.'

'Can't he come too?' Freddie sounded plaintive.

'It'll be a bit of a crush,' Romilly said. 'He might find it overwhelming.'

Freddie nodded, looking unconvinced.

Freddie and Romilly were still wearing life-vests. Mrs Dekker's sat on the end of her bed, the straps still tied round it.

'Perhaps you should put that on?' Romilly suggested. Mrs Dekker pursed her lips but fastened the vest around herself, pushing at the kapok-filled panels as though she could squash them flat.

'There's a whistle,' Freddie told her. 'So that you can let them know where you are if your lifeboat gets lost.'

'I can't imagine myself blowing a whistle.'

They made their way towards the gallery. The Franklins came out of their cabin behind them. Jack and Freddie grinned at one another. Perhaps Mrs Dekker would allow Freddie to play with another boy from First Class. But Romilly remembered the comments made by Mrs Franklin at the cabin door.

Captain Hutchings was a tall man with even, handsome features: he could have played himself in a movie. On deck, he was a calm, reassuring figure as he reiterated the points he'd made earlier about wearing life-vests at all times. Ahmed handed out cards to first-class passengers. Romilly studied hers. They were to go to muster point twelve in the saloon and their lifeboat was number six, on the starboard side of the boat deck, same side as the cabin. The captain explained how the lifeboats were lowered on their divots and told them where to find emergency life-rafts and lifebelts. 'But our escort is watching the seas at all times while we're in the danger zone,' he promised. 'They'll only leave us when we're out of German range.'

The sea was growing choppy now. Captain Hutchings nodded as he watched them grab railings. 'It could be rough over the next day. Some of you may find it a challenge.'

The Franklins were standing close enough for Romilly to hear Mrs Franklin sigh.

Romilly hoped neither Mrs Dekker nor Freddie suffered from seasickness and that she wouldn't have to look after them, bring basins, help them wash or change their soiled clothes. Freddie seemed unperturbed by the rougher sea. He was looking back the way they'd come, across the waves and spray. Without warning he kicked out at the railing, as though resenting the fact that Liverpool had been left behind. Mr Franklin tutted.

Mrs Dekker turned to Mr Franklin. She said nothing, but

her cold stare made him blink and look away. Romilly gave her a silent cheer.

'What is it?' she asked Freddie quietly. 'Are you missing the Cohens?'

He looked down at the deck.

'It'll be dinner soon. Perhaps you're hungry. I am. It makes everything worse, doesn't it?' Passengers were walking towards the companionway. 'Let's freshen up.' The Franklins had gone on ahead, thankfully.

In the cabin, Freddie threw himself down on his bed with a grunt. 'A stupid dinner having to sit up straight and do this and do that. Why won't she let me just eat with the others?'

Romilly threw a warning glance at the interconnecting door. 'Your grandmother wants to get to know you, Freddie.'

'She's not that interested in me.'

'This voyage will give you the time you need together. When you reach New York, you'll feel more at home with her. And your Aunt Ruth sounds kind.'

Ruth Belman had written a postcard for Freddie, which Mrs Dekker had handed over to him on the train. It sat on the dressing table with a colour picture of the Statue of Liberty on the front. It excited Romilly to look at it. Surely Freddie would respond to a city full of lights, copious food and attractions that were still open?

It wouldn't dull the ache inside him, not immediately, anyway. The ache would return when he was tired, when he lay down to sleep, when something or someone reminded him of what, who, he'd lost.

But he was being given another chance. So was she. They couldn't waste the opportunity. They'd both have to find a way of dealing with the past.

FOUR

'And find me a handkerchief, Romilly.'

Mrs Dekker had summoned her into the cabin to help her dress for dinner. Romilly located the handkerchiefs in the wardrobe drawer and selected a white square, bordered with lace. It reminded her of the handkerchief Aunt Ursula had dabbed against her cheeks at Mama's funeral, even though her aunt hadn't seemed that affectionate towards Mama during her lifetime. Her reaction to Mama's death seemed more shock than sorrow.

Romilly had never seen the surgery or more probably back room where her mother had gone in desperation at some point in the week or so before her death from blood poisoning. Even now, standing in Mrs Dekker's cabin, she was picturing a shabby door in some London backstreet, a disgraced physician taking Mama's banknotes, carrying out his work and sending her home, infection already seeding inside her. Days passing, Mama scared to go to their family doctor for help, telling herself it was all for Romilly's sake and she'd be fine with a bit of rest . . .

Mrs Dekker was saying something. 'Sorry.' Romilly gave herself an invisible shake.

'I was asking you to find me a bag.'

As she found an evening bag for Mrs Dekker, Romilly could still hear her aunt's voice in her head. 'In ordinary times, your mother could have lain low somewhere like Normandy, had the baby quietly, waited for Douglas to sort out the divorce and married him, preferably before the birth. People would have guessed but she'd have been commended for not rubbing it into people's faces. And you'd have been untouched by the scandal, Romilly. Decent men wouldn't have minded.' Because the object of Romilly's life had to be marriage with someone suitable?

'You have something suitable to wear yourself?' Mrs Dekker's voice with its foreign sounding rolled Rs and its hint of drawl broke into her thoughts.

'A velvet dress. Midnight blue. I'm afraid it's my only evening gown.'

Mrs Dekker nodded. 'That will do. Who knows what our fellow passengers will wear? Such a collection of people.'

Romilly returned to the cabin. Freddie had washed his hands and face. She washed herself, feeling a little awkward about removing her blouse and revealing her neck and upper chest in front of the boy to sponge herself, but he didn't seem to be paying her attention, absorbed in one of the comics he'd brought with him. She reapplied talcum powder under her arms before dressing. The velvet gown had arrived in her life just before the Christmas of 1939, when the war was very new and you could still just about have dresses made in luxurious fabric if you knew where to go. She, Mama and Douglas had dined out. Mama had worn a burgundy devoré silk dress and had never looked as beautiful, eyes sparkling as much as the new ring on her finger. Romilly hadn't worn her velvet dress again since then. Like most of her clothes, it seemed looser around the chest now but didn't gape enough to risk her modesty. Freddie looked up.

'You look posh.' Surprise was evident in his voice. She decided to take it as a compliment.

In the dining-room, they sat at a white-linen covered table, just the three of them. Freddie stared at the larger tables of children in the official group. Each time they laughed, Freddie laughed even though he couldn't have heard the joke. He was one of those children who was only half-alive by himself, a joiner-in.

'Those children should have had an earlier dinner setting,' Mrs Dekker said.

Mrs Dekker had been persuaded to leave Smoky in the cabin. It had taken until she'd drunk her first glass of Sancerre for her to stop complaining about the separation. Romilly thought the dog would be comfortable enough snoozing on the armchair. Romilly cut her veal escallop, barely needing the knife on the tender meat. The first course of watercress soup had tasted like nothing she'd eaten for a good year. Where had all this food come from? Perhaps she should feel guilty about eating like this. She hadn't the energy. Anyway, there were too many other things to feel guilty about.

Freddie was making short work of his lamb chop. 'Don't eat too quickly,' she warned him. 'You'll get a pain in your stomach.' He looked at her and for a moment his face softened. Perhaps his mother or Mrs Cohen had uttered a similar warning. The children on the escort tables were eating as quickly as Freddie, their chatter dying down as the food took all their attention. They'd reached the trifle stage when the red-headed official escort they'd seen earlier stood up. 'Ladies and gentlemen, boys and girls.' She gave them a full-beam smile from behind the bottle-glass spectacles. 'To celebrate this special night, we would like to invite you to a puppet show in the playroom after dinner.'

Freddie put down his spoon and turned to Romilly. 'We'll go?' She looked at Mrs Dekker for an answer.

'What do we know about those children?' Mrs Dekker shook her head. 'Best to wait until you get to New York to make new friends.'

'She seems to have everything well organised.' Romilly was fascinated by the young woman. She almost shone, her clear-skinned face untouched by a stroke of cosmetics, lit by some inner light. Girl guides, Romilly thought. Or Pony Club camp. Possibly church youth group. On her dress lapel she wore some kind of pin, probably denoting the organisation taking the children to the New World.

'Perhaps we could sit at the back, away from everyone else?' Romilly suggested.

Mrs Dekker frowned down at her wine glass.

'I want to go to the puppet show,' Freddie said loudly. 'I don't want to stay with *her* all the time.'

'Her name is Romilly,' his grandmother told him. 'Remember your manners.' She placed her napkin on the table. 'Come on. We're finished.'

'I wanted more trifle.'

'You've had enough, Freddie. We'll go back to our cabins now. Romilly will read you a story.'

Freddie didn't complain, but his face took on a fixed expression. Romilly hadn't known him for more than a few days but that was long enough for her to know that the puppet show mattered.

'Please,' she said to Mrs Dekker. 'I really think it would help him settle.'

Mrs Dekker's eyes widened. 'So, you're telling me how to care for my own grandson, young lady?'

A grandson she'd known for only a few days longer than

Romilly herself. Romilly was about to back down, to apologise. But Freddie was looking at her. Something less hostile seemed to have replaced his usual coolness. Poor kid, an hour of distraction and laughter would be good for him. Romilly forced herself to meet Mrs Dekker's glare. It was too late to fire her now: out in the Atlantic she couldn't be sent home.

'Are you coming to the show after dinner?' a bright voice asked. Romilly turned to see the young woman with the red hair standing behind her seat. 'Our puppeteers really need an audience.'

Something about her must have reassured Mrs Dekker. She nodded at Freddie. 'You may go. Romilly will accompany you.'

Freddie and Romilly followed the redhead out of the dining-room. 'Louise.' She turned, her hand extended. 'Louise Henderson.'

'Romilly Brooks. And this is Freddie Landau.'

'How do you do, Romilly and Freddie. You'll find our lot lively, but they're a good bunch.'

'Are the children going to family across the Atlantic?' Romilly asked.

'Mainly to host families. Most of them are from bombed-out areas of London and Liverpool. Their parents, if they're still alive, are desperate for them to go somewhere safe.'

But such a terribly long way away from home.

'How many of them are there?'

'One hundred and two.' Louise grinned. 'I spend my life counting them. We've split them into groups, each with a youth leader, but even so, keeping tabs on them is quite a job.'

Louise gestured at a group of dawdling girls, waving them along to the foyer, past the grand staircase. 'We're trying to give them a completely fresh start. As much fun as possible to distract them from homesickness and reassure them that the world's still a good place.'

Romilly looked away. 'Who's putting on the puppet show?' she asked.

'We've persuaded two men— one of them's old but pretty game. I had them signed up within minutes of leaving Liverpool. I thought we'd need something special for the first night.'

'You should be in sales.'

For a moment Louise looked flustered. 'What do you mean?' Her eyes swept Romilly's face.

'You're obviously good at persuading people to do the right thing.'

Louise grinned. 'Suitcases of samples and a different hotel every night? Sounds good.'

They paused by the staircase while Louise halted a small boy and did up his shoelaces. 'By the end of this voyage you'll be doing them yourself perfectly, James,' she told him, sending him on.

She turned to Romilly. 'Tell me about the lady you're accompanying. Is she family?'

'No. I answered an advertisement in *The Lady*. Mrs Dekker wanted a companion for her and her grandson on the voyage.'

'Are you staying in Canada?'

'New York.'

Louise's expression changed in a way Romilly couldn't read. They reached the playroom with its brightly painted walls and toys stacked on shelves. A little wooden theatre with red velvet curtains had been set up in the middle, rows of chairs forming a small auditorium. Romilly let Freddie run ahead.

'Is she nice to you, your Mrs Dekker?' Louise asked. 'She looks a little fierce.'

'I think it's because she's scared.'

Louise looked at her, eyebrows raised. Romilly thought again of Mrs Dekker's fiddling with her rings, the way she clenched her hands, the tightness in her voice when she said those things about the other passengers. 'She's Jewish,' Romilly went on, lowering her voice. 'Her daughter, Freddie's mother, is still in Prague. As far as anyone knows, that is. Freddie was sent to England before the war started.'

Louise sighed. 'When I think about what's happening on the Continent, it makes me even more certain . . .' Her voice became sterner, almost harsh. She looked at the clock on the wall. 'Goodness, we're running late.' She rushed ahead like a games captain preparing a lacrosse team for the match. Romilly detached Freddie from a gaggle of boys lining up toy soldiers in battle on the side of the improvised auditorium. He scowled at her.

'You're always spoiling things. I want to stay with them.'

'You know I promised your grandmother I'd sit with you.' Romilly was growing exasperated. She was trying to help him, but he kept blaming her for Mrs Dekker's restrictions.'

He made a face. 'Does she think I'm going to fall overboard? I'm not daft.' He looked as he had when he'd kicked out at the deck railings.

'Let's take our seats,' she said, to distract him.

They sat towards the back. Louise nodded at one of her male colleagues to turn down the lights, taking a seat at the side of the audience. An older boy stood up and blew a trumpet. The curtains drew back to reveal a farmyard, complete with a cow wearing a hat and a pig in a checked waistcoat. Freddie clapped his hands.

With just two puppeteers, presumably unpractised in puppetry, it was impressive they'd mastered the strings at all. The cow asked the pig if he liked her hat and the pig became increasingly cheeky as he replied, to the delight of the children. The show didn't last long: it must have taken the puppeteers hours just to rehearse the five minutes of dialogue or so. The curtains swung closed. The children clapped and cheered. Two men appeared from around the puppet theatre: the younger of the pair the one Romilly had seen on deck as they'd cast off, and an older man who beamed at the children as they took a bow and replaced their suit jackets.

Louise stood up and turned to face the audience. 'That's all for tonight, boys and girls. Our thanks to our accomplished puppeteers, who may now wish they had proved less gifted as I may call on them again.' She turned the full-beam smile on the two men. The younger feigned groans of dismay. The older gave another bow. 'It's been a long day for everyone and we all need to go to our cabins now. And what do we have to remember?' She put a hand to an ear.

'Sleep in our life-vests and clothes,' the audience replied in unison.

'And what else?'

'Remember our lifeboat number,' a small girl at the front called.

'That's right. And your muster point, the place where you meet up in an emergency. And remind me, if I'm standing looking towards the front of the boat, the bow, what do I call the right side?'

'Starboard,' a small boy called.

'Correct. And port is left. Once a day, you'll hear the siren you heard when we had the drill this evening. Stop whatever you're doing and go to your muster points.'

'Even if it's during prayers?' piped up a little girl. 'Or lessons?'

'Even then.'

'What about if it's when I'm on the lav—' With a single glance, Louise silenced the boy who'd spoken up, quashing the giggles around him.

She clapped her hands. 'Off you go. Don't forget to clean your teeth and wash your hands and faces.'

A future headmistress, Romilly thought. Kind but firm. A woman who'd take an interest in the people she taught, perfect for children orphaned or removed from their families.

'What are you thinking about, Romilly?' Freddie asked her. 'You look a bit weird.'

'Nothing.'

'Were you thinking about dead people?'

She flinched. He could be so direct. 'No.'

He turned to look at her more closely. 'What about those you left behind?'

'I didn't have any of those, really.' Nobody left to wave her off at Liverpool docks. Or even to see her off at Euston Station.

'So they died?'

She nodded.

'Once you've left people, they might as well be dead. Like my parents.' He kicked out at the bottom step of the staircase as they walked past it. 'I haven't had a letter from them for such a long time.'

'It might be hard for them to send post out of the country. Don't give up hope.'

He scoffed, looking older than his eight years. 'You don't know what you're talking about, Romilly Brooks.' He stormed past her as they reached the gallery leading to their corridor.

The ship was pitching slightly under her feet. It was going to be a more turbulent voyage than she'd expected.

FIVE

Trying to sleep while wearing the life-vest was almost impossible. The kapok stuffing prevented Romilly from rolling into her usual position on her side, one leg bent underneath her. At two in the morning, she gave up the attempt and switched on the light above her bed, reaching for her book and checking that she wasn't disturbing Freddie. He slept deeply, his breaths so slow, and even she could hardly see his chest rising underneath the life-vest. He looked very small in the bed. Her novel, the one she'd taken from the bookshop to read on Miss Jones's recommendation the very day before Mama had died, promising to write a review that could be pinned to the shelf for customers to read, didn't hold her attention. Something of London, of hospital disinfectant, sirens and empty houses, seemed to have left its scent on the pages, even though they described a country house in a peacetime summer where the murder hadn't yet happened and nobody was worried about more than organising a fête. She put the novel down on the bedside table. Her legs felt restless, she needed to stretch them to have any chance of sleep.

Romilly pushed the bedclothes back and got out of bed. Careful not to make a sound, she put on her dressing-gown over the life-vest and found her slippers. She took her cigarettes and lighter from her handbag. Perhaps she could find an unlocked door to the promenade deck and have a smoke. With a last look at Freddie, she placed the key in her pocket and opened the door to the corridor.

It was lit only intermittently with soft lamps. Not a sound emanated from any of the cabins. Of course, the curfew. You weren't supposed to move from your cabin after a certain hour, 11pm, she remembered, but nobody would notice if she walked quietly around for a few minutes, would they? The last two weeks had been a rush of organising the funeral with Uncle Simon, seeing lawyers, making sure she had the right papers. Then dashing back to the bookshop to apologise to Miss Jones for giving notice, with immediate effect, seeing the shock on Miss Jones's face, blurting out an account of what had happened and accepting commiserations and concern with little more than a dazed nod.

After she'd handed in her notice, she'd sat alone in the mews house that evening, the air-raids having ceased again, solitude pressing in on her like a physical pain. Her mother would never again turn on the wireless for the news or heat a saucepan of milk for a bedtime drink for them both. Never again would they discuss acquiring a cat who could take on what they hoped was a mouse in the pantry, but feared might be something larger. Her mother wouldn't ever sigh again as she wound up the kitchen clock that always ran two minutes slow by the end of the day. Romilly hadn't known what to do with the clock and had left it on the wall.

Now, surrounded by strangers, Romilly again felt an urge to explore *The Lucknow* alone, unobserved. She needed to make her new surroundings feel more like her own space, where she was Romilly Brooks, an individual rather than a cross between nanny, maid and governess, where she could either take out her recent memories and consider them quietly or distract herself by examining the ship alone. She stepped quietly along the parquet floor towards the gallery. As she reached it, a tall figure appeared in front of her. She froze. If it was one of the crew, she might be in trouble. She started to prepare an excuse for being out of her cabin.

'Good-night,' the figure said, in a voice that matched the elegant suit he wore. The wide-shouldered man who'd been on the deck when they'd departed from Liverpool and later acted as a puppeteer. What on earth was he doing up at this hour? He wasn't talking to her, it seemed, as he started a little as he passed her, recovering himself and nodding politely. His eyes were keen, seeming to take her in with a single sweep.

'Sleep well,' a female voice called, back at the end of the gallery leading to the staircase. The woman sounded young but her voice was deep. Under the gentle glow of the lights she looked somehow familiar, but Romilly couldn't place her. That distinctive dark bobbed hair would be hard to miss. The woman obviously hadn't seen Romilly in the shadowy corridor. Had the two of them been carrying out a secret assignation? Aunt Ursula sometimes talked darkly of people getting up to no good on cruises. Something about being on the high seas, in international waters, made them think indiscretions didn't count, Aunt Ursula said, curling her lip. And if the climate was hot, it disinhibited people. That wasn't going to be a problem on this crossing, though, Romilly thought. The dark-haired woman turned to the companionway down to the second-class cabins on the lower deck.

Romilly should go back to her own cabin. This silly act of rebellion in breaking the ship's curfew was pointless. If something happened, if the Germans shot at them, the crew would look for her in her cabin, that was the point of the curfew: knowing exactly where passengers were during the night. But perhaps she was more of a rebel than she'd imagined. She wanted to get the measure of *The Lucknow*, familiarise herself with the ship without distraction.

Her feet took her to the top of the grand staircase. She was aware of someone coming up the companionway behind her and she moved into the shadows. The dark-haired woman proceeded on down the passageway, seeming to head past Romilly's cabin. Had she been hiding from Romilly, waiting for her to walk on to the gallery?

Romilly went down the grand staircase to the foyer. The scent of lilies still hung in the air. She stroked the petals, feeling wide awake now. Perhaps she could find a newspaper in the library and smuggle it back to the cabin. If she returned it in the morning, it wouldn't be too bad, would it? Even if it was, she didn't care. If she was reprimanded by a steward and hauled in front of the captain they couldn't exactly throw her overboard. Though perhaps Mrs Dekker would think that an appropriate punishment.

As she walked through the foyer towards the library, she heard a door opening. Romilly stepped into the recess between two glass cases displaying necklaces and bracelets. A sliding door opened in what had appeared to be a mural on the wall. The older puppeteer from the show emerged, a set of beads clasped in his hand. He closed the door behind him and walked past Romilly's hiding place. She let out a breath. Another door opened and she heard him apologising, perhaps to one of the stewards, for breaking curfew, explaining that he came to the chapel to pray because he couldn't sleep. The men's voices faded away. Romilly counted to ten and stepped out from her hiding place. The mural on the sliding door was actually a depiction of a lamb in front of a cross. The Lamb of God: Jesus as a perfect sacrifice for man's sinfulness.

Romilly slid the door open and went inside. When she switched on the light, she saw she was in a small space, just a dozen chairs arranged in front of a simple altar, with a rail and kneelers in front of it, Christian in tone but multi-denominational, she guessed. Romilly thought of saying a prayer. For her mother? For herself. The Church of England didn't encourage you to pray for the dead. They were in God's hands. But if someone had died as her mother had died, having done what she had done, perhaps they needed an additional plea on their behalf?

Romilly was the very person who should intercede with God. Her mother had done what she had done because of her, not wishing the disgrace to fall upon Romilly. It hadn't been Mama's fault that Douglas couldn't marry her in time, that he'd been sent away somewhere where letters and telegrams couldn't reach him.

But had this actually been the case? Perhaps active service had caused Douglas to forget about the two of them, to extract himself from them? Maybe he now wanted to patch up things with his wife, although she was supposedly still living overseas? Or perhaps he was dead: shipped over rapidly to North Africa and killed in some desert. Mama hadn't been his official next of kin so she wouldn't have known. Romilly herself might never know what had happened to him.

Romilly touched the cool wood on the top of one of the kneelers. If God had allowed both Mama and Douglas to die, he probably didn't plan anything good for Romilly either. You don't think much of me, she prayed. Just don't let me mess up this chance I've been given.

Why would God even listen? She stood very still to see if a voice spoke back to her but all she could make out was the distant deep purr of the ship's engines below. Perhaps God was still reflecting on her own sin on the night of Mama's death. If she hadn't . . . If she'd come home on time and called an ambulance earlier on . . .

Romilly turned her back on the altar, sliding the door closed firmly as she left the chapel and leaving God to himself. Sleep, having eluded her, now wanted to claim her. She stumbled up the stairs to the gallery and along the corridor to the cabin, where Freddie slept on peacefully.

SIX

Almost immediately, it seemed, someone knocked on the cabin door. Romilly groaned and sat up, rubbing her eyes. 'Breakfast is served in the dining-room, miss,' Ahmed called.

Eight o'clock. In the next-door cabin, Mrs Dekker would be waiting for her to take Smoky up to the exercise deck before they ate. Freddie was already out of bed, pulling on his socks.

'Have you washed?'

He nodded. Romilly wasn't convinced, but there wasn't time to question him. She wet his comb and pushed his fringe off his forehead, then washed herself in the handbasin, instructing him to turn away from her while she sponged herself. A shower would have to wait until the evening. She dressed in her only other day-dress. At some point on this voyage she'd need to investigate the on-ship laundry arrangements, but not this morning. She knocked on the communicating door.

'About time, too,' Mrs Dekker said, calling her in. 'I was about to summon the steward to take dear Smoky up. He's made use of the balcony for now. You'll have to exercise him after breakfast.'

'I'm sorry,' Romilly said. 'I overslept.'

'Ahmed will knock on your door at half-seven tomorrow.' Mrs Dekker picked up her handbag. 'Let's go up now.'

Crossing the foyer, they caught up with Louise, leading a group of small girls. 'Morning, Romilly.' She spoke cheerfully, but faint shadows under her eyes suggested a disturbed night. Had her charges woken her? Her red hair was arranged as neatly as usual, Romilly noted enviously, aware that her own locks had probably needed more than the quick comb-through they'd received this morning. She couldn't help feeling inadequate in comparison with Louise, who seemed to manage so many children so effortlessly.

Louise put a hand to her mouth and yawned. 'Excuse me. Didn't sleep well. The girls were unsettled. I expect the healthy sea air will sort us all out, though.' She grabbed a girl's shoulder. 'Don't run, Maisie, love. You know the rules about how we behave onboard. Plenty of eggs and sausages for all of us.'

Mrs Dekker sighed loudly behind Romilly and Freddie.

'Hurry up, those girls will scoff all the food,' Freddie hissed at Romilly.

In the dining-room, they sat where they'd been seated the previous evening. A pot of coffee arrived almost immediately. On a table to Romilly's right sat the younger puppeteer she'd encountered in the corridor during the night. He sipped his coffee reading a newspaper, looking very relaxed. Where was the brunette he'd been talking to? Romilly glanced around the dining-room, spotting a young and beautiful girl who looked Spanish or Italian. No, not her: her hair was too long. An older woman with hair that looked the right length and colour sat with her husband. The woman laughed: a high-pitched cackle unlike the brunette's low tone.

Romilly gave herself a mental shake. She was falling into the very trap she'd promised herself not to fall into: looking for gossip, speculating. And what for – idle distraction? Gossip wasn't harmless; it could poison people. Leave them bleeding, dying of infection. Romilly stabbed at the yolk of her egg.

The three Franklins came in. Mrs Franklin gave them a nod that was almost friendly. Her son grinned at Freddie. Mr Franklin carried his life-vest and threw it down underneath the chair. 'Ridiculous to expect us to wear these damn things at all times.'

'It's only for the first few days, while we're in the danger zone,' his wife said, in soothing tones, waving at the waiter.

Mrs Dekker was saying something. 'I'm sorry,' Romilly said. 'I was . . .'

'Distracted, dear.' She bent forward and tapped Romilly's arm. 'And not for the first time this morning. Can I rely on you to pay attention? We're on a ship in dangerous waters. And I need you to prepare Freddie for New York.'

What did Romilly Brooks know about New York? But she thought she understood what Mrs Dekker was getting at: Freddie was to be presented as a little English gentleman rather than a boy who'd been fostered by East-End Jews. But why? Would New Yorkers really care how he spoke? Would a hint of middle-Europe or Whitechapel matter in Manhattan? Surely sounding English wouldn't help him fit in to his new school? But it wasn't her decision. Mrs Dekker had made it clear that she had been hired to do as she was told.

On the other side of the dining-room Louise stood up, indicating to the children that they should do the same. 'Back to our cabins to freshen up,' Romilly heard her say. 'Then lessons in the playroom until lunchtime.'

One of the older girls, who looked about fifteen, rolled her eyes. Louise twinkled at her. 'There are some good books in the library. You may choose one to read in place of lessons if you're quiet.'

The man from last night stood up, too. He nodded at Romilly as he walked past, wishing her good morning.

'He was one of the men doing that puppet show, no?' Mrs
Dekker looked at her sharply. 'He knows you how, Romilly?
Who is he?'

'I don't know his name. We bumped into one another . . . in
the passageway.' She'd been about to say she'd met him the
previous night but remembered the broken curfew. Best not to
admit to leaving the cabin.

'Be careful about the friendships you strike up onboard.'

Did Mrs Dekker suspect that Romilly was flighty enough to
strike up an onboard romance? Did she know about Mama and
suspect Romilly was somehow flawed because she was her
daughter? No, she couldn't have had time to research it all.
Romilly had given her Miss Jones's name and the bookshop
address as a reference, and Mrs Dekker would only have had a
day to contact her. She was probably just warning a single
young woman to be careful about strangers on a ship. Perhaps
she was right.

Mrs Dekker wiped her lips daintily with the napkin. 'We
should get going. No time to waste.'

'When can I play?' Freddie asked. 'There are games on the
deck later. One of the boys in the lavatories told me.'

'Romilly will take you out later. Perhaps you could play
quoits or something. No need to involve strangers.' Mrs Dekker
reached for her handbag. 'Come on.'

Surely Romilly and Mrs Dekker were really still strangers
to Freddie, too?

'I could ask whether any of the children are going on to
New York?' Romilly offered. 'It might be nice for Freddie to
make some friends who'll be there too?'

Mrs Dekker sniffed. 'My daughter Ruth intends sending
Freddie to the same school that his cousins attend. It's expensive.' The implication was clear but how could she know where
the escorted children were going? Perhaps some of them were
being fostered by well-off families.

They reached the foot of the grand staircase. Romilly wasn't going to let Mrs Dekker win every round. 'Freddie might find the sea air helps concentration. Perhaps I could take him out onto a quiet part of the deck?'

'Very well.' Mrs Dekker said. 'But don't imagine the sun will be out all day: I heard the steward talking of a storm. You may work out there for an hour, if there's no slacking.'

Freddie gave a half-skip of excitement. 'Make sure you concentrate hard,' Romilly whispered when his grandmother had gone on ahead of them. 'Otherwise, we'll be stuck in the cabin all day every day.'

'Let's take the lift up to our floor,' Mrs Dekker said. 'No need to keep going up and down these stairs.' It was a shame. Romilly liked going up and down the sweeping staircase, it made her feel like someone from a film.

In the cabin, Mrs Dekker handed Romilly a small pile of what looked like new exercise books and school textbooks, smelling of fresh paper and ink. She must have brought them with her from New York. There was a reading book, too, thank God.

'I will take Smoky up to the exercise deck myself,' Mrs Dekker told her. 'As you haven't allowed enough time, Romilly. Tomorrow morning, I expect you to be better organised.'

They carried exercise books and pencils to the open-air lounge at the stern of the boat deck, cordoned off for passengers to sit on deckchairs and enjoy the spring air. The sky was clear, though small clouds of varying shapes massed ahead of them. The horses on top of the waves galloped beside *The Lucknow*. For now, though, it was warm enough sitting on the sheltered starboard. Below, on the exercise deck, people played badminton and quoits. On the deck below that one, passengers strolled past, stopping to peer out to sea at the rest of the convoy. Mrs Dekker came into view with Smoky, breaking the rule about dogs on this deck. Romilly thought it would be a brave steward who'd challenge her. What must it be like to have such a disregard for other people's rules? And yet, there was something about the way the older woman clung to the handrail that made her look unsure of herself. Perhaps she hadn't found her sea legs yet.

Romilly pulled two deckchairs into upright position and commandeered one of the low tables. She had never given a lesson in her life. 'What were you doing at school in maths?' she asked Freddie, choosing the subject off the top of her head.

'Fractions.'

She extracted the maths textbook from the pile. He took it from her and flicked through the pages. 'We were doing sums like this.' A faraway look came into his eyes.

'Do this exercise, then.' She pointed at the page. He picked up a pencil and opened his exercise book, carefully writing the date on the top righthand side and underlining it with the ruler. He seemed to finish very quickly. She took the book and checked his answers. They were far too easy for him.

'You could check my times tables?' he said helpfully.

'Eight sevens?'

'Fifty-six.'

It took her a fraction longer than she would have liked to nod. 'Nine eights?'

He gave her a withering look. 'Seventy-two. I'm good at tables. Probably better than you.'

The wind had picked up again, trying to dash the books across the deck. Romilly grabbed at them. 'Perhaps we should do something else.' Mrs Dekker had asked her to check his pronunciation. She wasn't sure how she was supposed to do this: hold a feather in front of his mouth to make sure he said "white" and "while" instead of "vite" and "vile"?

'She wants you to make me sound like you, not like Mrs Cohen and her boys, doesn't she?'

Romilly nodded.

'She doesn't even sound American herself, not all the time. This is all stupid.'

She shrugged. They sat in silence. The lesson was slipping away from Romilly, along with any hope of exerting any kind of authority or even influence on Freddie. She looked at him, sitting hunched over, lower lip jutting out, arms crossed. She unwound her own arms, trying to look less defensive.

'I'm trying to make this better for you,' she said quietly. 'If we can keep your grandmother happy it's more likely she'll relax and let you have some fun.'

'You're just saying that because you can't be bothered with me. You want to read and lounge around.'

'Freddie! That's not true—'

'You're only here because she's paying you, aren't you? You don't really care about me. Mrs Cohen wasn't paid, just some extra money for my food.'

'Some of us can't afford not to earn.' She shouldn't have said that.

'You're saying you're poor?' He snorted. 'That's why you're leaving your country in the war?'

'Not poor, not like . . . some people. But I do have to work.'

'But not in London? Were you scared, Romilly?'

'Of the bombs? Once or twice. But that . . . That wasn't what . . . That wasn't why I wanted to leave.'

'You had a choice. I didn't. Because I'm just a child.'

'I'm sorry.' There didn't seem to be anything else to say. His face was pulled into a scowl.

'What you said yesterday about leaving people behind, how it made them feel almost . . . dead?' she said softly. 'Your parents, then the Cohens. You know your grandmother wouldn't be doing this unless she really thought it was the best thing for you, don't you?'

'I didn't want her to take me away. Nobody asked me where I wanted to be.'

'She cares about you.'

He shook his head. 'She doesn't know anything about me. She just turned up. Mrs Cohen would have kept me. She wanted me to stay.' He brushed a hand angrily across his eyes. Very slowly, Romilly placed her hand on the arm nearest her, expecting him to brush it off.

'I didn't leave anyone behind, but I do know about losing people.' Her words came out very quietly. She wasn't sure he'd heard. 'I'm excited to be starting again in America, but I miss—' She stopped for a moment, unsure that she wanted to talk about her mother. 'I miss my mother. She died two weeks ago.' Only two weeks. It felt simultaneously longer and shorter since she'd said good-bye to her mother at breakfast for the last time. Freddie lifted his head, his expression hard to read. He nodded and some of the distance between them seemed to fall away.

'So I know how you feel.' The atmosphere was becoming too intense for what was supposed to be a lesson. 'Read to me.' She pulled out the copy of *The Children of the New Forest*. He waved his hands in the air, the moment of connection between them breaking again.

'A boring old book. Can't you find us some more comics?'

'It's not boring if you get into it.' Perhaps it would be better to find Freddie a copy of *Tom Sawyer*. More American? Would they have it in the library?

Freddie read a page, stumbling over the name Humphrey. 'Who'd call their kid that?' He sounded disgusted.

Behind them came a male laugh. Romilly turned. The man from last night. 'Sorry,' he said. 'Very rude of me, but your companion has a point.' He was wearing a trilby and sunglasses, which he removed. His eyes were as inquiring as she'd noticed last night. She wondered how much of the conversation he'd heard.

'I can't seem to find anything he wants to do,' she admitted.

The man nodded towards the ocean. 'How about marine biology? Some of the passengers say they see whales out there.'

Freddie sat up.

'And there are books about sea creatures in the library. You could follow up any sightings with research.'

'Thank you.' Romilly was relieved to watch Freddie rush to the railing and stare out to sea. 'I was finding it hard.'

'Not a teacher by vocation?'

She laughed. 'Not really. As you can probably tell.' His raised eyebrows seem to ask more. 'I worked in a bookshop in London.'

'You should be able to think of a few more books to pique that young man's interest.' His clothes were good quality, she noticed. Fine wool in the suit he wore with a casual elegance. His shoes looked expensive, if not new, too. She'd got used to assessing shop customers.

'Freddie's grandmother chose this one.' She glanced at the novel. 'I was thinking of Mark Twain.'

He nodded. 'Where are you and your young Huckleberry-to-be bound?'

'New York.'

'An adventure. Planning to spend the war over there?'

She shuffled in the deckchair, unwilling to reveal herself as completely unpatriotic. 'Not sure. Freddie will stay. I'll have to see what happens.'

'Hard times now in America.' He picked up his newspaper. 'But a bright, hard-working person can probably make their way, with persistence.' She thought she heard a challenge in his words. Was he implying that she wouldn't be up to it?

'That's what I want: to make my own way in life.' She opened the book again.

'Freddie mightn't like that story, but it's appropriate for the times,' he said. 'Four children taking responsibility for themselves at a time of civil war. Chivalry, honour and bravery at a savage time. An appropriate read now, metaphorically.'

His expression was thoughtful. Thinking she wasn't very honourable or brave? No. This man didn't know anything about her. Anyway, he wasn't fighting the enemy himself, was he, in that suit of his?

'What's metaphorically?' Freddie asked, returning to them.

She thought for a moment. 'It's a way of making a story mean something about yourself or life. On this voyage you might face storms, things go wrong. But there are good bits too, like the food and the puppet show. Eventually you arrive in safe harbour. The voyage could be a metaphor for life: the difficult bits and the more pleasant parts.'

The man looked back to her from Freddie as she spoke. He extended a hand. 'Rudely, I haven't introduced myself. I'm Edward Witney.' She realised he was probably only in his late twenties.

'Romilly Brooks.' She shook the hand, which felt dry and cool. 'And this is Freddie Landau.'

'I'm sure New York will prove safe harbour to you both.' He brushed an imaginary crease from his perfectly pressed trousers. 'I must go down to my cabin and do some work myself. Life on the sea is making me idle.'

'Are you a frequent traveller?' she asked, trying to keep the question casual.

He gave her a sharp look before nodding. 'Business takes me back and forth across the Atlantic.' He looked down at *The Times* in his hand. 'Would you like this?'

'Thank you.' She wondered what kind of business would take a man of fighting age to America so frequently? But she reminded herself of her vow not to concern herself with other passengers' business. He picked up his life-vest and crossed the deck. Despite his apparent fitness, he walked with a slight limp she noted, his left leg in the well-cut trousers seeming to move stiffly. Perhaps that was why he wasn't serving in the armed forces.

Romilly read Freddie an article in the newspaper about rescue dogs helping to find people in bombed-out houses in Liverpool. 'I don't think Smoky would be very helpful,' he said, when she finished. 'Though he's small enough to wriggle down small holes to look.'

'You like him, don't you?'

He shrugged. 'He's all right.'

'I had a dog when I was about your age. He used to jump up onto the kitchen table and grab food. Once, my mother bought a very expensive piece of beef and he stole the whole joint. We found it in the garden.'

Freddie grinned. Romilly remembered her mother trying to discipline the spaniel and failing to do more than tell him she was very disappointed in him.

A gust of wind threatened to take the exercise books and newspaper and blow them across the deck. Freddie and Romilly grabbed at everything. 'Take it all down to the cabin. We can do some arithmetic there.' It was cooler now. She was almost glad of the bulky life-vest.

'I expect my grandmother's down in the beauty salon having her nails done,' he told her. 'She wouldn't know if we did something more interesting.'

'We have to do what we promised.'

He made a face. 'You should have your nails done too, Romilly,' he said, generously. 'Or your hair. Mrs Cohen always had hers set on a Thursday. It's red but she calls it auburn.' He blinked hard.

'She's lucky. My hair is what you call mousy-blonde.'

'I quite like mice,' he said.

As they entered the gallery, she asked him if he could remember their lifeboat drill.

'Muster point twelve in the saloon, lifeboat six, starboard,' he intoned. 'Where they have cigars. The boats are on the deck above, on the starboard side, the righthand side. See, I know it.'

'And you sleep in your life-vest, I noticed. That's good.'

He gave her a sidelong look. 'You got up in the middle of the night, didn't you? I heard you go out and come back after a while.'

'I needed the lavatory.'

Perhaps being a refugee meant you were on your guard, paying attention. She unlocked the cabin and he ran in and bounced on his bed.

'I wish we had bunks. If I was down with the other boys, I bet I'd be in a bunk.' He shot her a look that made it clear she was still on probation with him.

'We're in first class. Most people at . . . ' She'd been about to say 'at home' but London wasn't home anymore for either of them. 'Most people would love to have a cabin like this and all the food they give us at meals.'

He nodded grudgingly.

A siren sounded. Lifeboat drill. 'Come on.' Romilly suppressed a groan. 'Back up the way we came. We'll pick up your coat from the cabin in case you feel cold out there now the wind's up.'

They retraced their steps to the muster point in the saloon, where they were counted. The boat deck was the deck above, the lifeboats suspended on their divots so that passengers could climb into them. The ship's chief officer selected a group of adults and children and showed them and those watching how to climb in, lowering one of the boats into the sea. Crew members demonstrated the use of the Fleming gears: handles under the seats that propelled the boats, the chief officer telling the passengers what they were doing in a reassuringly clear voice. There were oars for rowing, but the handles were easier to find in a hurry. There were also emergency life-rafts: pallet-like wooden structures in a stumpy U-shape, with a footwell and two slatted seats, which would provide little shelter but would keep you out of the water until you could find a lifeboat. But this wasn't the *Titanic*, the captain told them. There were plenty of lifeboats, more than enough for every single passenger and crew member, and the drill for getting into them would be practised until everyone knew how it worked.

The lifeboat was raised again and the group got out, looking flushed and pleased with themselves.

Mrs Dekker clutched Smoky to her life-vest, eyes narrowed. 'Let's hope it doesn't come to that,' she said, as all the lifeboats were winched above their heads. 'Lowering boats full of people could be a much riskier procedure than they think.'

Romilly was wondering about Smoky. One of the stewards was eyeing the dog, apparently too nervous to ask Mrs Dekker what he was doing there. Surely if the ship went down Mrs Dekker would know her pet, despite his small size, would not be allowed in a lifeboat? The Franklins were standing behind Romilly. 'In the hair salon someone said the captain told them he wouldn't consider sending his own children on this voyage,' Mrs Franklin whispered. 'I hope we're doing the right thing with Jack.'

'You shouldn't listen to tittle-tattle,' her husband told her. 'We'll soon be out of the danger zone.'

Romilly stared out to sea, making out the outline of a freighter and, further away on the horizon, a larger naval vessel. The wind tossed her hair, blowing strands into her eyes. Perhaps it would lighten to a more interesting blonde if the sun came out while they were onboard. If Mrs Dekker allowed them out on deck.

'I wish we could throw off the convoy,' Mrs Franklin said. 'I'm sure they're slowing us down. We could make our own tacks, confuse the U-boats.'

'Don't let Jack hear your fussing, Cynthia,' Mr Franklin told her. 'Your nerves are getting to you.'

Mrs Dekker tutted loudly. 'Must I raise my voice to get your attention, Romilly?'

'Sorry, Mrs Dekker.' Romilly turned to her, fixing her face into what she hoped was a steady, attentive gaze.

'I was asking whether you'd seen the lunch menus for today?'

Had they been posted on the board outside the dining-room? Romilly couldn't remember.

'Soup of the day and roast chicken,' Freddie told his grand-mother. 'And apple pie. I always notice.'

The meal sounded the equivalent of a full day's food back in London. Romilly's mouth watered. She felt a rush of grati-tude towards Mrs Dekker for bringing her on this voyage.

At lunch Mrs Dekker seemed reflective. 'Did your mother tell you much about where she grew up before we moved to Prague?' she asked Freddie. 'We lived in Ruthenia, in the east of the old Austro-Hungarian Empire. It became part of Czecho-slovakia when the empire was broken up after the last war. And that was when your grandfather and I moved to Prague with your Aunt Ruth and your mother.'

'How did you come to move to New York, Mrs Dekker?' Romilly asked, curiosity overcoming her. She blushed. 'Sorry, I'm being impertinent. It just sounds . . . Well, like something from the pictures.'

Mrs Dekker gave her a gracious nod. 'When Freddie's grandfather died, I took on the management of the family glass-making business in our factory outside Prague.'

Romilly looked at Mrs Dekker, trying to imagine her as a woman running a business rather than lounging around on a liner.

'I was at a trade fair in Berlin when I met Jackson Dekker. He was in the glass industry too, a different kind of product, though, used in laboratories. We fell in love. He followed me back to Prague and courted me until I agreed to marry him and move to New York. My eldest, Ruth, wanted to come too. Irma, Freddie's mother, was at university and wanted to stay in Czechoslovakia.'

Mrs Dekker's was a later-life romance, like Mama and Douglas's: both widowed, both with daughters. Something seemed stuck in Romilly's throat. She looked down at the weave of her white linen napkin for a moment. 'That's a romantic story.' When she could look up again Mrs Dekker was nodding.

'A chance meeting around an exhibition stand when Jackson couldn't understand something a German supplier was telling him. I didn't speak much English, but I made Jackson understand that he was dealing with the biggest *zhulik* west of the Oder.' Her eyes flashed at the memory. 'I have an instinct for knowing when things aren't right.'

Romilly felt herself sit straighter and pay more attention to Mrs Dekker.

'It was challenging in America during the Depression. But Jackson and I concentrated on the products that would always be needed: the glass bottles and jars for food manufacturers. We didn't sack a single employee and came out strong.'

Freddie moved restlessly on his chair. 'Do you remember Prague?' Romilly asked, trying to engage him.

He nodded. 'Throwing snowballs with the other children in the courtyard. We had candles on Fridays but they didn't, because they weren't Jews.' He prodded his fork into the plate. 'Mrs Cohen has candles on Fridays, too.' He stopped, perhaps remembering that Mrs Cohen's Sabbath arrangements would now only be memories for him.

'Does Mrs Belman observe Sabbath in the same way?' Romilly asked Mrs Dekker awkwardly, not knowing much about Jewish customs and never, in fact, having met many Jewish people at all.

'Oh, Ruth's very secular these days. So am I. But we light candles on the Sabbath and we will do all we can to make Freddie feel at home.'

Freddie would be part of a family, with cousins, an aunt and uncle and a grandmother, and a new school and friends. She couldn't help but compare his situation with her own. All that was left to her were Uncle Simon and Aunt Ursula. Her uncle was kind, but since the death of Mama he'd seemed to find even making eye contact with her embarrassing. Aunt Ursula had never made a secret of the fact that she'd found Mama and Romilly oddities: living in their cramped mews house, with that man spending a lot of time there and Romilly burying herself away in a bookshop.

'It sounds a wonderful set-up,' she told Mrs Dekker, with feeling.

Mrs Dekker gave a slow nod. 'My life in New York has been a good one, especially when Jackson was there.' She looked around the dining-room, with its crisp white linen and palms and smiling waiters. 'Yet part of me is still a young girl in the Carpathians, fearing pogroms.'

'Pogroms?' Romilly asked.

'Organised attacks on Jewish settlements. Houses burned, families driven out, sometimes killed or . . . other things. Hitler wasn't the first to turn against the Jews, you know. I was always alert, even as a small child, looking for a way out.'

Romilly met her dark-eyed gaze. 'It's good to know where the exits are. The words were coming to her from somewhere. 'And where the nearest shelter is.' A flicker of recognition, perhaps almost sympathy, passed between the two of them.

'You have paid close attention to the drill here, Romilly.' The words sounded grudgingly approving.

'I like to know how to get out of a place.'

'Tell me about your own childhood, dear,' Mrs Dekker said, breaking her gaze. Romilly told her about the prosperous early years, with a father who did something in the City, a maid and a cocker spaniel called Bumble, whom they took for walks in Richmond Park.

'My father lost his money when the stock market crashed. Perhaps the stress affected his heart and we didn't realise because he died suddenly after what we thought was just a bad cold. It became . . . harder then.'

Mama had sat up late, trying to balance the cheque books and scribbling sums on a piece of paper. She rented out rooms in the house. The maid's hours were reduced and when the spaniel died, pleas for another pet were turned down. Knitwear was darned and sheets turned when they were worn. Mama took on a job as a secretary in a solicitor's office.

Romilly stopped there, before the arrival of Douglas in their lives. 'My mother died very recently of an infection after a routine operation,' she ended. Mrs Dekker bowed her head.

'Finish that trifle,' she told Freddie. Romilly traced her spoon around the cream topping on her own helping, remembering how Mama had come home one evening the spring before the war started.

'That man who came to have a document witnessed and asked me the way to the park,' her mother had said. 'He looked at the photograph on my desk of you and Bumble and told me he'd once had a cocker spaniel just like him. Well, I bumped into him later on when I was on the way home. We talked about the deer. He's asked me to meet him for another walk on Sunday, darling. Do you think I should go?'

Romilly, seventeen, preoccupied with studying for school certificate and whether or not she should blow her pocket money on a Tango lipstick, had thought the outing sounded so mundane as to be almost unworthy of comment. 'If you fancy a walk, why not?' She'd barely raised her head from the advertisement in the magazine, agonising over the choice of shades.

She couldn't tell Mrs Dekker about Douglas, how the relationship between him and Mama had blossomed. How he found the little mews house in Chelsea for them to rent in the early summer of 1939 and helped them sell the Richmond house. Mama had released capital from the sale. She could take the bus to her work in Richmond, but she'd be more central, making it easier for them to meet anonymously. He could visit her without the neighbours knowing, that's what Aunt Ursula had said, with a sniff.

'As you know, I worked in a bookshop,' Romilly told Mrs Dekker. 'I'd still be there now, I suppose, if my mother hadn't died.' She stopped.

'And was there someone?' Mrs Dekker asked. 'Someone particular in your life?'

Romilly nodded. 'But that's over now.' He'd written to her when he'd heard about Mama. She hadn't answered Philip's letter. He probably didn't even know she'd sailed away.

'You can leave it all behind.' Mrs Dekker's voice was so low Romilly could barely hear it. 'America is the place we go to forget all the bad things.'

Their eyes met again over the starched white linen tablecloth.

SEVEN

The morning sun slid between the centre edges of the curtains where they weren't quite pulled together. Vida put a hand over her eyes and thought about complaining to the steward. *Oh honey,* Jackson said. *Why be sorry for an extra hour of a beautiful morning?*

To be fair, she'd slept well, perhaps as well as she had since leaving New York on this mission of hers. Vida felt something almost like guilt. This voyage back wasn't proving too onerous with its abundant food, comfortable cabins and sea air. Only the awkwardness with her grandson prevented it from being acceptable. And the U-boats. She could work on the first niggle; the second was beyond her.

Freddie. He was the priority. She was only sixty-one, plenty of time to work on the relationship with him. She'd tended to see him as the child of her own adored younger child, a proxy for Irma. But he deserved to be cherished in his own right. She wasn't a bad grandmother to Ruth's twins, after all. But she'd known Lewis and Clara since the day they were born: two little bundles of fury, cradled in the pristine maternity ward. It would be different with Freddie without those early years together in the park or reading bedtime stories. She'd have to make more of an effort with him here on *The Lucknow*. The dog might be the way. She'd seen how Freddie looked at Smoky, how his shoulders dropped and his face softened when he was with the animal. In New York they could walk him together in Central Park. On *The Lucknow*, she and Freddie could perhaps take him out on the deck together. Good for her blood pressure. *Honey, the other thing that would be good for your blood pressure would be cutting back on the rich meals.* She snorted at Jackson's voice. He hadn't exactly held back at the table, probably cutting years off his own life.

On the chair, Smoky yawned and stretched. Still only seven o'clock. Vida could take him up to the exercise deck and stretch her own legs, spare Romilly the task. She wouldn't worry about getting properly dressed: just tidy up her hair and dab some lipstick on and sort everything else out when she returned to the cabin. How sensible she'd been to bring some of what New Yorkers called cruise-wear, including a wide-legged pair of slacks and sweaters. Probably not flattering in the same way a dress would be, but adequate. *You look wonderful whatever you wear.* How could Jackson's voice still be as clear in her head as it had been during their marriage?

She found the lead and took the dog up to the deck. The sea had calmed overnight. The light was almost blinding. Every line on her face would be clearly etched. She should have brought a hat to shadow it. But who would see her? The only people up here were half a dozen of the boys from the refugee group, chasing one another and watched by an older boy. The redhead must still be dressing the younger children. The boys looked the same age as Freddie. *Aw honey, let him play with those kids. What's the harm in it?*

If he'd been here, Jackson would have known each of those boys' names by now, where they were from, where they were going. He'd have dispersed candy and coins. While her second husband had been with her, Vida had felt herself expand into his view of life too: a generous, forgiving kind of place. She'd moved from being the wary girl from a distant eastern European town, widowed young, trying to make the glass-making business flourish. She'd become an American wife and business partner: challenged by the Depression but able, at times, to look forward with hope.

But hope wasn't the same as optimism. Jackson had died before Hitler marched into the Sudetenland and then invaded Poland. He'd been wrong to promise that she'd see Irma as often as she wanted – *hell, he'd ship her and her family over to New York once a year if she wished* – and that Vida could make the trip across the Atlantic every year herself. He hadn't expected the world to turn so dangerous.

She sprinkled sand from the bucket on Smoky's deposit and found the dustpan and brush so she could flick it overboard even though one of the Lascars was hovering and would have done it for her. As a girl she'd never had anyone to do things for her. Her mother had taken in washing. She'd always felt so scared that something of this early poverty would show if she carried out menial work herself. She'd never realised this about herself before. All these years when she'd insisted on having the best in life, she'd been frightened that any compromise would expose her for what she really was. A peasant. Well, this peasant hadn't done so badly and could clear up her own dog's mess without worrying people would look down on her.

Perhaps the morning sunshine was putting her into a good mood. *Atta girl, look after yourself, enjoy the sea air and spend time with Freddie.*

Vida felt the engines pulsing beneath them as she and the dog returned to the cabin. The ship felt sturdy, even as it was presumably moving at some speed through the ocean. The sun was out. Why, then, did she feel the return of her sense of foreboding as she unlocked her cabin? She stared at the intercon-

necting door to Romilly and Freddie's cabin, hearing sounds of
movement. At least this morning the girl seemed more organised. Vida unclipped the lead. Smoky returned to the armchair.
There hadn't been time to ask much about him, what kind of
dog he was. A mixture? Yet again she marvelled at his ability to
coil himself up into a tight ball. Did he feel the need to bind
himself together against some kind of threat? Even in this
comfortable cabin? Vida stripped down to her underclothes and
washed herself in the basin. A bath would be an evening treat.
She applied cream carefully to the creases around her eyes.
Romilly had fine skin, albeit of that pallid English tone that
probably came from spending so much of the autumn and
winter either indoors or sheltering from the bombs. A day or
two more of sea air would bring colour to her cheeks. By the
time she arrived in New York the girl would be quite the peach.
Perhaps the stunned expression on her face would be replaced
by something more purposeful, more befitting New York, where
you needed to look as though you knew where you were going
and were ready for anything. And yet those hazel eyes of Romilly's were sometimes watchful, too. Watchful was good.

At Romilly's age, Vida had known that life was full of
sudden reversals of fortune. You couldn't grow up Jewish on the
frontiers of competing empires without knowing this. She had
known to trust her instincts, that the small and inconvenient
voice whispering to you should be listened to.

Ach, she was just being paranoid again. But she'd always
trusted her instincts. Jackson had called her a witch. 'How did
you know the Pennsylvania plant wasn't a goer?' he'd asked. 'It
looked good. None of my guys sensed what you sensed until I
made them go back and have another look.'

The owner-manager's secretary who wouldn't meet their
eyes when she'd shown them into the meeting with him. The
rust around the taps in the ladies' room that belied the new

carpet in the office. 'Small things.' The back of her neck had prickled.

'Your hunch saved us a fortune, sweetheart.'

Vida looked out through the window. A destroyer sailed beside them, looking much closer to *The Lucknow* in the morning light. *There you are, they're looking after you.*

Vida returned to her dressing table and applied vermillion to her lips before rapping on the interconnecting door for the youngsters. Time to start the day properly.

EIGHT

After a day of studying and playing quoits with her on the deck, interspersed with large meals, Romilly was not surprised that Freddie willingly took himself off to bed at half-eight. Before he fell asleep, she read him more of *The Children of the New Forest* and he seemed to listen with some interest. Once or twice he even smiled.

After a moment's hesitation, she knocked on the interconnecting door. Mrs Dekker called her in and she found her sitting at her desk, writing letters. 'I don't know why I'm doing this, I'll see them all again in days.' She put the lid on her fountain pen. 'Do you have letters to mail, dear?'

'I'll wait to send postcards from New York.' She was uncertain as to who might welcome a card from her. Perhaps Aunt Ursula would be impressed by a postcard of the Empire State Building and show it off at her Women's Voluntary Service afternoon. Either that, or she'd regard it as an unpatriotic gesture. Seeking distraction from her aunt, Romilly looked at Smoky, stretched out on the mossy carpet. 'Shall I take him out for a final turn round the deck? Freddie's asleep.'

Mrs Dekker passed Romilly the lead from the desk. She stared at the dog and frowned. 'Do you think he's settling?'

What could she say? 'I haven't known him long, Mrs Dekker, but Smoky seems a born seadog.'

Mrs Dekker smiled, looking fleetingly more like her grandson. Was this what she was like with her daughter and the twins – relaxed, kindly? Romilly hoped for Freddie's sake that this side of her would surface more often.

Romilly and Smoky walked through the saloon, comfortably lit and full of men reading newspapers and talking in low voices. Out on deck, other people were letting their dogs off the lead so they could bound around and retrieve rubber balls. She clutched the lead more tightly.

'That's the most pampered pooch on board.'

Romilly spun around to see Edward Witney behind her.

'I don't think he lives in the kennels with the other dogs. Is that because he's so small they might think he's dinner?'

'Mrs Dekker says his nerves wouldn't be up to it.'

Edward was watching Smoky. 'He looks pretty relaxed. Did she bring him with her from America?'

'From the little I've gathered, she rescued him while she was in London.' The full story of Smoky's arrival in Mrs Dekker's life hadn't yet been told to Romilly.

'He seems to have survived the worst the Luftwaffe can do.' Edward offered her a cigarette from his case. She took one gratefully and he lit it for her. They walked along the deck, Smoky sniffing railings enthusiastically, wagging his tail at the other dogs. 'Whereabouts in New York does Mrs Dekker live?' he asked.

She told him about the block in Central Park West and how Mrs Dekker and her daughter lived in apartments one above the other. 'Good address,' he said. 'Convenient and comfortable. Lucky young Freddie. And Smoky, with that park to explore.

And you plan to make your own home there, too, Miss Brooks, you said?'

He was certainly inquisitive. Perhaps she should mind the questions, but she didn't, not really. He sounded just like he ought to, with that expensive suit. Public school, well-off. And yet, was there perhaps just a hint of an accent in his voice?

'If I can. They won't need me to look after Freddie permanently once we're safely in Manhattan.' The family hadn't spelled out just how long she'd be needed to settle Freddie in. A few days? A week? The full four weeks the visa lasted? She could be waiting on tenterhooks for Mrs Dekker and her daughter to hand her an envelope with her wages, their thanks and a dismissal. What then, she wondered again? She'd have her earnings plus a small amount from her savings account. There might be more money to come, Uncle Simon had said, once he'd finished winding up her mother's affairs.

How quickly, if at all, could money be cabled to America? She must be frowning – Edward Witney was raising an eyebrow at her. She composed her features. 'I'll just have to turn my hand to whatever I can find, won't I?' He was still looking at her curiously.

'Some people run away to America to escape.'

'That's me.'

'Sometimes judgements are passed. People say it's wrong to leave Britain.' He was asking a question, watching her for a reaction.

Romilly shrugged. 'Perhaps, if they still have families and friends there. I don't have anyone to stay for.' Was he trying to provoke a reaction from her? She didn't really care what he thought.

'What was your line before you left?'

'I worked in a bookshop.' She realised how vague it sounded. She'd need to up her game or she risked sounding like a drip. 'I can type and my shorthand isn't bad. I was thinking of studying book-keeping in the evenings.' There must be thousands of girls like her in New York, with smarter clothes and hairstyles. She set her shoulders. 'I was good at finding books a customer might like, selling them titles they mightn't have come across.'

'Good at selling, eh?' He gave her another one of his long, searching looks. She tilted her chin to meet his gaze. Let him try and make her feel she was making a mistake. Perhaps she was, but it was her mistake to make and nobody else's business.

'I have nothing to lose trying my luck in New York.' She spoke quietly, not even sure he'd heard until he nodded slowly.

'I'm going to give you this.' He reached inside his life-vest and jacket pocket to remove a silver cardholder. 'This bureau is in New York.' He handed her the card. No name. Just a telephone number. 'We'll talk more before we disembark in Montreal.' He replaced the cardholder, grunting with displeasure at the life-vest. 'I'll be so pleased not to have to wear this wretched object everywhere.'

'I used to think gas masks were the worst thing. Now I'm not so sure.' Mumbling a thanks, she put the card in her skirt pocket. As she and Smoky walked back to the salon door, she felt Edward's eyes on her back.

Romilly thought the gentle evening stroll would put her in the mood for sleep, but she found herself tossing in her bed again. Freddie's breaths were smooth. He might be more settled this evening, but she felt less calm. She turned another page of her novel and realised that she hadn't taken in a word. Already having broken curfew the previous night, she was pushing her luck leaving the cabin for a second time, but she couldn't stay in bed. If she was caught, she'd claim she was going to the lavatory.

It felt colder now. She pulled her dressing-gown over her life-vest and pulled Freddie's sheet and blankets up to cover his chest, then left the cabin silently.

Walking the corridor by night made her feel as if *The Lucknow* belonged to her alone, its captain and crew propelling her through the darkness. Reaching the gallery, she gazed down the staircase, lit in its dim night-time tones, but more restful than daylight. The murmurs of a group of Lascar stewards approaching the foot of the staircase sent her scurrying behind a pillar. They talked and laughed in their own language. What did they make of this voyage and the passengers? Maybe they just wanted to make money and go home to their families, leaving the grey Atlantic behind.

The Lascars passed through one of the discreet doors at the rear of the foyer leading, she presumed, to the galley and other service areas. Romilly made her way down the stairs and headed to the port side, towards the library.

Voices reached her, this time English ones.

Romilly darted behind one of the elegant painted screens at the foot of the grand staircase. A man and a woman came towards her. Excitement pricked her. That same woman again, the one with the dark hair and the accent she couldn't place. Romilly peeped more closely through the panels of the screen. As she thought, Edward was with her again.

'It's a truly masterful performance,' he said.

'You know me, give me a good role and I throw myself into it.'

'I've always said the West End's loss is our gain, Catherine.' Was Edward's voice less polished than it had been earlier on? The hint of regional accent sounded stronger now. It intrigued her, she squinted harder at him through the panels.

Catherine laughed: a deep, throaty laugh so contagious that Romilly found herself wanting to laugh in response. She turned away from the screen, cursing silently as she failed to grab a second look at the woman's face.

'Getting time alone is going to become harder once we're off the ship. We need to make the most of it.' Catherine sounded more serious. 'On the train, it'll be harder to find time alone together without curious eyes on us.'

Romilly flushed, feeling disappointed and not sure exactly why.

'We'll find a way. We have to.'

'So was she receptive, your little mouse? I had to dash down the companionway to avoid her last night.'

Romilly felt her muscles clench. Her mouth opened to protest, but she forced herself to stay still. 'Don't know yet, but I handed her the card.'

'There must be other girls?'

'Perhaps. Not on this ship. Something about this one makes me think she's right for the Rockefeller operation. She's got some spirit, if she chooses to recognise it.' Something rustled. 'In the meantime, I should pass some of these back to you. I failed in London,' he said. 'Most of the printers were bombed out or had ink and paper shortages. Or the finished result just didn't look authentic. At least if we have a supply of flyers each, we can try our luck with New York printshops.'

'Riskier, though.'

'Not for you with your chameleon skills. You can find a way to talk yourself out of tricky spots. I've never been as good.'

She laughed. 'No. You're coming along though, when you concentrate.'

'Hide them under your mattress.' A door opened. 'Damn, someone's coming. Are you clear on the next rendezvous?'

Catherine glanced over her shoulder. Romilly blanched, even though she knew she was invisible. 'Hotdog stand, Saturday, three pm. I hope whoever you've found for the male role has a gentle touch.'

'We're relying on acting skills rather than physical violence. Anyway, when did you ever shy away from a scrap?' Admiration in his voice. Whoever this woman was, Edward clearly thought well of her.

A breeze blew through the foyer. Romilly heard a metallic clanking. A cleaning trolley, she thought. The passengers might be curfewed, but the staff would still need to carry out essential cleaning duties. Papers flew. 'Grab them, quick,' Edward said. Romilly heard the pair dash around picking up flyers before they walked off to the staircase, their feet pattering away before the Lascar reached the foyer, Edward's footsteps noticeable with their uneven pace.

The Lascar looked up, but, seeing nobody, started to move chairs and tables. Would he move the screen? She held her breath. Someone else came in and started a conversation in their own language with its melodic rises and falls. Through the gap between the slats Romilly saw them walk away towards the rear of the foyer. One of the flyers had blown behind a chair, unnoticed by Edward. The Lascar picked up the piece of paper without looking at what was written on it and put it on one of the occasional tables, alongside the magazines advertising Florida vacations, sweeping the floor underneath the table. Romilly darted back behind the screen and waited to see if he'd move on, but he was taking his time, stooping down to dust the legs. He continued to the next table. There were half a dozen tables down here. He'd be working for ages. She couldn't wait any longer and the only other place she could hide was in the lift. But he'd hear the doors clinking open. Nothing for it but to make a dash for it. Romilly darted lightly up the staircase to the gallery, holding her breath until she had silently closed the door behind her, and on to her cabin.

Freddie was still breathing slowly and quietly. She removed her dressing-gown and got into bed. She was buzzing with questions. It took her an hour to fall asleep, tossing and turning in the unwieldly life-vest.

The steward's knock on the door seemed to come seconds after Romilly had dropped off. She looked at her watch and groaned. She'd hoped to slip down to the foyer before the ship was stirring to grab the flyer. Was it even significant? Important enough for Edward and Catherine to discuss in secret. She'd have to find a moment when Freddie was preoccupied and hope nobody else had found the dropped flyer on the occasional table before she did.

Romilly washed quickly and dressed. 'You were out of the cabin again last night.' Freddie sounded smug.

'I needed the lavatory.'

'We're not supposed to get up at night unless it's an emergency.'

She shrugged. 'Let's get your grandmother and have some breakfast.'

As they passed through the foyer, Romilly glanced at the occasional table. The flyer was still sitting on top of the magazines. 'You look pale, dear.' Mrs Dekker's gaze seemed to pierce Romilly's head.

'Just hungry.' She was unable to think of an excuse at this moment for going over to the magazines and removing the paper without being questioned.

In fact, she did have a good appetite this morning. Perhaps the famed sea air really did work wonders on people. Or else sheer curiosity did the same thing. It really wasn't any of her business, she told herself. All the same, as they ate breakfast, she couldn't help glancing around as people walked in and out.

'Looking for someone?' Mrs Dekker asked drily. 'Or are you actually going to eat that toast before it's cold?'

'Sorry.' She bit into the toast. The butter had melted to just the right degree and the marmalade cut through its sweetness perfectly. She hadn't yet become accustomed to the food on *The Lucknow* and it was enough to distract her from her quest.

Perhaps her pleasure was visible on her face. Mrs Dekker raised an eyebrow. 'Glad you're enjoying the meals.'

'They're wonderful.' She spoke without thinking: something she didn't often do in conversation with her employer, still wary of saying the wrong thing.

'Was the rationing bad for your family?' Mrs Dekker asked, looking as if she really wanted to know. She'd asked so few questions about London in the war.

'It made cooking interesting meals hard. My mother tried her best and became good at doing things with parsnips and potatoes. But when we left the table, we always felt that an extra spoonful would have been good.'

Freddie was looking at her with an expression that implied he knew what she meant.

She remembered Douglas praising Mama for a pie made out of potatoes and a tiny scraping of Cheddar. Assuming he was still alive, did he remember those meals the three of them had together, feeling like a real family as they sat around the table? She couldn't actually feel much curiosity about Douglas anymore. She looked at her watch. 'Time for us to get our books, Freddie.'

Mrs Dekker nodded approvingly. 'I don't think the deck will be suitable this morning, though.' Romilly looked out of the windows at the seahorses galloping across the sea. The sky was low and grey. No sight of the destroyer today: the visibility wasn't good enough.

'Can't we walk Smoky first?' Freddie asked, looking sullen when Mrs Dekker shook her head.

They left Mrs Dekker with a second cup of coffee. As they walked across the foyer, a small crowd clustered around the occasional tables, chatting about a bridge tournament. A woman put her crocodile-skin handbag down on top of the magazines. No hope of retrieving Edward's flyer without drawing attention to it.

Romilly spotted Ahmed heading towards the service doors at the rear. Telling Freddie to wait there, she walked on quickly. 'Would there be any way I could look at the passenger list, Ahmed?' If she couldn't get hold of that flyer immediately, she could at least find out who the woman was.

His eyes widened. 'Why would you want to do that, miss?'

'There's a passenger, Catherine someone or other, I never see at meals or out on deck. I'm just being nosy. There aren't many girls my age on *The Lucknow*.'

'Ah, it would be good for you to have more company, Miss Romilly. Miss Louise is always so busy with her charges. But a passenger called Catherine?' He frowned. 'This lady I do not know and we do not have many passengers onboard.'

'Could you look at the list for me?'

He looked doubtful. 'The captain shows the list only as required by the authorities. He has to be very careful, you'll understand.'

Passenger lists were perhaps seen as sensitive information. 'I only see Catherine at night. She never appears in daytime. You don't seem to know who she is. Isn't that something we should be worried about, Ahmed?' Since the start of the war they'd always been told to report suspicions about people.

Freddie was walking towards her. Ahmed nodded. 'I will ask the captain, miss. Do not worry yourself. Perhaps the lady is a bona fide passenger using, what is it called, a pet name for reasons best not examined.' With a bow, he left her.

'What was all that?' Freddie asked.

'Just checking I labelled our laundry bags correctly.' How easily the lie came to her.

'If you've lost my grandmother's clothes she'll give you a rocketing.'

'Everything's fine.' She spoke in a tone she hoped would end the conversation. 'Let's get our things and go to the library.'

In their cabin, Freddie insisted on opening the door to Mrs Dekker's to check on Smoky. The dog jumped down to the carpet and ran towards him, ears back, tail wagging. 'I wish we could take him into the library. Nobody would notice.' She felt his dark eyes on hers.

'Your grandmother probably wants to keep him with her.' Romilly shoed Smoky back into Mrs Dekker's cabin and shut the door. 'Let's get to work.'

The library was perhaps her favourite part of *The Lucknow*, she decided. The wooden bookcases filled with volumes, the tables and armchairs set back into alcoves, the newspapers and magazines hanging from their racks: it felt simultaneously stimulating and soothing. The newspapers were now days out of date, but she spotted a yellow-covered *National Geographic* on a rack and scooped it up for Freddie. He seemed to like colouring: perhaps he could reproduce one of the colour plates with his pencils. She directed him to a table in the furthest corner of the library and moved the chairs so they were facing into the alcove. 'We'll have to keep our voices down,' she told Freddie. 'People come in here to read in peace. Let's see what you can draw.' She flicked through the pages, finding a photograph of an American eagle.

'Appropriate,' Edward Witney said from behind her, making her jump. Under his arm he carried a leather portfolio case. Whatever his line, it was keeping him busy onboard *The Lucknow*. Did the portfolio contain more of the flyers? How would he react if she told him he'd dropped something in the foyer late last night?

'Did you have a pleasant night?' she asked, before she could say anything else. Something about the sea air was making her much more confident – some might say reckless – about speaking what was on her mind. Back in England she'd operated as girls her age were supposed to: minding her tongue, hanging back a bit, not drawing attention to herself.

He blinked. 'Oh, I went to my cabin after you and I met on deck.'

Romilly stared at him and thought he looked briefly disconcerted, but his composure returned almost immediately. He smiled at Freddie, reminding Romilly of a friendly vicar. 'Your teacher is planning a busy morning, I see?'

'Romilly's not a real teacher. My grandmother just wants her to make me sound posh. Don't know why that's important for Yanks. They don't know what posh is.'

Edward's laugh caused a few of the newspaper-reading gentlemen to look up.

'You don't think Americans will appreciate Romilly's work?'

'Why should they? They have cowboys and Indians and skyscrapers. Why would they care about how we speak in England?'

'Sharp, but perceptive,' Edward said. 'Some of them care about being posh, though perhaps not in all the ways the British do. But you're right, it's a large, diverse country. Lots of variety in people and wildlife. That's one of the reasons I like America so much, I suppose.' There was a real enthusiasm in his voice she hadn't heard before. But perhaps nobody in Britain had been feeling very enthusiastic at this stage of the war, with the bombing having lasted since autumn and the news never seeming to improve.

Romilly glanced down at the eagle in the *Geographic*: so fierce, with his talons and piercing eyes, with the mountains behind him, so completely suited to the wild and open countryside. Was that how she would have to be, too? Perhaps huddling in an air-raid shelter was safer than trying to be bold enough to take on America. But back in London the shame would still be there. Its grey twisting fingers would still pull at Romilly, reminding her of that night.

'The Americans should fight the Germans with us.' Freddie picked up a brown pencil to shade in the eagle's feathers. 'That's what Mrs Cohen thinks. She said they've got their bloody heads stuck in the sand. I'm going to tell them that when I get there.'

'I think we should get back to our lessons,' Romilly said. 'While you're finishing the drawing you can be thinking about the landscape the eagle lives in and the other animals who inhabit it.'

'Well intervened, Miss Brooks,' Edward said quietly. 'Though Mrs Cohen is correct.'

She swept one of the pencils off the table and bent to pick it up so she didn't have to expose her face to him. Her mixed feelings about him must be written all over it.

'He's like you.' Freddie watched Edward walked away.

'What do you mean?' She glanced at Edward's well-tailored figure. The limp seemed more pronounced this morning.

'You're both hiding something.' He replaced the brown pencil with a green one and drew in leaves on a tree.

'I'll look at the books to see if there's anything more we can read on American fauna, that's animals and birds.'

Freddie was sharper than she'd thought. If he knew she was hiding something, was it clear to Mrs Dekker as well? He was right about Edward Witney having secrets, too.

An elderly couple, probably Jewish from The Netherlands or Belgium, she thought, were reading travel guides, quietly reciting sections aloud to one another in accented English and nodding excitedly. Their clothes were expensive but had been carefully darned, she noticed. Their faces were lined but hope burned in the smiles they gave her as she passed. She wondered whether they had family in the States or whether they'd arrive as complete strangers in a new country. They were fellow adventurers, a desire to succeed in a new life uniting them with Romilly despite the age gap.

'Your little brother concentrates hard.' The man's words seemed to come out with effort.

'Oh, Freddie's not my brother. I'm just his companion.'

The couple looked at one another. 'What is a companion?' the woman asked.

'His grandmother employs me to look after him.'

They nodded. 'You do a good job,' the woman said. 'We thought you were family.'

Romilly thanked her. Freddie as her younger brother? What a strange thing to believe. She had no intention of growing any closer to him. And yet, there was something about the kid that could be quite endearing. He had a good sense of humour, despite all he'd been through. Which was a lot.

Romilly found a book about wildlife in North America and carried on scanning the shelves. She spotted a few novels she hadn't read, older ones that the bookshop didn't stock. A pang for her old job swept her. She'd liked the quiet, companionable days with Miss Jones, dusting the shelves and books, wrapping up orders for posting to customers, answering the telephone, helping the few people who still came in from the street to search for something to read, feeling real joy when she sold them something she knew they'd enjoy. Perhaps she would have longed for more excitement in time. Well, she certainly had that now. But wherever she went, there were always books, which was a comfort.

She glanced back at the elderly couple, noticing the leather travel pouch between them on the small sofa. In there would be their exit and entry visas and all manner of other paperwork they'd need. She hadn't seen the entry papers for America that Mrs Dekker had for them all, just her own visa, stamped in her passport and safe in the cabin. Suppose the paperwork hadn't been properly completed and she was thrown off the train at the border, left alone in Canada? Well, if that happened, she'd have to make the best of it, sneak herself across into the United States some other way. She wouldn't be that little mouse. Her lips pursed.

'You look fierce,' Freddie whispered when she returned to the table with the book. 'Like my eagle.'

Fierce she was going to be, if necessary. Something was going on here on *The Lucknow*. That flyer that she still hadn't read – she wasn't going to sit back without getting to the bottom of it all. Perhaps it was nothing at all. Edward and Catherine had talked about acting: perhaps he had some kind of interest in a Broadway show or something. He'd been a puppeteer that very first night on board the ship, after all. She was probably obsessing about something trivial. But the obsession was distracting her away from all those things she didn't want to think about anymore, so she was going to indulge it.

'Could I trust you to stay here quietly for five minutes?' she asked Freddie.

'Why?'

'It's personal.'

He didn't lift his head from his drawing. 'All right.'

'If you move, I'll have you keel-hauled.'

'What's that?'

'They pull you under the hull of the boat and drag you up the other side.' She winked at him and after a second he grinned. She caught a glimpse of the mischievous urchin he'd probably been back at Mrs Cohen's. She knew he wouldn't move. The two of them were starting to understand one another.

As she crossed the foyer, Romilly looked around quickly to ensure Mrs Dekker wasn't emerging from one of the shops or salons. There was a single man standing at the occasional table, looking as though he might sit down at any moment. 'Excuse me.' She took the top magazine and the flyer off the table, trying to make it look as though it was the Florida vacations that she was interested in. For a moment she pretended to flick through the magazine's pages. When she was sure the man wasn't look-ing, she murmured another apology and replaced the magazine on the table.

She read the flyer as she walked back to the library.

Romilly came to a halt.

NINE

Vida watched Freddie and the girl playing quoits on the deck despite the rocking of the deck and the wind blowing salty water into their faces. The game seemed to involve throwing rope hoops over a wooden peg. Freddie wasn't bad for a boy his age, almost matching Romilly's success. Each time she threw her hoop she stared at the peg so intently Vida could almost feel it heating up under her stare. Romilly's final throw was a success: a ringer, a spectator shouted. She raised her arms in triumph.

'Let's have another game.' Freddie scooped up the rope hoops. Romilly blinked, as though wanting to decline, but she said nothing. Did she consider herself so beholden to them she couldn't even say she'd had enough?

But then Romilly shook her head. 'It's too choppy.'

Freddie looked as though he had objections. Romilly pointed at the railings. 'We still haven't seen any whales yet. Shall we have a look?'

Folding his arms and letting out a sigh, Freddie allowed himself to be led away. Vida joined them at the railing, clinging to it as the ship lurched. The Franklins came to stand at the railings too. Jack and Freddie grinned at one another. 'I feel awful,' Mrs Franklin told her husband, her hand going to her mouth.

'You just need fresh air. Better for you to be out here than down in the cabin,' her husband told her. He seemed, annoyingly, to be one of those people who didn't suffer from the lurching. Romilly and Freddie seemed equally untroubled. Vida felt her own insides surge as the ship pitched. The voyage out had been calm, unusually so, the crew had told her.

'I'm going down to the cabin,' she told Romilly. Really, she should tell the girl to help her down: that's what Romilly's job was. But it was a shame to force her and Freddie inside. Freddie didn't seem to mind the pitching and the lashing spray, seemed to relish it. Was it safe out here? He was wearing his life-vest and lifebelts were pinned to posts along the deck. But if a child fell into these seas, he'd be gone in seconds. 'Take him down to the library if it gets any rougher,' she told Romilly. Freddie made a face that reminded Vida of his mother at the same age when she didn't want to come inside from the falling snow. Irma had always loved being outdoors, regardless of weather. The cells in Vida's body filled with a sudden pain so intense that she gripped the railing even harder.

'Are you all right, Mrs Dekker?' Romilly asked.

For a moment she couldn't answer, her daughter filling her consciousness. Where was Irma now? Still in their apartment? Or thrown out and interned somewhere, struggling to find food? Working, or were she and Josef no longer allowed to earn money to survive? Was her younger daughter cold, hungry, scared? And there she was, travelling further and further away from Europe, leaving her girl to her fate.

'Just need to lie down,' Vida muttered, turning her eyes to the horizon, hoping it would settle her. But the horizon itself seemed blurred and indistinct, the swells more threatening, reminding her of the peril Irma faced. She felt an urge to beg Romilly to come down to the cabin with her, to listen while she

told her about her life in Prague with the two little girls who
were now mothers themselves, about the summer excursions out
to the countryside to pick plums and cherries, the trips to winter
markets in the city when the air smelled of gingerbread and
candles. Perhaps some of the longing flashed across her face
because Romilly leant towards her, head tilted.

'Shall I come with you, Mrs Dekker?'

She shook her head. 'Stay with Freddie, take him down to
the forward promenade deck behind the glass.' He'd be safer
there.

The steward, Ahmed, stood by the door into the saloon.
'Would you like me to escort you, Mrs Dekker?'

She shook her head. 'Some tea, please, in my cabin.'

'And perhaps a ginger biscuit?'

She managed a nod as she walked into the saloon. The room
was still occupied, though the passengers smoking and playing
cards cast uneasy glances out at the sea.

Down in her cabin, she sat in the armchair, which Smoky
had vacated. The dog lay in front of the interconnecting door,
ears pricked. Waiting for the other two to return, perhaps.

Vida faced the window so that she could see the horizon,
which Jackson had once told her made seasickness less awful.
Perhaps she should have followed Ruth's urging and not made
this double voyage herself. An organisation like the one
employing the redhead might have brought Freddie to New
York. Or she could have arranged for someone like Romilly to
take complete responsibility for escorting the boy across the
Atlantic. She hadn't been sure about Romilly to begin with,
though she'd been the best of the candidates, the only one who'd
smiled at Smoky, curled up on the armchair in the hotel room
and the only one who'd asked about Freddie's likes and dislikes.
And looked a little shocked when Vida had told her she hadn't
yet met her grandson. The girl had grown on her. In New York
it would be interesting to set a good hairdresser on that dark-

blonde hair and buy her some new clothes. Of course, she'd only be there for a month, but it would be a project. Her figure was neat, if too lean for perfection. *She's not a doll,* Jackson chided her. *And if you're only keeping her on for a month, let the kid loose for some fun.*

Smoky gave a sigh and left his vigil by the door, coming to lie beside her. She picked him up. 'If I hadn't come to London, I would never have found you, *milacku.*' She hadn't used that endearment for years, not even when Ruth's children had been infants. It had belonged to the past, to Prague. 'When we get to New York, we are never leaving again,' she told him. 'I only did it because I was feeling so guilty. I left my Irma in Europe and went off with Jackson. We will stay at home. Apart from, perhaps, a trip to Florida for some winter warmth,' she conceded, hearing Jackson's laugh. 'Freddie will like the beach. You will come too, Smoky. The sunshine will do you good.'

Ruth would tell her she doted too much on the dog. Probably true. She hadn't ever intended having a pet. It had been on her first morning in London, a city she'd never visited before, that she had rescued him. She emerged onto Piccadilly to find it grey and dusty, as though they could never completely clear up after the bombs that had only just stopped falling regularly. On the sidewalk, the pavement, as the British called it, a woman, middle-aged, smartly dressed, was taking a wicker carrier containing a small white dog towards a waiting taxi. Vida stopped.

'Michael says I must have him put to sleep,' the woman told her between tears, not even seeming to realise Vida was a complete stranger. 'We were bombed out and we can't have pets in our rented apartment. It's terribly smart but they don't like dogs. He's only two. I just...'

Vida's hand had been stretched out before she'd even noticed herself doing it. 'May I take your dog? I'm going back to

Manhattan,' she said. 'On a liner.' What? What was she saying? Had she lost her mind?

'But he hasn't got papers...'

'I'll sort the papers. The concierge will know what to do.' Jackson had always had utmost faith in concierges.

Emotions floated across the woman's face: relief, doubt, pain.

'I like dogs.' Vida hadn't had a dog since her childhood but suddenly knew that she loved this animal. 'I'll walk him every day in Central Park. On the liner he'll be in the cabin with me.'

The taxi driver tooted the horn. 'Are we having a meeting in the street?' he asked.

The woman extended the wicker basket to Vida.

'You can trust me,' Vida said. 'Here, this is where I live.' She extracted a card from the holder in her handbag. *Mrs Jackson Dekker* and her address. 'What's his name?'

'Smoky.' The woman's fingers loosened on the handle. 'He's good, comes to a whistle. Doesn't bark.'

'He will love Manhattan,' Vida said firmly. 'And he will have my grandchildren to play with.' The woman let out a breath and turned to the taxi.

'I'm so sorry. I won't be needing to go to the vet after all.' With a last whisper to the dog and muttered, sobbing, thanks to Vida, she walked away.

'Well,' Vida told him. 'This has been quite the visit, Smoky. I think you need a biscuit and some water and I need a strong coffee, if this city still runs to such a thing.'

Honey, Jackson laughed. *Ruth will think you're mad.*

In a world where armies could pour into other people's countries and kill anyone they wanted, rescuing a dog the size of a hand muff hadn't seemed like insanity to Vida.

Ahmed brought her tea and the promised ginger biscuits. 'The sea is growing calmer now, madam,' he told her. 'But the captain says it will be rougher again tonight. If you wish for fresh air, you should take the opportunity.'

'I shall have my hair done, I think.'

'Would you like me to make an appointment for you, perhaps in 25 minutes?'

How clever he was at knowing how long people needed to drink their tea. She found herself smiling and thanking him. When she'd finished, she gave Smoky a pat and promised him an excursion on the deck later.

The girl in the hair salon seemed to know what she wanted: washing and setting her hair with quick, nimble fingers and without too much chatter.

Freddie and Romilly hadn't returned to the cabin when she unlocked the door again. She hoped Romilly was finding something educational for the boy to do but couldn't seem to muster up as much anxiety about his lacking polish. Tomorrow Freddie could leave his studies and play. Perhaps even with one of those escorted children, though that might be going too far. The boy Jack in the cabin next door might be suitable. Though Vida hadn't missed the look his parents had exchanged. They knew she and Freddie were Jewish and they knew it in a particular way.

Vida sat in front of the mirrored dressing table and pulled at one of the freshly set waves of her hair, watching it spring back into place. Not bad. She could return to New York without feeling a fright. She felt refreshed, restless, even. Sensing a need in herself to do something she hadn't done for years, she found herself leaving her cabin again and heading down to the foyer and across to the library. It was one of the smaller public rooms and gave off an air of quiet studiousness.

In a corner, Freddie and Romilly sat with books and magazines. Freddie was drawing something, his cheeks still pink from being outside on deck. Disappointing that he wasn't reading something improving, but then why shouldn't the boy perfect his art? Irma had been a keen artist at his age and her talent had taken her into the world of designing interiors for some of the wealthiest families in Prague. That had been before the Nazis arrived, of course. Perhaps Freddie had inherited some of his mother's talent. Vida wanted to go over and look at his drawing, but that would interrupt him and it seemed almost unkind. Romilly was flicking through what looked like a guidebook, occasionally pulling at a lock of her hair. Perhaps she should book a hairdressing appointment for the girl while they were onboard. Shampooed and trimmed, possibly set, the hair would actually be quite attractive. It had a natural wave to it. Both Vida's girls had had thick dark hair. Ruth's was still without a single grey. Vida's had only started to turn in her early fifties.

Romilly lifted her head from the guidebook and looked at Freddie's drawing, saying something that made him grin. The two of them seemed to have formed a rapport. Was that good? Suppose Freddie was upset again when they said good-bye to Romilly as they inevitably would do once the boy was settled in.

Vida pulled an atlas off a shelf and sat down with it, turning to the pages covering Central Europe. She found the town of her birth, the mountains she'd hiked in as a girl. She tracked her family's journey west to Prague after the Great War, then the routes of her business trips to Berlin, Milan, Paris and Amsterdam. She flicked back to the British Isles and traced the route of their voyage from Liverpool, around the northern tip of Ireland and out into the immensity of the ocean. Where were they now? Somewhere in the middle of the North Atlantic, Greenland above them to the top of the page, Newfoundland ahead of them. At some point, perhaps around now, or while she was having her hair done, the Royal Naval ships accompanying them would have turned back to escort a convoy back to Britain.

They wouldn't exactly blast foghorns, would they, to announce their departure? She closed the atlas and returned it to the shelf, pulling out an illustrated history of the United States, looking at the drawings of the men in animal skins on their horses, the construction workers in overalls building skyscrapers and railways; such a busy, busy country.

A country that couldn't busy itself fighting for the stricken of Europe. She could understand them, of course, not wishing to shed anymore of their sons' blood after the First War and having many citizens of German and Italian background to consider. But even if the moral argument didn't sway them, wasn't it in their own interests to crush the Nazis, who would surely limit American ambitions? Markets, markets, it was all about markets. If you couldn't sell to the world because the Germans stood in the way, wouldn't that make a commercial case for fighting, too?

These thoughts distracted her so completely that she didn't notice Romilly and Freddie tidying their papers and standing up. It was only when they walked out of the door that she checked her watch. She'd been here for an hour, reading and thinking. Jackson would have laughed: *Not like you to be daydreaming, you're always such a busy bee, Veed.*

Vida returned her book to the shelf and walked quickly out in pursuit of the pair. Crossing the foyer, they met Edward Witney. Romilly jumped like a scalded cat when he raised his hat to her. Interesting. Did she have a crush on the man? He was an elegantly presented figure, that was for sure. But the way Romilly's shoulders stiffened made it uncertain that it was actual attraction she felt towards Mr Witney. Had he made an unwelcome pass at her? If that were the case, Vida would have a word with him. When her girls had been Romilly's age she'd been able to warn off unwanted suitors with a glare. Romilly walked on, her hand going towards her skirt pocket, as though she was worried Mr Witney might be trying to steal her purse.

Looking at her more closely, Vida decided Romilly didn't dislike Edward Witney. The studied refusal to make eye contact with him suggested something else. But what?

The ship sailed on smoothly, yet Vida felt, even more strongly since leaving the library, instinct warning her to pay attention. Her hand went to the ring on her little finger. The nervous tic had almost ceased while Jackson was in her life. The war had brought it back. Observing small interactions between other people seemed to trigger the compulsion.

Stop fiddling, she heard her long-dead mother scold. *Control yourself, Vida.*

You're fine, honey, Jackson told her. No peace from the voices in her head. She must have muttered this aloud because a passing Lascar gave her a worried stare.

TEN

Romilly was never away from Freddie's sharp eyes. The flyer crackled in her skirt pocket, but she dared not take it out again. The words she'd read on it were printed on her memory, anyway. *AMERICA FIRST COMMITTEE. Save our sons! Protect our neutrality! There's still time to keep us out of war.* Details of a rally to be held in Manhattan itself.

Edward was organising rallies to keep Americans out of the war? He didn't want them to join in the fight to stop Hitler? This rally, were things like that really going on in America? She tried to recall if she'd seen anything about the anti-war movement in the newspapers. All she remembered was Douglas talking about isolationism once at dinner, explaining the complexities of the European situation for Americans.

Romilly needed to know more about the America First Committee. She knew there were American newspapers in the library but this afternoon they'd all been off the racks, read by other passengers who seemed to be deliberately lingering over stock market and sports reports. While Freddie was sitting on his bed reading a comic, she knocked on the interconnecting door. 'Would it be all right for me to leave Freddie while I go back to the library?'

'Again?' Mrs Dekker's eyes narrowed.

'I'd like to have a quick look at the American newspapers.'

'You are keen to familiarise yourself with the country?'

'It's a good way to prepare Freddie.'

Mrs Dekker nodded. 'Very well. Keep the door ajar so I can keep an ear open for him.'

In the library, Romilly found the American newspapers returned to the stack. Most of them were now a week or more out of date and well fingered by previous readers. She took a stack onto one of the desks by the door. The *New York Times* told of a rally held by the America First Committee in Wilmington, earlier in April. There'd been trouble, someone in the crowd had protested and a fight had broken out and the police called. The committee seemed concerned that America would be dragged into a European war, with American lives at risk. Any move to involve the country in the conflict should be resisted.

How was Edward Witney tied up with this? Puzzled, she returned the newspapers to the rack and went back to the cabin to smarten herself up for dinner. She found Freddie sitting in with his grandmother, playing a card game. Smoky lay on the rug at Freddie's feet. Romilly hoped her surprise didn't show on her face. Mrs Dekker put down a card and held out a hand. Freddie grudgingly handed her a matchstick.

The brief lull hadn't lasted. This evening, the sea reminded them again how capricious it could be. As she dressed, Romilly heard rain showers and spray dashing against the windows of the cabin. It was comforting, being inside while outside all grew dark and stormy. She didn't feel seasick, she realised, or scared. Not so much of a mouse after all. Freddie came into the cabin when his grandmother wanted to change for dinner. He seemed to share her sense of calm, turning the pages of his comic and only reluctantly agreeing to brush his hair and wash his hands and face.

She put on the blue velvet dress, adding the life-vest, and found her lipstick, which she had stuffed into an evening shoe. She hadn't worn the lipstick since that night with Philip, back in another universe a million years ago. Normally she just brushed her hair and pinned it back, but tonight she combed it more carefully and parted and pinned it on the side, so that the fringe half-fell across her brow. 'You look older.' Freddie put down his comic. 'I like it.'

'Thank you, kind sir.' She felt more self-assured this evening. Perhaps the sea air was helping. 'You might just pull your socks up and then you'll look very respectable yourself.'

'Even my grandmother might think so?'

'She might.'

He made a scoffing noise. 'I don't think she'll ever think I look right. She says that Lewis, that's my cousin, is a good inch and a half taller than me and pounds and pounds heavier. He's only a few months older than me.'

'You're probably just due a growth spurt. I had one and almost overnight everything was too short for me.' She remembered Mama frantically letting down skirt hems. How old had she been then? About Freddie's age?

The cabin tipped. A glass, fortunately empty, slid across Romilly's bedside table, hitting the little rail around the edge.

'I should check that your grandmother isn't too uncomfortable. Make sure your life-vest is tied up properly, Freddie.'

Mrs Dekker answered the knock from her armchair, where she sat looking pale.

'Shall I ask Ahmed if you can dine in your cabin, Mrs Dekker?'

'I shall be fine. But I can't possibly leave Smoky alone. Look at him.' The dog cowered in a corner, tail between his legs. 'He'll have to come down to the dining-room with us.'

'They said no dogs in the—'

'I know what they said.' Mrs Dekker pointed at the wardrobe. 'Somewhere in there I have a leather shopping bag. Fetch it for me, will you?'

Romilly did as she was asked. 'You're going to put Smoky in there?'

'I can't think of another solution.'

'I'll stay down here with him. Ahmed will bring me sandwiches.' She felt she should offer although she really wanted to go into the dining-room and face Edward Witney, find a reason, if she could without anyone noticing, to hand him his missing flyer and ask him innocently why he had it.

Mrs Dekker's face softened momentarily before stiffening. 'I paid a lot of money for our tickets. Smoky will go where I wish him to go. He'll be no trouble in the bag. You can carry it for me. Is my grandson ready?'

Her grandson. She still seemed to find it hard to refer to Freddie by name. There were only two more days left at sea now: there'd have to be more than a single card game to bring them closer to one another.

'What's in the bag?' Freddie asked as they walked out. Romilly put a finger to her lips and told him, under her breath. He gave a broad smile. 'That's great. We shouldn't leave Smoky by himself. He might think we're never coming back for him. Can I carry the bag, Rom?'

'Best if I do.' He made a face but accepted what she said.

Walking across the dining-room to their usual table, Romilly heard the familiar tones of Mr Franklin at the table next to them. 'The navy's left us now. So we must be more than halfway to Canada.'

'Can't see why they couldn't have stayed with us all the way,' his wife said, in between mouthfuls of soup.

'I think the Royal Navy knows better than you what's best, my dear.' Mr Franklin lifted his gaze as the Dekker party sat down, giving them all the briefest of nods. Jack and Freddie grinned at one another. Perhaps Mrs Dekker would allow Romilly to suggest to Mrs Franklin that the boys could play together under her supervision. Mrs Franklin seemed to have softened towards them. A game of ping-pong with Jack would be more fun for Freddie than playing with a girl more than ten years older than he was.

The storm continued to blow as they ate. Some of the diners finished quickly, turning down further courses and returning to their cabins. Occasionally, the tan leather bag at Romilly's feet lurched slightly. She hoped the waiting staff wouldn't notice, tossing pieces of bread in from time to time to keep Smoky occupied.

Edward was sitting alone, as usual. Romilly peered at him when he wasn't looking. This evening, his attention was mainly fixed on Louise and her party of children and fellow escorts. Her efforts to keep them reasonably quiet seemed to amuse him greatly. A few days' good rations and respite from bombs had built up their energy levels. Any initial shyness was dying down. A bread roll flew across the table. A glass tumbled over. Louise retained her composure but looked relieved when an older girl interjected in no-nonsense Cockney tones, threatening to lock up the offenders in the hold 'until you bleeding well stop showing yourselves and your country up'.

Edward's lips twitched. Mrs Dekker was looking at him, too. He nodded as he met her eye. 'Polite young man,' she told Romilly. 'Even though he's not in uniform. I wonder why not?'

'I noticed he limps a little,' Romilly said. 'Maybe he's unfit for active service. But it is strange.' She stole another look at him. Perhaps she was making too much of the America First committee flyer and of his meetings with the stranger.

'Mrs Dekker,' she said loudly enough for Edward to hear. 'Do you think America will join the war?'

'Goodness me, what kind of a question is that to throw at a person?' Mrs Dekker looked shaken by it. Edward was still watching them, expression fathomless.

The leather bag at Romilly's feet shifted. Edward's eyebrows shot up. He reminded Romilly of a schoolboy about to lose himself to laughter in front of a stern teacher. Freddie stifled a giggle. If the waiters noticed the dog there'd be a scene. Romilly put down her napkin. 'I'll take Smoky up to the exercise deck.' She looked meaningfully at the bag. 'I think it's time for a leg-stretch.'

'Don't you want your ice-cream?' Freddie sounded incredulous as she picked the bag up. 'Can I have it?'

The dog seemed relieved to be released from his prison. She kept him in the bag until they were up the grand staircase and companionway, then up to the lounge and saloon. When they were safely out on the exercise deck, she let him sniff as he pleased, keeping him on the lead but moving with him.

'Last breath of sea air before you go back to your charge?'

Louise stood behind her.

'And before the storm gets going again. Are you taking a break, too?'

'I'm off duty for an hour while the stewards play ping-pong with the children and the younger ones are having stories read to them by the other escorts.' Louise let out a long breath. 'We're trying to get them into a very calm bedtime routine.'

'Are they homesick?'

'Homesick and still suffering the after-effects of the air-raids in many cases. Most mornings we're changing wet beds. They have bad dreams. What about your Freddie?'

'Nothing like that, so far.' She realised she'd been fortunate.

Louise nodded. 'He may wait until he's safely across the Atlantic before he can let himself react. Apparently, that's sometimes the case. Stiff upper lips can get you through it for a while, even if you're a kid.' She stretched out her arms overhead. 'But I didn't come out here to talk about my wards.'

'Enjoy the respite while you can.'

'I'm going to miss *The Lucknow*. I doubt I'll be sent back home on anything as glamourous. Probably some old merchant ship, stuck in a tiny smelly cabin next to the galley.' She looked at Romilly. 'What about you? When do you go back?'

'I'm hoping to stay in America. Probably very unpatriotic of me.'

Louise shrugged. 'It's going to be a long war. If America comes in, you can do something to help from that side.'

'You think they will?' She thought of the flyer, which she'd placed under her pillow before coming up here. Her velvet dress didn't have pockets.

'Hope so. We need all the help we can.' They had reached a bench and sat down, Smoky sniffing at something invisible underneath them. Romilly put the leather bag down beside her on the seat.

'Were you always involved with youngsters before the war?' Romilly wasn't usually one to ask personal questions, but Louise's friendly face invited enquiries.

She laughed. 'I worked in the British Museum. The Assyrian section.'

Douglas had been an Assyrian devotee, could talk for hours about them. Romilly tried to remember what he'd told them. 'Which period?'

'Don't get me started, I'll bore you to death. Everything in my section was packed up and sent to a mine in Wales. One of the saddest days of the war for me. So, they didn't have anything for me to do at the museum.'

'From a museum to stopping bread roll fights – that's quite a contrast.'

'Life's more interesting when it throws up different roles.' She smiled at her own joke but her expression was still friendly if a little more guarded. Did she think that Romilly was feeling sorry for her? 'What about you, Romilly? What were you before you sailed on *The Lucknow*?'

'I worked in a bookshop.' Romilly laughed. Louise looked at her quizzically. 'It seems so mundane, so safe.'

'Enjoyable work?'

'I love books and I liked the customers. There was talk about me eventually becoming a partner, but the war made it impossible.'

'So, you left your bookshop and set sail for the New World?'

'Not quite like that.' Her fingers tightened on the lead. 'Other things happened.' All at once. Just in a single night. Louise was looking at her, interested. 'My mother died unexpectedly. Not in an air-raid, after an operation. There was no reason to stay.'

'I'm sorry. So, you were alone in the world? No young man?' From anyone else it might have sounded nosy, but Louise was so easy to talk to. 'Or had he joined up?'

'He was about to.' Romilly hadn't thought about Philip much at all: he didn't seem to belong to the world she'd fallen into.

'Once men put on uniform there's no point hanging around for them, it could be years they're away. If you're not really serious about someone, it's best to make your own plans.' The words were firm but the tone kind.

Louise looked at her watch. 'Goodness, if I want to have my longed-for hot shower in peace, I'd better get down there.' She raised a hand in farewell. Romilly sat on one of the small benches placed around the deck. Smoky sniffed happily beside her. She hadn't thought much about the night her world had fallen apart, but now its events seemed to be unfolding in front of her, as though she was in a cinema, watching them.

Philip's parents were about to shut up their house in West Kensington, had already left town and were just waiting for him to go off to his training camp before they locked it up for the duration of the war. After Romilly and Philip had been to see *That Uncertain Feeling* in Leicester Square, he asked her to come back with him for a nightcap. It sounded so grown up and sophisticated.

She'd told Mama about the cinema trip at breakfast, telling her not to wait up that night. 'You look weary.'

'Just this cramp.' Mama sounded distracted. 'And I seem to have a bit of a fever. They sent me home early from the office, so I'll have an early night.'

'I won't wake you when I come in. I won't be late back.'

'Have a lovely evening with your young man.' She tried to smile but put a hand to her abdomen. As she walked to work, Mama was on Romilly's mind, but the day was busy and the film distracted her. When Philip suggested going back to the house afterwards, she couldn't see what difference it would make to her mother.

Mama would be sleeping. She wouldn't know if Romilly came in at midnight rather than half-ten, or might think there'd been a localised raid, which sometimes happened, meaning she'd been forced into a shelter. They'd grown used to carrying on with the bombs and it wasn't as bad as it had been back in the autumn and winter.

'I found a bottle of brandy this morning,' Philip said, as they went down into the Tube. 'I thought you could wish me good luck.' She had only known him for a few weeks. He'd come into the bookshop to buy a present for his mother and she'd directed him towards a detective novel. He'd returned the next day to buy a book for himself and as nobody else was in the shop, they'd talked for an hour, by which time she'd agreed to meet him for a walk the following weekend. They'd kissed, clumsily, in a bus shelter at the end of the walk. More kisses had been exchanged the first time they'd gone to the cinema and tentative explorations of one another's bodies had occurred. They both knew that the nightcap would lead to a further exploration. Romilly thought she knew where the boundaries lay. Things would go so far and no further.

In the kitchen, already dusty and half-empty, he rooted around in a cupboard for the brandy, along with two glasses: not proper balloons but tumblers. He lit a fire in the drawing room with the last of the wood. They sat together on the sofa, not even bothering to remove the dust sheet. A siren sounded. They didn't move. 'Those planes are coming over further south-east,' he said. 'Westminster, I'd say. Or the other side of the river.' Their shoulders were just touching. Philip's hand was resting on her thigh, close to the knee. He moved it up an inch. Bombers rumbled somewhere miles away. 'Heading towards Holborn. Or Fleet Street. We can go into the shelter if you want?'

Romilly wrinkled up her nose. 'Let's leave it. Do you have a cellar?'

'Full of god knows what, but yes. We could run down there if they come closer.' They sipped the brandy. Romilly didn't really like the way it burned her throat, but it made her feel pleasantly sleepy. She found herself slumping towards him.

'Sorry, not used to spirits,' she muttered.

'My fault.'

'I'm not a kid. I chose to drink it.'

His hand moved another inch up her thigh, underneath her skirt. He stroked the top of her stocking. 'Do you mind me doing this?' His voice sounded thicker. She shook her head, feeling warm, and at the same time relaxed and aroused. In the distance bombs crumped, too far away to worry about. She let him push her gently back onto the sofa. 'May I kiss you?'

'You're so polite. Yes.' The kiss was sweet, tasting of salt and brandy and something she hadn't tasted before and couldn't name. The kisses became deeper, more urgent. She was half in and half out of her body. He was pulling at her clothes and she was undoing buttons for him. The boundaries had been breached. She hadn't meant this to happen.

The all-clear sounded. They sat up. Romilly put a hand to her undone blouse front.

'Another moment and I couldn't have stopped,' Philip said. Another moment and she wouldn't have wanted him to. The fire had gone out. Her head was clear. He was looking at her, face solemn. 'You're the first,' he said. 'You *would* have been the first, I mean. Obviously. I didn't think, I didn't presume. Oh God, I'm making a mess of this.'

She put a hand on his shoulder. 'You thought I'd let you go all the way?'

He nodded, flushing. 'I'm so sorry. You're not that kind of girl, I know. I don't know what got into me.'

Tomorrow he'd go to the training camp. Weeks, months, would pass. He'd be posted somewhere. Shot perhaps. Or blown up.

'You'd be careful, wouldn't you?' she said, slowly.

His answer was another kiss, deeper, more urgent. They fell back onto the sofa. Clothes dropped to the floor. Their breaths rose and fell. Romilly's skin no longer prickled from the chilly air but seemed to be heated by its own internal furnace. There was a brief stabbing pain between her legs sharp enough to make her gasp and make him stop briefly, until she'd pulled him closer again.

It was over. Her heartbeat slowed. Philip lifted himself off. He put a finger on her cheek. 'I never dreamt this would happen. I kept thinking I might be killed and I'd never know what it was like.'

'I thought like that, too.' They sat together, looking at the embers of the fire turn from orange to grey to black. She wasn't in love with him, but she liked the way he made her feel. 'I should go.' She scooped her clothes off the floor.

'I'll walk you home.'

'No.' She put a hand on his arm. 'Early start for you tomorrow. Don't want you getting into trouble on the very first day because you missed the train.'

He laughed and then grew more serious. 'I don't know when I'll be back in London again, Romilly. I'll write when I find out.'

'Do.' She touched his lips with hers.

Walking back through the dark streets she felt light, free. She'd done something she never have dreamt she had the nerve to do. Would Mama guess? Hopefully she'd be asleep. Was it true people could tell by looking at you that you'd shed your virginity? She wasn't sure how she felt about what had happened. Not ashamed, not surprised. Shouldn't she be feeling more? Perhaps she was too tired to process it.

She unlocked the front door and heard the last ring of the telephone Douglas had installed just before he left. She ran to the table to pick it up in case there was still a connection, but it was too late. The line was dead. The house was dark and even colder than normal, the blackouts not pulled down. She turned on her torch and saw a note on the table. *Doctor came to house and insisted that I go into hospital. Please could you bring me a fresh nightdress after work tomorrow?*

The telephone rang again.

It was dark now, the contrast between sea and sky had blurred into a uniform grey. The deck rolled more than it had before dinner. A solitary star appeared briefly between the clouds. Sirius, she thought. Her father had taught her how to recognise the dog star. Venus would be out there, too, she knew, obscured by cloud. She rubbed her arms, clad only in the thin velvet sleeves. At least the life-vest kept her abdomen warm. Romilly peered out into the greyness to look for the other ships in the convoy, but it was impossible to make them out. The wind gusted so aggressively that she clutched the bottom of the bench.

'I'd get down to your cabin. This isn't going to be a comfortable night.'

Edward, appeared suddenly like an apparition. Something about him made her angry. 'Where's your companion tonight?'

He looked surprised. Let him. He was up to something and she wanted to know what.

'The dark-haired lady? Does she prefer to eat in her cabin at mealtimes?'

'I don't know who you mean.' He was still only displaying mild puzzlement. He brushed spray from the back of his neck.

'Twice now, after curfew, I've seen you with a woman I never see anywhere on the ship in daylight.'

He took a step towards her. She realised the two of them were alone out on the deck with the sea pitching and spitting at them.

'A young woman? Old? British or American?' The amused expression had returned to his face. Her sense of irritation with this man grew stronger.

'Young. English. Northern accent. Manchester, perhaps?'

He shook his head regretfully but not before she noticed how he blinked at each part of her description. 'You and Louise Henderson are the only young British women onboard *The Lucknow*.'

'I know what I saw.'

He gave a half-shrug. Damn him, making her out to be a

fantasist. 'And what about the piece of paper you dropped last night in the foyer when you were talking to her?'

'Paper?'

'Advertisement for a rally. America First Committee, whoever they are.'

A mixture of shock and annoyance crossed his face. He muttered something under his breath before regaining his usual detached manner.

'Your accent slipped a bit just then. Why have you got their advertisements? Who are you?' She stood up. She was a fool, confronting him like this when they were alone. He was stronger and bigger than her, could flip her overboard and nobody would ever know what had happened. She ought to have gone straight to the captain and told him what she'd seen.

'You could have reported me, Romilly. They'd have taken all the details. But when you arrived in Montreal, or perhaps before, as soon we're in Canadian waters, someone would have taken you aside and told you that you'd made a mistake.'

'But I didn't, I—'

'Or that you'd seen something it would be better for you to unsee. A very foolish error.' He sounded angry again, with himself, not her. 'You can still go and see the captain now. I won't stop you.' He stepped aside. 'It's your right, your patriotic duty, to report anything that's not quite right. Anyone who might be working for the enemy.'

'Are you?'

'Working for the Germans?' He now had flecks of colour in his cheeks. 'What do you think?'

She shrugged. 'If you were any good, I mightn't be able to tell.' Her voice sounded remarkably steady. Perhaps she should make a dash back inside.

'I'm not working for them. But I'm interested in all they're up to in North America.' He looked her square on and his accent was like crystal again. 'It's my job to know which side is winning the public opinion war. Can we just leave it like that?'

But the conversation with Catherine had made it sound as though he was doing more than keeping an eye on what was happening. 'You're setting up events. Or certainly printing documents to deceive. Who exactly are you, Mr Witney?'

Now he really would scoop her up and push her overboard into those inky waves. How long would it take her to die? He gave a regretful nod, as though acknowledging her mistake.

'Mrs Dekker and Louise Henderson know I'm out here.' The words came out breathlessly. 'Louise just left me. And the Lascars are always watching people come and go onto the decks. They'll have seen me come outside, and then you, too. And those people you said would want to talk to me in Montreal, well, they'll be wanting to talk to you, won't they? Not good if your work is so secret.'

'I work for the British government.'

She hadn't expected that but didn't want to let it go. 'That could mean anything. You work for them in New York?'

'Most of the time. Occasionally in Washington, too.' He stared at her, as though trying to make up his mind about something. 'Romilly, Miss Brooks, I could spin you some line but I won't insult your intelligence. In the morning I'll show you proof of who I am, but for tonight, I'm going to ask you to forget it all. And not to tell anyone what you saw and heard.' He paused. 'Perhaps you and I should spend less time breaking curfew.'

'And meeting people who don't exist. Like Catherine.' She'd kept the name until now and was pleased to see him blink.

'You're sharp, aren't you? Observant.'

'At school everyone thought I was a goodie-goodie. A mouse.' She looked at him as she said the last word and was pleased to see him looked discomfited. 'I just like to watch people before I know whether I can . . ' She let the sentence trail off.

'Trust them.' He nodded. 'You'll find Americans are happier with more open personalities and less reserve.'

'I'll bow to your superior knowledge. Though you're not a good example of an open personality yourself. Why is that? Why are you a spy? Who is Catherine?'

He moved his hand as though he was going to put it over her mouth before dropping it. 'Sorry, but please don't use that kind of language, even in jest.' He looked far less amused by her now. 'Telephone that number I gave you when you get to New York.'

The business card. She'd forgotten about that. 'That's something to do with your work? Why are you so interested in me and what I'm going to do when I reach New York?' Her body was telling her conflicting things. Part of it screamed at her to leave the deck and go down to her cabin where there were other people around. Lock the door. Part wanted to stay up here with Edward, even though it almost certainly wasn't a good idea.

'Good question.' He took a step towards her and this time she knew he wasn't going to throw her overboard. 'I'm a stranger on a ship. Even if you didn't suspect me of all kinds of things, you'd be wise to be cautious.'

'Stranger on a ship sounds like a soppy film.' The words came out sounding high-pitched. He was standing so close to her that she could feel his breath on his face.

'You and I don't belong in soppy films.' In another moment he'd be extremely close, actually touching her. In another moment she'd have given herself away.

'I should go and see to Freddie.' She pulled the dog towards her. Edward put a hand on her shoulder. It felt warm.

'Whatever you may think of me, Romilly—'

But it wasn't about *him*, it was about how she thought about herself. Only weeks ago, she'd let herself slip into Philip's embrace. Now she was, to her consternation, feeling similarly strong impulses about this man. Whom she wasn't even sure she actually liked. All the same, she let him pull her towards him. Heat seemed to radiate between them. She hadn't noticed how cold she'd been feeling. Their mouths seemed to meet before she'd even realised what was happening. She wasn't resisting him, she was melting into him. She was lost in a place she hadn't been for weeks, somewhere where nothing else mattered apart from the moment. She felt warm, alive. He wasn't wearing his life-vest, she noted, and his suit jacket was smooth, the muscles of his arms and shoulders strong beneath the fabric. All the nerves in her body seemed to light up. She was alive again.

A yellow flash lit up the sea and sky. Before Romilly could register it, something crashed below and behind them. No, not a crash, an explosion. Brief, but building in fury. From inside the saloon came the sound of cups and glasses falling and shattering. Wood creaked and groaned.

The Lucknow shook, pulling Edward and Romilly apart. Behind Romilly, the door to the saloon blew out, almost knocking her over but for her lurching out of range. Edward grabbed her by the arm to stop her falling.

'What was that?' But she knew the answer to her own question. The sulphurous flash—that was no explosion in the boiler room. This was the disaster that wasn't supposed to happen because they were out of range of the U-boats and no longer required a naval escort.

She shook her arm free of Edward. 'I've got to go down and get Mrs Dekker and Freddie, take them to the muster point.' They might not remember the emergency drill. Mrs Dekker hadn't seemed to take it seriously.

'Your muster point is in the saloon, like mine. Don't waste time going down to the cabins. Listen.' The alarms were screeching now. The dog whimpered.

'I can't leave them down there.' *The Lucknow* was still trembling. The lamps in the saloon flickered and went off, replaced by the sickly emergency lights. Romilly glanced out to sea. Surely the rest of the convoy must be out there? But they wouldn't, couldn't come to their rescue. There'd been a comfort in seeing the outlines of the ships, but everyone knew if there was a U-boat strike, the others had a responsibility to move out of the danger zone as quickly as possible, leaving the stricken vessel to wait for rescue.

The *Lucknow* was alone.

ELEVEN

Edward was still holding her shoulder. 'You're in your life-vest, go straight to the lifeboats.'

'I have to get Freddie and Mrs Dekker.' The alarm was shrieking now.

'Don't risk going down to the cabin,' he urged. His accent, she noted, was again slipping into something less polished, more urgent.

'I must.' Something whined, just discernible above the creaking of the ship and the shrieking alarm. Smoky. The dog was standing, head cocked, looking up at her. She picked him up.

'Freddie and Mrs Dekker have been to the drills, Romilly – they'll know what to do.'

'Mrs Dekker didn't go to all of them. Freddie's very young.'

'They would have made her go to them before, on her voyage out. The steward will look after them.' But she shook her head.

The saloon floor was tilted to starboard, only by a few degrees, but enough to send all the brandy glasses and coffee cups to the edges of tables, where they were only prevented from falling to the floor by the rails. Passengers blinked, looking at one another. A few weren't wearing life-vests and patted their chests as though only just realising it. Mr Franklin, who must have come in here for a post-dinner brandy and smoke, rose from a leather armchair. 'But we're in the safe zone,' he said. He was without a life-vest too.

'Nobody told the Germans that,' Edward said.

'What do we do now?' Mr Franklin looked baffled.

'You collect your family and bring them to the muster point.' Romilly passed him, making for the companionway down to the cabins.

'Which one are we?'

'Muster point twelve. In here, by that little table.' Hadn't he listened to a word of the drills? 'Lifeboat six,' She pointed upwards. 'Is up there once we're assembled.'

'Couldn't you bring my wife and son up here?' Mr Franklin asked. 'You're going down to get your people, aren't you? And we're only just in the next cabin.'

'Be a man and fetch your wife and child yourself,' Edward told him, in a tone Romilly hadn't heard before. They headed towards the companionway. Plaster trickled from above them. Some of the light fittings had come away from the walls and dangled by their wires, like end-of summer flower stems caught in a storm. The emergency lighting emitted a sickly lime glow. Romilly's ears rang, Edward was saying something but she couldn't make out the words. She followed him down the steps to the top of the corridor leading to their cabins. The door was jammed. He pushed his shoulder against it, managing to open it just enough for them to squeeze through and walked with her to the cabin. 'Grab Freddie and go up to the saloon. Don't let them waste time fiddling around with personal belongings. Just get warm clothes, the passports and visas. And hurry.'

She nodded at him. His smooth, affable features were tighter now, but he still seemed calm. 'It'll all be fine,' he said.

'We've practised the drill often enough.' A light above them fused. Romilly smelled burning metal.

She had left the cabin key with Mrs Dekker because her dress had no pockets. She rapped on the door. Freddie opened up, his face pale.

'I'll see you at the lifeboats.' Edward moved away. She wanted to ask him which number his boat was, but he'd already gone.

Mrs Dekker sat on Freddie's bed, holding his hand. '*Ach*, there you are, Miss Brooks. I was worried.' She might have been worrying about a tardy guest. She was doing it for Freddie, keeping control so he could, too.

'Did you see the torpedo strike, Romilly?' Freddie's eyes were wide. 'That's what it is, isn't it?'

'I saw a flash.' She put Smoky down and went to the wardrobe. 'Come on, we need to go to the muster point.' She pulled out his jacket.' Put this on over your jumper. And you'll need a hat and gloves.' She looked over to Mrs Dekker. 'Do you have the passports and visas?'

Mrs Dekker patted her chest. 'Safely in my coat inside pocket.'

Romilly needed her own papers; she grabbed them quickly before pausing. Something Uncle Simon had said, something he'd given her, that she'd stuffed in with her underwear: a stained canvas wallet with strings attached: 'Used it during my spell in India. You can tie it round your waist if the natives look unreliable and it's waterproof, too.' She found the canvas object in her drawer, took the papers out of her handbag and placed them into the wallet, hoisting up her clothes so she could wind the ties round her waist, heedless of exposing her underclothes. The skirt of her velvet dress swished back down her ankles. No time to get changed into something more practical.

She pulled out slacks from the wardrobe, kicked off her shoes and pulled the trousers on under the skirt, replacing her heeled shoes with her brogues. Mama's rings were safely round her neck on the chain. She removed her life-vest and put on her coat, replacing the vest quickly. She needed a hat and gloves too. It was all taking too long. The ship lurched and creaked, its heel more marked now. Where were her gloves and hat?

Ahmed banged on the door. 'Up to the muster point now.' Gone was his gentle deference, his tone was calm but stern. No time to find the hat but her gloves were in the coat pocket. The burning metal smell was acrid in her throat. She picked up the silver photograph frame that held a picture of her parents with her as an infant, ripping the back of the frame off and putting the photo into her slacks pocket with the passport and visa. They only just fitted but the pocket buttoned up so she knew they couldn't fall out.

'Let's go,' she told Freddie and Mrs Dekker. Her foot caught in the dog's lead. What were they going to do with him? The dogs down below in the kennels would surely be left to go down with the ship. Freddie was stuffing pencils and paper into his shorts pocket.

'Where's Smoky?' He looked round. 'We're not leaving him here.'

Mrs Dekker made clicking noises at Smoky. 'Come here, dear one.' She picked him up. No time to dispute this now. Either Smoky would be allowed onto the lifeboat or he wouldn't. Arguing about it now wouldn't change things. 'Where's the bag?' she asked Romilly, who stared at her for a moment.

'It was on the deck with me. Must have gone.'

The burning smell was becoming more intense and the carpet in the cabin felt spongy. Water must already be seeping in through the torn hull below or from a burst pipe.

'I have him.' Mrs Dekker patted the front of her life-vest.

As they walked into the passageway the ship listed and groaned again. Freddie grabbed Romilly's hand. 'It's all right,' she told him, echoing Edward's earlier words. 'We know what to do, don't we?' She made herself smile at him, hoping the smile was more reassuring than it felt. 'We paid attention in the drills, we'll be fine.' Behind them the Franklins were coming out of the cabin. Mr Franklin had obviously made his way down to his family.

'We should have taken more of the dollars,' he hissed at his wife. 'If you'd given me another moment to open the safe.'

'We can't spend them if we've drowned,' she told him. They passed a wall-mounted clock. Less than fifteen minutes had passed, Romilly calculated, since she'd left the exercise deck. A quarter of an hour and everything had changed utterly. Ahmed pushed past them, arms full of life-vests. 'Excuse me, ladies, young sir, you must hurry. There is no need for panic but the captain says the damage is serious.'

Freddie squeezed her hand. 'Don't worry, another ship will pick us up, Romilly. Perhaps we can go back to London.'

Mrs Dekker's face tightened as she heard the words. They'd reached the door leading onto the gallery. It had jammed. Ahead of them Louise stood with a group of life-vested girls. Shouting at the passengers to move aside, one of the young Lascars came from behind carrying a spade from the fire bucket. He wedged the handle into the small opening and wedged it so it stayed open.

The foyer below looked deserted as Romilly looked down the sweeping staircase. Were they ahead of the other passengers who must also be heading up to the lifeboats? The pots containing the palms had toppled over, the soil tipping out and mingling with sea water, staining the mahogany floorboards. The grandfather clock still stood upright but its pendulum no longer swung. The hands were stuck on the time the torpedo had struck *The Lucknow* and the deck was too tilted now for them to move. She turned back to check Freddie and Mrs

Dekker were following. Smoky lay still in Mrs Dekker's arms. Nobody seemed to have noticed him yet.

Below them a babble of voices rose. The passengers from the lower decks had reached the foyer. 'I can't see the boys anywhere.' The panic was evident in Louise's voice, the usual self-assurance gone. 'They should be up by now.'

'What were the cabin numbers?' a male voice called to her from behind Romilly. Edward. He must have snatched up his valuables from his own cabin and grabbed the life-vest he was wearing. Louise told him the numbers.

'I'll go down and see if they need help.'

'But I should, they're my responsibility.'

Edward shook his head at her. 'Stay with the girls, they need you.' *The Lucknow* shook, plaster falling from the ceiling. Mrs Franklin screamed.

Edward moved through the jammed-open door to the top of the grand staircase. He'd be making for the companionway down to the lower deck where the boys must have been preparing for bed. Suppose it was now underwater?

Ahmed led the group up the companionway leading up to the saloon. The ship lurched to port. Romilly grabbed the handrail and the neck of Freddie's life-vest at the same time. People fell around them, some toppling down the steps. Louise fell, putting a hand out to steady herself in vain, children dropping around her, calling out. The emergency lights flickered on and off. Romilly turned as far as she dared and saw Louise on the ground. She groaned and sat up, putting a hand to her head. Her red hair seemed to move above her temples, exposing a darker, shadowed area. Blood? It wasn't blood, Romilly saw, it was hair: dark, straight locks. Louise pulled her red hair down to cover it, looking around to see if anyone had noticed.

Her eyes met Romilly's just as the emergency lights came on fully. Her red hair was just as it had always been. Had Romilly imagined that escaping dark head of hair?

The ship listed again, this time to port.

Someone was shouting from above them, telling them to stay where they were – the lifeboats on the starboard side had jammed against the hull.

'Let us go to the port-side lifeboats then,' Mr Franklin shouted from behind Romilly. Despite his ungainly proportions he'd managed to cling on. His wife and son clutched the banister behind him.

'All hands are needed to clear the starboard boats, sir,' came Ahmed's answer, his voice still calm but with an urgency to it. 'Stay here and await further instructions. The situation is under control.'

As though in contradiction, something deep below them gave a metallic groan that built up to a high-pitched creak. The ship lurched to starboard, as though trying to balance itself. 'Perhaps that will free the lifeboats,' Mr Franklin said. The group on the steps were battling the shifting gravity, clinging both to the rails and to one another as they tried to balance.

'It's the bow,' Mrs Franklin said. 'It's lifting. The water must be pushing through to the back of the hold and the boiler rooms.'

'What do you know about the ship's layout?' Mr Franklin sounded less confrontational, as though he was trying to reassure her.

'Your wife looked at the diagrams on the walls,' Mrs Dekker said. 'I saw her while I was doing the same thing.'

So Mrs Dekker had been paying attention after all. Romilly hadn't noticed. People could surprise you.

Perhaps the sea had already pushed its way into the lower deck cabins where the boys in Louise's party were accommodated. If Edward had managed to get down there, he'd be facing tons of water pushing through the hull.

Mrs Dekker was still clinging on. Romilly looked for Smoky: surely she must have dropped him? But there was the dog, just visible beneath her life-vest, where she must have managed to stuff him. 'Let me take him for you,' she whispered.

'It's fine, dear.' Mrs Dekker nodded at her. 'Just keep holding on tight to Freddie, won't you? Oh.' She blinked, as though spotting someone she wasn't expecting to see. For a moment Romilly thought she might be going to say something to this invisible person. But she nodded her head. 'Just hold on. We're going to be just fine.' She spoke as though she really believed it.

Romilly's knuckles were turning white and her hands were cramping. She let go of the banister for a second to grip Freddie's life-vest with her other hand so she could flex her fingers and increase the blood flow. 'Hold my life-vest strap, Freddie.'

'I don't like it when the lights go out,' he whispered.

'Nor do I.'

'It looks haunted.'

'No ghosts here, it's too new,' she said, in a bracing tone. But she was remembering not ghosts but being in an air-raid shelter once when the lights had briefly failed during a raid. Someone had screamed that they'd taken a direct hit, that they'd be buried alive, tons of earth and brick piled above them. Panic had risen in her. Mama had been there with her. She'd tutted, saying it was a nuisance not being able to see to read her book, just as she'd reached the part where the heroine realised she was about to go up the altar with the wrong man. Immediately Romilly had felt her panic slip away.

This time it wouldn't be rubble that would suffocate them, but the cold, grey weight of the Atlantic, pressing into their lungs. And her mother wasn't there to reassure her. She was the one who'd have to do the reassuring. Mrs Dekker was calm but seemed frozen, like an automaton. Freddie was young and vulnerable. How could she know she'd be up to the task of looking after him? She hadn't proved herself in the last emergency, failing to even notice that her mother was dying.

To distract herself, Romilly looked down towards Louise again. Her hair looked as red and as well arranged as always. Had she imagined what she'd seen? Louise had organised the girls in her party so that they were holding onto one another's life-vests with one hand and to the banister with the other, somehow managing to balance on the tilted steps. She was telling them jokes in funny voices and the girls were giggling. Many of them must already have come through some fierce air-raids, just as Romilly had. Did prior horrors toughen you up or just jolt an over-stimulated nervous system even more when something else happened?

Mrs Dekker was loosening her life-vest. 'This really is too tight.' As she undid the strap, the ship lurched again. Smoky wriggled himself free from her, leaping down from her chest onto the stairs.

'Don't let him go.' Freddie wriggled himself free of Romilly's grip. Before she could grab him, he was two steps below her.

'Stop him!' Romilly yelled to the people below. 'Don't let him go after the dog.'

Freddie was small and nimble, evading arms, seemingly unbothered by the tilted angle of the steps. He clambered down to the jammed-open door to the gallery.

'Smoky's running down to the foyer,' Freddie called. 'I'm going down to catch him.'

'Freddie!' Mrs Dekker's voice was anguished. 'Leave the dog. Come back.' Her voice carried but there was no answer.

'I'll go after him,' Romilly told Mrs Dekker.

'Don't go.' Mrs Dekker tried to grab her arm. 'There'll be a steward down there and they'll catch him.'

But Romilly was already clambering down, muttering apologies to the passengers clinging to the banister, squeezing past them. No sign of Freddie on the grand staircase. The emergency lighting wasn't enough to give much of a view of the foyer beneath. 'Freddie!' she called. From the companionway behind her she could hear passengers shouting at her to stay where she was, someone would bring Freddie back up. But there was nobody else down there now: just a dark void. Perhaps the water had risen too high. She walked to the top of the staircase, clinging to the balustrade and following it round as it curved down into the steps. The ship creaked and trembled, as though wanting to throw her off. At least she was pulled towards the banister rather than being thrown off. From above, a Lascar called to her to stop. 'No crew down there, miss, too dangerous. Wait for help.'

Why wasn't she waiting? Because she'd seen Edward disappear to the lower decks. He hadn't reappeared. Nobody had come from down there in the last twenty minutes. Freddie might be all alone with nobody to help him. The Lascars would all be trying to right the starboard lifeboats or loading passengers onto the boats on the other side of the ship.

She'd never planned to do anything on this voyage except make it safely across the Atlantic to America, but here she was, about to slide across the slanted mahogany-floored lobby that felt like an ice-rink beneath her feet. Which way, though?

'Freddie?' she called.

'Romilly, we're in the library.' His voice seemed to come from a long way away.

'Hold on, I'm coming to get you.' The library was on the port side of the lobby. To reach it, she had to cross what seemed like an infinite slippery slope. At least she'd changed out of her evening shoes. She made it, inching her way across and against the slant. The display cases housing jewellery and handbags still hung from their fittings, but the painted screens where she had hidden had toppled over. Romilly picked her way across them and into the library.

Freddie was kneeling down, clutching Smoky's collar with one hand and clinging to one of the chairs that were fastened down to the floor. He was motionless, as if too scared to move.

'I'm here.' She put a hand on his shoulder and shook him. Freddie?' He still seemed frozen. She shook him a little harder.

'He was so scared, he ran in here and hid behind the chair.' The dog's lead was still fastened to his collar. Good.

'Let me have him. We've got to hurry. It's not safe down here, the ship—' This time *The Lucknow* rocked so severely that she only just had time to grab the railed edge of a bookshelf. Freddie flew across the library floor, his feet and arms waving as he tried to stop himself. He grabbed at one of the fixed tables and managed to halt his descent.

'I'm fine,' he said, gasping. 'Where's Smoky?'

'Safe. Come on, do you think you can get back up to me?' She tied Smoky's lead to the life-vest belt and leant forward as far as she could, reaching out an arm, stomach lurching as she realised just how far the ship was now listing. 'Let go of the table and try to jump up to me.'

'I can't.'

'You have to.' The slippery surface of the parqueted floor made it hard for him to propel himself upwards. His first attempts resulted in him simply falling onto his chest. She wanted to tell him to hurry – the lifeboats must have been freed now, they'd be loading passengers in. 'One more try.'

This time he lunged forward, higher up the floor. He slipped back but not before she caught his outflung hands and then his life-vest. She pulled him up.

'I didn't know you were that strong.' He patted Smoky.

'Nor did I.' Her heart pounded. *The Lucknow* groaned and trembled. Books pattered off the shelves, the rails at the bottom not tall enough to stop them falling. 'Come on, we've got to hurry.' The foyer was twenty or more feet away. They'd have to cling to the bookcases and that wasn't going to be easy with the dog.

'Freddie...?' Surely he'd agree to leave Smoky now?

He looked her directly in the eye. 'I left my parents to come to England. I left the Cohens. I'm not leaving Smoky now. He's the only thing good that's happened since my grandmother made me leave. You go if you want, I'm sick of leaving people behind.'

Romilly nodded. 'Come on, then. Hold on to my life-vest strap with your right hand and grip the bookshelves with your inside hand. I'll have to let go of you now.'

Smoky's lead was still fastened to the belt of her life-vest. He'd have to scrabble for purchase on the slippery parquet. Beneath them came the sound of a muffled bang. Water poured into the bottom of the tilted floor, probably rising from the lower decks. What of the boys down there? And Edward?

'Don't look down.' She tightened the knot tying Smoky's lead to her belt. Foot by foot they moved upwards towards the foyer. They reached a break in the shelving where an alcove housed another chair. The water was still flowing in rapidly. Romilly took a breath. The door to the foyer still seemed as far away as it had. Were the lifeboats still stuck on the starboard? If so, everyone would be rushing to the port side and there wouldn't be enough boats for all of them. Perhaps she and Freddie had already been given up for dead.

The ship listed again. Freddie was breathing heavily behind her, clinging to the chair. 'Come in front of me,' she told him. 'I'm going to help you grab the next shelf.' At least if he slipped, she'd have a chance to catch him. He crawled over the chair. Romilly bundled him across the gap to the shelf. 'Keep going,' she said. 'Don't wait for me. Make for the foyer. If I'm not behind you, cross to the staircase. Go back up to the gallery and then up to the saloon. If there's nobody at the muster point, go on up to the boat deck.'

Even if the others weren't waiting at the muster point, they couldn't all have got away in the boats yet.

He looked from her to the dog.

'I won't leave him,' she said. 'What you said about leaving

people behind – I know what you mean.' She tried not to think of the people, and dogs, certainly abandoned below them in the lower decks. Freddie stepped carefully along the parquet, clinging to the shelves and reaching the library door, thankfully hinged on the other side or else he wouldn't have been able to get round it. Romilly made a jump from the chair to the bookshelf. Her feet slipped and she fell onto her side. Smoky's paws scratched as he tried to hold himself on the surface. She pulled herself up and tried again. This time she managed to grip the floor. Romilly repeated the move until she reached Freddie at the door leading to the foyer. The grand staircase itself was empty: its starboard side half submerged now. No chance of making it up there – they'd have to go up the port side and cross to starboard at the gallery level. 'Hello?' Romilly's shout went unanswered. She realised that the alarm had stopped. How long had it been silent? Did it mean the lifeboats had left?

'They've gone without us, haven't they?' Freddie's face was ashen and she wasn't sure whether it was because he was cold or because the realisation that they might have been abandoned had hit him. She put her arms around him.

'If they have, we'll find a life-raft. Remember how they showed us the cases and how to undo them?' Would she even be capable of launching a raft from the deck of a ship so heeled as *The Lucknow* now was? Or of getting Freddie down a rope ladder into it? But she had to keep him calm, had to keep herself calm.

The greeny-yellow emergency lights increased the queasiness inside Romilly. It wasn't seasickness; it was knowing that everything that happened from this point onwards would be up to her, her responsibility. Fleetingly, Douglas's face came to her mind. He'd told her that he couldn't wait for them to be reunited in the future and for her to tell him all the things she'd done in the interim. He wouldn't have expected this attempt to leave a sinking, now-lethal ship, to be one of them.

'What?' Freddie asked. His lips were blue, she noticed. 'You laughed.'

'Was I? Probably just my teeth chattering.' She looked at the slanting foyer floor. How on earth were they going to get across there without help?

He was fiddling with something. The whistle on his life-vest. He put it to his lips and a piercing shriek filled the foyer. Smoky whined, ears back. Freddie stopped, listened, and blew the whistle again. Nothing. Nobody. It was down to her. She glanced at the small shivering boy.

'If I can get across there, I'll find something we can use to pull you over.' She undid the dog's lead from her belt and handed it to Freddie.

'It would be better for me to do it. I have a lower centre of gravity because I'm small. Mr Cohen taught me that. It means it's harder for me to overbalance.'

'I can't let you do it.' Romilly couldn't bear seeing him scrabble ahead of her across that greasy slope. She'd been brought on this voyage to look after him.

'But if we hang on here the ship will sink and I'll drown anyway. So will you.'

She set her shoulders. 'Me first.'

'Because you're a lady.' He smirked. 'You don't look like one at the moment with those slacks under your dress and blood on your face from when you fell over.'

At least he had enough energy to joke. 'You're not exactly the picture of a gentleman yourself right now.' She reached out and squeezed his shoulder. 'Let me do this. Wait here.'

Romilly's neck and shoulders were rigid. She forced herself not to hunch forward, but crouched low, back straight, adjusting her balance every few paces as her right leg dipped towards the water, fixing her gaze on the bottom of the staircase, stomach lurching as *The Lucknow* rocked again. A crash jolted her, losing her rhythm. Her right foot slipped. The huge gilt-edged mirror, positioned at the halfway point where the two sides of the staircase met, had fallen from its fixtures. It balanced on the top step for a moment before falling onto the stairs and racing towards her like a toboggan.

'Romilly,' Freddie screamed. 'Watch out.' She moved to the right, the mirror missing her by inches as it slipped across the floor and into the water. She'd lost her balance, couldn't regain her grip. Plants in copper pots and plaster rained down on her, she was slipping down the floor into the water. She tried to reach forward and grab the leg of a table fixed to the floor. The ship trembled again and she missed the leg, sliding further away from the stairs. Freddie was still screaming at her.

'Take this.' A man in uniform was at the bottom of the staircase, clinging to the banister with one hand and reaching out with a boat hook in his other. She clutched it and he pulled her in, Smoky reeled in behind her. Her rescuer was the captain, she saw, face covered in oil and grease, his uniform ripped. 'And now you, young fellow.' Romilly grabbed the banister while he leant out towards Freddie. 'Take a run at it, don't stop.'

There were feet between Freddie and the boat hook, his shoes were sliding on the surface. Behind him Smoky skidded on the lead. Romilly closed her eyes. But then she felt Freddie grab at her leg. She opened her eyes and clutched the top of his life-vest, pulling him up. He was still clinging to the dog's lead. Smoky jumped up onto the step, panting hard.

'Thank God.'

'Miss Brooks, isn't it? And Master Freddie Landau.'

'I thought you were going to drown, Romilly.' Freddie said. 'At least you didn't have Smoky with you, though.' He looked at her. 'Only joking. You can let go of me now.'

She looked up at the captain. 'Have the lifeboats left, captain?'

'Most of them. Come on.' Begrimed as it was, the captain's face was still reassuring, the exemplar of calm authority. He held out his hand to Freddie. 'We might just make the last boat on the port side. If we don't, I'll launch a life-raft for the two of you.'

'Won't you come with us?'

He looked away without answering. Romilly picked up Smoky. 'I'll pretend I haven't seen that dog,' the captain said. 'If something that size can be called a dog.' He winked at Freddie. She placed Smoky inside her life-vest, loosening the straps a little. She could feel the patter of his heart against her chest.

Romilly could sense the water below them coming closer, could hear it rippling. The sulphurous smell was more marked now. 'Keep moving,' the captain said. They clambered up the slanted staircase, reaching the midpoint where the flights merged, and carrying on up to the gallery. The captain halted. The floor between them and the door to the companionway to the upper decks fell sharply to starboard. Romilly had hoped they'd hear the voices of those who'd been waiting for lifeboats. Some of the lights up here were still working. The captain used his boat hook to grab the side of the door, which appeared to be jammed an inch closed. He jumped forward, launching himself at the door and wrenching it open. The metal creaked. He turned and held out the boat hook for Freddie and Romilly. When it was her turn, she loosened the belt of her life-vest and wedged the dog between it and her coat before springing forward to catch the boat hook. The velvet skirt of her dress ripped. 'You must have been a long-jumper at school?' the captain said. 'Good leg muscles on you.'

'I was pretty useless.'

'You don't know your own strength. Were you a good swimmer too?' The way he asked, so casually, it made her swallow. The school pool had been a frigid place, but she hadn't been a bad swimmer. The North Atlantic wasn't a calm pool, though.

They picked their way up the staircase, carrying on to the

deck above the saloon where the lifeboats should have been waiting for them. *The Lucknow* shivered beneath them, a low thunderous groan rising from its lower decks like a huge animal crying out in terminal pain. No shouts or whistles reached them. The captain tugged at the door to the deck and they followed him round, clinging to the door until they could grab the railing. The tilt was more pronounced.

'There's nobody here,' Freddie said, looking around. 'They've left us!'

They looked up at the empty davits and dangling ropes. The boats had all gone. All Romilly could see was the darkness of sea and sky, intermittently pricked with stars. No moon to illuminate the ocean.

'Are there still boats on the starboard?' Romilly asked, raising her voices against the roar of the wind.

'Not that we can launch.' The captain gave her a smile that made it seem as though this was just mildly inconvenient, nothing more. 'I'll find you a life-raft and make sure you both get down the ladder safely onto it.'

'You won't come with us?' she asked again. He looked at her steadily.

'I shall return to the bridge.'

'Romilly.' She turned to see Edward behind her, a stream of crimson running down his right temple onto his cheek. The deck was too slanted, too slippery to move across quickly, but somehow she managed to find herself holding on to him without knowing how she'd managed it. She realised she'd been looking out for him without noticing, all the time she'd been in the library and foyer with Freddie.

'You went down to the lower deck?' she asked. He felt frozen in her arms, but his breath was warm on her cheek.

'I was too late. Two of them had already got out, were trying to swim for it. We managed to get them up the companionway and they ran up to the lifeboats, I think they'd have got there in time. The others... I swam down the corridor to see if I could undo the cabin doors, but when I did, I saw it was hopeless.' He looked away. 'Some of the cabins were right in the torpedo's path.' No words were adequate. She let him go, noticing how torn and sodden his clothes were. He'd lost his life-vest. He saw her looking at him. 'A Lascar needed it, tiny chap, couldn't swim.' He gave a shrug. 'I've always been strong in the pool.'

Those wide shoulders.

'I see you've still got your little pretence at a dog?'

Smoky's nose protruded from her life-vest.

'We should find you another life-vest,' she said. Freddie saw one lying abandoned on the edge of the deck and handed it to Edward. The captain had opened a cabinet housing a life-raft, pulling it out onto the deck. She hadn't misremembered it: the raft was really little more than two benches facing one another, set across a shallow footwell, but with oars and basic supplies, and ropes to cling onto. At the drills they'd explained how to fire the flare gun also stored in the footwell.

'Come on,' the captain said. 'There's not much time now.' Edward fastened the vest. Romilly stepped forward to help the captain with the raft, more of the details of the emergency drill coming back to her.

As she moved towards the raft, the world split itself into two and someone turned off the sound for a few seconds. Voices – urgent, loud – broke into the silence, briefly, Freddie's hand thrust itself into hers, and then it was quiet. The deck was rushing down to meet the water.

Romilly was flying, the stars bursting out of the clouds momentarily, close enough to touch, free of the dying ship. She smashed down into something heavy and dark. The cold crushed against her, pushing all the air out of her lungs. The silence now was absolute, almost like a respite after the groans and clanks of the dying ship. Freddie floated beside her, his mouth opening and closing, bubbles flying up from his mouth.

She must have let go of his hand but now she took it again and thought that he moved his head towards her as she did.

It was peaceful, but the pressure in her chest warned her that she needed to abandon the darkness and peace and push herself and Freddie up towards the light she could still make out above them. They were rising now.

Black flecks passed before her eyes. She was in a race to reach the light before the black flecks merged into one single darkness, before it just became too easy to let the silence consume her. She kicked out hard, pushing her free hand down over and over again to speed their ascent. She was in a Cornish cove, having jumped off a rock, sunk too far in the chilly water, scared but knowing that her mother and father were sitting on the sunny beach, watching out for her. Any second now she'd emerge from the sea.

'You gave us a bit of turn, darling,' her father would say, a jerky note in his voice. 'Did you go in too deep?' He would never have let her drown – he was waiting to see whether she could manage herself before he rescued her. Her father had been a brave man, a decorated soldier from the Great War. She'd always wanted to feel she'd inherited some of his bravery.

I went in too deep, but I'm going to be all right. She was fooling herself, the pressure on her chest had gone beyond pain now. A feeling of acceptance swept through Romilly. This was the end. She'd tried to run away from shame but perhaps if you were destined to die, death would seek you out. She looked at Freddie, trying to indicate that he shouldn't be scared, that she wouldn't leave him.

The light burst around them. Romilly drew a rasped, agonising breath, the frigid air burning her chest, forced back to life. It hurt, it was too much. She wanted to be back in the quiet darkness. She'd let go of Freddie. She'd failed. He'd been claimed by the ocean.

Freddie surfaced beside her. His mouth opened, lips blue.

She clutched his shoulder, her arms moving like stone. He coughed and water ran out of his mouth. Still alive. The bows of *The Lucknow* rose above them. The water was churning around it. They'd drown in that froth.

'Swim!' she shouted. 'Get away from the ship.'

She didn't even know if he *could* swim. Some instinct was making him kick and strike his arm out. Romilly rolled onto her side and, grabbing the neck of his life-vest with one hand, found herself mimicking what the swimming coach at school called lifesaving stroke. In a pool it hadn't been hard: flat water, no freezing waves breaking over your head, no darkness all around. Her strokes took more energy than she possessed. They weren't putting any distance between themselves and *The Lucknow* and the cold was paralysing her, consuming her body and her mind. The ship's bow now formed a pyramid. She stopped, sensing that any warmth from her body was wasting itself on her extremities. The ship paused for a moment, almost vertical, as though composing herself before her terminal plunge. From inside came the groan of tortured metal. And screams. There were still people in the ship. Bile rose from Romilly's stomach. The ship groaned again and its lights flickered on and off as though its dying brain was pulsing out one last defiant signal. Or perhaps it was a farewell. Romilly closed her eyes.

The screams stopped. Her limbs could no longer move. She let her head tilt backwards. The clouds parted for a second and she opened her eyes and glimpsed the stars.

'Where's... Mr Witney?' Freddie gasped, '...life-raft?'

He was talking, that was good. She wasn't sure she had the strength to reply. She forced herself to pay attention. Waves, tower-like, crashed around them. Even if Edward was only yards away, they'd miss him. The same went for the raft.

'And... Smoky?' Freddie's voice was fainter now. His eyes looked glazed over. She shook the neck of his life-vest. 'Stay awake.'

'Did you let go of him?'

She put her spare hand down her life-vest, expecting to touch cold fur. Breath warmed her fingers. 'He's alive.' Perhaps some ancient instinct or the shock of the cold had made the dog shut himself down as they plunged deep down into the ocean until it was safe to draw breath. 'He's all right,' she tried to say, but the words caught up before they came out of her mouth. The waves and wind were making it hard to hear her own voice.

Freddie smiled. Even now, in the fury of the sea bubbling around them, the cold overpowering them, he could smile.

He pointed at something. '...raft.' It was only feet away from them. The captain must have managed to release it a moment before *The Lucknow* sank. He wouldn't have had time to return to the bridge before the ship went down. Romilly propelled them towards the raft, her legs feeling heavier at each kick. If she didn't grab it quickly, she knew it would be too late: they were racing against the cold, which would kill them as ruthlessly as a torpedo. They'd been in the water for ten minutes, she thought, but already thinking was becoming hard, as though her brain was too slow to process information. She grabbed at the rope slung along the raft's side, failing to hold it at the first attempt. She tried again and managed to do it.

The raft would provide no shelter at all from the wind and waves, but it was better than waiting to freeze. Neither of them would last more than a few more minutes if they didn't get out of the sea. She pulled at Freddie, trying to manoeuvre him to the side of the raft so she could push him up. A wave plucked him away from her. She clutched at the strap of his life-vest as it shot past her, feeling the skin on her palm blister. Before the next wave could arrive, she shoved him into position and he managed to wriggle up onto the raft. He lay in the footwell, motionless. Had he passed out? Just as she was opening her mouth to try to scream at him, he came to and dragged himself up onto the seat, looking small and weak. His legs would feel like hers, no longer fully part of her body, appendages that didn't respond to the mind.

She used the last of her strength to kick herself up the raft. From inside her life-vest Smoky yelped. She must have squashed him. Giving herself a second before she moved up to the seat she saw her breath condensing at each exhalation. Romilly pushed up again. Her legs held her for a second before they lost control. She slipped off the bench back down into the footwell, the raft rocking. Freddie gasped.

'Sorry.' Her arms felt like lead pipes. Ignoring their stiffness she pulled herself up onto the seat opposite Freddie.

'Blow... whistle, first... what they told us.' He lifted the whistle to his lips but no sound came out. Romilly grabbed at her own whistle. Her lips were stiff from the saltwater and it hurt to move them. She didn't seem to have air in her lungs to blow into it. Eventually she managed to produce a faint shrill which probably nobody would hear. Her body was shutting down. She needed to force the blood around her limbs.

Should she row? Her arms were cramped. She tried to move her hands down towards the oars beneath the seat and her muscles screamed out pain. Another wave lifted the raft. Her eyes were too full of salt water for her to see much. Where was Edward? Trapped on the ship as it sank? Drowned as he fell into the sea? The lifeboats had come off the port side of the ship. Was that the same side she and Freddie and the raft had entered the water? Her mind felt too numb to work out whether she was rowing in the wrong direction. Flares. So that people could see them. The flare gun was . . . Where? Under the seat. She reached down for it. The raft rose and dropped suddenly. Romilly retched, nothing left in her stomach to vomit. Freddie called out something to her. She grabbed the seat of the raft with both hands as the wave tossed them off its peak. She closed her eyes, visualising them flung off the raft, lost to the sea. When she opened them, Freddie was handing her an oar.

'I don't know which way we should row.' It seemed too hard to work it out – even speaking seemed to be difficult now, the words slurring on her tongue. She wanted to let her chin sink onto her chest, to rest, to close her swollen eyelids. Although she was shivering, she no longer felt cold. Was that a bad sign? Just one moment to recover and then she'd be all right.

'You're in charge, Romilly, you've got to tell us what to do.'

She could barely hear Freddie's words. She tried to take a stroke with the oar, but it rippled over the surface of the sea. Wreckage from the ship floated towards them, objects she couldn't make out, joining them in whatever voyage it was they were taking. Her fear was fading away; she felt at peace. All she needed was a moment's rest and—

Something hit the side of the raft.

'It's Mr Witney.' Freddie was tugging at Edward's life-vest. 'Mr Witney, Mr Witney, get out of the water. Help me, Romilly.'

She put down the oar, reluctant to bring herself back into life because it needed more of her than she could give. Inside her, very faintly but clearly, a voice was telling her to come back into the moment, into the cold and fear. She leant forward and grabbed Edward under his arms.

'Kick,' she told him. 'You're too heavy for us to pull you up.' He didn't move his legs but the raft shifted down and then up, sliding him onto the base. She put a hand on his neck and thought she could make out a faint pulse. 'Help me turn him over.' The waves were now determined to toss the three of them out of the raft. Edward was heavy, his clothes drenched, and they couldn't take both hands off the seats at the same time. It took minutes to turn him. His right temple was bloodied. He must have hit it again as he fell into the sea or reopened it against a piece of wreckage as he bobbed in the waves. She placed a hand tentatively on his life-vest and pushed, uncertain what exactly she was trying to do: squeeze the water out of him?

'Shake him,' Freddie said. 'He's got to wake up.'

Edward's unconscious weight was making the raft even harder to manoeuvre. Every time Romilly removed her hand from him so that she could sit up and row, he slipped back towards the edge. She tried to pull his knees round so he was wedged into the footwell. The numbness in her hands had spread up her arms. They wouldn't move as she wanted them to. Frustration made her blink tears from her eyes and the salt liquid made them sting even more.

'Hold him,' she told Freddie. If she didn't use the oar to keep the raft steady one of the waves would throw the three of them into the sea. She looked down at her arms and willed them to respond to what she was asking them to do.

TWELVE

'Wake up.' Freddie shook Edward's shoulder. His legs still dangled over the side of the raft, drenched with every wave that hit them. 'I think his eyelids moved.' Freddie looked up at Romilly. She broke off her rowing to store the oar carefully behind her feet and bent down to Edward. His eyes were opening.

'You're safe,' she told him. 'On the raft.' Calling it safe seemed optimistic. The clouds had closed up again and a mist hung over the sea. Each wave still threatened to dislodge them from the raft and she hadn't found the flare. Freddie had managed to blow the whistle, but it hadn't been answered. 'Don't leave us!' she shouted at him. The need for him to stay with her cut through the numbing cold.

Edward struggled to sit up. Freddie had found the water canister and held it up to him. With shaking hands Edward drank. 'Thank you.'

His voice was shaking but his pupils were normal, Romilly noticed, dimly remembering first aid training right at the beginning of the war. If he'd been concussed, perhaps he was coming out of it? She noted too that Freddie's face had a blue-grey cast. He hadn't looked like that when they'd clambered onto the raft.

Something moved under her life-vest. The dog. She risked taking both hands off the seat and undid the straps.

'What are you doing?' Edward rasped.

Speaking was still too much effort. She shook her head and pulled out the dog, pointing at Freddie. 'Warm.'

Even above the roar of the sea she heard Edward's rasped attempt at a laugh. ' . . . bloody dog? . . . don't believe it?'

She was almost too weak to pass Smoky to Freddie, who was bedraggled and shivering but looking more alive than she could have dared to hope. 'Water.' She pointed at the canister. 'Then under your life-vest. Help him.' She looked at Edward.

Edward's eyes narrowed. Perhaps he thought she'd gone mad, that the blast and the ship going down had driven her out of her mind. 'For warmth,' she tried again to explain.

He nodded, taking Smoky from her. There was no room under Freddie's life-vest so he pulled out a second tarpaulin from under his seat and wrapped it around the boy and dog. Romilly worried that binding his arms like this would affect his balance but keeping Freddie warm seemed more important.

A surge struck the raft. Romilly clung to the rope strung across the edge of her seat, her stomach rolling over. Edward was clutching Freddie. 'We need to swap so that I'm opposite the two of you, we're unbalanced,' he shouted.

This raft was no more than wooden slatted seats, uncovered, impossible to steer. Their eyes met in a silent acknowledgement that they wouldn't make it unless they found a lifeboat. Given that wreckage from the ship still followed their course, other boats might be drifting in this direction too.

'They'll find us.' She shouted the words out in defiance, but the wind twisted them into a plea. She wanted Edward to answer and tell her that a rescue ship would be on the way. He said nothing, handing her the water canister when the surge died down briefly.

'Drink.' He had to shout for her to hear him. 'In . . . cold . . . hard to tell . . . dehydrated, but you must . . .' Romilly took a sip. Until the water filled her mouth she hadn't realised just how thirsty she was. She felt more alert for the liquid but also more aware that she was shaking. She picked up the oar again. At least she could row, keep the blood moving.

'Which way?'

He nodded over his shoulder. 'Just before the ship went down, I spotted flares coming from over there.' The roar of the wind died down briefly and she could hear him. 'I watched the stars whenever they came out from behind the clouds to keep my bearings.'

All Romilly could see were towers of waves. The sky was a mass of charcoal cloud.

'I wonder if my grandmother is in lifeboat six like we were supposed to be?' Freddie seemed to be asking the question of nobody in particular.

'She'd already gone when the captain took us up to the boat deck,' she answered, between strokes. 'If they couldn't get onto our lifeboat there, Ahmed would have found another boat for her.'

'They didn't wait for us to come back.'

'We don't know what happened.' A thought struck her, making her taste bile. Suppose Ahmed and the group of passengers including Mrs Dekker had waited in the lifeboat for them, wasting precious minutes? Perhaps the boat had still been hanging from the divot when the ship went down and they were dragged under with it? And it would be because she'd let Mrs Dekker take Smoky with her instead of insisting that she left the dog in the cabin. The dog had run off and everything else had gone wrong.

Edward leant across. 'Just concentrate on the here and now. Don't worry about anything else. You've been heroic, Romilly.' He coughed as he finished speaking, doubling over.

'Me?' She could laugh, even when her body had resumed its shaking and the teeth in her mouth were rattling against each other. 'I don't do heroics. I just want to survive.'

He muttered something she couldn't pick up as the wind rose again, something about using it. 'No time to explain more.' They rowed on in the direction Edward had pointed. His strokes were strong. She just tried to do her best. They could be travelling in circles, though. The stars were still invisible. They had no compass.

After what seemed like hours but was perhaps just a single hour, he shouted at her to stop. 'Rest. Drink more water. There may be emergency rations somewhere.' He nudged Freddie. 'He's fallen asleep. Dangerous.'

Freddie woke, emitting a wail. 'I thought I was back at Mrs Cohen's. But I'm still here.'

'How's Smoky?' Romilly asked, as distraction.

She could see his hand moving underneath the tarpaulin. 'He was whimpering. But he just licked me.'

Edward handed Romilly his oar and bent down, reaching around in the base of the raft. 'Here we are.' He drew out a tin. 'Emergency rations.' Inside there were biscuits and malted milk tablets. He passed one of the latter to Freddie. 'This will pep you up.'

'Can Smoky have one?'

'They might make him thirsty.' Edward looked at Romilly for corroboration. She shrugged. 'Very well, let him have one. We'll help you pull him out to have a drink later.' He sounded like his calm, polished self again.

He was trying to keep Freddie calm, too. On this fragile raft, any hysteria could mean the boy toppling in. Besides, hysteria would be a waste of energy. They chewed on the tablets. They weren't bad. *The Lucknow* had gone down with all that food on board: loaves of bread, sides of beef, crates of oranges, all now resting on the seabed. People had drowned on the ship and there she was, lamenting the lost rations. Well, she'd never claimed to be anything other than what she was. She just wanted to get through the war as comfortably as possible. And see where that had got her: falling into the depths of the ocean rowing a raft through a storm with her arms throbbing with exhaustion, so cold that she probably couldn't even remember her own name. Edward was staring at her. She shrugged.

'Did I laugh? It's the sheer absurdity of it all.' Perhaps she was warming up a bit if she felt so self-aware again.

A quick answering nod of agreement from him before he handed her back her oar. 'Come on.'

Her hands were blistering in the salt water, the gloves too sodden to protect the skin. She rowed, falling into a daze, staring at nothing, no longer even feeling cold or pain. Edward muttered something. 'What?' she shouted to him.

'Just need . . . moment.' He swayed on the bench, one hand going to his head on the side where the temple had been struck.

'Catch him,' Freddie shouted. 'He's falling off.' She caught him by the shoulders.

'Edward? You can't fall asleep now.' She shook him hard.

'No good. Must have hit head harder than I . . .' His pupils were dilated again, as though he'd been drinking. 'Let me go.' He didn't sound like the elegant man now. He was like an ordinary serviceman who knew his time was up.

'Don't be stupid.' She shook him harder. 'You're going to be fine.'

'They'll have to listen now.'

The words were slurred. He must be delirious.

'Convoys mean deaths. Civilians. Children. One day soon .

. . American ship.' He closed his eyes. She took his hands, so cold they hurt to hold. 'Do you . . . the card?' He raised his voice against the crashing waves and for a second she thought he might be recovering. But when she nodded his voice faded. 'Ring when you reach New York. If Catherine doesn't . . . Tell them . . . you instead.'

'Louise was Catherine, wasn't she?' How long ago it seemed that Romilly had admired her as the bright, efficient red-haired children's escort. And all the time she'd been someone quite different: a dark-haired earthy woman with a stage background.

Edward looked at her, his face white as the crests of the waves. She tightened her grip on his hands. 'Let me go,' he said. 'Freddie needs you. I'm . . . deadweight. Harder for you.'

'I can't manage alone.'

'You can. You already have.' She had to lean forward to hear him. The raft tilted. Freddie gasped. Edward must have retained some final strength because with a single twist of his shoulders he detached himself from Romilly's grip, slipping off the raft. A wave picked him up, dashing him away. He vanished into the dark before she could blink.

'Edward!' She couldn't lose him.

A hand tugged at her sleeve. 'We have to row, Romilly.'

Edward must still be close to them. In a moment she'd see him, could row towards him, drag him in to the raft . . .

'Romilly.' Freddie was shouting. Under his life-vest she could see the bulge of the dog. 'I can see a lifeboat.'

Waves rocked them. Romilly clutched the seat. This raft wouldn't stand up to the waves and wind. They'd be washed away like Edward. She picked up the oar.

'That way,' Freddie shouted, pointing. 'They're blowing the whistle.'

'We can't just leave him.'

The sky burst into a flash of red. A flare. There it was in

front of them. Lifeboat six. 'It's ours,' Freddie said. 'I can see my grandmother.'

'Blow your whistle,' she shouted to him. At the sound of the blast, the lifeboat turned towards them. Romilly spotted Ahmed rowing at the bow, Mr Franklin behind him. Mrs Dekker sat in the middle of the boat, beside Mrs Franklin and Jack. She saw them and her face seemed to collapse.

'Grandma, *bubbe,*' Freddie called. She shouted words back in a language that Romilly couldn't understand.

A wave picked up the raft, tossing it against the side of the boat. Someone shouted. 'Don't come closer, you'll tip us over.'

Mr Franklin. It would always be Mr Franklin.

'We're full. No more spaces.'

'This is lifeboat six,' Romilly shouted back. 'It's our lifeboat.' They'd battled their way up from the library. They'd fallen into the water and scrabbled onto the raft. This was their place, their lifeboat, as shown to them in the drills. 'It's ours,' she shrieked. 'Our names were on the list.'

Mr Franklin pushed at the raft with his oar. 'We picked up other survivors. We set off our flare to attract a rescue ship. Try another lifeboat.'

'What other lifeboats?' Romilly shouted back. 'This is the only one we've seen.'

'It's lifeboat six, it's ours,' Freddie said. 'Let us on.' He was trembling and Romilly didn't think it was just with cold.

'My grandson and Romilly are coming into this boat,' Mrs Dekker said. 'They are both slight, we can move up for them.' Voices rose in support of her.

'They're in a raft, they can find another lifeboat.' Mr Franklin was still pushing at them.

'Tow them behind us,' Jack Franklin suggested.

'The boy will be washed away,' Ahmed said. 'He's so small. It's a miracle he is still there. The young lady, too. The raft gives them so little protection.'

'You swap with them, then,' Mr Franklin said.

'Tony,' his wife said. 'Be reasonable. A little boy and a girl?'

'Should have got themselves into the boat when they were supposed to, shouldn't they?'

They were going to push them away, let them float off on this crate. Romilly tried to find words to plead, to reason.

'Enough.' Mrs Dekker spoke in a tone that rang out against the roar of the sea and wind and silenced them. 'I shall take the life-raft. You can tow me behind you. There'll be plenty of room for the pair of them without me.'

'Madam, I beg you,' Ahmed began, but Mrs Dekker was already standing up, more agilely than Romilly could have imagined, grabbing her oar, pulling the raft back towards the boat.

'Pass Freddie to me,' she shouted to Romilly. 'Then you and I will swap places.' Mrs Dekker's face was resolute, set.

'I'll stay in the raft.' She could hold on now, couldn't she? If she was towed, it wouldn't be so tiring. She could perhaps curl up in the footwell, ask for another blanket.

'You're exhausted. I'm surprised you can even sit up.' Mrs Dekker held out her arms. 'Come, Freddie.' The boy clambered over the edge of the boat into her embrace, one arm outstretched, the other presumably still clinging to the dog underneath the tarpaulin. Romilly had never seen them so close before. Mrs Dekker closed her eyes and kissed the top of his head. Amazement filled her face as she looked down. 'And Smoky, too? Well, well, what a miracle. How did you manage that?'

'Romilly saved us.'

'Indeed, she did.' Mrs Dekker pushed Freddie gently down into the seat beside her. He clung to the side of her life-vest. She took off his tarpaulin and wrapped him in a blanket, before replacing the tarpaulin. The roar of the wind and sea seemed to lessen. Romilly could hear what Mrs Dekker was saying.

'Now Romilly, I must give you these papers.'

'No, stay in the lifeboat, Mrs Dekker.' But Mrs Dekker pulled a leather wallet out from under her life-vest. Our passports and papers. And one of my rings, which you must be sure to give Ruth if for any reason you arrive in New York before me.' She handed them to Romilly. 'Come on, move, girl.'

Romilly was so cold, she didn't have the strength to argue. 'I'll swap back with you when I've warmed up.'

Mrs Franklin was saying something, Ahmed joining in with words of agreement. 'We need a gentleman to swap places with the young lady in the raft. We must not let Mrs Dekker do this.'

'She's not a young woman.' Mrs Franklin was getting up. 'Let me take her place.'

'You'll do no such thing.' Mr Franklin put an arm around her shoulder, clamping her to him.

'Not you, Mummy,' her son pleaded.

'Ahmed should go,' Mr Franklin said. 'He's staff.'

'I have no problem with that, sir, but can you navigate the lifeboat? It would be hard for me to do it from the raft, but I could perhaps give instructions.'

An old man, in dark clothes with a little cap on his head, seemed to have stirred from a trance. 'We need Ahmed to stay. I will go to the raft if I can leave some precious objects in the boat?'

'Enough, rabbi.' Mrs Dekker's shout was clear across the roar of the wind. 'I have said what I am going to do, and I shall do it.' She gently undid Freddie's fingers from her life-vest and reached out for the rope on the side of the raft. 'Let's move before the next huge wave arrives.'

Mrs Dekker and Romilly passed each other between boat and raft, eyes meeting, some brief flash of understanding passing between them, perhaps more of an urgent plea. And Romilly saw in Mrs Dekker's expression all that she had missed in the preceding days. Mrs Dekker loved Freddie. He was everything to her. 'I will get him to New York,' she told Mrs Dekker. 'I'll keep him safe and warm.'

Romilly sank on the wooden boat seat, holding the objects Mrs Dekker had given her, still looking at her. Mrs Dekker gave her a brief, almost ironic, smile, making her look very young, even though her face was grey, and brine crusted around her eyes and mouth.

A cry from Freddie made her look up. Mrs Dekker had vanished. Romilly wiped a gloved hand over her eyes, but still the life-raft floated empty just feet away.

'Where's my grandmother?' Freddie screamed. 'Find her.'

'There she is.' Mr Franklin stood up, holding out a hand. Another wave took Mrs Dekker, dashing her away. She reappeared, kicking out towards the raft.

Romilly leant out towards her, dropping the wallet and ring to the floor of the boat. 'Take my hand.' Mrs Dekker's hand, wrinkled, still wearing some of her rings, reached out to Romilly's. For a moment, their fingers touched.

'Look after Freddie.' The words were barely audible. 'And you, Romilly . . . whatever . . . nothing to be ashamed of.' The sea grabbed Mrs Dekker, pulling her away. She rose again, her face now frozen into white stillness. She gasped once and smiled again, this time as though spotting someone she'd been waiting for a long time. She vanished.

'Vida?' For the first time, Romilly used the woman's name, calling it in desperation. 'Vida? Lift an arm. Blow your whistle. We'll find you.'

'She's gone.' Mr Franklin pulled Romilly back into her seat. 'Sit down, you'll have us over.'

As though to emphasise the finality of Mrs Dekker's disappearance, the clouds parted, revealing the moon, low in the sky now. Romilly made out objects floating along beside the lifeboat, remnants of their brief stay on *The Lucknow*. The grandfather clock from the foyer – how had that managed to remove itself from its wall fixtures and float out of the sinking ship? One of the velvet-upholstered chairs from the saloon. The puppet theatre from the children's playground. Piles of clothes – no, they weren't just garments, they were people, face-down, dead.

'She can't be gone. Where is my bubbe?' Freddie turned to Romilly.

'I don't know.' He stared at her, blank eyed. Romilly knew what it was like to try to grasp such a sudden loss, how every fibre of the body resisted it, insisted it couldn't be right. *She can't be gone, she was here just a few hours ago, I was talking to her . . .*

'Row.' Someone pointed to the levers beneath her seat. 'We're drifting.'

A switch pulled in Romilly's head. She couldn't think about Mrs Dekker or her mother now. An instinct from somewhere inside her she didn't recognise made her remove a glove and reach below the seat, pick up the ring and wallet and place them both in her coat pocket under her life-vest, before she pulled the levers, Fleming gears, they were called, she remembered from the drills. All that mattered was moving the boat.

Her mind wasn't here in the boat, in the present. She'd survived flames and fire twice now: in the Blitz and from the torpedo. Now there was this threatening icy paralysis, slowing her down, which had to be fought. Someone was singing a hymn. Romilly remembered the tune and words and sung it huskily. Ahmed shouted at them to pull harder. No longer was he the smiling servant who brought you whatever you wanted – he was the driver, the master who issued orders, who shouted and threatened.

Pull because you want to live. Because Mrs Dekker was right. Mama's shame isn't your shame. You deserve another chance. She pulled hard again, feeling the blood run hot and painful through her veins. Tears fell down her cheeks and crusted over, stinging her face. This greed for living hurt. She hadn't even known she possessed it. Edward Witney had noticed it in her before she herself had. She wished she could slump back into the numbness she'd felt in the life-raft before they'd run into Edward but there was no turning back now.

The icy water had baptised her into a new life.

THIRTEEN

The girl died the next morning. They thought she was about eight, one of Louise's group. How she'd come to be on lifeboat six was a mystery. She hadn't said much, if anything. They'd struggled with her about an hour before she died, when she called out, saying she was burning up, pulling at her clothes.

She'd grown quiet after that, wrapped in a blanket, huddled up in the stern between two elderly men, who did their best to keep her warm, talking to her, singing to her.

Romilly knew it ought to appal her that the girl had died, that she ought to feel it in her heart, but it seemed impossible to connect with that part of her. Freddie stared at the girl, not seeming to respond. Romilly checked that the tarpaulin and blanket were still wrapped around him securely and pulled him into her arms again.

At first it seemed they'd have to cast her body off the boat without even knowing her name, but Romilly dug around under her life-vest and coat and found a label. JENNIFER SMITH. Mrs Franklin asked if they couldn't keep Jennifer, wrapped in a blanket, on the boat.

'We cannot keep the dead with us,' Ahmed said. 'We do not know how long we will be here.'

'But it's cold,' Mrs Franklin said. 'So she won't . . .?'

'We have no way of returning this child's body to her family, if she still has one,' he said gently. 'Perhaps a rescue ship will find the remains later and bury them. But we must concentrate on the living. I will note Jennifer's details.' Ahmed had a black notepad that he wrote things in every now and then.

Freddie was pulling something out from under his life-vest. At first, Romilly thought it was Smoky, but it was the toy rabbit she'd seen in his suitcase. Somehow, he'd taken it out before they'd left the cabin and she hadn't noticed. He handed it to Romilly.

'You want me to give it to Jennifer?'

He nodded. 'So she's not alone.' He sounded detached, but she knew that the handing over of the rabbit reflected emotion he couldn't express for a girl he'd probably never even spoken to. Perhaps he was too physically exhausted to feel much now. Or the separations from his mother and then Mrs Cohen and the loss of Mrs Dekker had taught him to keep grief under control in case it overwhelmed him. Romilly removed Jennifer's life-vest and placed the rabbit in her coat pocket. She replaced the life-vest, hoping that perhaps her body would be recovered. Ahmed was looking around the passengers. Romilly couldn't work out what he was asking. But Mrs Franklin understood.

'Someone needs to say a prayer for her?' The passengers looked at one another.

'Obviously I'm not a Christian.' The rabbi sounded apologetic. 'I can say prayers though?' 'Would it matter to her family, do you think? I wouldn't want to offend.'

'No,' Romilly said. 'You're commending her to the same God, aren't you?' The other passengers nodded, as though Romilly was some kind of authority.

'I'll try to make it acceptable.' The rabbi turned to Jennifer's body, placing his fingers gently on her forehead. 'Jennifer Smith, we are filled with sorrow at your passing, but we entrust you to your loving Father. May you rest in peace. We will not forget you.'

Ahmed added something in his own language. Romilly picked out the word Allah. The passengers bowed their heads for a moment before he pulled the blanket over the girl's face. He and the rabbi gently lay her onto the water, now calmer and quieter.

Ahmed pulled out a notepad from under his life-vest and made notes with a pencil stub. 'Does anyone know what the time is?' Romilly's watch had stopped, she saw, when she looked at it. Her old life had frozen at the point she'd entered the water.

Ahmed finished the note-making and looked up at Romilly. 'We must keep Freddie warm, missy. It's the cold that's the enemy now, not the Germans.'

Freddie patted his chest. 'I'm warm.' Romilly shot him a warning look: best not to remind them about the continued presence of Smoky, assuming the dog was even still alive under all the layers. He was still shivering intermittently. Was that good? Did it mean your body was still able to do what it needed to do?

The elderly rabbi had rowed when asked to row, taking over from the younger passengers for short periods. When he himself was relieved for the last time, he sat in the stern of the boat, a gentle smile on his face, wrapped in a blanket, shaking his head when he was offered water or malted milk tablets or a mouthful of condensed milk from one of the tins they'd found in the boat.

Romilly didn't even notice he'd died until she asked him to

move slightly so that she could hold Freddie up to pee over the stern. She touched the rabbi's shoulder and he fell gently, almost apologetically, onto the floor of the boat. She found his passport in an inside pocket of his coat and repeated his own funeral prayer to him and Ahmed added his blessing.

Freddie looked in the small bag the rabbi had brought with him onto the boat, pulling out a long shawl with Stars of David on it. 'He should wear this.' They didn't want to lose another blanket to the sea and Romilly thought they should keep the rabbi's long coat, so Ahmed and Mr Franklin lifted the rabbi into the water with just the shawl over his suited shoulders and face. He floated beside the boat for a few minutes, as though reluctant to leave them, before drifting away. Once again, Ahmed wrote the details in his notebook.

'We didn't say the prayer for bubbe,' Freddie said.

'Do you know the prayer?'

'I can't always remember it.'

'Just say what you do remember.'

He murmured words in a language Romilly didn't know as she bowed her head, muttering an amen at the end. 'She did love me, didn't she?' he said. 'When she came to get me, I hated her at first, Romilly. But she just wanted me to be with them.'

'I think you and she would have got along very well in New York.'

'She couldn't smile a lot because she was worried,' he said. 'I thought it was because she didn't like me. She smiled at Smoky, though, and that showed she was a good person.'

'People don't always let you see what they really feel. Not to start with. But she showed us when she gave up her seat in this boat.'

He fell silent. Then sat up straight, looking surprised. 'I think Smoky just wet me. It feels nice and warm, though.'

At least the dog must be hydrated enough to produce urine.

'I should have wet you instead of going over the end of the boat, Romilly,' Freddie said. 'To warm you up.'

Jack Franklin managed a feeble guffaw from the bench in front, where he slumped against his mother. Romilly herself couldn't remember the last time she'd relieved herself. Perhaps in the water, before they'd found the life-raft. How long ago was that now? This was the following evening, wasn't it? The sun was dipping down to the west. This time yesterday she'd been in *The Lucknow*'s library, trying to find out what Edward and Louise, or Catherine, were up to. If she'd known what was about to befall them all, what would she have done differently in those final hours? Stayed in the dining-room for her trifle, ballasting herself with valuable extra calories? Making sure she could locate her felt hat in a hurry? She'd lost her own gloves somewhere. Someone had given her another pair, thick wool mittens, too small for her but wearable. Perhaps they were Jennifer Smith's. Romilly felt a mixture of guilt and relief that they'd been removed before Jennifer's body had been released to the sea.

More debris from *The Lucknow* was floating past them, caught up in some current that made it sweep along, faster than they could row. More of the deckchairs. A table. A body, facing up. Ahmed leant out and pulled it towards them with his oar. Romilly recognised the elderly Polish man who'd been Edward's fellow puppeteer and who had prayed in the ship's chapel late that first night. Ahmed murmured something and gently pushed the body away from the boat. Romilly watched it drift away. She should feel something, anything, at seeing the man's corpse, but there was nothing left inside her for feeling.

Freddie coughed. Romilly handed him the water bottle and he drank. 'My chest feels tight,' he said. 'Can we loosen this a bit?' He pulled at the life-vest straps. She took the empty bottle and put it under the seat and adjusted the straps. Smoky licked her fingers. If anything, the vest was tied too loose. She wrapped the rabbi's coat more tightly around herself and Freddie. Even with the double layer of blanket and coat, she felt no warmer. She wasn't scared anymore, though. Fear took up too much energy.

If she could just rest for a moment she wouldn't even think about thirst or cold. She'd just drift, drift, drift away. In their old house, the one Mama had sold after she'd met Douglas, there'd been a hammock strung up between a beech and a maple. She'd liked to lie in it on summer afternoons and sway, sometimes half-opening her eyes to look up at the sky. She'd stay there for hours, until her mother called her in for dinner. She felt warm now, too warm. Her hand went to the coat, to pull it off.

Someone shook the hammock and tipped Romilly out. She gave a start, opening her eyes, wincing because they were glued together with saltwater and discharge. 'You drift off to sleep, you die,' Mrs Franklin told her. Romilly felt like screaming at her to leave her alone, that she wanted to drift off, but she didn't have the energy.

'There's a ship,' Freddie said. Everyone looked where he pointed.

'There's nothing there,' Mr Franklin said. 'You're hallucinating, boy.'

'I can see it too,' Ahmed said. 'Pass me the flare gun.' Romilly felt her brain waking. She reached down for the empty condensed milk tin at her feet, removed her mittens and pulled off the label. Pointing one exposed metal side at the setting sun, she angled the reflected light back and forth in the direction of whatever it was Freddie and Jack could see. Three shorts, three longs, three shorts.

'Good girl,' Mrs Franklin said. 'Keep going.'

Her flashes probably didn't even look like a Morse signal.

'They're not stopping,' Freddie said. 'They're going on. Why aren't they coming to us?' His voice rose to a shout. Romilly was surprised he still had the energy.

Jack was silent for a moment. 'Perhaps we didn't really see anything at all.'

Ahmed hesitated. 'Should I fire this? Or wait until we are more certain? I do not want to waste it . . .'

'Fire it,' Mrs Franklin said. He fired the flare. Romilly thought of Guy Fawkes Night at home, back when overhead explosives didn't drive you down to a shelter. She put down her condensed milk tin. Nothing to stay awake for now.

'We still have some water.' Ahmed switched back into the mode of attentive steward, tempting his passengers with delicacies.

Mrs Franklin was looking at the woman sitting beside Jack. She'd been quiet for hours now, her body slumped against the side of the boat. A lock of dark hair fell down the back of her life-vest. She was the woman who'd eaten her breakfast at a neighbouring table in *The Lucknow*'s dining-room, the one with the high-pitched cackle.

'I gave her some water about an hour ago, but she didn't drink it,' Mrs Franklin said.

'Take off her coat before we let her go,' Mr Franklin said. Jack moved in closer to his mother and she put her arm around him as the body was released to the sea. Ahmed noted the name and time in his notepad. Romilly wondered how his fingers could still move sufficiently to do it. This time, nobody had the energy for any prayers.

'She wasn't supposed to be in this boat.' Freddie sounded angry. 'Not in lifeboat six.'

'It doesn't matter,' she told him.

The skies darkened. Romilly looked up for Sirius. The storm had now burned itself out. It promised to be a clear night and the star was already blazing.

A grey form the size of a London bus emerged yards from the boat on Romilly's side, arcing itself up, over and down into the water, sending up spray. Her mouth opened in a silent scream. Her muscles must have tensed and woken Freddie, who sat up, his body stiffening beside her. The shape arced again, further away this time.

'It's a whale. Remember Mr Witney said we might see them?' He coughed. 'There's another one.' Freddie pointed it out. He tapped Jack's shoulder, but Jack moaned and didn't look up. 'Don't worry, Romilly. I don't think they're going to eat us.' A spasm of coughing stopped him from saying more. Romilly gazed out at the ocean to see if the whales would reappear. But if they were still out there, they remained under the surface.

Someone passed her and Freddie another blanket. It smelled oily. She was surprised that the odour made her feel nauseous when nothing else in the boat, not the unwashed bodies or the smell of urine and vomit, had yet turned her stomach.

Ahmed was counting the water cannisters, making calculations in the notebook, torch propped up beside him. She looked down to count the cannisters at their feet.

Ahmed muttered numbers to himself. To keep her brain working, she forced herself to make calculations too. Four passengers had gone now? If you counted Mrs Dekker, but then you had to add on Freddie and Romilly, which would mean . . . it would mean . . . if you added everyone together and took off those they'd floated away, it must mean something. Except she really couldn't work it out. And now there seemed to be more people in the boat. Her mother sat beside her, dressed in a summer frock. Her father was there, too, wearing a Panama hat. Mama had a wicker picnic basket on her lap.

'Don't worry, you were never good at maths.' Her father smiled gently.

'We've kept Douglas's baby,' Mama told Romilly. 'He's in the picnic basket but we're going to float him overboard to spare us the embarrassment. It was Aunt Ursula's idea.'

Romilly struggled to tell her mother she couldn't do this.

Someone was shouting. Romilly forced her eyes open.

The sky had lightened to grey. 'Wake up, Romilly.' Freddie was shaking her. She tried to ask him what was wrong, why he sounded so agitated, but her words were coming too slowly.

'The ship's coming for us after all.'

She looked around the other passengers, many of them slumbering, those that weren't, glassy-eyed, dull. 'Shine your torch, Ahmed.'

'It's a mirage, missy.'

'It's real.'

'Be quiet, Miss Brooks,' Mr Franklin told her. 'We need to rest, we're exhausted.' Ahmed looked from him to Romilly.

'Shine the torch,' she told him.

He switched it on. 'I cannot see anything.'

'Over there.' Freddie pointed to the starboard. 'Look, the lights.'

'It would sound its horn,' Mr Franklin said.

'It wouldn't want to alert U-boats,' his wife told him.

'Blow your whistle,' Romilly told Freddie urgently.

Freddie blew a sharp blast. 'Nothing's happening,' Jack said.

'Either they're not stopping for us or they can't hear us,' Mr Franklin said. Romilly's eyes hurt as she tried to keep the ship in view but it wasn't coming closer, it seemed to be moving away. 'It's hopeless. We'll never get out of this boat.'

'Blow it again, Freddie,' Romilly told him. 'Keep flashing the torch, Ahmed.'

'Save the battery.' Mr Franklin sounded deflated, half his usual size. 'It's not coming to help us.'

'No,' Romilly said. 'We have to keep trying.'

Then the ship's lights signalled in some kind of code. Slowly, so slowly Romilly wasn't sure it was happening, it changed direction, cutting across towards their port side. No doubt now. A rush of emotion shot through her nerves, painful and exhilarating. It was a mistake, the ship would turn away again any moment, she could hardly bear to watch it. But it kept coming.

'Get the lines ready,' Romilly said. 'We're safe now.' Her voice shook as she said the last words.

PART 2

FOURTEEN

'Sorry we can't take you all the way to New York City.' The US naval lieutenant who'd given up his cabin for Romilly and Freddie stuffed more of his possessions into a duffel bag to make room for them. 'But at least we can get you safely to Halifax.'

The American cutter that had pulled the occupants of lifeboat six out of the Atlantic had been heading north on a voyage to southern Greenland.

'Looking for potential weather station sites,' they told those they'd rescued. Romilly had been beyond the capacity to ask questions or even care who was scooping them out of the water. Someone was helping them onto a ladder, pushing them up each step, hands were reaching down to pull them up. Mrs Franklin was too weak to climb: she was in a stretcher, being winched up. Freddie was already on the deck.

Then the crew were pulling the tarpaulins, blankets and coats off them, untying their life-vests on the deck. 'Holy Mary.' A male voice sounded stunned.

Smoky tumbled out onto the deck, looking like a piece of white knitting left out in the rain.

'Is that actually a dog?' another American voice asked. 'Alive?'

Mrs Franklin pulled herself up from the stretcher and stared. 'I don't believe it. You had your dog all that time?' Jack Franklin looked at Smoky, then away. Romilly knew he was thinking of his own retriever, left to go down with *The Lucknow*.

'He was so small we thought . . .' she started. Peculiar things were happing to her legs, they didn't seem to be working like legs and she was sinking to the deck and someone was shouting to take them all below deck to be checked over, pulling her gently to her feet.

'Don't take her coat off until she's below deck, just the shoes.'

'Freddie . . .' She tried to turn around. 'Where . . .?'

'Right behind you, just taking his shoes off too.'

Freddie was shouting. 'Smoky has to come with me, he needs me.'

'He'll be fine in our hold, sonny. We'll towel him down and we'll give him some food and water.'

Freddie's cries continued, quieter now, he was clearly lacking energy.

'I promise we'll look after him.' Another voice spoke up. 'He's like a lucky mascot.'

Romilly, Freddie and Mrs Franklin were taken below deck. Romilly's legs and arms hurt, and she swayed as she descended the steps.

'Your circulation is starting to work and it won't feel good,' a man in uniform who must have been some kind of medical officer told her, placing a thermometer in her mouth. 'That bruise on your arm is nasty but will heal.'

She hadn't noticed that her arm was so bruised.

'The cuts on your legs and the scratches on your hand are superficial.' He removed the thermometer and peered at it.

'Low temperature, but not dangerously so.' He put a stethoscope on her chest. 'Heart's doing well. How long were you both in the water?'

'It's hard to remember. Perhaps ten minutes? It seemed like longer.'

And then you were in open boats for, what, 48 hours?'

'Something like that.' The time in the raft and lifeboat seemed impossible to quantify. Ahmed had made notes in his pad, she remembered.

'Hmm.' The medical officer waved at a younger man. 'Find any clothes you can for her to change into and escort her to the showers. Guard the door while she and the other females use them.'

'I have to wait until Freddie's been seen,' she said. 'Before I go, I have to know he's all right.'

He was too busy to reply, nodding before he moved on to Freddie. He examined his fingers and then placed a thermometer under Freddie's tongue. Then he listened carefully to his chest with a stethoscope. 'Heart's good but he'll need a close eye on him. We'll change him into warm clothes down here.'

Someone else came in with a bundle of clothes. 'Smallest things we could find, sir.'

Romilly helped Freddie remove everything he was wearing and rubbed his arms and legs with the towel she was given. He swayed in her arms. She dressed him quickly in the underwear, shirt, jersey and some kind of trousers that had been found for him.

'Low blood sugar. Lay him down.' The officer pointed at a couch. 'Find more blankets for him and bring him something warm and sweet to drink. And young lady, you need to get yourself some hot food right this moment, that's an order.' He turned away to attend to Jack Franklin.

'I'll come back later for you,' Romilly whispered to Freddie, placing a hand on his head. 'I promise I won't be long.'

'Come this way, miss,' a young lieutenant told her. 'When you've showered, I'll show you where you'll be sleeping and then we'll get you something to eat.' He handed her a set of clothes. 'I'm afraid they're not really designed for women, but they're warm.'

She tried thanking him but found the words hard to put together. He nodded at her kindly.

The shower was tiny, designed for serving men, but it felt like an en suite at the Ritz to Romilly.

She pulled off her clothes, rinsing her brassiere and underpants under the tap. Her stockings were beyond redemption: they looked like strings. The slacks were probably past saving too, she wasn't sure about the dress. Under the hot shower, her body stung. She noticed bruises and cuts and that her temple still throbbed, but nothing worse than that. Romilly turned off the shower and dried herself. Replacing her wristwatch, she remembered it had stopped at the moment she'd fallen into the Atlantic. Would it be repairable? Around her neck, Mama's rings still hung on their chain. She put a hand on the wedding ring. The gold felt warm to the touch. A strange rage came over Romilly and she wanted to snap the chain and throw the rings away. If her mother hadn't died, she wouldn't have been on *The Lucknow*, seeing what she'd seen, Edward, Mrs Dekker, the rabbi, Jennifer, washed away. And the woman on the lifeboat whose name she would probably never know. She'd seen people dug out of the rubble at home, but she hadn't felt the same sense of somehow being responsible for them.

The flash of emotion left as fast as it had come. It wasn't Mama she was angry with. She just needed a human face to pin her fury and fear onto and some anonymous German on a U-boat was too hard to picture. She felt guilty because she had lived, because she'd been helped. Guilt and anger felt remarkably similar, she recalled from the days just after her mother had died.

She dressed in the set of dark-blue work pants, as the Americans called them, and sweater. When she opened her mouth to clean her teeth with the toothbrush also included with her bundle of clothes, her lips were so cracked and dry she could barely insert the toothbrush. In the small square of mirror above the basin, she saw the reflection of someone who might have been her older sister or cousin.

The lieutenant was waiting to walk her to her quarters. 'We're so grateful,' she managed, at last. Ahmed came out of another door, nodding at her. Gone was the confident steward of *The Lucknow*, then the captain of the lifeboat, who'd urged them on, who'd noted the deaths, who'd measured out the water ration. He looked thin in the clothes the American crew had given him, hollowed out, anxious. Their eyes met. She didn't know what to say to him: there seemed too much to express.

'Thank you,' was all she could manage, and she hoped it was enough.

He bowed. 'And I thank you too, Miss Romilly.'

'Me?'

'You kept calm. You helped. The lifeboat needed a girl like you.' He walked away towards the galley.

The lieutenant showed her into a cabin. 'I'll come back later and take away my things, but we thought you might want to lie down. Or would you like something to eat first?' He looked at her face and smiled. 'OK, food first.'

To her surprise she found Freddie sitting at the mess table already. 'I heard they had doughnuts,' he said. 'I didn't want to miss out.'

He looked surprisingly buoyant, colour starting to reappear in his cheeks. 'The doctor said I could have something to eat if I went back to the sickbay afterwards.'

Mugs of soups arrived. Freddie looked disappointed. 'Soup first,' Romilly told him. The soup warmed the core that the hot shower hadn't yet touched. She started to look around, at the crew members who served them, looking at them wide-eyed.

'You sure were lucky we were close,' one of them told the group. 'A few more hours out there and those kids would have been—' he looked at Mrs Franklin and stopped.

'We lost a child from our lifeboat out there,' Romilly said. 'Jennifer.'

'We didn't see her body in the boat?'

'We had to let her go,' Mrs Franklin told him. He bowed his head and left them, returning immediately with a plate of doughnuts.

'We were lucky indeed,' Mr Franklin told the steward. 'Where were you when you got the radio signal?'

The steward didn't seem to have heard the question.

'They were probably on their way to sniff out locations for new air bases in Greenland,' Mr Franklin whispered as they enjoyed mugs of soup. 'All a bit under cover. This isn't a naval ship, it's a coastguard cutter, but there are US naval personnel onboard, like that young lieutenant. I heard a few Canadian accents, too.'

So perhaps the Americans really were thinking they'd have to enter the war? Edward would be pleased. She found herself looking around the mess, just in case they'd found him too.

Freddie ate a second doughnut and seemed to flop on the narrow bench. 'Come on,' Romilly told him. 'Back to the sickbay with you.'

The medical officer had finished checking the rest of the passengers. Jack Franklin was sitting up, pulling on a woollen jumper. 'Doughnuts in the mess.' A bout of coughing stopped Freddie from saying more.

'You must have stuffed so many in you choked yourself,' Jack told him.

'I knew I'd have to get them before you scoffed them all.'

The medical officer looked at Freddie. 'I've heard all I need to change my mind: you don't need to stay in the sickbay, sonny. This young lady can have the pleasure.' He turned to Romilly. 'If you find he's not easy to wake up in the morning, you need to come and find me. Or if anything else makes you worried, miss.'

She'd run out of ways to thank their rescuers. He looked at her curiously, perhaps wondering as others had what her relationship to Freddie was. 'Have you heard anything on the radio about any other children being found?' she asked quietly as Freddie and Jack exchanged boasts about cakes and sweets once enjoyed in a single sitting. 'Or a young woman a little older than me? And an Englishman, late twenties?'

'We haven't. But this is a big old ocean, and the currents work in mysterious ways. There's even a chance the Germans might have picked them up.'

'Why would they do that? They tried to kill us.'

She must have sounded vehement – he blinked. 'I guess so. Anyway, miss, best you concentrate on what you're going to do when you arrive in Nova Scotia?'

'Nova Scotia?'

'That's where we'll drop you before we continue our reconnaissance. You can go on to New York from there. Or would you two rather just go back to Britain?'

'My grandmother wanted me to go to New York so that's where I'll go,' Freddie said firmly, looking around.

The medical officer ruffled his hair. 'That's the attitude, sonny.'

'But what about Mrs Cohen?' Romilly asked hesitantly when they were alone in the cabin and Freddie was lying in the top bunk. 'I thought you wanted to go back to her?'

'Bubbe, in the lifeboat, she . . .' He lowered his head, shoulders slumped. 'When we first met she didn't seem to care much about me. But she did. She wanted me to be safe. She wanted me in America.'

Mrs Dekker had given up her life for Romilly to bring

Freddie to America. Romilly's eyes went to the leather wallet on the bottom bunk which contained Mrs Dekker's and Freddie's papers. Her own papers in Uncle Simon's canvas wallet were dry. She removed Mrs Dekker's documents carefully, placing them on a towel, so they could dry out and not crack. Mrs Dekker's own passport, Freddie's, a visa for Freddie and a copy of the letter she'd written to Romilly, officially appointing her as Freddie's companion for the duration of the voyage and a period of up to one month after arrival in the United States. There was also a copy of Freddie's birth certificate, his mother's birth certificate and Mrs Dekker's own birth and marriage certificates, as well as documents that looked like official approval for Freddie to be fostered by his aunt Ruth for the duration of the war and medical certificates. So much, in one wallet the length and width of a paperback book. If it had fallen into the Atlantic, Romilly felt sick trying to imagine explaining who they were.

'I wish they'd let us have Smoky in here.' Freddie sounded drowsy.

'He's warm and dry in the hold, with water and food. He probably just wants to sleep in peace and quiet.'

She waited for a reply, but Freddie was asleep. She thought she detected the hint of a catch in his breath but he rolled over and took shorter, quicker breaths and she couldn't hear the catch anymore.

Romilly combed out her hair. Some of the saltwater still seemed to linger and it gave the hair a thickness that was hard to tame. She hung her velvet dress and slacks over the chair. They'd almost dried and could probably stand up by themselves now. Her brassiere and pants dangled over the side of the bunk, she was too weary to care about Freddie seeing them. Her coat was hanging up on a peg but would probably take far longer to dry. She remembered the photo in her pocket and retrieved it. Perhaps if she left it on her towel it would dry out gently and her lost family would come back into focus.

Her legs were going to fail. The two steps to the lower bunk were almost beyond her. The wet locks of her hair ought to be drier before they hit the pillow, but she couldn't wait any longer before she slept. No ghosts came to trouble her, but she woke a little before dawn with a start, just in time to stifle a cry, not sure where she was, heart racing until she remembered she was on the cutter, safe.

'Not too late to change your mind,' the lieutenant said. They were on the deck, Romilly still wearing the work pants and sweater she'd been lent. Two junior crew members were sweeping the deck behind them. There was something soothing about the long, rhythmic swishing of the brushes. 'We heard from the Royal Navy again. There's a ship sailing back to Greenock in Scotland. It's got berths for you two if you want to give up your dream of America and return to Britain. We can make a slight detour to meet it?'

'Freddie and I want to carry on. He's got papers allowing him to settle with his mother's family. Mrs Dekker may be dead, but her daughter will still want him brought to her.'

'And you?'

'I'm still Freddie's escort. He needs me to get him to New York.' The sea sat almost flat and benign this morning, as though pretending that it had never been the monster that had nearly killed them.

'People talk about you. The girl in lifeboat six. They said you were assured, kept your head.' He grinned at her. 'You're going to America, Romilly, the land where people don't look anxious at compliments. You just need to smile and say thanks when people praise you.'

Romilly laughed. 'You're probably right that compliments

aren't dished out at home. We're always worried about people becoming big headed.' They stood in companionable silence. He was easy to talk to, she thought. Not reserved like so many Englishmen were before they knew you properly. But he knew when to be quiet, too.

'Thanks for all you've done for us,' she said. 'Finding us warm clothes. Giving up your cabin. Keeping an eye on Smoky.'

'Wish it was all more luxurious. Not like *The Lucknow*, I guess.'

'I don't feel in the least nostalgic about *The Lucknow*.' She shuddered. He looked at her solicitously. 'Quoits on the deck and three-course dinners didn't stop us being torpedoed.'

'You and Freddie will be able to tell the folks at home just what war means.'

She thought of Edward's leaflet, of his hints about his work. She couldn't let herself think of Edward now and allowed the memory of the leaflets to distract her. 'There are rallies, aren't there? Telling people not to let America join the war?'

He nodded. 'There's a lot of resistance, some of it under-standable. Some driven by less respectable concerns.'

'I suppose if I was an American I'd wonder what was in it for my country.'

'When we saw you and those children in the boat, I don't think there was one of us on this ship who wouldn't have wanted to take a shot at the Nazis.' He rolled his eyes. 'Even O'Leary, our engineer, who thinks the only good Englishman's a dead one.'

He left her to carry out his duties. Romilly stared out to sea again. By now, Uncle Simon would have received a telegram telling him she'd been rescued. And Freddie's aunt in New York would know that her mother had died and her nephew had lived. Had Edward's family received a similar telegram? Assuming he had family? Assuming they'd found him, or his remains? She stared out at the water, as though trying to look for him. She'd only known him a few days, it wasn't like losing Mama. But the thought of him drifting alone into the ocean was too much to consider. She'd add it to the container of things she couldn't bear to open while she was on this ship, surrounded by these amiable strangers. It wasn't really a container at all, she hadn't safely shut up all her emotions, she knew. It was a flood heading for her, unforgiving and unyielding. She wasn't ready for it now. None of the other survivors had expressed emotion in public. Perhaps they wept or raged in their cabins. Or perhaps, like her, they still felt as if it wasn't the time for it. Not yet.

She scratched an arm, the coarse naval material irritating her skin, which had felt like sandpaper since her immersion in the Atlantic, finding the scratching soothed her and took away some of the panic.

'I'm starving,' Freddie said, running up to her. 'Do you think they'd have something we could eat in the galley?'

'Come on,' she told him.

They found the other survivors sitting at one of the fixed-position tables, fried eggs and bacon in front of them. Freddie nodded at Jack and sat down next to him.

'Freddie, I can't manage both my eggs, help me out.' Mr Franklin pushed his plate towards Freddie, who shook his head.

'He probably remembers you told his grandmother there wasn't room for the two of them on the lifeboat and what happened next.' Mrs Franklin shot an acid look at her husband.

'I didn't behave well in the boat.' Mr Franklin pulled his plate back and stared at the eggs.

Romilly opened her mouth to agree with him. And stopped. 'You didn't kill Mrs Dekker, the Germans did,' she said. 'They torpedoed a ship full of civilians and forced those who survived to take to lifeboats during a storm.' The others at the table blinked and looked at her. Perhaps she did sound strident.

'They'll pay for it.' She pierced the yolk of one of her eggs and watched it bleed.

'I was a coward, Miss Brooks,' Mr Franklin said. 'Don't like to admit it in front of my family, but there you are.'

Mrs Franklin put a hand on her husband's shoulder. 'None of us felt at our best out there on the sea.'

'She did.' Mr Franklin nodded at Romilly. 'Just a slip of a girl, backing Ahmed up.' He glanced at the steward, who sat at the end of the table. 'A female and a Lascar, and they were the best of us.'

'Mr Franklin,' Freddie said. 'I would like your eggs, if you're sure.' Mr Franklin's face relaxed as he passed the plate over.

'Will you two be all right when we reach Halifax?' Mrs Franklin asked Romilly.

'We have our visas, everything looks in order.' She remembered that their train journey was now starting hundreds of miles from the original disembarkation point at Montreal. And what would happen when they reached Grand Central Station in New York? Would Ruth Belman know they were on that particular train and come and collect them? Mrs Dekker's wallet had not given a telephone number, only an address for Ruth.

She ate her toast and thought it through. The money Uncle Simon had given her was in her purse, now at the bottom of the sea. Mrs Dekker had placed dollar bills of different denominations in the wallet along with the entry papers and the rail tickets from Montreal to New York. They seemed to have dried out fairly well. She'd have to make do with them.

The Franklins were travelling on to New York, too. 'Wish the ferry still ran direct from Nova Scotia to New York,' Mr Franklin said. 'But they wound it up when the war started.'

His wife shuddered. 'When we disembark at Halifax, I never want to get on another ship in my life.'

Freddie coughed. 'Sorry, egg got stuck in my throat,' he said.

Mr Franklin looked at him benevolently. 'You boys, you bolt your food.'

All the lifeboat passengers were examined again by the ship's medical officer before disembarking.

'Should help speed you through immigration if we say you haven't got any infectious diseases,' the doctor said, placing a stethoscope on Freddie's chest. He listened, raising an eyebrow, and looked up at Romilly. 'Do you know this young man's medical history?'

She explained that she hadn't known him long.

'I'm probably just listening to a little congestion.' He picked up his fountain pen and tapped it on the desk, looking down at the form he was filling in. 'I'm not going to write anything down. I don't want to do anything that might raise issues.'

'Issues?'

He didn't answer immediately. 'Let's just say that America has always been keen to keep infectious disease out of the country.'

'They might think Freddie's got something like tuberculosis, you mean?' TB was what everyone feared.

'I haven't,' Freddie said. 'They checked me over before I left Prague and my grandmother took me to a doctor in London. The doctor didn't find anything wrong with me, not even nits.'

'When you reach New York, have Freddie's aunt arrange an examination with a paediatrician. She's bound to know one, knowing good doctors is a hobby of New Yorkers.' He put down his pen, looking at her. 'If Freddie leaves us for a few minutes, I'll give you a last quick examination.'

When Freddie had gone, he made her lie down on the couch and examined her, looking awkward as he checked her glands and reflexes and looked at the bruises on her limbs. 'Haven't had a woman to examine for some years.' He told her to sit up and listened to her chest and checked her blood pressure and temperature. 'That bruise is fading and the cuts look better. I think you may be one of the naturally robust, Miss Brooks.'

'Me?' She heard the astonishment in her voice.

'You have excellent lung capacity and a strong ticker.'

'Perhaps I shouldn't have made up excuses to get out of cross-country running at school.'

'A little more fat on your bones would have helped with the cold. Try to eat red meat and drink milk when you're in New York. And oranges will be good for both of you, too. Gather they were sparse in London. I very much doubt Freddie has TB, but sometimes infections can set in later on, so build him up.'

When they landed at Halifax, the Canadian officials were meticulous on behalf of the Americans, requesting papers many of those from lifeboat six could no longer provide in legible form. Some of the passengers would have to wait in Halifax until the British authorities could provide duplicates. Romilly's visa was examined along with Freddie's and handed back to her without comment.

She spotted Ahmed exiting the immigration buildings ahead of them and caught up with him. On the cutter, he'd kept himself to himself, always sitting at the end of the table and rarely speaking, perhaps uncertain as to where he fitted in now as he was no longer crew nor a passenger of *The Lucknow*. 'What will happen to you?' she asked.

'The shipping company has wired funds for me, miss. I will stay in the seaman's refuge here. They say they will find work for me on a ship returning from Halifax to Britain.'

'And the other members of crew?' The boy who'd been on the deck when she was exercising Smoky. The waiters at meals.

The crew who cleaned the ship at night. Those who worked the engines . . .

'There has not been much word yet. We were not clad for the cold, stormy weather and I fear that few will have survived unless they were quickly rescued.'

'I'm so sorry. And the escorted children?'

'Miss, it wasn't good, the little I heard. They found a boat with six of the girls in it. The adults had done their best, but two of the girls died. And the boys . . .' He looked down.

'I know that most of them didn't get off the ship. But there were a hundred or so children, weren't there? Some of them . . .?' She trailed off.

'There may be a few we haven't heard about yet. Sometimes the communications take time.' He put a hand briefly on her arm. Aunt Ursula would have had a fit, but Romilly placed her other hand on top of Ahmed's, acknowledging what they'd shared on the lifeboat. 'I will miss you and young Mr Freddie,' he said.

'We wouldn't be here if it wasn't for you.' He gave her a bow.

A friendly policeman took Freddie and Romilly to a guesthouse. 'I'm biased, of course, because she's my aunt, but you won't find a more comfortable place in Halifax.' He looked at Smoky. 'She doesn't usually take pets, but I'll have a word.'

The landlady took Freddie's shorts and jumper –well dried out on the cutter and worn again after the first night – and Romilly's velvet dress and slacks. In the morning, she returned all the clothes: sponged, aired and pressed, refusing any thanks. Romilly still felt she had to choose between wearing an evening dress or her slacks. Clean and darned as they were, neither outfit looked quite right for travelling to New York. Freddie, on the other hand, looked fit to be presented to Mrs Ruth Belman of Central Park West. She decided on the velvet dress, although the salt water seemed to have streaked the fabric and the rips, though repaired, were visible.

The landlady handed her a pair of lisle stockings, which looked a little strange under the velvet but were probably better than bare legs. 'If you could give me another day, miss, I could find you another dress. My friend's girl is your size. But I can't go over there until tomorrow.'

'I can't wait another day. Freddie's aunt will be desperate to see him. But thank you.'

'That was good quality velvet.' The landlady shook her head. Romilly remembered going to the dressmaker with her mother. They'd pulled roll after roll of velvet and taffeta out to unfold and examine. The blue they'd chosen – somewhere between a royal-blue and navy – had brought out the colour of her eyes, Mama said. And the dressmaker had been skilled; the finished gown, probably an extravagance her mother couldn't afford, had given her more of a figure than she possessed in reality.

'When you had the dress made you could never have imagined what would happen to it,' the landlady said.

FIFTEEN

They had to pay more for the train ticket from Halifax to Montreal. Romilly raised another silent prayer of thanks for Mrs Dekker's dollars, which appeared to be acceptable payment in Canada. The ticket clerk bit his lip as he took them. 'You should travel free, miss, after what you've been through. If it was up to me, you would.'

They settled into the carriage. Romilly still half-expected to be thrown off the train. Some piece of paper would be missing, some magic words, known to Mrs Dekker but not to her, would be lacking.

When they changed train in Montreal and headed south for the US border, the American immigration officials entered the car, examining passports and papers all over again. Suppose Freddie coughed? Suppose they asked Romilly for a more official proof of employment than the letter of appointment and the temporary visa? Would they just take them off the train and leave them in Canada? What would she do then? She'd have to telegram Ruth and ask her to help.

And then there was Smoky. He'd been secreted onto the train under Romilly's coat, where he still rested, on the seat next to her. Would they expect a dog to go into quarantine and, if so, how would she arrange that? Mrs Dekker's wallet had contained no papers for Smoky. Perhaps she'd imagined she could secrete him into the country under her coat. Romilly couldn't think of any other option now. Keep him hidden. She prayed that Ruth was a dog-lover. She wanted to a laugh at their predicament. So much could go wrong if the officials, now only feet away from them, asked certain questions.

The survivors from *The Lucknow* seemed to have been seated all over the train. Even Mr Franklin might have been a reassuring presence now. The coat beside her moved. Romilly put a hand on it, trying to settle the dog. He whined. A woman sitting further along turned her head, looking puzzled. Romilly smiled back, trying to appear unruffled.

The immigration officials were standing in front of them. Romilly pulled out their papers from the wallet, trying to fix an expression on her face that was simultaneously respectful yet confident. She and Freddie had done nothing wrong, she reminded herself. They were entitled to enter the country and she needed to buck up. The officials studied the passports she handed to them, holding the page with the visa stamped on to it up to the light, as though suspicious it might be forged.

'You were employed by the deceased Mrs Dekker to accompany her and this young man to his aunt's home at this address on Central Park West?'

'That's right. I have the letter of appointment here.' She held it out, but they didn't take it from her.

'Why couldn't your grandmother look after you herself on the voyage, sonny?' the official asked Freddie. 'Why'd she need Miss Brooks to help?'

'She liked to rest in the afternoons and have her hair done,' Freddie said. 'I think she found London a bit scary and it wore her out.'

'The bombs,' Romilly said. Perhaps useful to remind him

that they'd come from a battered city, even though Mrs Dekker probably hadn't experienced an air-raid on the days she'd been in London. She felt the coat beside her shifting slightly and forced herself not to look down at it. Smoky had been placid so far but these officials had already been in the car for twenty minutes.

She couldn't bear to look at the man in front of her, staring over his shoulder into nothing.

'Do you have your own birth certificate with you, miss?'

She shook her head. 'It was on the ship.' She'd picked up her passport and the family photograph but forgotten to go to her handbag and pull out her birth certificate too. A fly entered the carriage, circling the compartment, hovering over her lap. Any moment now Smoky would move again or whine.

'My birth date is the ninth of January 1922,' she said, although he hadn't asked. She heard him flick through the pages of her passport.

The other man was looking at Freddie's papers. 'This boy came from Czechoslovakia but was living in London? Why'd he want to go on to New York?'

'My grandmother thought London wasn't safe,' Freddie said.

The man grunted, flicking through Freddie's birth certificate and all the other papers Mrs Dekker had collected in the wallet, medical certificates, transit visas from his journey to London on the train just before the war, sponsorship forms.

The fly landed on her coat. Before she could stop herself, she flicked it off reflexively, catching the dog's head. Smoky whined. The officer looked at her.

'Romilly really hates flies,' Freddie said. 'She makes those noises when she swats them.'

The official handed back the papers and wished them a pleasant trip.

Romilly breathed out but tried her best not to show Freddie how nervous she felt.

'I didn't even want to come here,' Freddie said, when the officials had gone. 'But when the Germans torpedoed us, it changed. Now, I really, really want us to get to New York.'

She touched his hand briefly. 'I know what you mean. The torpedo changed everything, didn't it?' It had ripped through the metal of the ship and thrown them into the sea. It had also torn something out of Romilly herself, filled her with an emotion she hadn't known before. Vengeance, pure and simple. She wanted to get her own back for having missed seeing her mother so ill, for the air-raid that had excused her staying at Philip's when she should have gone straight home. Vengeance for Mrs Dekker, thrown into the North Atlantic. And for Edward, too. She had barely thought about him in the last twenty-four hours, but now he almost seemed to be sitting with them on the train, smiling that half-appraising, half-amused smile of his.

'You've changed, Rom,' Freddie said. She'd noticed the shortened version of her name he'd taken to using. She liked it.

'Have I?'

'You looked, I don't know . . . floppy when you first met us. Now you look like someone who expects things.'

'Expects things?'

'Like my grandmother. And Mrs Cohen. People are a bit scared of them sometimes. Or were.' He dropped his head, probably remembering that his grandmother could no longer scare people.

'You sound like a wise old man.'

'I just want to know why they're fierce.'

'Perhaps we all have to be a bit fierce, Freddie. Just to get by. Not all the time, not with everyone. But when it matters. Most people are kind.'

'Like the landlady in Halifax. And Ahmed.' He rested his head against her shoulder. It felt warm.

'And the lieutenant who gave us his cabin.'

'Most of the time people will be kind to us and we'll be friendly, like Smoky,' he said. 'But when we have to be, we'll be the tigers of New York City.'

'The tigers of New York City. I like that.'

She must have dozed for part of the journey. When she woke, the window to her left blazed with the setting sun. Romilly looked at her watch, before remembering it no longer worked. It was in her coat pocket, but goodness knows what she'd do with it. It would be impossible or expensive to repair. Now she felt a pang. Her mother had given it to her for her sixteenth birthday.

They couldn't be far from the city, though. Already the countryside was taking on a more preoccupied slant: more cars on roads, telegraph poles. Passengers had filled the carriage while she slept. The men wore suits and hats and carried folded mackintoshes. The women were dressed for entertaining, carrying small evening bags. Their eyes fell curiously on Romilly and Freddie in their put-together outfits. Smoky whined on her lap. He couldn't have been off the train for hours and hours.

'It's all right,' Freddie said, seeming to understand what was on her mind. 'You were asleep when we stopped. I took him onto the platform. He needed to make a big puddle. And the guard gave him a bowl of water and a sandwich.'

'A sandwich?'

'The guard said his wife always packs too much food for him. Smoky doesn't need to be hidden now and he won't do anything bad.'

Suppose the train had pulled away, leaving her asleep on it

and Freddie alone on the platform with the dog? 'I'm sorry I didn't wake up, Freddie.'

He shrugged. 'You look after me and I look after Smoky.' He coughed, covering his mouth. Romilly remembered what the doctor had said about keeping an eye on Freddie's chest. Could he perhaps be coming down with something after all? But he seemed bright and alert.

A man was approaching them. No hat. Romilly sat up and rubbed her eyes. Mr Franklin.

'We changed carriage at Albany.' He pulled a face. 'Some obviously German Americans boarded the carriage and started talking about the war. I thought I might resort to violence . . . Anyway, how are you two?' His face wore the bashful expression he'd worn ever since he'd offered Freddie his fried eggs on the cutter.

'We're fine, thank you.' She couldn't feel anything against the man now.

'Where'll you go when we reach Grand Central, Romilly?'

The use of her Christian name seemed to mark the mellowing of their relationship. 'I'm hoping Mrs Dekker's niece will be there to meet us. Otherwise, we'll make our own way to her apartment.'

'You have the wherewithal to do that?' Mr Franklin reached inside his jacket for his wallet.

'There's no need,' she told him. All resentment towards him had gone now, but she couldn't take his money.

'It seems the least we can do,' he said. 'A friend wired me money to Halifax. There was just time to withdraw it from the bank before we left.'

She kicked herself for not doing the same thing. Surely Ruth Belman would have wired them funds? She was so bad at knowing what to do. But the dollars in Mrs Dekker's wallet would be enough for a cab.

'I hope you and Freddie find a warm welcome and that you

both settle into your new home.' He held out his hand and she took it.

'We'll go on to Chicago once we've had a few days resting in a hotel,' he added. 'Of course, we haven't got any of the right clothes or any of my business papers. Or our dog. But . . .' He shrugged. 'We're safe. And we're here. Better get back to Mary and Jack now – they're down there.' He nodded to the rear of the carriage.

She nodded. 'Don't change carriage next time German Americans start talking about the war,' she said. 'Tell them what happened to us. And I'm sorry about the dog.' He bowed his head slightly as he moved away. Then he stopped.

'Car,' he said. 'They call them cars here, not carriages. You've got to adapt, Romilly.' She laughed as he walked on.

They were passing over a bridge now, water glistening below. Lights were coming on in the buildings ahead. Freddie stared out of the window. 'Look, Rom. No blackout.'

It seemed so decadent: a city advertising itself like this, unabashed, just . . . there. The railway line cut along the side of streets, very close to the buildings in places. She could see people in offices, walking up fire escapes into apartments, whole rooms illuminated. Cars pulled up and parked, fully ablaze with headlamps.

The people on this train wouldn't struggle in blacked-out streets, tripping over kerbs, at risk of being run over by cars with meagre lamps. They wouldn't worry about putting together the few rations they'd obtained into a halfway adequate meal.

The buildings themselves seemed to stretch up into the sky further than she could have imagined, blazing light from offices and apartments.

'They don't have to worry about bombers,' Freddie said, reading her mind. A man folding up a newspaper ready for arriving at their destination gave him a look Romilly couldn't interpret.

Then they were underground, the view from the windows gone. Around them, passengers reached for coats and bags, women snapped open compacts and inspected their features, talking all the time about shows and movies, restaurants and the friends they were meeting. At home in London, conversations in public places were more muted. Perhaps they'd always been like that or perhaps there was simply less to talk about, unless you wanted to dwell on rationing, bombs and the progress of the war. She and Mama had gone to concerts in the National Gallery and talked about them on the Tube on the way home, but their voices had been low. People here seemed unabashed about saying whatever they wanted. Romilly couldn't help but listen in, hoping they didn't notice.

They all had bags – purses, the women called them even when they were big enough to be handbags. Romilly's remaining possessions were now easily transported in her coat pockets.

Everyone else in the carriage – car, as Mr Franklin had reminded her to call it – seemed to know where they were going and what they were going to do when they got there. The few days on the cutter had made American accents seem more familiar. Hearing these civilians talk about peacetime life using words that were different from the ones used at home made Romilly feel dizzy, though. Movies and movie theatres. Candy and vacations. She wasn't just on the other side of the world – she was on another planet.

They passed into a tunnel and the train slowed. The terminus must be close now. Romilly stood, tipping Smoky gently down onto the floor, shaking out her coat and brushing down the skirt of her dress. Despite the Halifax landlady's valiant efforts, the velvet still smelled of salt and oil. She had no idea what the temperature would be like outside in New York on a spring evening. At least she and Freddie had their coats. The train gave a gentle shake and stopped.

Romilly picked up Smoky, still feeling naked without a bag of some shape or size to carry. They walked up the steps into the concourse, blinking at the lights, the noise, the people bustling around them, just as they had when they'd entered *The Lucknow*'s foyer. Her eyes went up to the high ceiling: this was a temple rather than a public transport terminal, surely? Smoky wriggled under her arm. She put him down on the floor and hoped he wouldn't relieve himself until they were outdoors.

'Will my aunt be here?' Freddie asked.

'I don't know. She may not know what time we were arriving. Do you know what she looks like?'

'I saw a photo. Dark hair, about your size.' They looked around. Nobody seemed to be looking back at them or interested in them. They didn't have a telephone number, Romilly remembered again. Perhaps she could ask the exchange how to find the number. But working out how to do this and pay for the call when she only had large denomination notes, seemed too hard. The lights and noise from the concourse were dazzling her; she couldn't think.

'Nobody's expecting us, Rom.' Freddie sounded very small.

'Never mind.' She tried for a positive tone. 'We'll just go straight there.' Where did one find taxis? But there was a sign, so she led Freddie towards a line of people waiting, stopping for a second to blink at the lights on a tall Art Deco building piercing the sky behind the station, its top shaped like a fine, layered pyramid, with an upside-down sewing needle shaft on top.

'It's an address on Central Park West,' Romilly told the driver, who was sitting on the left side.

'Number?'

She told him.

'Got it,' he said, moving off. 'Don't let that dog, if that's what it is, do anything on my seats or floor.'

Romilly and Freddie sank back into the seats. She felt

almost numbed by the view of streets outside: the traffic on the wrong side of the road; the steam rising from ducts, presumably from the underground trains – no, *subway*, that's what it was called here. They were driving north, she thought, from the streak of red sunlight occasionally visible between the buildings to her left, which rose so vertiginously they might have been at the bottom of a series of ravines.

The driver cursed at other drivers and at the lights switching to red. He seemed to be in a hurry. While they were waiting for the lights to change, he turned his head. 'Where are you two from?'

'London,' Romilly answered, 'though Freddie here came from Czechoslovakia before then.'

'Czechoslovakia, eh?' She wasn't sure whether this made them more or less acceptable.

'Something happen to you?' She could see his eyes on hers in the rear-view mirror. She'd forgotten the scratches on her hands he'd have seen as she opened the passenger door and how dishevelled she must look.

'Our ship went down.' The thought of having to describe it all again seemed to require more energy than she had, but the effort to persuade Americans to join in the fight had to start straight away. 'A German torpedo hit us.'

'We fell into the sea when the ship sank,' Freddie said. 'We had to find our lifeboat, but it was dark and cold.'

Now the driver was paying attention, so much so that the car behind him hooted its horn because he hadn't been quick enough moving off the green light. A square full of illuminated billboards advertising beer and cigarettes, with people milling around made him slow again. 'A German torpedo, eh?' he said. A tram, if that's what they called them here, whistled past inches away. Romilly glimpsed a woman reading a book and two boys of about her age laughing. Ahead of them a building with lights on it advertising Coca-Cola and peanuts rose in the fork between the street they were on and another splitting off to the right.

'Is something special happening?' Freddie asked, his head turning as though on a swivel as he took in the crowds.

'It's Times Square, sonny. Something's always happening.'

Freddie looked impressed. He wouldn't have known Piccadilly Circus in London before the war, when a similar bustle and air of anticipation cracked through the crowds.

They moved through the traffic and left the square behind. The taxi drove more rapidly now, taking them around some kind of large circular junction. To the right, a space opened up. A park: Central Park? If so, they'd be heading up the western side, she thought. Mrs Dekker's apartment probably wasn't far now. It overlooked the park and Ruth's apartment faced a side street, though a well-regarded one, Mrs Dekker had told Romilly.

They passed paper sellers. That at least was like home. Yet people walked differently here. They weren't eyeing the white lines on pavement edges in case they toppled into the road. They weren't scurrying home or to a shelter before an air-raid started, but anticipating meals without rationed food in rooms where curtains didn't need to be drawn at dusk and blackouts pulled down. She saw what seemed to be a mother and daughter, chatting as they strolled, arm in arm. The younger woman said something that made the older one stop and tap her on the arm, shaking her head, but laughing as she did. Romilly had to look away.

She couldn't do this. New York was too bright, too untouched by war. How could she ever behave like these people who had nothing to fear? She was only nineteen, but perhaps she'd been battered too much for this new start. That berth on the ship back to Greenock had been offered to her. She'd been a fool to turn it down. Uncle Simon would have let her stay with them, would surely have insisted, if it was just for a few months until she found a job and lodgings.

The driver hooted at a car and muttered a curse, jolting Romilly out of the panic. *The girl in lifeboat six,* they'd called her. Romilly forced herself to sit up straighter in the taxi seat. She had to do this. What was the alternative: a return to the smashed-up buildings of London and the life she'd left behind? Anyway, Freddie needed her to settle him in with his aunt. She couldn't have left him with strangers in Halifax. She'd wanted to go to New York and now here she was. Freddie was sitting up straighter, eyes slightly narrowed, as though something inside him was waking up to the city, responding to its rhythms. Smoky sat between them, ears pricked, sniffing. Both of them looked ready to take the city on. If they could face what was on offer, so could she.

They were slowing, pulling up opposite an apartment block. 'The entrance is just across the street,' the driver said.

Romilly took a bill out of Mrs Dekker's wallet. 'How much do we owe you?'

He shook his head. 'No charge, kid.'

'Oh. Why?'

'Darned if I know. Now, get that dog out of my cab.'

'Thank you,' she said, scrambling out behind Freddie. 'Thank you very much.'

He drove off with a screech, as though maddened by his own kindness. Romilly put Smoky down and he lifted his leg, producing a puddle. Romilly looked to her right, about to cross the road. A car hooted her. 'You need to look the other way,' Freddie said. She checked again and they crossed. A doorman came out, looking as though he was going to shoo them away. 'Mrs Belman is expecting us,' Romilly said. 'This is her nephew, Freddie Lauder.'

'And you are?'

'Romilly Brooks.'

The doorman's face was impassive. 'I see, Miss Brooks.' He nodded at a boy in white gloves. 'We'll let Mrs Belman know you're on your way up. Please go to the elevator.'

The boy opened the wrought metal doors of a lift, mirrored, softly lit, reminiscent of the one on *The Lucknow*, and pushed buttons, motioning them inside. Romilly felt herself trembling and wanted to run away, to leave Freddie and the dog, and disappear into the night. She'd never anticipated meeting Ruth Belman like this, facing her without Mrs Dekker. The door closed behind them. Too late. The lift – elevator, Romilly remembered to think of it – stopped at the first floor. Romilly swallowed. The doors opened.

In front of them stood a woman in her thirties dressed fashionably in a navy cashmere ensemble, her dark hair arranged in a sleek low coil around her neck.

'Freddie?' She stood back to let them out. 'It's really you?' Her voice shook. She seemed moved at the sight of him. 'The photos we had of you are so old now and you look so big.' She put a hand to her chest. 'And Miss Brooks, I assume.' She smiled and looked genuinely pleased to see Romilly. Her gaze went down to Smoky.

'Mrs Dekker's dog,' Romilly said.

'My mother had a dog?' Ruth Belman's large dark eyes were wide, but her attention was on her nephew. She knelt down and threw her arms around him, seeming to crumple as she embraced him. 'Oh, Freddie. We thought . . . Never mind what we thought. It's just a miracle you're here.'

'Smoky needs a bowl of water and something to eat.' Freddie let his aunt embrace him before wriggling free.

So did Romilly and Freddie. Her throat was dry. No matter how much she drank, she still seemed to taste brine in her mouth, as though the Atlantic had seeped into her cells and would only retreat little by little. Something about the mirrored lobby of Ruth's house, the vases of cut flowers, the soft rugs, was taking her back to *The Lucknow*. She could almost feel the sway of the deck underneath her feet.

Ruth was absorbed with Freddie, seeming to find it hard to take her eyes off him. 'Thank you,' she said to Romilly, in a shaking voice, letting him go at last, her eyes refusing to leave him. Of course, she'd never seen her sister's only child before. 'Come in, come in. You must both be starving and exhausted. A meal first, I think, and then perhaps a long bath and a good sleep?'

A manservant who might have been southern European or possibly South American hovered behind Ruth. 'You have no bags, miss . . .?' He tutted at himself. 'Oh, of course you don't, please forgive me.'

'Give Alfonso the dog to look after,' Ruth told Romilly. 'Goodness me, I never thought we'd have a dog . . .' She gave a laugh that was half a cry. 'Anyway, come in, come in.'

She took them into a dining-room, table half-laid half-cleared, with two places still set. 'We didn't know when you were arriving. I've been on the phone all afternoon to the British consulate and the Canadians trying to find out where you were. I'm so sorry I wasn't at the station to meet you in the car. We thought it would be tomorrow now.' Her words were tumbling out in a rush.

'I should have telegrammed,' Romilly said. 'I didn't think . . . I was just so absorbed with getting on the train.'

'You concentrated on exactly the right thing, dear. Getting here was all that mattered. We heard about all those children who didn't . . .' She broke off, looking at Freddie.

'It's all right,' Freddie said. 'I know that most of them died.' He said it coolly, almost matter-of-factly.

She thought back to how he'd reacted to Jennifer's death in the lifeboat. Was that how children reacted to tragedy, perhaps? Or was he still trying to process what had happened? Romilly knew she hadn't quite taken in the full enormity of the torpedo strike. Perhaps all your attention needed to be diverted to recovery before your brain could encompass the loss. Or were children able to dip in and out of trauma in a way older people couldn't?

A woman who seemed the same ethnicity as the manservant brought in bowls of soup and bread rolls, clucking her tongue sympathetically at Freddie. 'Eat, eat,' she told them. She looked at Romilly. 'The boy is calm because you have stayed calm for him, no?' She nodded. 'We thought he'd be distressed – perhaps he will be later.'

The soup was chicken and there was real butter for the bread. The first spoonful Romilly took stuck in her throat and she thought she wouldn't be able to swallow it, but somehow she did. As the food hit her stomach, she was suddenly ravenous, tearing through bread rolls, chasing mouthfuls with gulps of water. Deep inside her there was still a cold void.

Romilly thought that would be the complete meal, but the servant brought in plates of beef steaks and potatoes, enough to feed a family in London for a week. Romilly found herself unable to eat more than half what was served for her, putting down her cutlery with a muttered apology.

'Lina,' Ruth called to the servant. 'Could you please run Freddie a bath and bring him his new pyjamas?'

'My twins are out with my husband Louis,' she told Romilly. 'Because we thought it would be tomorrow you arrived, I let him take them to a movie. Lewis and Clara were getting over-wrought with the news of their grandmother and then getting excited about Freddie.'

Ruth hadn't really asked about her mother. Romilly wondered whether she was supposed to extend her condolences for the death of Mrs Dekker. She wasn't even sure how to do it. But when Lina took Freddie off for his bath, Ruth turned to her with an expression that was half-distressed, half-enquiring. 'I held off in front of Freddie, didn't want to upset him again after what happened with Clara, but I have to ask you about my mother. We only had the briefest information, just saying she'd died.' Her voice shook.

'I'm very sorry about Mrs Dekker.' Romilly looked directly into Ruth's eyes. 'It must have been a terrible shock for you.' She could have mentioned the loss of Mama, said she understood, but she held back, not feeling she knew Ruth well enough. 'Let me just give you all the papers. And she passed me a ring, too.' A moment was needed before she could tell Ruth everything. Romilly stood up and took the wallet and ring out of her coat pocket. Ruth had been eyeing the coat as though wishing it out of the dining-room. She handed both objects to her.

Ruth flicked through the papers as though she couldn't understand them. 'Oh, look.' She pulled a lock of hair out of the wallet. Romilly hadn't noticed the lock before. 'This is mine, and my sister's, plaited together. I remember her cutting it when we were little girls and both of us had long hair. Imagine her taking it all the way to London and back. My mother always surprised me.' She blinked hard and Romilly saw that her eyes were full of tears. 'I just can't believe she's gone.' She touched the ring.

'Mrs Dekker surprised me too,' Romilly said, without thinking.

Ruth looked at her inquiringly.

'She was so brave.'

'Was she?' Ruth was staring at her almost hungrily. 'We kept telling her she didn't need to go to London for Freddie, that it was reckless to make that voyage twice in wartime.'

'She didn't find any of it easy, even before the torpedo hit. But she was selfless.'

'Selfless?'

'In the lifeboat,' Romilly added. 'What she did there.' Her brain was trying to form words into sentences.

Ruth sat taller. 'My mother made the lifeboat? When they

said she was unaccounted for, I imagined she hadn't made it off the ship at all.'

'She did. She gave up her place on the lifeboat to go into the raft.'

Ruth frowned. 'I don't understand?'

'As she moved across from the boat into the raft, a wave caught her. We tried to pull her out, but the sea was too strong for us.'

'She . . . ?' Ruth frowned. 'Why? Why would a woman her age move from a proper lifeboat into a raft?'

'There wasn't room for everyone in the lifeboat. They'd picked up other survivors and were going to push Freddie and me away on the raft.'

'You didn't leave *The Lucknow* on the same lifeboat?' Ruth's eyes narrowed.

'We were separated.' For a moment Romilly was back there, in the library with Freddie and the dog, hearing the ship groan around them, knowing that time was trickling away. 'Freddie and I didn't . . . make the lifeboat before it was launched.' She tried to frame the events leading them down to the library, but it was like pulling memories out of treacle.

In her own mind she hadn't yet gone through the sequence of events between the captain helping them up to the grand staircase, meeting Edward on the boat deck and finding herself in the water. The only way to explain was to be factual. 'Freddie and I were flung into the sea as the ship went down.' She sounded mechanical. 'We found a raft, but it was flimsy, exposed. We needed to be on a lifeboat – we were so cold.' Cold. The word didn't seem to encompass what it had felt like on the raft. 'Holding on was becoming impossible.' Skip over the bit about Edward releasing himself into the sea. 'We found our boat, number six. But they said there wasn't room. They'd picked up other survivors. Mrs Dekker insisted on swapping with us.'

Ruth's lipsticked mouth opened and closed. 'But Freddie is small. He could have sat on her lap.'

Romilly nodded. 'Your mother and I were going to swap places for a while. I was so cold, you see.'

'And the other people in the lifeboat? The men? They didn't say anything?'

'They were frozen too. I think . . .' She stopped, trying to put herself back into that moment where Mr Franklin was telling Ahmed he should sit in the raft, when the rabbi had offered, when Mrs Dekker had silenced them all.

'What do you think?' Ruth was twisting a ring round her finger, just as her mother had done when she was feeling tense.

'They couldn't be the people they wanted to be.' She remembered Mr Franklin giving Freddie his fried eggs when they were safe on the cutter, saying he'd been a coward. 'They felt bad about it later. Most of them weren't young, though.'

'And you, Romilly? How did you feel?' Ruth's brown eyes were fixed on her. Her voice was neutral. She picked up the salt cruet and turned it round in her hand.

'I couldn't believe it, when she disappeared, I thought she'd resurface and the people in the lifeboat would change their minds and swap with her.'

'Or that you might change your mind.' Ruth replaced the cruet on the table.

Romilly looked at her.

'And swap back with her? After all, my mother did it for you, didn't she? If she'd been saved after she fell in, would you have insisted on giving her your place in the boat?' Vertical lines had appeared between Ruth's eyebrows. She turned away from Romilly, winding her arms around her chest as though trying to contain herself.

The roar of the sea and wind, the frigidity of the air, the way the oars blistered her hands: for a moment Romilly was back in the lifeboat. It had been bad in there but better than sitting on the raft. She knew they – she – would have died in the raft if she'd been on it for much longer. And she hadn't wanted to die, she'd wanted to live. 'I hope I would have swapped back with Mrs Dekker,' she said. 'That's easy for me to say, sitting here in this warm apartment. In the lifeboat, after hours in the cold, I can't be sure. I hope so.'

'Yes, that cold, that terrible, terrible cold.' Ruth stood up, a manicured hand going to her lips, blinking hard, as though trying to experience what her mother had gone through.

But Mrs Dekker hadn't been immersed in the water before she'd been loaded into the boat. She'd been dry, wearing a fur coat. Taking to the life-raft in the storm would have been perilous, but the exposure wouldn't have felt like it had for Romilly and Freddie, already sodden and exhausted from their swimming and rowing. Mrs Dekker had understood this and that's why she'd offered to swap places with Romilly. Ruth, in this warm, comfortable apartment, did not. Romilly felt her jaw stiffen as she forced back the words that wanted to come out.

But perhaps it was Romilly who didn't understand. Perhaps she had taken advantage of Mrs Dekker and ought to have refused to move from the life-raft. The bruise on Romilly's leg seemed to throb as she tried to work out who had been right.

'Freddie should be finished in the bathroom now. Nina will run you a bath and you can have a good night's sleep. I will provide you with new clothes: we're almost the same size. In the morning, Alfonso will take you to the British Consulate.'

'I'm not to stay with Freddie for a few days?'

'If you need funds for a ticket back home to England, we can sort that out.'

'I thought I was to help settle him in?'

'I'm of the opinion that it's kinder to children to have a clean break.' Ruth smiled at her, looking tired and older than she had just half an hour ago. 'He'll settle quickly with his cousins and once he starts school, he'll be into a new routine. Of course, we'll pay you what was agreed originally.'

Nina was coming back into the dining-room, a towel over her arm. 'You ready, miss?' Romilly followed her down a corridor and around a corner into yet another corridor to the bathroom, still not processing what Ruth had told her. The bathtub was filled with what would have been three days' rations of bathwater at home. Soap and bottles of liquids for hair were lined up on the edge. She undressed, removing her papers, watch and photograph from her pocket, and got in. Might as well get herself as clean as she could before they sent her away. Because her services had just been terminated, hadn't they? She hadn't misinterpreted what Ruth had said. Of course, Mrs Dekker hadn't spelled out how long exactly she was originally to stay with Freddie, but Romilly had inferred weeks, if not the full month the visa allowed her.

Again, her mind hovered around the lifeboat, picking out details of the scene she'd described just now. Had she been too keen to swap places with Mrs Dekker? If she'd stayed in the raft, would someone else other than Mrs Dekker have offered to swap places with her? Perhaps the other survivors had found Mr Franklin's objections so unreasonable they'd been waiting for him to capitulate and let both Romilly and Freddie onto the boat.

Had she been wrong? At the time, it had felt reasonable, but Ruth obviously felt differently. But now? What were the options? Weep against Ruth Belman's decision? Beg to be allowed to stay in this apartment with its thick rugs and ample food?

She wasn't going to beg. It would be a waste of energy and she'd simply be putting off the inevitable. The Belmans hadn't promised her permanent employment. Even if they had, would she want to limit herself to the plush confines of the apartment, punctuated, perhaps, with trips out with the children to the park, school and museums? It would be a comfortable, cosseted experience, but there was more she could be doing.

Let them take her to the Consulate tomorrow. If the people there couldn't help her stay on in New York, she'd slip away and sort something out herself. With the wages due from Ruth, she'd probably have enough for accommodation for a week, somewhere far humbler than this part of Manhattan. How easy was it to find casual work in this city if you had a visa specifying employment here, for Mrs Dekker's family. Would another employer check the conditions?

And what about Freddie? How would he feel about her being sent away? How did she feel? At first, she'd seen him as a slightly vexing kid. But they'd found a sense of kinship, there was a bond between them.

Questions ran through Romilly's mind like sparks. She closed her eyes, sinking back into the warm water and thinking it through. She sat up. How could she have forgotten the card Edward had given her on board *The Lucknow*? She'd put it in her velvet dress's pocket. Had it survived the landlady's laundering and repair in Halifax?

Romilly reached over the rim of the bathtub and pulled the dress across the tiles towards her. She could feel the card in the pocket. She extracted it. The numbers were still just legible. Perhaps Mrs Belman would let her use the telephone before she left the apartment. Edward was gone, but perhaps she could explain that she had briefly known him.

Romilly sat up and placed the card on the side of the hand basin beside the bathtub. The threads were badly worn where she'd rubbed against the lifeboat's wooden seat and where the oar had caught her each time she took a stroke. The rips had been neatly darned but were visible. People must have been eyeing her on the train and wondering if she'd escaped from a circus or an asylum. The thought made her laugh out loud and she hoped Nina was out of earshot.

She'd worn the dress to dinner that last night on *The Lucknow* and felt proud of herself, worthy of the ship's comfort and elegance. Its soft folds had wrapped her as she stood on the deck with Edward and she'd sensed a power in herself, understanding why some clothes could make women feel they could do anything they wanted.

Romilly let the dress fall through her fingers onto the tiled floor. She'd buy herself her more clothes, and they'd make her feel the same way she had standing on that deck.

SIXTEEN

'You're leaving me here?' Freddie spoke with a fury more intense than she had seen before. 'Just going off without me?'

Ruth stood behind Romilly. 'Miss Brooks was only ever employed to help your grandmother on the voyage over here, Freddie. Which she has done now, with great attentiveness.'

'What does that mean?'

'She took good care of you. Now she needs to get on with her life.'

Freddie turned his back on her. 'Are you going back to England, Romilly?'

She tried to shake her head slightly. 'We'll see what the Consulate has to say.' She managed to move around and make direct eye contact with Freddie.

'I thought you and I were tigers.' His eyes misted over.

It took her a moment to remember the conversation on the train. 'We still are.' She tried to take his hands but he pulled away. 'Hopefully, I'll still be in the city.' She glanced at Ruth. 'Perhaps we could meet occasionally?' Ruth nodded.

'What about Smoky? Are you sending him away with Rom, too?' Freddie asked his aunt.

'The dog can stay. Alfonso has already taken him to the park this morning. You and the twins can walk him there too, after school. Oh,' she turned at the sound of voices. 'Here they are. Freddie, this is Lewis and Clara.'

Lewis was curly-haired, taller and bigger than Freddie. He bounded towards his cousin, talking loudly, asking questions, seeming delighted at his arrival. Freddie looked at Romilly. She nodded.

'Gently, Lewis,' his mother told him. 'Have your breakfast quickly.'

Clara was almost the size of her brother, but calmer, quieter. 'We saw your dog,' she told Freddie. 'He's great. I always wanted a dog. Can we walk him later?'

Freddie seemed to relax a little. How pale he seemed beside his cousins.

'Are you coming to school with us?' Clara asked, as she sat down at the table.

'Not today. Freddie's going to rest,' Ruth said.

Clara stopped. 'Our grandma died. Did you see it?'

'Clara.' Ruth's face paled. 'I told you not to talk about that.'

Freddie folded his arms, as if holding himself together.

'I'm sorry' Ruth put an arm around him. 'She's not being unkind, Clara just can't understand what happened to her grandmother. We told her the Germans wouldn't attack passenger ships.'

How could Clara understand, Romilly thought, a child growing up insulated in an apartment like this? She still didn't understand herself why *The Lucknow* had been torpedoed. There were no guns on the deck.

'Bubbe was smiling.' Freddie slipped free of his aunt. 'When she floated away.'

'You're wrong.' Clara spun round on her heel. 'She wasn't *happy*. She wanted to come back to us.'

'She wasn't happy, but she wanted to help us. She wanted

to help Romilly. I could have just sat on her lap but bubbe didn't want Romilly to stay in the raft.'

Ruth's lips tightened. 'Your grandmother was a kind woman.'

'She said Romilly was going to stay with us for a while. I don't know why you're sending her away.' Freddie's arms seemed to tighten around his body.

'It's all right, Freddie. I think I'm ready to find something else.'

'Everyone always leaves me in the end.' He sounded resigned yet angry.

'I'm not going to leave you, honey.' Ruth managed to wrap her arms around him again. 'This is your home now. We're your family.' He let his aunt hold him, but his eyes stayed on Romilly.

She wanted to tell him that this was not what she wanted, either, but anything she said could be turned against Ruth. And Freddie had to love Ruth, it was his best chance of happiness, living here with her and her family. 'Your aunt will take good care of you, Freddie. This is the home your grandmother wanted for you. It's what your mother would want, too.'

Ruth stood up, releasing Freddie. She didn't seem able to look at Romilly.

'The cab is here,' Alfonso said, coming into the dining-room.

As they walked towards the elevator Ruth turned to a table by the door and handed Romilly a long white envelope.

Her wages.

'Thank you.' The envelope was thick and smooth in her fingers. She hadn't felt pre-war paper like that for a while now. She was safe, able to support herself for long enough to find work. She pointed at her dress. 'I'll have this cleaned and returned to you.' It was an obviously expensive silk garment that made Romilly feel as if she should be going to a smart race-course. When she'd tried it on, the dress had flopped around the chest and waist, but Nina had whisked it away to a sewing machine somewhere behind the scenes and taken it in. Romilly's brogues had been passed as still acceptable and she wore them with a pair of Ruth's stockings, which appeared to be almost new, no darns. Her underwear had been removed while she was in the bath and laundered.

Ruth put up a hand. 'Keep it, dear.' Did she feel that an act of charity was appropriate? Romilly wanted to protest but not within earshot of Freddie.

Romilly knelt down in front of Freddie, forcing him to make eye contact with her. 'I haven't forgotten anything we talked about. You settle in with your aunt and uncle and cousins.'

'You don't care, you're leaving me, too.'

'I don't w . . . I'll be around.' She had been going to say he was among family, but they were still strangers to Freddie. Yet again, the people, the person he'd become accustomed to were letting him go.

'Can I write to you?'

She glanced at Ruth, who shrugged. 'I'll let you know my address,' she told Freddie. He flung his arms around her neck so tightly she thought she might choke. He smelled of clean cotton and talcum powder. 'Say good-bye to Smoky for me,' she whispered as she released herself, feeling a pang at the dog not being out here to give a final pat. She remembered something else and turned back to Ruth. 'When we were rescued, the doctor said Freddie needs to see a doctor. About his lungs, he's been coughing. The doctor said it was very important you make an appointment as soon as possible.'

'I will call the twins' doctor.' Ruth was trying to smile.

Now was the moment for Romilly to ask her if she could use the telephone to call the number on Edward's card. But something told Romilly not to make the call here. How did public telephone boxes even work in New York? She'd need to change some of the notes into coins. Presumably, if she found a post office, they would explain the process to her.

Alfonso picked up her coat, which Nina had obviously deemed fit to retain, unlike her dress and slacks. It had been folded on a chair, looking as if it had been sponged and pressed, but looking faded. 'Fine day, you won't need this. I'll bring it down for you, miss.' She was about to tell him not to worry, she could manage to carry the coat herself when something in his expression stopped her. Romilly nodded a thanks to Ruth and followed Alfonso into the open elevator. He closed the door behind them.

'Mrs Belman is very upset about her mother,' he told her, without preamble.

So, she'd been right to think that she was being dismissed early because of what had happened in the lifeboat.

'Make sure you tell us where you are. That's what Mr Belman told me to say to you. If you get into difficulties, let him know.'

'Thank you.' She wouldn't ring Mr Belman, though, as he'd obviously agreed with his wife that Romilly didn't belong here, even for a few days. Let them throw her out. She wasn't going to explain what it had been like on that raft, how much it had cost her to get Freddie onto it. She wasn't going to plead with them. She wasn't going to explain what had happened in the lifeboat, or before that when they were making their way to the lifeboats and Smoky had run off and Freddie had followed him. She hadn't gone through all that to plead with these rich people to let her stay in their plush apartment.

'Nina packed this for you.' He handed her a paper bag. 'Sandwiches. In case you have to wait around. Mr Belman's number is written inside the bag.' He put up a hand, stopping her from thanking him again.

At the street level, Alfonso didn't leave her to the doorman but took her out and saw her into a cab himself, settling the fare in advance. 'Mr Belman told me to sort it all for you. Nina and I will keep an eye on little Freddie. He'll settle in quickly. School's a good one.'

In the morning light she could see clearly into the park as they drove along: a large green space with trees and people strolling around in it. A good place for a walk, Smoky was going to enjoy running around in it. It would have been fun to watch him scamper around with Freddie. She could return for a walk here herself unless the Consulate or the American authorities sent her straight back to England like a misdirected parcel. On her right, they passed huge buildings which seemed to be hotels, though they looked like palaces with their pinnacles and turrets. Despite everything that had happened at the Belmans' and the uncertain future facing her, her attention was caught again and again by what she could see outside.

They were heading south. Romilly glimpsed the same Art Deco skyscraper she'd seen the previous evening as they'd left Grand Central Station. 'What's that one called?' she asked the driver.

'Chrysler Building. The other one's the Empire State building.'

It looked even taller than the Chrysler. As well as this pair, many tall, light skyscrapers rose in front of her, forming bold geometrical outlines. London had been grimy during the Blitz, and even before: its old buildings stained by centuries of coal dust and smoke. These New York buildings seemed to greet the morning with optimism, as though nothing bad could happen here.

The driver pointed out some kind of radio centre where stars came to record, and she craned her neck as they passed it. He told her the names of the big department stores where you could apparently buy anything your heart desired. Again and again, she oohed and aahed, hating herself for feeling stupid, a tourist who wasn't even supposed to be here. Trams rattled along. The driver cursed at one of them, calling it a darn streetcar and Romilly noted the name. Taxis, or cabs, as they seemed to be known as here, sounded their horns almost constantly. Men rushed down subway steps, looking as though they had a hundred important things to do before lunch. Even outside Whitehall at the worst of the Blitz, where civil servants and uniformed officers bustled around, Romilly couldn't remember such an air of purpose in London. And those not rushing to work also seemed to be enjoying their leisure in a heightened way. She saw girls her age sitting at high stools in cafes: milk bars. They were talking animatedly, leaning into one another, laughing. Romilly felt a pang of loneliness that she brushed away. She couldn't resent the girls, though, for enjoying themselves, but she wondered if they had any idea what was happening outside America.

The city changed its mood several times as they moved south: the age of the buildings, the signs on the shops and the people walking on the sidewalks, as the driver called the pavements, differing in their clothes and demeanours. Romilly saw people with dark faces, more than she'd seen in London. They weren't so present on the smart avenues, though she spotted some in uniforms like Nina's and Alfonso's, presumably working as domestic staff or drivers.

The sky was clear and blue above the buildings. As she looked down the streets crossing this thoroughfare, the morning sun blazed down on her left. It was the kind of spring day that made Romilly want to get out of the taxi and walk for miles. Sometimes, the city seemed to run out of steam. They passed blocks that appeared only half-complete or already abandoned, lined with dingy shops, buildings with fire escapes hanging limply off them and empty lots between them that might once have hosted shops or houses. Then they'd drive a block or two further and the city seemed to gather itself together and bustle along again.

'You trying to get home to England?' the driver asked as they waited on a light.

'I'm actually trying to stay in New York.'

'Good luck with that.' He sounded as if he genuinely meant it. 'I wouldn't want to live in England with all those bombs falling and Hitler glaring at you just across that little bit of sea.'

He probably thought she was a coward. Well, only a few days ago he might have been right. She'd run away from London, from her life, in fact, when she'd boarded *The Lucknow*.

When the taxi dropped her off outside the imposing building that looked as though it belonged in Rome, she entered a huge domed hall and asked the receptionist for the British consulate. Perhaps they'd allow her to make the call to the number on the card on one of their telephones. But just like the Belmans' apartment, it would be too public. She hadn't thought this through properly. The sensible thing would be to find a post office with private telephone booths.

In the meantime, she'd wandered towards a huge staircase. Romilly paused for a moment to stare up at the murals on the domed ceiling with their painted oceans and sea deities. The confidence that the waves could be conquered, that steamships could safely travel from one side of the globe to the other made her feel dizzy. A similarly confident and splendid staircase had carved itself up *The Lucknow*. And the ship had steamed past Liverpool's Three Graces, those buildings that spoke of assurance and mastery of the seas, to its doom. Just a single blaze of yellow as the torpedo struck to remind the passengers that they were just frail flesh. Vulnerable. Out of their natural habitat. She clasped the rail, trying to pull herself out of the North Atlantic on the night of the sinking, to reground herself here on solid ground. Her mouth seemed to be full of salty water, she was falling into darkness, couldn't breathe. She needed to get out of here, she wasn't in control of herself. Her legs were shaking. She might actually be sick . . .

'You're going in entirely the wrong direction,' a male English voice told her. 'Come downstairs with me, quietly and without drawing attention to us.' A hand was placed on her shoulder. What she thought she was seeing was all part of the same mirage, the same dream, it wasn't happening. It couldn't be him, he'd been floating away in the sea, already unconscious.

Edward Witney steered her back through the hall and out of the building. All the time her mouth was opening and closing. She was seeing ghosts. Her legs felt numb. 'I need to sit down.' The words came out in a gasp. The air outside was fresh April air, the ground was firm underneath her shoes, but she was drowning, seeing ghosts, people who'd been left behind in the North Atlantic.

'Over here.' He, the ghost, steered her across a busy street. If he was some kind of spectre his grip on her arm wouldn't be as tight, would it? The bright daylight made her nausea more acute. He turned into a side-street, taking her inside some kind of café and sitting her down at a table. She tried looking at him, blinking hard. And still the face she saw was Edward's. She touched the table, which was solid, cool. The voices of the customers were real, too, and so was the occasional backfiring of a car outside.

'I don't understand.'

'Try not to flop, Romilly.' He put a hand on hers and it felt warm. She wanted to grab it, but her body still wasn't following instructions properly. 'I'm ordering you a strong coffee. And a doughnut for your blood sugar.'

'You . . . How . . .? I thought you'd . . .?' She and Freddie had seen Edward drifting off, stolen by the cold. He must be an image conjured up by her moment of panic on that staircase. But that smile of his hadn't changed: weighing her up at the same time as finding her somehow amusing. She closed her eyes for a moment. When she opened them, he was still there.

'Drowned? I thought I'd drown too. I was barely conscious when I found myself colliding with a lifeboat, literally bumping into it. It can't have been that far away from your raft. Fortunately for me, they poked me with a boat hook to check whether I was still alive. I must have shown some flicker of animation because they hauled me in and wrapped me up in blankets. I asked them to look for you. They found an empty raft.' For a second, his composure seemed to dissolve.

'We were already on lifeboat six.' She still couldn't compose herself enough to say too much, to tell him about Mrs Dekker.

The waitress arrived with a pad to take the order, looking from Edward to Romilly and back, as though seeking reassurance that she wasn't going to cause any trouble or disgrace herself by being sick.

'But how did you get to New York so quickly?' Romilly asked. 'It seemed to take us ages.'

'You say "us"? Freddie's all right?'

'I don't know how he managed, but he survived.' The words seemed completely inadequate. She passed over the time in the lifeboat, still finding it unbearable to revisit, telling Edward about the voyage to Halifax and how they'd waited until the next day for a train. Her response to him seemed inadequate. She wanted to tell him how she'd felt as he'd drifted away, unconscious. She couldn't possibly tell him how his appearance now was making her feel. She wanted to run her hands down his perfectly tailored suit jacket, feel his heart beating, the warmth of his body.

'Twenty minutes, half an hour, that's about the maximum they say you can survive in seas like the one we were in. For children it's a much, much shorter time. We must all have been at the limit.'

'Just sitting in the lifeboat was too much for some people.'

Again, she faltered, not wanting to tell him what she'd seen. He would have seen the same.

He nodded. 'I imagine you find it hard to describe too. Perhaps try to write it down, though. They say it helps. You did well to get Freddie through the experience.' His voice became brisker. 'I hope his family are grateful.'

'What happened once you were in the lifeboat?' she asked, not able to tell him what had gone on with Ruth.

The waitress brought them coffees and doughnuts, looking relieved to see Romilly showing signs of animation. 'A British rescue ship found us,' Edward said. 'Within hours. We seemed to drift the right way, which was lucky for me as I wasn't in good shape. Luckily, they took us to a merchant vessel in a convoy heading west, not back home again.'

Edward must have been in the city for days already, judging by his poised appearance and the pressed suit and immaculate shirt. 'My ship sailed directly to New York. In fact, other than being a little dishevelled, with a mashed-up forehead and minus my luggage, I can't complain.'

'How is your head now?' He'd arranged his hat so it tipped over his right temple. He sipped his coffee, looking at her.

'It's no trouble at all now. But you must be tough, Romilly. You don't actually look as bad as I thought you would.' His voice was softer again, losing some of the brisk cheerfulness.

'I'll take that as a compliment of sorts. I'm fine.' The coffee hit her bloodstream. She followed a mouthful with a bite of doughnut, feeling the sugar course through her bloodstream, her powers of reason starting to return to her. He really was here. Her heart could stop pounding.

'You're looking less floppy by the second.'

Edward pulled out his cigarette case and offered it to her. She hadn't smoked since she'd arrived in New York. She took one. She didn't recognise the brand. 'That's better.' She drew on it again greedily.

'So young Freddie? And the wretched hound, did he make it?'

'He did.'

'Where are they both now?'

'Both safe in Central Park West.'

'But you're not with them?'

Romilly looked down at the cigarette resting in her fingers.

'Ruth Belman doesn't want me there. She . . . I think . . . It was because of what happened on the lifeboat.'

'What was that?' He asked the question very gently.

She drew on the cigarette again before telling him briefly what had happened to Mrs Dekker when she'd swapped places with Romilly. 'She thinks her mother wouldn't be dead if it weren't for me.'

He blew out smoke in a discreet puff. 'Grief will do strange things to people.' He gave her a sidelong look. 'It's probably not so much that she blames you, more that she associates you with her mother's death. It's hard for her to have you around for the moment.'

'You think so?'

'Mrs Dekker made that choice to swap places with you of her own free will.' He rolled his eyes. 'From what I saw of that lady, nobody could make her do anything she didn't want to. She made a rational, humane decision. Her daughter will come to terms with it. She could be feeling guilty, too.'

'Guilty?'

'That she let her mother make the voyage in the first place.'

The matter-of-fact dismissal of what had happened with Ruth made her feel better, as though Ruth's reaction belonged to Ruth and wasn't for her to worry about. Was that the masculine way of dealing with problems: not making them your own unless you had to?

'So, Romilly Brooks, what now?' He leant back in his seat, eyes creased as he looked at her, his air of unruffled calm completely restored to him. 'You didn't telephone. Perhaps the card was lost at sea?'

'I still have the card. I wasn't sure about calling from a public place or the Belmans' apartment.'

He looked approving. 'What were you doing at the Consulate: begging a return ticket?'

'I was going to ask them how I could stay here. I wasn't sure about my visa now I've left the Belmans'. Or about how to find a job.' She shrugged. 'Perhaps they need typists in the Consulate.' It all sounded feeble as she related it.

He raised an eyebrow. 'You think you'd like that kind of work? Administration? All that typing? Chasing bits of paper?'

'Better than nothing. If it helps the war effort.'

'You really do sound quite the patriot.' He narrowed his eyes at her, as though weighing her up. She felt herself bristle.

'Being blasted out of a ship will do that to a person.'

'Quite.' He tapped the cigarette end on the ashtray. There were questions she still wanted to ask him, mainly whether he'd been at the Consulate quite by chance, but something made her hold her tongue, wait for him to reveal more about himself. 'You'll remember the flyer you, erm, retrieved?'

She nodded.

'The anti-war rallies. Just before we were interrupted so abruptly, I told you a little of what was concerning us about our American friends' response to the war.' His voice had lowered.

'They don't want to join in.'

He nodded. 'The task of persuading them remains an onerous one.' This morning his accent was the polished version.

'Who exactly is involved in this task of persuading Americans to join in? On the ship you said you worked for the government?' She frowned. 'Am I not supposed to ask questions?'

'You pulled me on to your life-raft, you're entitled to ask. I may not be able to answer all of them.'

He might have been talking to a work colleague. Had he

forgotten what had happened between them on the deck of *The Lucknow* just before the torpedo blasted through the hull?

'Louise was part of the team.' He examined the cigarette stub. 'I always think of her as Catherine. I was fairly sure she'd died. Confirmation came today.' The tone of his voice was flatter. 'That was one reason I was at the consulate.'

'I'm sorry. Did she even make it onto a lifeboat?' It was no surprise that Catherine had died when so many others were unaccounted for, but all the same a sense of coldness rippled down Romilly's spine. Sudden death was no rarity at this stage of the war, but she remembered how Catherine, in her Louise guise, had entertained the children at the puppet show, and how the two of them had talked on the deck that last night.

'Catherine made it to a lifeboat. But she gave her coat up to one of the children. Then her gloves and hat. Exposure got her.'

It was so arbitrary. Romilly was the same age as Catherine and had also been on a lifeboat and had been soaked before she'd reached it. And yet she'd survived, and Catherine hadn't? Was it because of the blanket and the rabbi's coat she'd wrapped around herself and Freddie? Or because she'd pulled on that pair of slacks before she'd left her cabin? Or because their lifeboat had been picked up before Catherine's? So many variables. 'I only knew Catherine briefly as Louise, but I liked her.' Liked her more in her Louise guise, to be fair. The little mouse reference still prickled Romilly a little.

'A lot of what she told you was true. Catherine worked for the British Museum. But she was also a talented actress. She could have had an Equity card and acted professionally, but her love of antiquities won out.'

That's what he'd meant when he'd talked about her acting skills that night when Romilly had overheard them: he wasn't speaking figuratively.

'She was also a Marxist. Or had been in her younger and

wilder university days. Unfortunately, that last fact made Catherine unacceptable to the Americans.'

'That's why she changed her name and appearance.'

'I think she grew rather fond of her auburn locks.' His face showed a flash of emotion. 'I think she really became Louise, too. Wholesome and responsible. As Catherine she was rather more complex.'

'Was she . . .? Were you?' She blushed.

'Involved?' He looked away over her head. 'There was someone in the RAF. A Pole. The poor chap will just be finding out about her death by now.' Romilly could picture it, the telegram appearing after days of scanning the survivor lists in the newspapers, stomach churning.

'What was Catherine going to do here? Obviously, something connected to whoever works at that telephone number on the card you gave me?'

A party of men and women came over to the table beside them, talking loudly, glancing curiously at Romilly in Ruth Belman's silk dress and her battered old coat. Edward shook his head in warning. 'Another time.' He put his cigarette case into his jacket pocket. 'I may be able to help you with some temporary work,' he said casually. 'While I liaise with the people you were going to call at that number. They're a British organisation.'

She felt relief sweep her. 'I have my wages from the voyage but I'm not sure how long they'll last here.'

'You worked in a bookshop in London, didn't you?'

She laughed. When he lifted an eyebrow, she explained. 'The bookshop seems like something from a different world. It was so . . . orderly, even when we couldn't fulfil customer orders or there was broken glass and plaster dust to clear up after a heavy night.' The job had seemed all she needed at the time. She'd been content. But she was no longer that girl.

'Far too quiet for someone like you, Romilly.'

'Someone like me?' She looked at him, waiting for him to explain what he meant, but he stood up.

'Stay here for a moment. I'm going to make a call.' She watched him say something to the girl at the counter, who nodded towards a telephone on the wall. She couldn't make out what he said, but the call didn't take long.

'There's an elderly lady in Murray Hill,' he said, sitting down. 'That's north of here but south of Central Park, on the eastern side of Midtown. She lives in a largish old house but she's moving out of New York to her Connecticut place later this week. She's shutting the house up and wants someone to sort through her books. She can't take them all with her.'

'The books we sold in Chelsea weren't antiquarian.' She remembered opening the cardboard boxes, smelling the fresh paper and print. Nostalgia swept her briefly. 'I don't know much about that side of the business.'

'A dealer will be coming in for the valuable books. The old lady just wants anything that's obviously not worth much put aside to go to a hospital or sanatorium or whatever.' He frowned. 'What is it?'

'You said my job in London was too quiet for me, but this sounds just the same. Don't think me ungrateful, I enjoy working with books.' In fact, part of her felt relief at the thought of slipping back into quiet, solitary work.

'It's a stop gap. While I set things in play. And if you only have a temporary visa limiting you to working for a family, you need to go somewhere where you're out of view for a while.'

'It all seems very convenient for me.' She was looking at him. 'Was it just a coincidence you happened to be in the consulate enquiring about Catherine as I was coming up the stairs this morning?'

'A fair question. I did need to get confirmation about her death. But I'm friends with one of the clerks. I buy her pastries. She keeps an eye on the front desk, tells me if she sees anyone going up the stairs I should know about. I wasn't far away when she telephoned. I worried you'd lost the card when the ship went down.'

She'd lost almost everything else except for the card: clothes, books, only Mama's rings, a broken wristwatch and a photograph remained apart from it. She put a hand to her neck to check the rings were still hanging on the chain. But she couldn't think about her material losses now, not when she'd just heard about the loss of this other woman who'd so perplexed her on the ship. And there were other preoccupations on her mind too. 'Who exactly are the people at that number on the card?' She kept her voice low so nobody else could hear. 'Do you work for them, too? Who exactly are you?'

'Not here.' He was eyeing her dress. 'You probably lost all your work clothes on *The Lucknow*?'

'Ruth Belman gave me this dress. It must be something she wore for lunches out.' Ruth Belman probably frequented smart Manhattan restaurants for light meals with her women friends. This wasn't the kind of dress you wore to eat doughnuts.

'You might need something simpler to work in. Though that frock could come in useful for other projects. I'll take you to Macy's on the way up.'

She was pleased that the taxi driver had pointed it out to her this morning and she didn't have to ask what Macy's was. 'No need for you to do that. I have my wages.' She patted her pocket, where the envelope of bank notes was a reassuring presence. 'And I can choose my own clothes, thank you all the same.'

The smile he gave her was a mixture of approval and amusement. Something shrewder, too. 'I think you're going to be just the ticket for our work.' He took out a notebook and pencil. 'I was going to introduce you to Mrs Macpherson, the book owner, but as you say, you can probably do it yourself.'

'Who is she?'

'A naturalised Scot, married an American and lived here for about a hundred years but retains an interest in Britain. And in Britain's interests.'

She took the address from him. 'Thank you, I appreciate it.' They sounded like distant acquaintances, not people who'd embraced and kissed like they had.

He was rising, putting his cigarette case in a pocket. 'When will I see you again?' she asked. He might vanish from her life as smoothly and suddenly as he'd appeared on that staircase at the consulate. The thought made her want to clutch at his arm. She folded her own arms to prevent herself from doing this.

'Probably fairly soon. We need to find you somewhere more permanent to live. Mrs Macpherson can put you up for a night or two, perhaps longer.'

They stood on the street. He hailed a cab and gave the driver the store's address in Herald Square, opening the door for her. 'It's a fair walk from there to Mrs Macpherson's. And you'll have all your shopping to carry. Sure you wouldn't like a parcel-carrier and guide?'

'Oh, all right.' A wave of relief that he would stay with her a bit longer passed over her. She hoped he didn't notice. If he wanted to be cool with her, she couldn't let herself down by appearing needy.

When they were sitting side by side in the back of the taxi, she again felt an urge to touch his hand to see if he was really there. Did she even know her own feelings about Edward Witney? He was back, very much alive. On the deck of *The Lucknow*, they'd been in one another's arms, mouths joined. Romilly examined the memory forensically. She hadn't imagined the moment. It hadn't been falsely generated by shock following a trauma. Perhaps Edward remembered it as part of an old existence smashed apart as the torpedo ripped through the metal of the ship, something to be put aside now?

A mixture of regret and shame curdled in Romilly. She was like a schoolgirl, mooning over lost kisses when a ship had gone down and so many people had died. She made herself concentrate on the view out of the cab window, noting street names. It was more randomly organised, this southern part of Manhattan, more like London, with streets running in patterns that had evolved naturally. As they drove north, New York's thoroughfares took on a grid design. Women were stepping out in spring fashions that Romilly had glanced at in the magazines onboard *The Lucknow*. She saw several girls her age wearing block-heeled shoes with a single lace tied high on the arch, some in white leather, which looked fresh for a sunny morning. Romilly felt a deep longing for shoes like that: impractical, fun. Why hadn't fate chosen her as a girl who could just buy spring clothes and laugh in the sun, without the memory of *The Lucknow* shadowing her?

The taxi swerved to avoid a crossing pedestrian. Romilly and Edward lurched towards one another. Where their arms and shoulders touched, Romilly felt a tingling. Did he feel it too? He looked at her, his eyes more serious than they had been before. She wasn't imagining there was still something there. The driver swore and the moment was lost.

'I expect you're delighted I'm with you and can bore you by pointing out the sights. We're on Broadway, as you'll have noticed.' Edward pulled himself away. 'We'll stay on it for blocks and blocks. It's the oldest thoroughfare in Manhattan and it's thirteen miles long. On your way down from Ruth's you'd have joined Broadway at Columbus Circus, at the bottom of Central Park.'

He was telling her this as though it mattered, so she paid attention as he went on to point out subway stations and describe the most useful lines. Somewhat to her disappointment, the rail and road routes he highlighted weren't to the grand sights or museums and galleries but to less glamorous

places: waterside warehouses, or areas in neighbouring
Brooklyn and New Jersey.

The taxi slowed. Macy's was a huge store, she realised, as
the driver dropped them off, even larger than she'd noticed
earlier on, seeming to occupy almost a whole block. They
walked through the leather goods and cosmetics sections,
towards the elevator up to women's fashion. Romilly breathed
in the smell of leather and scent, still perceptible in London
stores, but fainter now and often promising goods that could no
longer be purchased. In New York, everything still seemed
available. She felt a lightness, a sense of anticipation she hadn't
felt since before the war. Her mother had taken her shopping at
the start of each season or school term. The stores had offered
the prospect of transformation. As the war progressed new
clothes had been less present in Romilly's life.

The shoppers in Macy's seemed very sure of what they
wanted, moving confidently towards assistants and pointing at
spring gloves, hats and evening purses to be passed to them for
examination.

'You'll need a bag, won't you?' Edward asked, pausing
before they reached the elevator. 'Won't you have cigarette
cases and lighters, and powder compacts, purses and lipsticks
and god knows what else like most women do?' She wondered
how many women's handbags he'd been familiar with.

Yet the bag he selected from behind a counter looked more
workmanlike than anything else. It was like a smart satchel,
with a long strap, so could be worn over a shoulder. He was
giving her a meaningful look. 'Oh.' She nodded. 'Yes, that
would be useful.' For carrying seditious flyers? He let her pay
for the bag, seeming to take her at her word that she had money
for it. When she opened Ruth Belman's envelope, it seemed to
contain more dollar bills than the amount Mrs Dekker had said
she'd pay her. They went up in the elevator to the ladies' fashions and he sat on a small sofa while an assistant helped her

choose a fine woollen dress in a spring-like pale blue, plus a light plaid skirt, one white and one blue blouse, and a cream cardigan to try on, seeming to gauge her size with a glance. Romilly looked at her reflection in the full-length mirror, Mama's rings glinting on their chain above the open neck of the white blouse, seeming to approve.

She thought she was finished, but Edward had other ideas.

'You'll need slacks as well, if you don't mind me being so specific,' he said when she came out of the changing room. 'The pair you were so fetchingly wearing under your evening dress in the sea are probably now out of action, I imagine. And a new jacket. Something for spring, but warm enough for night temperatures. That coat of yours is about to give up the ghost. Let me cover the cost.' He lifted a hand to stifle her objections. 'There's an expense account I can use. If you spend all your money on clothes now you won't be able to pay your rent after you leave Mrs Macpherson's.'

She returned to the changing room and tried on slacks and jackets, choosing a practical navy pair of the former, and a checked light-grey spring jacket with a belt, adding a white beret to the pile of clothes at the assistant's suggestion. Instead of changing back into Ruth Belman's silk dress, she wore her new blue dress down to the footwear department, where she chose a pair of white shoes, with a single laced bow on each arch like those she'd seen on the sidewalk. With stockings, they were comfortable.

He looked her up and down. 'Before you looked like a debutante who'd fallen on hard times, but now you look like someone who fit to take on Manhattan.'

'Is that good?'

He smiled and a slight blush covered his face. She hadn't often seen him look discomfited.

Romilly also needed underwear and night clothes. 'You could wait for me here. There are other things I want to buy.'

She certainly wasn't going to let him pay for these things. She felt almost dizzy, not able to remember the last time she'd bought so many new things at a single time.

He seemed to guess she needed privacy and took himself off with her parcels. When she found the department, she was overwhelmed by choice. The shelves were full of garments, the racks almost groaning with things to touch and try on: silks, cottons, flannels. Mama would have loved this excursion. She wasn't going to think about her now, though. She touched soft satiny slips to wear under dresses and warm flannel pyjamas, trying to work out how much things cost in pounds, shillings and pence, feeling almost mesmerised. An assistant gave her an armful of brassieres to try on. Damn it, she thought, looking at her reflection, she'd buy a couple of these and if she had to live on bread and water or sleep on a park bench because she had no money, it would be worth it. She was going to start her new life feeling fresh and bright.

Romilly went down the staircase, finding Edward waiting for her by a rack of lipsticks. 'I assumed your essential purchasing would end up here.'

'Have you shopped with many women?' She thought one of the rosy-pinks would suit her. Or perhaps a red, to look more assertive? She took them both. And a powder compact.

'I've heard it said that shopping can be therapeutic for women,' Edward said, dodging the question, as the assistant wrapped her choices for her. This time she tried to pay as accurately as she could, using her change. Edward watched her as she counted the money out and gave it to the assistant to send up with the receipt by pneumatic tube to the cashier.

'Good, you're learning how this country works.'

'There are still other things I need, too.' She nodded towards the door. 'I'll meet you out there.' He nodded, holding out a hand to take the latest set of parcels. In the toiletries department she picked out talcum powder, toothbrush and paste, soap and a bottle of something called Drene for washing her hair. So many essentials had been lost when the ship went down. None of them had been expensive, but they'd been hard enough to put together in London. Perhaps there would be some kind of compensation payable for lost personal effects? Old Romilly would never have thought of this. New Romilly would make a note to claim anything she was owed. Except that she didn't own a notepad and pencil, let alone a pen. She'd almost reached the door but turned around and bought a large notebook with a marbled-effect cover, and a box of pencils. The notebook was rather larger than she'd need for keeping a list of expenses, she noted, not sure why it was she'd chosen it rather than a cashbook.

Edward rolled his eyes when she reappeared. 'Remind me never to go shopping again with someone who's lost all her worldly goods.'

'I never thought I owned very much until I had to replace it all.'

'We mourn the human losses the most, of course. But losing personal possessions matters too.'

'I shouldn't really complain. Not when all those children died.'

She put a hand to her neck, checking that her mother's rings were still there. Freddie had given that toy rabbit of his to Jennifer before they'd floated her away from the boat because sending her away without anything of her own seemed too stark. During the Blitz, Romilly had seen people raking over the ruins of houses, snatching at a single surviving cup or book to take with them as a memento of the life they'd once had, the family they'd once shared it with.

He put out a hand to hail a taxi. 'That's a message for our American friends, too: how would you feel if you lost everything down to your children's clothes or the tools you need for your work?' He narrowed his eyes, as though imagining how he could use the idea.

'Americans might think that was another good reason for staying out of the war,' Romilly said. 'To spare themselves those losses.'

'They might indeed. That's the president's problem. Roosevelt sees what Hitler is, he gave that big speech last month when he announced the Lend Lease program.'

Romilly remembered reaction to the announcement of Lend Lease. 'People at home were relieved he was going to give us the destroyers and planes. But my mother said we'd be paying for them, either now or for years into the future.'

'This war will cost us dearly. But we won't win without America. Roosevelt wants to bring America in. But he has to tread a delicate path. Let's get on to Mrs Macpherson's.'

'Could we walk?' She felt dizzy from the constant jumping into taxis, buzzing her from one side of the city to another. 'It would help me get a sense of New York.'

'In your new shoes?'

She wriggled her toes. 'They're very comfortable.'

He eyed the parcels. 'We should be able to manage all these between us.' The shopping redistributed, they headed in what seemed to be an easterly direction. Romilly's stomach rumbled. Nearly lunch time. She remembered Nina's sandwich, now stowed inside her new bag. Edward's limp seemed more pronounced.

'Could we sit down for a moment? I have my lunch. I'll let you have half.'

'We can make a bit of a diversion to Bryant Park.' He took her north up Sixth Avenue five blocks, as she was learning to calibrate New York distances. She could have slowed down, stared into every shop window, watched the people coming out of offices for their lunch, the girls in their spring-wear, all glossy-haired and lipsticked, the shoe-shine boys, the delivery men with their rapid talk, punctuated by hand gestures, but Edward seemed to want to press on, despite the limp. Perhaps Mrs Macpherson had set him a firm starting time for Romilly.

'That's the New York Public Library,' he said as they arrived, noticing her blink at the tall, narrow-windowed stone building on the far side of the park. 'You should visit it. You'd enjoy burying yourself in all those books. It's quite splendid inside too.'

They sat down on a bench. Romilly offered him half her sandwich. He took it appreciatively. A large amount of turkey, something Romilly hadn't seen since Christmas 1939, was stuffed inside, along with mayonnaise and lettuce. If she ate like this on a regular basis, Romilly feared her new clothes wouldn't fit her for long. There was a bottle of Coca-Cola in the bag, too, which they shared. It all seemed very companionable. On the deck of *The Lucknow* they'd melted into one another in that kiss, following her accusations. Despite that moment and despite the hour – possibly less – they'd spent on the life-raft before he'd let go, with all its physical and emotional intensity, she barely knew this man. And yet surely an experience like that would speed up the time that would take? Unbidden, the magazines Mama had sometimes indulged in came to her mind, with their tips for the lovelorn. *Want to light a romantic flame? Try a torpedo and immersion in the North Atlantic!* Her lips twitched. Fortunately, he wasn't looking. A blob of mayonnaise fell onto her chin and Edward grinned.

'Hope you remembered to buy new handkerchiefs in Macy's.'

She glared at him and wiped it off with a finger. This picnic didn't feel particularly romantic.

'I hope Mrs Macpherson doesn't give us lunch as well,' he observed. 'At this rate, I'll be needing new clothes too.'

He still looked lean. The blue-grey eyes looked brighter against his face, which was still windblown from exposure. But for the almost-invisible scar on his temple you'd never have known that he'd been almost dying in the sea such a short time ago.

'At the moment I feel I could eat any number of lunches.'

'I'd worry about you outgrowing your new clothes.'

'Don't you concern yourself with my clothes.' She decided she wasn't going to let him become over-familiar with her. She still didn't know if she really trusted him, despite the way her heart had nearly burst out of her chest when she'd turned to see him standing behind her on the staircase to the consulate. The kiss on the deck might still be so vivid in her memory that she could almost taste his mouth, but it was better to keep everything on a friendly, professional basis – with lines drawn.

'A fair point. Anyway, we'll keep you so busy you'll not have time to put on weight.' He kept shifting the conversation to the 'we' from himself personally. Perhaps he felt the same way she did about not becoming over-familiar. All the same, it niggled at her.

'Tell me more about Mrs Macpherson.' Romilly's stomach was pleasantly full. She wanted to stretch out on the bench in the now comfortable sunshine and sleep like a cosseted cat.

'She's a member of The Ladies British-American Protection Alliance.'

'Raising funds for what? Spitfires and Lancasters? Bring and buy sales?' She folded the brown paper bag. 'Or do you mean they . . . influence policy? Ladies' luncheons to lobby politicians' wives?'

'That kind of thing.' He looked amused.

'And that's what you want me to do, once I've finished sorting out Mrs Macpherson's books?' Her heart sank. 'I don't think I'd be very good at that kind of work.' She heard dejection in her own tone. 'I've never really—'

He raised a hand to interrupt her. 'You won't be entertaining over-poached chicken fillets wearing Ruth Belman's frock.' He stood up. 'Don't worry, Romilly. I'm lining something up for you that will be far more interesting.' He stretched out his leg, grimacing slightly and flushing when he saw Romilly had noticed. 'An injury from before. I must have struck the leg on debris as the ship went down. It's set me back a bit.'

'When you say before, what happened?' She asked cautiously. Sometimes men didn't like to talk about how they'd been wounded.

'We were waiting for evacuation on a beach in northern France when a German plane took exception to us.'

Dunkirk, she guessed. He must have been one of the thousands and thousands of servicemen taken off the beach when France had fallen.

'Nothing too serious, but Manhattan sidewalks can be unforgiving.'

In more than one way, she thought. But Romilly was up to meeting the challenge.

SEVENTEEN

Mrs Macpherson had something of Mrs Dekker's very upright, you could say rigid, posture. But her face was slender, almost austere. She looked Romilly up and down and Romilly was glad she'd changed into the more workaday pale-blue dress she'd bought at Macy's. 'I'll find you an apron. Don't want that frock of yours getting dusty. It looks new.' She gave Romilly a questioning stare. Perhaps, coming from ration-afflicted England, she wasn't supposed to be wearing new garments? She probably ought to have worn the new slacks rather than the dress. Although perhaps Mrs Macpherson wouldn't approve of women in trousers. Too late now, anyway.

'You should have seen what she was wearing before she bought that frock,' Edward said. 'Fit for the smartest society.'

Romilly started to explain about the borrowed dress. 'Ruth Belman's dress?' Mrs Macpherson gave a dry laugh. 'I can imagine.'

'You know Mrs Belman?' Romilly asked.

'Her mother, Vida (may she rest in peace), more than Ruth.' Mrs Macpherson's features softened. 'I heard on the grapevine that Vida had been lost when *The Lucknow* went down. Amos and I didn't know the Dekkers well, but we dined with them once or twice when both husbands were still alive.' She paused. 'It must have been a terrible experience for you on that ship, Miss Brooks.'

Romilly bowed her head, not knowing what to say. 'At least I'm safe now,' she managed.

'And the little boy, too. Mr Witney tells me you were responsible for him safely reaching a lifeboat.'

'I don't . . .' She didn't know what to say, remembering Mrs Dekker's sacrifice. She wondered whether word of Mrs Dekker swapping places with her was yet known outside the family. Perhaps Mrs Macpherson was silently judging her too, despite the kind words.

'Anyway,' Mrs Macpherson continued, more briskly, 'I gather you've had lunch, so we'll take you straight to your room before you start in the library.' She nodded at her maid, who stood in the hallway. 'Mr Witney can take a cup of coffee before he goes on his way.'

Dismissed, Edward grinned at Romilly. 'I'll be in touch when I've got some accommodation suggestions for you,' he told her. 'I'll also put further thought to your employment and visa.'

'I can put you up for two nights while I'm still in town,' Mrs Macpherson told her. 'Or longer, if you don't mind being in the house by yourself after I've moved out and the telephone and electricity are switched off.' The maid took her up two flights of stairs, to a bedroom. The room had already been stripped of most of its furniture apart from the bed and a clothes rack, which looked forlorn amid the wallpapered walls and silk drapes. Romilly put her shopping bags on the bed. 'There's a washbasin behind that door there if you want to freshen up. The library is one storey down. Come down when you're ready.'

Romilly found the small en-suite with a lavatory, basin and shower inside it. She brushed her hair with her new brush and applied her new pink lipstick, feeling herself sliding into an altered persona: the working girl, rather than the refugee. Only a few days ago she'd been in that lifeboat and they'd been pushing the bodies off into the sea. And only weeks ago she'd still been in London. Now, here she was, working for someone she'd only just met in a city so far away from home. The suddenness of it all hadn't completely hit her yet. It had all worked out so smoothly, but it couldn't be this simple, could it?

Her mind went back to Freddie. How must he be feeling? She would have to find a way of telephoning the apartment and asking to speak to him, make sure he was settling in. Surely Mrs Belman would allow that?

Down a floor from her room, she found the library, panelled in dark oak like the hall and housing bookcases that reached from the ceiling to floor. A red Persian rug was laid across the parquet. Mrs Macpherson was sitting at the desk.

'Seventy years in this house.' She nodded at Romilly's surprise. 'That's right: married at seventeen and brought here from Edinburgh as a bride. But Amos and I had no children. I don't need as much space these days, so I'll shut it up for now. I think change is on the way.'

Did Mrs Macpherson mean the war? 'Perhaps one day I'll open it up again.' Her eyes softened as she looked around the room.

'Won't you miss living here, Mrs Macpherson?' Though it was a house that seemed to turn its back on the spring sunshine outside.

'As you will have observed, this house is built on the vertical and, as I age, I find it hard. I'll live in our Connecticut place. I can always stay in the Knickerbocker if I need to come up to town.' Seeing Romilly's surprised expression, she added: 'That's a hotel, dear. Some of the names here do startle one at first.'

Romilly tried to estimate just how many thousands of books there were in the room. Most of them looked leather-backed, but two bookcases housed dust-covered hardbacks that looked more contemporary. Romilly took a step towards them, feeling a pang as she spotted old favourites of her mother's and some titles she'd sold in the shop. Would she ever return to London to take their old family books out of storage? Until now she hadn't felt anything resembling homesickness.

'I've already removed what I want to take to Connecticut and sent it on. My set of Walter Scott, of course. The Jane Austen and Henry James. Your task is to divide what's left here into two: first editions or anything that looks valuable, and the books without merit, either literary or to a collector. Books the casual reader might buy for recreation.' Mrs Macpherson sniffed. 'I'll sell them at a charitable bazaar for the cause.'

The latter group probably included books Romilly had enjoyed reading by torch in an air-raid shelter. Presumably, Mrs Macpherson herself had once enjoyed them too. Or perhaps her dead husband had been the one who'd liked to read for sheer enjoyment.

'The cause is the British war effort?' she asked.

Mrs Macpherson looked surprised. 'What else? The dealer will quickly review any books you place in the crates for the bazaar, just in case he wants any of them, but this way we'll save time.' She stood up. 'You might as well start now. I'll have an apron and gloves brought up to you, but you can acquaint yourself with the task in the meantime.'

Wooden crates were stacked in the middle of the library, on a white sheet. Romilly walked to the shelves. Someone had been an avid reader of detective novels. She flicked through copies of Dorothy L Sayers and Dashiell Hammett, placing them to one side if they were first editions. Who knew if they'd eventually become collectors' items? The scent of the paper instilled a sense of serenity in her. She sat, cross-legged on the floor, absorbed in the books, finding it hard not to open them up and read. She might have been back in London, chatting about last-night's air-raid with Miss Jones. Was the shop still open? She'd left in such a hurry there wouldn't have been much time to replace her. Perhaps the shortages had finally made the bookstore unviable. If she could fly across the Atlantic to tell Miss Jones what had happened to her since she'd left, how would she even begin to explain? Embarking on a voyage with two people she'd never met before. The comforts of *The Lucknow*. The wariness she'd felt for Edward and the contradictory feelings out on deck that last night. The frigid shock of the water and how it had grabbed her round the chest, threatening to crush all the air out of her lungs. The fight to get to the lifeboat. Edward floating away. Mrs Dekker's hands with their rings on the fingers reaching out to her. Jennifer and the kindly rabbi. The improvised funerals. The cutter and its crew.

She let out a breath to release the images, her mind going to the new notebook she'd bought this morning. Perhaps she could write down some of what she'd seen. Romilly returned to her task.

Soft footsteps at the door roused her an hour or so later. The maid stood behind her with a tray, which she set down beside Romilly. 'Tea with milk to add, the way the British drink it. And shortbread. Mrs Macpherson said you might like it.'

'Thank you.' The maid switched on the lamps and lit the logs in the fireplace. Romilly poured the tea and added milk. The maid left her. The shortbread tasted of real butter, each mouthful dissolving as it reached her tongue. She wiped her fingers on the napkin and carried on with the sorting. Perhaps Edward was wrong about her. Or she was wrong about herself. If she could find quiet, stable permanent work like this, she might be happy. Perhaps she didn't really crave excitement and purpose, after all. Old Romilly, back in London, had been happy enough. But old Romilly had died when the ship went down. The one who'd replaced her was more restless, more demanding, she admitted.

The maid returned to take the tea tray and Romilly barely noticed her come in. She alternated between standing up to take armloads of books onto the Persian rug and sitting cross-legged to check them. She no longer had a watch, she remembered with a pang, but there was still a desk clock in here. At five she sat back on her heels. In front of her rose towers of books. She'd cleared a whole bookcase, floor to ceiling. How long was she supposed to carry on working this evening? Romilly wandered out to the stairs and up to her bedroom. Washing her hands of the scent and dust of old books at the basin she looked at her face in the mirror. The walk from Macy's had given her some colour and now her hair was properly brushed she looked more like her old self, albeit more guarded and determined around the eyes.

On her way downstairs again, she met her benefactress. Mrs Macpherson's features were even more finely drawn and lined under the light of the switched-on chandelier.

'Take a stroll, Miss Brooks.' It was more of an order than a suggestion. 'It'll be light for a while. It can be rough in the blocks from here towards the East River, if you don't know the area. Turn right out of the house. Head back into Midtown.'

Romilly went back upstairs to collect her bag and outdoor clothes. Perhaps she could remember the way back to the park where she'd had lunch with Edward.

Outside the house, she turned right, as instructed, reaching Park Avenue and walking along it, admiring the store window displays and the women emerging from the doors with parcels and an air of purpose. She made a left turn a block later, cutting across Madison Avenue, feeling a sense of solidarity with the people moving along at a brisk but not rushed place. On Fifth Avenue, she reached the library on the side farthest from where they'd sat at lunch and admired a pair of marble lions. She wondered what time it closed but had had enough of books this evening, preferring to stay in the radiant light.

Romilly turned right along 42nd Street and realised she'd been here before as soon as she saw Grand Central Terminal. It had barely been twenty-four hours since she and Freddie had arrived here. As she walked along, the Chrysler Building drew her eyes again, already feeling like an old friend in this city she had dropped into like a bird migrating to an unfamiliar place.

Another right turn set her on the way back towards Mrs Macpherson's house. She could do another hour on the books, perhaps, impress the old lady with her industriousness. Might be worth obtaining a glowing reference in case whatever Edward planned for her fell through.

The newspaper boys were selling the evening papers, chanting about *extra, extra* and *read all about it*, wearing large caps and slipping coins from pedestrians' palms at the same time as they swept papers under their arms. A pang for the accents of the London newspaper boys swept Romilly and she slowed. She eyed the headlines for news of the war: a habit that had become ingrained in her at home. Nothing obvious, at a glance. Perhaps it really didn't matter as much to people here. And why should it? On an evening like this when the air was soft and inviting, when you had a restaurant table booked or a movie in mind, or when you were just planning on going home to your family, eating your evening meal with the wireless switched to your favourite sport or light entertainment programme, why should you worry about what was happening the other side of the world? Even in London people had switched off from it all, allowed themselves distraction. Her night out with Philip came to mind. She had to focus hard to even bring his face into view but thinking of him brought down a crashing wave of guilt. She ought to have gone straight home after the cinema. She shouldn't have stayed on with Philip, using the air-raid as an excuse, letting him, letting herself, go so far. If she had gone home earlier, Mama . . . She hadn't even been sure what she'd been running away from: all the guilt she'd felt about Philip had blended with the shock of knowing Mama had been pregnant and it all become part of the same enormous boulder pressing down on her.

She passed another boy, wearing the cap they all seemed to sport. As he handed a passing man a paper, she saw a headline on the front page that took her mind off her guilt. 'You want a paper?' the boy demanded. 'Or you just going to read it all standing there?'

She took the purse out of her bag and held out a few coins for him to select what he thought appropriate, feeling too flustered to ask the price and find the correct coin. He gave her a scornful look, but what she read on the front page completely took her attention.

'*Mass Rally for America First in Chicago.*' Beneath it, there was a photograph of what looked like thousands and thousands of people, arranged in lines and reminiscent of the news footage of Hitler at Nuremberg. Chilled, she looked again. The people were seated, she told herself, not standing. Not raising an arm in salute. Yet some of the audience wore bands around their right arms. Banners dropped from impossible heights. Some of the men wore a uniform that reminded her of the Germans. She must have muttered something aloud in horror. A man in a trilby turned and stared at her, tutting, but a woman with dark hair and bright, enquiring eyes under a tilted hat brim gave her an approving nod.

Was the woman perhaps Jewish like Ruth Belman? How many were there like her in the city. Romilly wanted to grab her sleeve before she walked on, ask her whether she was *actually doing anything about it*. The report below the photograph told of a Charles Lindbergh addressing the rally. The name was familiar to Romilly. Searching her memory, she remembered. She'd been six or seven when Lindbergh had flown solo from New York to Paris, the first to complete the feat. Her father had been down in Devon on a business trip and claimed to have seen him fly over. Her parents had kept the newspaper cuttings and when she and Mama had packed up the old house to move to Chelsea, Romilly had flicked through them. She had fleeting memories of a handsome young man in a flying suit. He'd had a tragedy in his life, too, she recalled, a child kidnapped and killed? Why wasn't he standing up for the boys and girls like Freddie, innocents threatened for nothing more than being the wrong race? Or for all the children on *The Lucknow* who'd died because of the U-boat's torpedo?

She wanted to throw the wretched newspaper into the gutter where a banana skin and cigarette paper lay, but folded it up to take back and read. Looking around, she realised she hadn't been paying attention. She'd continued east, towards the river Mrs Macpherson had warned her against, finding herself in an area that didn't look at all like the fashionable avenues running north to south. It made her think of what Edward had told her on the ship, that America had had its own harsh Depression, worse, in fact, than what had been suffered in Britain. Shop fronts were boarded over. Men hung around in the street, some of them Black, some perhaps from Central America, Puerto Rico, Mexico, maybe? Poorly dressed, thin, looking as though they had nowhere in particular to go at the end of the day. A few children threw a ball around, dressed in shabby clothes. Ahead lay what looked like huge warehouses, men hanging around, looking at her curiously. An odour of something both animal and metallic reached her. Slaughter-houses, perhaps?

London had many rough parts: the docks, other parts of the East End. And poverty as bad as this was certainly no stranger to the city. But it didn't have this sense of abrupt transition between areas.

Romilly turned around, re-orientating herself against the omnipresent Chrysler and Empire State Buildings. She was heading west now, and the sun was setting. She lifted a hand to her eyes to shield them from its brightness. This city on an island would be a hard place to get to know. Tonight, she felt almost dizzy with trying to understand it, to make sense of its strangeness.

But she'd do it. She had to.

EIGHTEEN

'It's all happening a little more quickly than we imagined,' Edward said. 'But it's too good an opportunity to miss.'

Romilly rubbed her eyes and stared at him. She was sitting back on the Persian rug in Mrs Macpherson's library the following morning. In front of her rose another tower of books. The shelves looked denuded now. Her fingers felt dry from the dust picked up from the old volumes. 'What's too good to miss?'

'An America First rally. This time almost on your very doorstep, the Manhattan Center. Less than half an hour's walk from here. We weren't expecting another rally so soon. Lindbergh's keeping himself busy.'

She remembered the newspaper pictures of the rally she'd seen. 'When?'

'Thursday.'

Romilly stood up, wincing as she stretched cramped legs. 'So soon?'

'I know.' He gave an almost apologetic sigh. 'What was going to take some time to teach you will need to be accomplished more quickly.'

'You mean what Lou—Catherine was supposed to do?'

'Yes.' He pulled two of the chairs that hadn't yet been packed closer together and they sat down. 'I don't think Mrs Macpherson will mind you taking time off your work for me to explain.' Between them she felt an intimacy, as though enthusiasm for the cause had warmed the air between them again. 'Catherine was going to picket the America First rallies as a protester, armed with placards.'

'Was that so very out of the ordinary? Presumably it's lawful to protest?'

'As you say, nothing so unusual in someone protesting. But there was a bit more to it than that.' He swallowed.

'What exactly was she going to do?'

He shifted in the chair. 'There were several projects we had in mind. One of them was that while she was shouting outside the venue and waving her placard, and in full view of the cameras, she was going to be knocked down by an America First thug. We were hoping it would make the front pages.'

Romilly sat straighter. 'I think I can see where this is going.'

'People don't like seeing women struck.'

'For good reason.' She crossed her arms around herself.

'It's all staged, though. I told you Catherine was an actress by training? She was also skilled, unusually for a woman, in certain martial arts. And fencing.'

Of course she was, Romilly thought.

'She knew how to move on stage, how to make it look as though she'd been struck.' A pause. 'We don't have long, just days, but some of those basic skills are things you can learn, Romilly.'

'Learn how to be hit?'

'Learn how to make a small blow look more serious, how to fall so you don't actually hurt yourself.' He put a hand to his right temple. His hair was swept back today and a scar was visible now.

'It sounds . . . slapstick. Like Laurel and Hardy.'

He rolled his eyes. 'There are elements of that, admittedly. But you wouldn't be on view very long. Another member of our team would escort you off, saying they were taking you to be checked over by a doctor. The apparent America First thug would also disappear quickly into the crowd. It would all be over in moments, but the pictures would travel the nation.'

'Surely if it's not a proper punch people will realise?'

'It's for the cameras.'

'People will be persuaded by photographs?'

'This is a very visual country. Images speak to people.'

'Can't we just show them photos of Freddie and tell them what happened to him?'

She felt ashamed as soon as she said it. Freddie's ordeal oughtn't to be made a newspaper spectacle.

'Believe me, the story of *The Lucknow* is being retold in many different ways.'

By people who hadn't been on board the ship? Reporters? Or had Edward himself written about it?

'You missed the papers the day after it went down. So did I, but I saw the clippings in the office. And the discovery of, unfortunately, more bodies is genuinely shocking people as the papers report it.'

Romilly thought of the missing children and decided she couldn't ask him which bodies had been recovered. Memories of Jennifer and the rabbi drifting away from the lifeboat made her shiver. 'But you need even more?' More than the sinking of a civilian ship?

'We always need more. At the moment, the war is a tragedy – for other people living thousands of miles away. We need something immediate and local. We're researching where the press photographers are likely to be on the night. We also have a few tame photographers who'll send any good pictures to the news agencies.'

Romilly had never thought of herself as a particularly strong or brave person. But perhaps the plunge into the North Atlantic had shown her that she possessed more physical courage than she knew. Yet everything she'd done had been done instinctively, in response to immediate danger and to survive, along with Freddie. This was something less visceral, more calculated. It required a different kind of courage, she realised. Because it wasn't just about pretending to be hit. It might mean being caught up in street violence, arrest. Possibly deportation. No temporary work visa would cover something deceptive like this, she imagined.

Edward was picking his trilby off the desk. 'You don't have to do it. There'll be other occasions. We're asking too much of you too soon. Forgive me, Romilly.'

'How do I learn to do this fighting?' The words were coming out before she consciously realised she was agreeing.

He examined her, eyes searching her face, as though assuring himself of her resolve. It took a while before he nodded.

'We have a contact. He coaches actors on Broadway in stage fighting. Trained with Errol Flynn's coach. You'll have seen those films?'

Of course she had: swashbucklers and pirates. 'And where do I go to learn these . . . moves?'

'He'll come to the house. It would be better if we could get you to a gymnasium, but not many women show up at those places, so he's agreed to come here.'

'When?' She felt dizzy at how swiftly Edward had organised everything.

Edward stood up. 'I just need to telephone and leave a message that you've agreed to do it. Mrs Macpherson's dining-room is pretty well empty now, so I thought we could go down there.'

'What, now?'

'Lucky you're in your slacks already.' He looked at her

trouser-clad legs. Romilly felt herself blush. He'd kissed her. He'd seen her in the ocean, her clothes clinging to her, but something about their proximity in this room was different.

'Danny will be coming over too.'

'Danny?'

'He's the Irish-American lad who's going to pretend he hates the British even more than he says he does. He's an actor who's returned from the West Coast.'

'A film star?'

'Don't use those words in front of him. His head will swell. He hasn't worked for a while, but he's good.' Edward opened the door. 'Just give me an hour or so, Romilly.'

She stood at the window to see him walk off. The leg must be less painful today – she could barely notice the limp.

Romilly worked on, occasionally lifting her head from a book to wonder what on earth she'd just agreed to.

The front doorbell rang. Romilly stood up. The door was already opening as she went downstairs, Mrs Macpherson herself letting in Edward along with two other men. The first was slight, almost like a dancer. He introduced himself as Raoul, a choreographer and fight scene director. The second, younger, physically more of a presence, was Danny. He shook her hand with a brief greeting.

'Come this way.' Mrs Macpherson led them into the dining-room. It had been emptied over the last twenty-four hours, its parquet floor now bare. She touched Romilly's forearm, turning her back on the men and lowering her voice. 'I'm not sure exactly what is planned, but I sense it's not altogether safe. You're certain you're happy to go ahead with this, dear?'

'Nothing's felt very safe during the last year,' Romilly answered.

'That doesn't mean you actively have to court danger.'

She felt a sudden warmth for the elderly woman. 'I won't do anything that doesn't feel right.'

With a nod, Mrs Macpherson closed the door behind her, leaving Romilly with the three men. 'You can act the cameras,' Raoul told Edward, without preamble.

'Imagine this is the main entrance to the Center.' Edward pointed at the window. 'Lindbergh is likely to pull up in the street outside here.' He stood back to the right of the window.

'And the press?'

'We can't be sure where they'll be. If I can get one of our photographers in there, I will, but the official press tend to get the best spots.'

'Unpredictable angles between these two and the cameras, who could be anywhere on the sidewalk or in the road itself?' Raoul shook his head, pacing up and down.

'It's important Romilly and Danny don't look as though they've been briefed to stand in certain places. We have to make it look unstaged.'

Raoul continued his loops of the dining-room, looking at Romilly and Danny, stroking his smooth chin. 'Originally, I was going to suggest Danny threw a false punch at this young lady that would look pretty convincing. But you're not on a stage where there's a static audience. Someone will see through it.' He put his hands on Romilly's shoulders and moved her backwards and forwards and side to side, looking at Danny, before letting go of her. He shook his head. 'Let me try this.' He took Danny's arm and moved it across Romilly, making her step backwards and to the side. 'No, no.' He sat down. While his eyes scanned the three of them, he tapped a hand on the table, sighing.

'You can't do this inside the auditorium?' he asked Edward. 'We'd have more certainty about camera angles.'

'Much harder to organise. The event is ticketed. The two of them would have to be seated separately, but in positions where they could both easily move towards the stage.'

Raoul nodded. 'And harder for them to escape at the end.'

He stood up and walked around the room again, looking at them. 'Not a punch.' He rubbed a finger over his bristled chin. 'It's going to have to be a slap round the face. It's less obvious.' He turned to Danny. 'Usual format.'

Romilly shifted her weight from one foot to another, eyeing Danny. 'Don't worry.' He placed his left hand on her right cheek. 'I haven't slapped a woman in my life and I'm not about to start.' His fingers were warm against her skin. 'You mean something like this,' he said to Raoul, over his shoulder.

'As Danny's right hand slaps the hand he's put on your face, move your head and cry out,' Raoul told her. She stared at him. 'Let me show you. Like this.'

Raoul moved in front of her, pushing Danny back and putting his left hand to the young man's cheek. As he struck his own hand with a loud slap, Danny moved back with an exclamation. 'The noise you hear is me smacking my hand, not Danny's face. But he has to move at exactly the right time to make the audience think he has been struck.' Raoul stood back. 'Try it yourself now, Miss Brooks.'

'Miss Brooks has probably never hit a man round the face.' A smirk curled over Danny's face. 'Where she comes from, I imagine they're far too polite.' Something about his tone made Romilly feel she could learn quickly. She placed her left palm on Danny's left cheek and struck it so hard with the other that her palm turned red. The cry Danny let out sounded genuinely startled.

'I think I'll pick it up,' she told him, with an innocent smile.

'Jesus, I think you will, too.' His eyes were wide.

'That slap was good, Miss Brooks, but we need to rehearse it from different angles and with different timing,' Raoul said. 'You may only have seconds to do it, when conditions are right. You need to be watching one another closely, but not making it obvious that you're doing so.' He looked at Danny. 'You need to make sure there's nobody standing behind Miss Brooks' left shoulder who'd notice Danny's palm on her face before the other hand makes contact. That's where you're exposed. And Miss Brooks, you need to come across as angry and then immediately scared. A very quick change of expression. After you cry out, you need to look shocked, put your hand to your cheek as if it hurts.' He demonstrated, his face expressing such distress that Romilly could almost believe he'd been hit. 'This man, this rough Irish hoodlum, has struck you: a young, unarmed woman.'

'You're breaking my heart,' Danny said.

'I don't think I'll have to act angry. Not so sure about the scared part.' Was Danny always so rude?

'Mr O'Donnell, you need to be . . . savage. You hate this woman. You regard her as everything you despise. You want to punish her and you don't care who sees you do it, because you are full of righteous anger.'

'Mr O'Donnell seems to be in character already.' Romilly heard the asperity in her own tone.

'She wants to pull your country into war on behalf of Britain's empire, Danny,' Edward said. 'You remember what your parents told you about why their ancestors left Ireland, the Famine.'

'I grew up with those stories. And, of course, I tune in to Father Coughlin every Sunday.'

Romilly looked at Edward. 'Irish priest in Detroit. He broadcasts on money lenders, Jews, international socialism, communism and is vehemently against entering the war. Hugely important figure in American Catholic life.'

'He sounds . . . interesting,' Romilly said.

Raoul cleared his throat. 'Enough background. They are not method actors, there isn't time.' He waved Romilly and Danny back into position. He made them repeat the actions again and again, standing in different positions, then approaching one another from each side.

'That's the first bit,' he said. 'Not bad. You need to practise.

There's the option of taking it further.' He put his hand into his pocket and drew out a small bottle. 'I'm not sure about this.'

'What's that?' she asked.

'Theatrical blood, as used on Broadway last week for a production of *Macbeth*.' He gave a thin smile. 'In reality it's a mixture of Hershey's sauce and food colouring.'

'Hershey's sauce is chocolate sauce,' Edward told her.

'It's a real art to know how to use the blood realistically. You'll have to be very quick lifting a handkerchief to your face. When you pull it away, there's blood on your nose.'

Doubt must be plastered all over her face.

'Suppose they interview me? The newspapers?' She thought of something even worse. 'The police? If they take me into the station, they'll surely see it's fake blood? And they'll know I'm British?'

'That won't happen.' Edward stepped forward. 'You will fade away into the crowd, telling anyone who asks that you just want to go home and rest, you don't need a doctor, you're just terribly shaken.' He touched her arm, the first time there'd been contact between them since he'd taken her by the shoulders on the steps up to the Consulate. 'But it's up to you. If you don't want to do this, that's good enough for me.' His forehead was creased. Did he think she wasn't up to this? He ought to know her better by now. Hadn't she and Freddie called themselves tigers?

'I'm game. But no chocolate sauce. It sounds too . . . staged.'

The men looked at one another.

'The kid's right.' Danny sounded as though it cost him to admit as much. Her shoulders stiffened. He couldn't be much older than she was.

Raoul nodded. 'Catherine could probably have managed it, but Miss Brooks has so little time.'

'Catherine was a professional,' Danny said.

'Thanks for reminding me,' Romilly said, icily.

'All right,' Edward said, before Danny could reply. 'We'll keep it simple.'

'We don't need props.' She turned to Danny. 'Let's try it again.'

'Well, you're keen, I'll give you that.' He looked amused.

'Must be my rank amateur enthusiasm.' She moved her lips into a cold, brief smile.

Someone knocked at the dining-room door. Edward opened it. 'Forgive the interruption.' Mrs Macpherson's precise, still-Scottish, respectable tone seemed incongruous after what they'd been planning here. 'There's someone to speak to you, Miss Brooks. They say it's urgent.'

'For me?' Was it the police, come to lock her up for outstaying her welcome. She followed Mrs Macpherson to the front hall. 'Alfonso?' Ruth Belman's manservant already seemed to belong to a past life, although it had only been yesterday he'd seen her into the taxi to the Consulate and handed her the sandwiches. She realised she still had the folded paper bag with the telephone number in her new satchel.

'Miss Brooks.' He looked pale. 'I'm glad you are home.'

'It's not my . . . How did you find me?'

'The British Consulate thought you might be here.' He gave Mrs Macpherson a quick look.

'What is it?'

'Freddie. His chest . . . He's in the hospital. Mrs Belman asked if you could come there with me. Now. He's not . . . they don't know if he . . .' Alfonso motioned towards the door. 'I have a taxi outside to take you to him.'

NINETEEN

'Freddie said his chest hurt,' Ruth Belman said. 'He was coughing more as the day progressed.' She wound the silk scarf she wore around her neck. 'I'd already booked him an appointment this afternoon with the twins' physician, Dr Stein, just as you said we should. Thank God I did.' She swallowed. 'I noticed he was breathing fast, as though he couldn't get enough air in. He actually vomited in the doctor's office and seemed . . . absent. Dr Stein sent us straight here and called ahead to tell them Freddie was coming in. He slipped into unconsciousness as we got him out of the car.' She dropped the scarf into her lap.

Romilly sat on the other side of the bed. Freddie lay with a transparent tent over his chest, into which an oxygen hose was fed. He was asleep, looking smaller than he had only yesterday, blue around his lips. 'The ship's doctor said there might be something wrong with his lungs.' She'd been so caught up in the prospect of working for Edward in this undercover capacity that she'd forgotten to ask Mrs Macpherson if she could telephone the Belmans and speak to Freddie. He was ill and must have thought she didn't care about him.

Ruth nodded. 'Dr Stein said seawater got in, probably just a small amount but enough to inflame the lungs. That in turn caused even more fluid to enter the lungs, making it worse.' She spoke mechanically, repeating words she'd been told, but her hands shook. She picked up the scarf and began to wind it round and round again. 'It's a form of drowning. Freddie came out of the sea, apparently safe, but the damage was already done. He was asking for you just in the car on the way here. And last night he had nightmares and wet the bed.' She looked at Romilly as though there were questions she wanted to ask about the sinking.

Romilly didn't know how much had been described in the newspapers. She hadn't talked about it in detail, not even to the sympathetic lieutenant on the cutter. Buying that notepad yesterday she'd thought of writing down some of her memories of the night and the following thirty-six hours, putting them into order, facing them again, explaining them to herself. 'I don't think I really understood what happened to you and Freddie, how it was you weren't in the lifeboat from the start?'

Romilly nodded, then took a deep breath. 'We got up to the deck with the captain, ready to launch the raft. Just as we were doing it, Freddie and I were flung off the deck. Then we were falling down into the water,' she said, unable to describe what it had felt like to drop down into the dark, the quiet, the bubbles floating upwards, the enveloping cold like a clamp around the chest. 'I thought we might never surface again. Freddie was next to me. We surfaced. I must have let go of his hand at some stage but there he was, next to me. He seemed fine. Frozen, of course, and shocked. But breathing. The life-raft was close by. We were lucky. Or else . . .' They would have died within minutes.

'Why on earth weren't you in the lifeboat with my mother? There must have been drills? Or was there panic on board?' Ruth didn't sound interrogatory, more puzzled.

Romilly thought of Smoky, safely back in the Central Park West apartment. If she told Ruth the dog's role in what had happened, would she get rid of Smoky? Freddie would be devastated. But she found herself unable to gloss over what had happened. Freddie might die, a victim of the torpedo, just like his grandmother. Ruth had to know the truth. She told her briefly.

'So Freddie ran down to the library after the dog and you went after Freddie, and that's why you missed the lifeboat launching. That dog.' Ruth let out a sigh. 'That wretched dog was the cause of all of this. If he hadn't run off and Freddie hadn't gone after him . . .'

'I'm not sure. A lot . . . went wrong, even for people who got off the ship in their lifeboats. The exposure. Some of the children . . .' No point in telling Ruth about Jennifer Smith. 'The dog seemed to keep Freddie's mind off what was going on.'

'He sure seems to dote on it.'

'Smoky's a link between London and America. A living creature who needs looking after. The rest of us are always telling Freddie we're protecting him from something or other: Hitler, the bombs, the ship sinking.' She could hear the fervour in her own voice. 'He's just a child, with no control over anything that happens to him. He can look after Smoky and feel that he's responsible for something, that he can keep him safe.' Romilly bit her lip. 'I'm sorry, it's not my place to say all this about your nephew.'

But Ruth nodded, looking reflective.

'I should have found a hospital in Halifax myself. Had Freddie admitted.'

Ruth was shaking her head. But Romilly's instinct had been wrong, hadn't it? She'd been trusted to look after Freddie and she'd let him down. She'd failed to notice the signs of serious disease with her mother, and she'd failed again with Freddie. Something about Romilly made her incapable of taking care of other people.

'Dr Stein said the doctor you saw was right to warn you so

we could have Freddie examined properly in New York. He probably wasn't coughing as much before? A hospital in Nova Scotia mightn't have found anything.'

Romilly tried to remember. 'The cough cleared up while were in the guesthouse in Halifax and if he was coughing on the train, it didn't seem to be any worse than it had been.'

'Children's illnesses don't always progress smoothly. Sometimes they seem to be getting better and then they slip back suddenly into a more serious condition. If you hadn't told me to make the appointment urgently, we might still be back in the apartment with Freddie, thinking he'd caught a bad cold as he lost consciousness, instead of already being on the way here.' Ruth was trying to smile, trying to make her feel better.

Romilly sat back. 'He needed this.' She pointed at the oxygen tent. 'We were in Canada, not the end of the world. But I just wanted to get us to New York as quickly as I could. I thought we could sort everything out if we could just make it to where we were supposed to be, to here.'

How naïve she'd been, pinning so much hope onto New York.

'Hardly surprising, given what you both went through in London and then when the ship went down.' Ruth swallowed. 'Romilly, Freddie owes you his life. It's a miracle you both survived that cold water, but he wouldn't have managed to get onto the raft and then lifeboat if you hadn't been there. I was a fool sending you away. I owe you an apology.'

Romilly looked at her.

'I . . . wasn't very hospitable to you.' Ruth sighed. 'I was upset about my mother, and I lashed out at you because she died and you didn't. But it wasn't about you, it was about me. I felt so guilty about letting her sail to London.'

'Guilty?'

'I was convinced she'd be killed in an air-raid. Instead . . .' She let her arms drop. 'She chose to swap places with you, knowing you'd rescued Freddie and you were exhausted and frozen.'

Romilly was trying to say something. Ruth shook her head. 'My response was completely unjustified. I hope we can be friends?'

Romilly nodded, suddenly feeling shy. 'I'd like that.' She took a breath. 'I wish I'd made her stay in the boat. Or that someone else had got up to swap with me. But your mother . . . she was so determined.'

Ruth gave a half-laugh. 'When she set her mind on something, it was hard to stop her. We told Mama not to go to London. We could have relied on you entirely. Freddie was safe with you to look after him. But my mother?' She sucked in a cheek. 'Well, I think she made the voyage because it made her feel better about leaving Irma in Prague all those years ago when she married Jackson. Irma was a grown woman, she could make her own decision about staying in Europe.' Ruth slumped back in the uncomfortable hospital chair, closing her eyes briefly. 'But Mama always felt she'd abandoned her.'

'So bringing Freddie to America was a kind of recompense?'

'She probably wouldn't have admitted it, but I think so. She hadn't managed with Irma, but she could bring Irma's son over. That's what I tell myself, anyway.'

Freddie stirred and they both sat up, watching him, hoping his eyes would open, that the blue around his mouth would fade. But on he drifted, lost in whatever space he had fallen.

After a moment Ruth spoke again. 'I was hoping you'd come back with me tonight and stay with us?'

Romilly shook her head. 'I've got a job,' she said. 'With accommodation.' She felt a small prickle of pride that she'd acquired these things for herself.

'In a house that's being taken apart because Phyllida Macpherson is moving out to Connecticut after about a century.' Ruth gave the ghost of a smile. 'Yes, news travels fast in Manhattan. It can't be very comfortable?'

It certainly wasn't like the soft-sheeted, plush-carpeted guest room at Central Park West. 'There are still things I need to finish. But thank you.'

Ruth switched her attention back to the bed. 'Apart from the oxygen, there's not much they can really do for him. The fluid and the inflammation are so hard to treat. All they can do is support his breathing and hope his own strength pulls him through.'

Romilly looked back at Freddie, still the colour of watery blue ink around the mouth. 'He's a strong boy. It was two days between the ship going down and us being rescued. He didn't give up. Not even when people older and stronger than him did. We saw . . . things.' She shuddered, remembering Edward floating away, and then Mrs Dekker. Jennifer. The rabbi. The elderly Polish man floating away from *The Lucknow*.

They sat in silence for a moment.

'Just let him know the dog's all right,' Romilly said, fiercely. 'It'll be the first thing he wants to know when he wakes up.'

Ruth nodded. 'Smoky's got a permanent home with us, don't worry. My kids will be delighted too.'

It seemed time for her to go but she felt reluctant. Did she really imagine that by lingering at Freddie's bedside she could keep him alive? That she had some magical hold over the boy?

A nurse came in. 'Visiting is over now. Mrs Belman, you may remain in the waiting room in case the doctor wants to talk to you. Miss, you'll have to leave now.'

'Will you let me know?' Romilly asked Ruth. 'If anything changes? I'll come back tomorrow, if . . .' If Freddie was still alive. She leant over the oxygen tent towards the boy. 'Smoky wants you back, Freddie.' He looked smaller than he had on the life-raft, as if he was cocooning himself in an earlier stage of his childhood. 'Come back to us,' she said, quietly.

She muttered a quick good-night to Ruth and made her way to the elevator and down to the street. As she'd travelled north in the taxi, she'd tried, despite her panic, to note where they were going. They'd edged up the east side of Central Park, heading to the high nineties. Now, as it grew dark, she was glad that she'd paid attention and that this part of the city was so logical to navigate. As she walked south, the weariness she felt sitting beside Freddie eased. She breathed in the evening air from the park, hinting at new growth on trees and spring flowers, trying to put her worry about him aside. This evening he was in the safest place he could be. She would keep telling herself this. She would keep pushing back the wave threatening to crash down on her.

She wondered whether Edward, Danny and Raoul were still at Mrs Macpherson's or had given her up. Perhaps her abrupt departure from the house had made them doubt her commitment to the cause. They were fools if they thought that. Freddie's sickness simply underlined how much the Germans needed paying back. Helping in some small way to persuade America to enter the war was a good enough way of doing that.

Walking on the sidewalk were men and women on the way home from work or heading to restaurants and movie theatres. She wanted to stop them, ask them if they knew what was happening out in the Atlantic and across Europe? Did they think that a force that had already unleashed such evil would hold back from attacking them, too? They might believe themselves safe in their big city, but they had ships on the North Atlantic that could be torpedoed. They had coastal towns and cities that were in range. They had borders with countries that might not prove themselves allies. Suppose Germany decided to declare war on America before it could happen the other way round?

A headline on a newspaper caught her eye. Another senator speaking on the isolationist side. She felt like ripping it out of its owner's hands. Her features must be set grim – a man on the sidewalk coming towards her stepped out of her path and dipped his hat to her, eyes wide. Well, who said you always had to look pleasantly neutral? Or present yourself as a demure young lady when you'd seen a child such as Freddie gasp for breath in the ocean and survive, only to slip away once he'd reached safety?

She hadn't pushed the wave back as far as she'd hoped.

Romilly emerged from her angry reverie with a jolt, realising she'd passed the square where she and Edward had shared her sandwich, and the library adjacent to it. Time to turn off left to Mrs Macpherson's. The buildings here were familiar now. As she reached the house, a dark shadow sitting on the stoop moved towards her. Romilly gasped. 'Relax, kid.'

Danny.

'You left in quite a hurry. How's the boy?'

'Not good.' She realised her eyes were pricking and she felt shaky.

'Hey.' Danny took her arm and led her to the steps. 'Sit here. Take a moment. What exactly happened to him? Your Mr Witney didn't say much, just that the kid was on *The Lucknow* too.'

'When the ship went down we all fell into the sea. Water entered Freddie's lungs.' She explained how you could drown after you'd been taken out of the sea, apparently fine. Danny whistled.

'Poor kid.'

'I think he's quite resilient to have survived at all. I'm hoping that will make a difference.'

Danny nodded. 'I had all kinds of things when I was a kid. Some of it serious: diphtheria once. Mammy always said I was a tough one and I'd pull through. As you can see, I did.'

'You certainly look . . . robust.' His shoulders were broad

and although he was slim, he had some heft to him. They were sitting close enough for her to feel the warmth of him.

'Now I'm not working on movies out west I'm earning my bread on the waterfront here, heaving cargoes around. Never been so strong as I am now.'

Romilly was recovering. 'How do you come to be involved in . . . all this? Do you know Edward Witney's, erm, group?'

'His group?' Danny gave a guffaw. 'I'm no part of it. Hand for hire, that's me. Raoul got me into it. I'm just a down-at-heel actor who looks like what he is: Irish. Anti-British.'

'Anti-British?' She still didn't fully understand.

'Aw, don't worry, Romilly Brooks, I'm not going to throw you under a streetcar or into the Hudson. I guess you can't help your nationality.'

'Why don't you like Britain?'

'You don't know much, do you, kid?'

'Probably not. But I'm a quick learner.'

'You showed me when you pretended to hit me.' He smiled and the smile gave her a flash of how he might light up a movie screen. 'Now that *would* make a good picture for the papers.'

'Not so good for the cause, though. Nobody would believe I was intimidating and abusing you.' He was probably strong enough to do her some serious injury. Romilly swallowed. 'But go on, tell me why you hate us all?'

'As Edward Witney said, too many starved family members were staggering onto land here a few generations back in the Famine years.' The geniality in his features hardened. Now she could imagine him as a gangster. 'They teach you about that in school in England, Romilly Brooks?'

'No,' she admitted. 'But surely that doesn't matter now that Hitler needs defeating? Surely anyone can see he has to be fought, regardless of who we are and what happened in the past?'

He shrugged. 'My enemy's enemy, as they say.' He stood up

and yawned. 'I'll method-act my part, as Raoul would say. An Irish-American born and raised on the Lower East Side, who will do anything to oppose the hated British Empire.'

'I see.'

'So when I slap you I will look as though those generations of hatred are behind the slap.' His eyes glinted in a way that might be expressing humour or real fury. How could she tell? He was just an actor, after all, working for money.

She glared at him. 'And when I recoil, I shall make you look like a thug.'

He guffawed. 'You look better when you're riled, Romilly. Perhaps old Edward knows what he's doing after all. He's got a good record for choosing his female team-mates.'

'Catherine?'

'Uh-huh.'

She was being over-sensitive to feel, once again, that she was a poor stand-in for Catherine.

'Were they together in New York for long?' she asked casually.

'Not sure.' He snorted. 'I think he chose her for more than one role.'

'What do you mean?'

'They were up to something back in January. Icy as hell on the streets but those two wouldn't have felt the cold as they went home.'

Edward had said Catherine had a boyfriend in the RAF. 'You mean . . .?'

He snorted. 'I saw them bundling themselves into a cab one night just off 42nd Street and they certainly seemed to playing a closer role.'

He stood up. 'Anyway, no gossiping. Must be getting home. No point in working unpaid overtime.'

She felt a real prick of dislike for him and not just because he'd told her what he'd seen. 'Tell me, if one of the pro-

German groups in the city approached you, would you work for them?'

He shrugged. 'As I said, no movies for me at the moment, so I'm just a hand for hire. Easy money.'

'That's no answer. Freddie's one of the lucky children, you know.' He looked at her, frowning. 'So far I've heard of about seven of the others surviving. There were 103 on board *The Lucknow* including him. But as you say, easy money for you to work for the pro-Germans if you think that's an acceptable loss.'

'Get a good night's rest, Romilly.' He nodded, raised a hand in parting. Despite his solidity he moved quickly into the shadows. The night swallowed him up.

Good riddance. She almost wished she'd shouted it after him.

TWENTY

By lunchtime the next day, Romilly had finished sorting the last piles of books. She sat back on her heels, feeling a mixed sense of accomplishment and regret. It seemed sad that a library collected over so many decades was being split up. On the other hand, the distraction from worrying about Freddie had been welcome. Ruth hadn't been in touch. Romilly had to assume that he was stable.

Mrs Macpherson seemed to have gone out on a final whirl of administrative errands. The maid wasn't able to say when she'd be back or when exactly they were leaving for Connecticut. 'She never tells us exactly what she has in mind,' she told Romilly. 'Very independent lady.'

'I need to thank her.'

'If you miss her, I'll tell her for you.'

'What will happen to you now?' Romilly asked.

'I'm going to the farm with Mrs Macpherson. She's keeping me on.' The maid looked at Romilly curiously. 'What'll you do now? The house is all yours for as long as you need, although the electricity will be cut off, and the telephone, Mrs

Macpherson said. You could go shopping.' She reached into her apron pocket. 'Mrs Macpherson left you this.'

Her wages in another of the thick ivory American envelopes. She'd been so relieved to have somewhere to stay in New York she hadn't thought of pay. She took it gratefully. At some point, if she stayed in New York, she would need a new bank account. When she'd taken the job in London, Mrs Dekker had told her what she'd be paid, but she'd barely noted the amount, she'd just wanted to get out of the country. It wouldn't be safe wandering around with all this cash she'd accumulated.

'I don't like to go far. I'm still waiting to hear news from the hospital.'

'About the little boy?' The maid's face softened. 'I heard you went to visit him. Don't worry, honey, I'll be here for the rest of the day. If anyone calls, I'll be sure to take a message for you. The telephone won't be disconnected until later on. Go look at some pretty things in shops or galleries. Treat yourself.'

Romilly smiled. 'I'd like to see more of the skyscrapers.'

'You been down to Lower Manhattan? Cross the bridge and come back over from Brooklyn.'

'Good views?'

'Uh-huh. Take the subway down to City Hall Station in Brooklyn, it's pretty, too, with all the tiles and glass. Then walk back across the bridge. Take you half an hour and you can gawp at Lower Manhattan. Wait, there's a map somewhere.' She vanished into the back of the house, to the kitchen, Romilly presumed, returning with an old street map that also showed the transport system, and gave Romilly instructions about the Lexington Avenue Line. It sounded a simple enough journey, with no changes. She opened the envelope. A ten-dollar bill and five ones.

She walked down to the 33rd Street station and took the Lexington Avenue Line southbound as instructed, getting off at

City Hall Station and admiring the arches, skylights and tiles, which seemed too elegant for everyday travellers. Or perhaps she'd just got too used to London tube stations, with their rows of camp beds at nights, sheltering people from the bombs. Brooklyn, from what she could see from this angle, had the same half-finished look as some of the parts of Manhattan she'd walked through: a contrast with the elegant subway station. But perhaps it was smarter further in from the bridge. No time to explore further today. A passer-by directed her to the steps to the bridge's elevated walkway and she headed back towards Manhattan.

Wind blew her hair into her eyes and she was grateful for her new beret. In front of her, the ziggurats and triangle-topped towers of Lower Manhattan beckoned to her, looking almost white in the light, the taller Empire State and Chrysler Building standing sentinel behind them. These buildings were audacious. They weren't temples or cathedrals or palaces, they'd been designed for people to work and live in. Well-off people, perhaps, but not princes or prelates.

Below her streetcars and motor vehicles hooted and clanked and roared, but she barely noticed them. Instead of the half an hour to cross the bridge, it took her almost an hour, stopping as she did to peer at the skyline, or turning round to look back towards Brooklyn. Romilly remembered how she'd thought of sending Uncle Simon and Aunt Ursula a postcard of the Empire State Building. *I am alive. I am here.* She could probably buy the card on her way back to Mrs Macpherson's, write it and post it. They might be pleased to hear from her, reassured that she was all right. She thought of Aunt Ursula's expression that last time she'd seen her, that relief on her face as she'd waved Romilly off – the socially-embarrassing niece conveniently taking herself to the other side of the Atlantic. Perhaps she'd wait a day or two to send a card. Thinking of her aunt and uncle had been a mistake – it had jolted her out of pure enjoyment of the Lower Manhattan skyline, taken her back to feeling haunted and lost on that train heading out of Euston to the Liverpool docks.

She gazed down at the water, at the ships and tugs, at the white wakes they left. Her legs were starting to shake. Nausea hit her, as though the walkway and the section below where the motors roared might dissolve and plunge her into the depths so that she might never rise up to the surface again. How could she when she wasn't wearing a life-vest? She'd sink to the bottom, only to rise again when her lungs were full of water and every thought and memory in her consciousness had been pressed out. A passing girl of her own age glanced at her anxiously. Romilly tried to smile, walking on, her eyes on the buildings ahead of her, concentrating on the geometric shapes and angles, the shadows cast by the sun, anything but the water. She wasn't on a liner, she wasn't under attack. The bridge held her. She wasn't going to drown. Her legs regained their strength. She pushed her shoulders back and stepped out.

She reached the Manhattan side feeling that she could have walked all the way up to Mrs Macpherson's now the water was behind her. Only the worry that she might have missed a call from Ruth about Freddie made her turn into the subway to speed her back north.

She almost ran the blocks back from the station to the house in Murray Hill, where she found her hostess had returned. Mrs Macpherson sat on a fold-up chair in the entrance hall, suitcases and boxes around her.

'I've hired a car to drive me to the farm,' she said, barely greeting Romilly as she came in. 'I'm afraid I couldn't manage the train with all of this.' She nodded at her luggage. 'I suppose I will have to think about employing a man to drive me in the country.'

'You'll need a car and a man to drive you, ma'am,' the maid said firmly over her shoulder, as she left the hall.

'Thank you for letting me stay,' Romilly said.

Mrs Macpherson acknowledged the thanks with a brief nod. 'We've left your bed made up. When you leave, strip the bed and leave the sheets in the kitchen. Apparently, we've left you a small amount of food to tide you over until you go – where is it exactly you're going?'

'I don't know yet.'

Mrs Macpherson gave another nod as though this was the correct answer. 'I expect Mr Witney has it in hand.'

The maid came back into the hall. 'I heard the car pull up, Mrs Macpherson.' She wore a coat, hat and gloves, looking as smart as one of the women Romilly admired on the streets outside. Opening the door, she let in the driver, who started moving suitcases and boxes down the steps to the sidewalk.

Mrs Macpherson stood up. 'Good-bye, my dear. If things become . . . awkward for you, I could put you up at the farm for a short period.'

'Thank you.' Romilly didn't like to ask for a telephone number or address.

'Mr Witney can put you in touch.' Mrs Macpherson handed her the front door key and walked out, without as much as a backward glance at the house she had spent so much of her life in.

'There were no messages for you about the little boy,' the maid said as she left. 'You look after yourself now.'

Romilly stood at the door as the two women got into the car, which looked long and shiny and very American in the dusk. She lifted a hand in farewell and watched the car pull away. Funny, she'd only known Mrs Macpherson for a few days but she felt abandoned. Having rushed off last night to the hospital she hadn't had a chance to ask Edward when she'd see him again. She still had his card, she reminded herself. Mrs Macpherson's telephone receiver sat on the floor, the console table having been removed. When Romilly lifted it, the telephone was dead. She really was alone now, even though she was surrounded by millions of people.

She hadn't been alone since the days and nights immediately after Mama's death. The nights had been the worst – she'd almost wanted an air-raid so there was reason to go down to a shelter and be with other people. Even on the lifeboat there'd been others with her.

No need to feel like a scared kid. She'd have a quiet night in. The crates of boxes hadn't been collected yet, she saw, walking upstairs, so she could borrow a book and curl up on her bed. Lose herself in a Dashiell Hammett story perhaps. Or write in that notebook she'd purchased, ostensibly for noting down expenses. It was really designed for something more creative, more descriptive. She took it out of her bag and ran her fingers over the marbled cover. It had been years since she'd written anything of any length, probably essays at school. Now, she felt an urge to express whatever it was that had overwhelmed her this afternoon. Perhaps if she described the terror she'd felt on Brooklyn Bridge it might be contained on the pages and she could examine it rationally.

She sat on the floor in her room, pencil in hand. Other than a schoolgirl diary, she'd never written much outside the classroom. She wondered where to start: with the ship going down? Or before, standing high up on the deck, watching the people on the quay in Liverpool? But the sense of panic from standing on Brooklyn Bridge was so vivid it seemed to demand a description. *It was only on that bridge, safe in New York, days and days after we were torpedoed, that I felt all the fear, as though I'd been storing it up inside me and now it had to come out. Or perhaps because I couldn't afford to be scared while I was trying to get us to the lifeboat.*

She let the pencil form the words it wanted to write, stopping only when the dark made it impossible to continue. Romilly stood up and drew the curtains and turned on a lamp.

Thank goodness the electricity was still on. Writing it all down should have left her with a sense of release, but she felt as though she'd only just pricked the surface. More of the emotion was welling, about to breach the little gap in her defences. She'd held it back all these days since the cutter had picked them up, but it was still there, waiting for a chink. What she'd felt on the bridge this afternoon was just a warning. *When the cutter rescued us, they gave me a sailor's clothes to put on and I felt warm at last. But it takes longer to feel properly safe again. One small thing: a sight, a smell, a sensation, can send you back out to the Atlantic . . .*

Her words petered out.

She'd run a bath. Relax. She'd already showered in the small bathroom adjoining her bedroom here, but now Mrs Macpherson had gone, there'd be no reason for her not to use the tub in the main bathroom on the first floor, which she'd spied walking up and downstairs to her room. Running up to fetch her towel and soap, Romilly was relieved that the electricity supply was still on and the lights worked. The water ran hot when she ran the bath, but she told herself not to overdo it: the furnace downstairs in the basement might be running out of fuel.

The bath wasn't as relaxing as she hoped. Her ears were pricked for any sounds. Ridiculous: she'd seen the locks on the front door and presumably any other entrances were equally well protected, given Mrs Macpherson was elderly. But Mrs Macpherson hadn't lived here alone, had she? When her husband had died there'd always been a servant somewhere in the house. Back home in the Chelsea mews cottage Romilly herself had always known that her mother was around, or due to come back in. She had never spent a night alone in the house other than that night when her mother had died. Something about being here alone was pulling her back to London, to the night with Philip, the air-raid, hearing the telephone ringing in the house on her return, finding the note on the table. And then later to the hospital.

It had been almost dawn when Romilly had come back from the hospital. She fumbled around in the kitchen drawer where they kept emergency cash to pay the taxi driver. Coming back inside, she'd pulled down the blackout blinds, before sitting at the kitchen table, staring at the paper parcel containing her mother's clothes and handbag.

The cups, saucers and plates from breakfast still sat on the draining board. Very unlike her mother not to put them away. She must have gone back to bed after Romilly had left for work, or collapsed onto the sofa, telling herself the fever would pass, putting off the telephone call to the doctor. All for Romilly's sake. Mama had waited and waited, hoping that the infection would pass, that she wouldn't have to seek medical help.

The sister in the hospital had been rushed when she took Romilly into a side room. Clearly the nightshift had been long and arduous, with air-raid casualties coming in. Her voice was clipped as she told her that they hadn't been able to save Mama. Then she'd looked Romilly in the eye for the first time and her face had softened. 'Your mother was talking about you, right to the end.'

'I should have been with her. I didn't know it was so serious.'

The sister nodded. 'She wouldn't have wanted to tell you much.' Her face took on a grim expression. 'Keep the details to yourself. Tell anyone who asks that your mother had post-operative sepsis. Say she was in for a routine procedure, if they ask.'

'I really don't know what happened.' She felt so foolish, so blind.

The sister let out a long sigh.

'Your mother procured an abortion.'

Romilly felt her mouth open, but no words came out.

'Had she lived she might have been prosecuted. Even now, even with all this,' the sister nodded towards the blacked-out window, 'the newspapers publish sensationalist stories.' She put a hand on Romilly's arm. 'Is there anyone else in your family?'

'My uncle.' Simon, who showed a brisk but kindly interest in them but didn't approve of Douglas. 'But, I can't . . . Are you sure that's what happened? It can't be right. Not my mother.'

The pity on the sister's face was even more marked now. 'You'll need your uncle's help with the funeral arrangements. Tell him what happened, nobody else.'

She hadn't told Uncle Simon what had happened but perhaps Aunt Ursula had worked it out because he seemed to know when they both took the train down to London. 'That man has cast shame on you both,' Uncle Simon said. 'He's left a blot on my sister's reputation.'

That seemed to matter more than Mama's life having been lost.

The memory made her mouth flood with bile. If she was going to succeed in her new life and make this whole adventure work, she had to shed this sense of guilt. She closed her eyes and let herself float back in the tub so the back of her head was resting on the end of the bath. The water held her, warm, soothing. Romilly hadn't realised how weary she was. She drifted off.

She woke suddenly, her head banging against the edge of the tub, liquid running over her forehead. She felt as she had on Brooklyn Bridge: suspended above dark water. The water was pulling her down. Lights flashed above her. Bubbles rose from her mouth. She was back in the North Atlantic and this time the water wasn't going to let her go. When she'd stood on

Brooklyn Bridge it had flowed beneath her, reminding her of its presence. Now it had her completely trapped. Her arms flailed around, banging against the sides of the enamel bath. Romilly opened her mouth to scream and it filled with soapy water. She pushed herself up, water running down her face, panting, gasping. With shaking legs, she pulled herself out onto the bathmat and scrubbed at herself with the towel, not waiting until she was fully dry before she replaced her clothes, not bothering with stockings and leaving her hair unbrushed, only delaying to pull the plug from the bath so that the water would vanish. Her wet feet slipped on the tiled floor as she ran out of the bathroom. Her bag was by the front door where she'd left it. She grabbed jacket, beret and front door key and let the dark swallow her up, tearing along the streets, only relaxing when she'd reached the lights and bustle of Fifth Avenue.

Romilly stood in the doorway of a store selling men's clothes, receiving bemused looks from pedestrians and a newspaper boy. She knew she looked a fright, her hair dripping down her shoulders, her beret placed on her head any-old-how. She took a moment to scrape her hair back off her face and turned away quickly to apply a slick of lipstick to her mouth, hoping nobody noticed. At 42nd Street she headed west, blinded by the dazzle of theatres and restaurants, dizzied by the noise of taxis screeching up and disgorging their passengers, dressed up for the night, talking about collecting tickets from box offices and ordering interval drinks. Sometimes a streetcar would rattle beside her and she'd stare at the people inside as though they were ghosts.

She found herself on Broadway and then heading north through Times Square, maintaining a straight course to the point where those coming towards her had to jump out of her way.

A building with lights on it advertising Coca-Cola and peanuts veered up above her, reminding her of the stern of a ship. *Walgreen Drugs*. The store was still open. She stopped, brought back into consciousness by her feet, which had blistered because she hadn't pulled her stockings back on before putting on her new white shoes. The blocks she'd walked had been too far in new shoes, which had torn her heels and the tops of her toes into ribbons. She took the shoes off, holding them by the laces as she went inside. Finding one of the ever-helpful New York assistants, she asked for something for the blisters. Romilly paid for the antiseptic and tin of sticking plasters called Band-Aids without being fully present. She let the girl help her to a chair and dress her feet, thanking her absently when she'd finished and replacing her shoes, which were bearable if she placed each foot on the ground slowly and deliberately.

As Romilly left Walgreens, she passed a line of people waiting to be served a milky drink from some kind of fountain. It smelled malty, familiar. Without warning, she was sitting back in the lifeboat, eating one of the emergency malt ration tablets, the waves tossing them, spray blinding her. Freddie was falling into the sea. She couldn't hold him.

The store seemed to pitch beneath her feet. Desperate to leave before she fainted, she tugged off her shoes again, her fingers shaking so much she could barely undo the laces. She almost ran out to the sidewalk, which felt cold and hard under her bare soles. People stared curiously at her plastered feet. She glared at them.

Romilly lowered her eyes. Continuing up Broadway, she barely noticed as her surroundings grew intermittently quieter and then louder as though the city was drawing breath before breathing out the noise of car horns, newspaper boys' calls and the rattle of the streetcars, exhaling steam from its subway vents. While she was moving, she lost the fear that she was going to fall into a dark vastness of water.

At Columbus Circle she crossed almost without paying attention to the traffic or the toots and shouts she attracted.

Romilly carried on north, the park to her right, looking steadily forwards until she reached Ruth's apartment block. The same doorman was helping an elderly man into a taxi. He waved the vehicle off and started at the sight of Romilly, no longer in a sea-stained velvet evening dress, now wearing a smart jacket and beret, but her feet bare, carrying her shoes. Perhaps he thought it was some particular British eccentricity to turn up dishevelled in the evening. The thought made her want to laugh but she controlled herself.

'Miss Brooks?'

'I have to see Mrs Belman. I need to know how he is, Freddie.' This was what had driven her out of Murray Hill, she realised now. As much as her own terror of the bath water passing over her face, it was not knowing about Freddie, a fear that he had finally been snatched away by the water, which had played a long game with the boy, letting them believe he'd been saved, only to taunt them with a reversal.

'You'd better come inside, miss.'

Once inside the lobby, he stopped. 'May I get you something to put on your feet?' She looked down at the plasters.

'I forgot that my shoes were new. I shouldn't have walked so far.'

He nodded. 'New shoes will do that to your feet if you don't wear socks or stockings. You need to rub a bar of soap over the leather to soften it, that's what I tell my kids. Let me see what I have.' He went behind his desk and reached into a drawer, pulling out a pair of satin slippers. 'Someone left these in the elevator – they never claimed them. They might fit you?'

'Thank you.' The slippers were only a little too big.

'Nina and Alfonso told me what you did for that little boy.'

'They did?'

'Young Freddie kicked up quite the fuss after you left. Told everyone you'd pulled him out of a flooded library on the ship and saved him.'

'I didn't stop him from getting water in his lungs. He could still die.' She followed him to the elevator.

'Perhaps. Perhaps not. But for sure he'd have died in the Atlantic if you hadn't been there. He wouldn't be safe in a hospital now.' The wrought iron door closed on his face, watching her with a calm solicitude. She mumbled thanks and hoped he'd heard. He must have called ahead because Alfonso was standing in front of her as the elevator doors opened.

'Miss Romilly. Come in.'

She tried to read his face for news. He looked concerned but that might be because she'd turned up unexpectedly like this.

'Mr Belman is in his study. He said to show you in.'

'Mrs Belman?'

'Still at the hospital with Freddie.'

So Freddie was still alive. She felt her legs shake. Alfonso took her arm. Nina appeared, tutting, 'Your poor feet. Those Band-Aids need changing.'

'I'm sorry.' She must look like such a wreck. She *was* a wreck.

'I will bring a bowl of water and a towel to Mr Belman's study.'

'No, please, I won't keep him long. I don't want to be any trouble.' She was talking like an automaton because her mind was trying to catch up. She was safe, Freddie was safe.

'He will not mind.'

Mr Belman's study with its wood panelling reminded Romilly of a room from an English country house – almost incongruous when the apartment sat above a busy New York thoroughfare. It was a welcoming room. Romilly felt her pulse slow. He was a tall, thin-faced man with spectacles, a little round-shouldered, a few years older than his wife. He stood up as she came in, concern on his face.

'Romilly, Miss Brooks, I'm Leon Belman.' He extended his

hand, sounding anxious but welcoming. 'Do sit down. Alfonso will bring you a sandwich and a glass of something to revive you. I gather you walked quite a way to ask after Freddie?'

She flopped onto the chair. Nina came in with a towel and bowl, and a small first-aid kit. The water was lukewarm and something aromatic had been sprinkled on it. Romilly sank her feet into it gratefully. Quietly, Nina dried her feet and redressed it with plasters. Through Romilly's mind flashed the memory of her mother doing the same thing for her when she'd worn a new pair of school shoes that had rubbed her feet. The recollection brought another stab of pain.

'How is Freddie?' Romilly asked Leon Belman. 'I'm sorry for just turning up like this. I just . . . I need to know.'

He was shaking his head. 'Of course you do. Ruth tried to telephone Mrs Macpherson's to tell you, but she'd already disconnected the service, so Ruth was going to send a message to you by taxi. You beat us to it.' He smiled. 'Freddie seems to have turned a corner.' Some of the tension left her shoulders. 'He's still wearing the oxygen mask, but they hope to remove it tomorrow.'

Relief blanketed Romilly. She found herself unable even to express relief, unable to speak. She closed her eyes briefly, nodding. Alfonso returned with a tray of food. She found herself suddenly ravenous, trying to remember her manners.

Mr Belman looked amused. 'Mrs Macpherson probably didn't leave you much food?'

'I didn't actually go into the kitchen to look.'

'That house probably has its charms, but from what I've heard, I sure wouldn't like to spend the night in it alone. Anyway, you don't have to. Ruth will want you to sleep here tonight.'

The thought of the comfortable bedroom she'd slept in that first night made her feel she might actually melt with relief. But she couldn't stay here with the Belmans. She had to be in the

Murray Hill house in case Edward and Danny needed to find her. She certainly hoped Edward would need to find her but would be happy not to see Danny again once their stunt was completed.

'You can call anyone you need to inform,' Mr Belman told her. 'Help yourself to the telephone.'

Staying here still didn't feel right, though. As though to nudge her into making the decision, the study door pushed open and the tip of a white nose inserted itself into the opening. Smoky came in, greeting Romilly with a small bark and a wind-mill-waving tail. She hadn't heard him bark before. Perhaps he was pleased to see her. 'I missed you.' She knelt down to pat him. The dog already seemed glossier, eyes brighter.

'I'll leave you with your sandwich.' Leon Belman stood up. 'Whenever you feel like it, the bedroom's ready for you. Ask Nina if you need anything.' He paused. 'We thought my mother-in-law was mad, you know, insisting on going to London herself. Ruth argued and argued with her. She blames herself for what happened.'

'Neither Mrs Dekker nor Mrs Belman launched the torpedo that struck us.'

He swallowed. 'I have to admit, Miss Brooks, that when we first heard of British passenger ships going down, it seemed sad, but what would you expect, going to war? Perhaps humans are selfish and only take things seriously when it happens to them? I gather from more recent press coverage that the Germans say they didn't know *The Lucknow* was carrying civilians?'

'They should have looked more closely, shouldn't they? In any case, killing civilians doesn't usually bother them.'

Mr Belman looked serious. 'We heard stories of the Blitz. And before that, of what happened when they invaded Poland and France.'

'Do you think America will come into the war?' The old Romilly wouldn't have dreamed of asking an older man she'd only just met a blunt question like this. He took his time to reply.

'There are some powerful voices telling us to stay out.'

'Charles Lindbergh?'

He nodded, still standing in the doorway. 'Back in '27, I stood out on Fifth Avenue to watch Lindbergh's victory parade when he returned from his transatlantic flight. He didn't just fly through the air, he walked on it. I can't believe he's whipping up people like this at his rallies. I wish . . .' He fiddled with his tie. 'I wish Lindbergh could meet you and Freddie.' His face hardened. 'But he's an intelligent and well-informed man. He has children himself. It obviously hasn't made any difference. Equally, he has Jewish friends. Or had them. And yet he has said there are too many of us in this city and we do not need more. I cannot understand him.' Puzzlement was written on his open features.

'Lindbergh understands America, though. People don't want to join the fight.'

'Not all of us. Some of us see entering the war is inevitable.'

He left Romilly to finish her sandwich. She dried her feet. Smoky sniffed at them but found the aromatic scent too much for him, retreating to lie by the desk. Nina, returning for the tray, nodded at the empty plate. 'I will bring you a slice of apple pie, too, miss. You've an appetite. That's good. Look at you – nothing on your bones. Your room is ready.'

'I should go back to Mrs Macpherson's. I haven't finished my work.'

'Anyone who needs you that badly will probably know to try here, won't they?' Nina fixed her with a look that made it clear she didn't expect a rebuttal.

Back in the room she'd had before, Romilly collapsed into bed and slept without dreaming for nine hours.

TWENTY-ONE

Ruth was at the breakfast table when Romilly, washed, dressed and wearing the satin slippers on her feet, went into the dining-room. Dark shadows hollowed out her eyes, but some of the furrows and lines had gone. Her more relaxed features reminded Romilly of Mrs Dekker's expression that very last moment of her life, when the sea was pulling her away – strangely more at peace than she'd ever looked before. 'Romilly, great to see you. Good news – Freddie will be back with us this afternoon. A remarkable recovery, they said.'

Romilly couldn't speak.

'Our ancestors carved out a living in the Carpathian mountains. They were a hardy lot. Mama used to tell us all about them. Freddie must have their blood in him. I hope my two have inherited some of that hardiness, too.' Ruth stood up. 'Just making sure they're ready for Leon to drop off at school on his way to work. Then you and I can have a good chat. Make this apartment your base, come and go as you wish.' Ruth's whole posture had softened towards her. Romilly felt herself relax with Ruth, too. Perhaps because she knew so few people in this city, or because of the frank conversation in the hospital, Ruth now seemed almost like an old acquaintance. If she'd lived, Mrs Dekker would perhaps have become a friend as well. Her family and Mr Dekker had clearly doted on her.

'Was he a kind man, Mr Dekker?' Ruth looked surprised by the sudden question. 'I'm sorry, I don't mean to be nosy.'

'You're not. This is New York. We like discussing people. Jackson was a darling.' She peered at her. 'Why'd you ask?'

Romilly struggled to find words.

'Did my mother talk about Jackson?' Ruth asked.

'Sometimes. I could tell they'd been happy together and that talking about him made her, I don't know, feel reassured.' But it had been something more than that.

Ruth gave her a look that conveyed understanding of what Romilly couldn't express. 'She used to say she could hear his voice in her head after he died. I told her she needed a shrink, but she said it gave her strength.' For a moment they were silent.

'I think there were times on *The Lucknow* and then later, in the lifeboat, when she felt he was with her. It was strange, but I think it helped her.'

'He had a very distinctive voice. He could make a roomful of people turn round to look at him but never seemed to raise it.' Ruth blinked and smile. 'My mother, on the other hand, could certainly raise her voice. She was peculiar like that: sometimes soft as a kitten, but so demanding of everyone. It was her childhood, always expecting trouble to come down on them. And then, in the last years, seeing things getting very bad for Jews again, knowing Irma couldn't escape, it made her frantic. Her way of managing her fear was to be very strict even when she cared very much about people.'

'Perhaps Freddie heard his grandmother's voice when he was in hospital.' Did that sound daft? But Ruth nodded.

'If Irma and I were sick as children she'd bring us soup and lemonade but there'd be a fierceness too, as though it was a slur on her mothering abilities that we'd fallen ill.' Ruth's smile became a grin. 'My mother was probably telling Freddie off, telling him he had to wake up. Vida Dekker's grandson simply couldn't slip away.'

'I should probably go back to Mrs Macpherson's and check everything's in order with the books I've been packing up.' Edward must be wondering what was going on. 'I'll find a telephone later and ask for news of Freddie.'

Alfonso came in. 'There's a gentleman for Miss Romilly.'

'For me?'

'A Mr Witney.'

Edward – here? 'Oh. Excuse me.' She stood up and followed Alfonso out. Edward stood in the entrance hall, trilby in hand, looking around at his surroundings with interest.

'How did you know I was here?' she asked.

'And good morning to you, too. You weren't at Mrs Macpherson's and this seemed the most likely place to find you. I was a bit concerned. Has there been any news about Freddie?'

In the brighter light of Ruth Belman's apartment his features looked freshly minted, his eyes more blue than grey.

'Last night, I . . .' She couldn't explain about the panic she'd felt in the bath, and later on, standing on Brooklyn Bridge. 'That house of Mrs Macpherson's felt a bit empty, that's all.'

'That place could be a haunted house set.' His eyes were still on hers, holding the gaze.

'I was worried about Freddie.' She told him about Freddie's turnaround.

'That's wonderful.' He actually beamed, his eyes showing real warmth.

'Would your friend like coffee?' Ruth came to the door of the dining-room.

'That'd be kind, thank you.' He held out a hand. 'Edward Witney. I met Romilly and Freddie and Mrs Dekker on *The Lucknow*. My condolences on the loss of your mother, Mrs Belman.'

Somewhat to Romilly's relief Ruth thanked him and vanished to supervise her children's departure. In the background came thumps and shouts as they located bags and coats and promised their father they were almost ready. Perhaps in a few days or a week Freddie would be joining his cousins in this morning rush, complaining that someone had taken his exercise book or his pencils or asking Nina if anyone had seen his shoes.

They sat down at the table. Smoky came into the dining-room and made straight for Edward, who patted him. 'I've come to the conclusion this dog is a Maltese terrier crossed with a guineapig. Lucky for him he was small enough to fit down a life-vest but tough enough to survive the cold.'

'I think Freddie willed him into surviving. In turn, he helped Freddie, kept him warm, gave him something else to think about.'

'Distraction can be the best way to get children through things.'

She looked at him, surprised.

'I've got a cousin with children. Yes, I'm actually Uncle Eddie, can you imagine?' Perhaps that was why Freddie's emergency hospitalisation had touched him. He looked softer when he talked about his family. And she didn't believe it was just down to his social skills.

'Do you spend much time with them?'

'Not since the war started. I was serving in the Expeditionary Force at first, as I said. Before then I'd been here in New York. I'll catch up with them when I can.'

Ruth came back in. 'I need another cup of coffee. I don't know why getting those two ready for school each morning is such a business.' She poured herself a cup. 'I know I'm spoiled, with Nina to help. My mother used to roll her eyes at me. Of course, she never had any trouble getting Irma and me ready for school in Prague before she set off for a day's work at the glass factory.'

This came as no surprise to Romilly.

'I can remember my mother telling me I'd be the death of her first thing in the morning,' Edward said. 'My sister was always clean, pressed, ready to go. But no, not me.' The accent had slipped very slightly. She had the feeling that Edward and his sister hadn't been getting ready to attend some smart preparatory school, but somewhere more down to earth, probably in the north of England.

'You work in New York, Mr Witney?' Ruth reached for her cigarettes and offered them around.

'In the International Building at the Rockefeller Center.' He shook his head politely at the cigarettes and looked at Romilly. 'I must head over there now. I was wondering whether Romilly fancied walking with me? We could cut across Central Park?'

'I'd like to,' Romilly said. 'The problem is...' she looked down at the slippers she was still wearing. 'My new shoes destroyed my feet.'

'Ah, those very elegant white shoes.' Edward looked amused. 'I did wonder at the time but didn't like to say anything.'

Ruth looked puzzled.

'I acted as bag-carrier when Romilly replaced her lost clothes in Macy's,' he explained.

'We have closets full of shoes here. Mine and my mothers. Why don't we see if anything would fit?'

Ruth left the room. Edward smiled at Romilly. 'Ostrich-skin pumps, do you think?'

Ten minutes later Ruth returned with Nina, each carrying an armful of women's shoes of different descriptions.

'Some of these are my mother's. She's . . . she was a size larger. I don't think she wore most of these more than once.'

Romilly tried on pumps and brogues but settled for a mint-

condition pair of white tennis shoes. 'Like a Chelsea art
student,' Edward said.

'Did Mrs Dekker play tennis?' Romilly asked.

'She joined a club one summer. Jackson played. Mama liked
the shady club house terrace. She'd sit there with iced tea,
working out who was misbehaving and who was about to pull a
fast one on their business partner.'

'All from observing tennis matches?' Edward looked
impressed. Mrs Dekker would perhaps have been suited to his
line of work.

'She could tell whether a player was over-praising his
doubles partner for no good reason. Either they were licking
their boots, about to ditch them or sleeping with their wife.'
Ruth looked apologetic. 'Sorry, that was Mama, she could be a
bit sharp.'

'Will you be back for lunch, Miss Romilly?' Nina asked,
coming in to remove plates. 'Or dinner?'

'Please say you'll be back?' Ruth asked. Edward watched
her carefully as she agreed to return. 'Stay until Freddie's fully
recovered,' Ruth added. 'It was what we planned, anyway,
before . . .' She swallowed.

'I . . . I'm not sure.' She looked at Edward, but his face was
blank.

'Well, we know where to find you if there's any news about
Freddie and you're welcome any time,' Ruth said.

'Thank you.' It seemed extraordinary, Romilly thought, that
she could have grown so close to Ruth after what had happened
when they'd first met.

She felt like someone different again as they strode
into the park. To her relief the blisters on her heels and
toes, still in Nina's Band-Aids, weren't troubled by the
walk.

'It's a very comfortable berth,' Edward said, 'the Belmans'
place. And, of course, your visa still covers you for staying here

and helping with Freddie.' He was watching her. Romilly said nothing.

He took her arm, pointing out the landmarks, telling her the names of buildings she hadn't yet identified, making her laugh with a running commentary on the people they passed. A few passers-by gave them second-glances. Romilly put a hand to her face, was there a smut or a lock of hair out of place? She'd checked herself in the mirror before leaving. Perhaps, it dawned on her, people were looking at her because she and Edward were in some way appealing? They were smartly dressed, enjoying a walk. It seemed strange not to be pitied; strange but refreshing. He seemed to know what was on her mind.

'I always think people are staring at me because I'm limping a bit, despite my best efforts. But when I'm in London I think they look at me because I'm not in uniform.'

She hadn't thought of how difficult it would be to suspect people thought you were shirking your male duty to fight.

'People like to dress well here. And if they see you've put in some effort, they approve.'

'Your suits are certainly very smart. Not sure about my tennis shoes.'

'You're drawing eyes for the right reasons, Romilly.' It was the closest he'd ever come to expressing approval for her appearance. She felt herself grow a bit taller. Her hair blew over her face and she pushed it back with her spare hand. Hair was one matter she had still to attend to.

A newspaper boy walked past, shouting out headlines. 'Germans win battle at Thermopylae.' Romilly felt the mood grow sombre.

'Like something from the Ancient World' Edward sounded thoughtful. 'Those classical names.'

'They just keep coming and coming.' The sunny park seemed overcast. 'Thermopylae today, all of Greece tomorrow.' The grey uniforms and tanks of the Germans were shadowing

New York itself. She was aware of Edward watching her. 'Do you think we can push them back?'

He didn't reply at first. 'I don't know,' he said eventually. 'Not now, anyway.' He looked at his watch. 'We should step out. I have a meeting.' He sounded more clipped, more controlled. Perhaps work was on his mind. 'I'll leave you in the Rockefeller Plaza, if you don't mind. You'll be going to Mrs Macpherson's? The plan is to meet Danny and Raoul there this evening, to run through plans for the rally. If you're still on?'

The rally. The feigned blow. She had to concentrate to remember all the details and what she'd rehearsed with Danny and Raoul. Freddie's sudden hospital admission felt like a wall between then and now, as though weeks had passed instead of a few days. They were walking out of the park now, heading down Sixth Avenue.

'I'll be there.' The words came out clipped. She'd been hoping this walk together would bring back that previous intimacy between them. He'd praised her appearance, but it felt more as if they were still friendly colleagues.

Edward stopped.

'What?' she asked, releasing her arm.

'Of course you're tired, still finding your feet here.'

She frowned at him. 'I said I'd be at the meeting, and I will be.'

They'd reached a large Art Deco building, Radio City. Edward stopped. 'The International Building, where our office is, is the other side of the Rockefeller Center.'

'Not in the music hall with the Rockettes?' She was looking at the posters of the dancers.

'That might be fun, if distracting.' The girls in their tight-fitting, scanty outfits would certainly take your mind off work, Romilly thought. 'Walk through with me and you'll come out on Fifth Avenue, you'll easily find your way back to the Macphersons' from there. Must seem like home turf now.'

'Yes.'

He looked at her, inquiringly. Something was bubbling up inside her. She didn't know quite what it meant yet. They crossed the plaza, huge buildings all around. Romilly put a hand to her head. Not a headache, not quite, more as if something inside her brain was telling her she was going to have to make a choice.

'See you this evening, six o'clock,' Edward said.

She raised a hand in farewell.

As she watched him walk away towards the entrance the sense of being pulled in half intensified. She wasn't sure how she could do this.

TWENTY-TWO

Instead of going straight to Murray Hill, Romilly drifted into a marble-clad, stained-glass windowed cathedral on Fifth Avenue. It reminded her of the old cathedrals back home, although a quick examination of the guidebooks at the front told her St Patrick's was less than a century old. Women in black veils, she couldn't remember what the veils were called, knelt and said their rosaries.

Still uncertain what had drawn her inside, she found herself looking at the candles arranged in racks in front of various statues. Romilly wandered around the cathedral, finding herself in what seemed to be a chapel dedicated to the Virgin Mary. She waited behind an elderly woman who pushed a coin into a slot box and lit a candle, kneeling and making the Sign of the Cross and praying devoutly, lips moving.

Feeling awkward, Romilly copied her, adding a coin to the box, lighting her candle and kneeling in front of the Virgin. They hadn't been a church-going family. She hadn't knelt in a church for years. Nor had prayer featured much in her life and she had never addressed it to a plaster statue before. She didn't know what to say. Memories of her mother filled her. Thoughts of the hours spent with Philip came to her for the first time since the ship had gone down. Mama and her father. She let the statue grow fuzzy in front of her eyes. 'I'm all right,' she told them, silently. 'I survived.' She tried to picture Douglas, too, wherever he was. At some point he'd be discovering that Mama had died. Then she thought of Aunt Ursula and Uncle Simon, because, well, they were family too and had surely been anguished at the sinking of *The Lucknow*. She tried to express gratitude for her own life, and for Freddie's, and to Mrs Dekker for sacrificing her place in the lifeboat.

'I'm pulled in two directions,' she continued silently. 'On the one hand there's Freddie. On the other, there's a cause much bigger than just individual people. It's hard to know which way I should go. But I don't feel guilty anymore for what happened to you, Mama. I know you would hate that.'

To her surprise, Romilly found her cheeks were damp. When she rose, she wiped them with her sleeve. She listened to see if she could hear any internal guidance but there was only the sound of hushed voices and quiet footsteps. The same elderly woman was watching her curiously.

Romilly felt lighter when she re-emerged onto Fifth Avenue. Nothing had changed – she still wasn't sure what to do – but it felt as though some burden had been lifted from her shoulders. Maybe Mama, too, had felt some kind of relief following her visit to the church in Chelsea and the feeling had stayed with her in her last hours.

Having sorted out the spiritual aspect of her life, Romilly was aware that the physical side needed attention. New York didn't seem to lack hair salons. She found one where the women entering and leaving didn't all seem to be either prosperous matrons or rich debutantes. 'I don't have a lot of time,' she explained at the reception desk. 'Perhaps just an hour?'

'Hmm.' A girl of about her age appeared from the salon floor and examined her from each side. 'Quick wash and cut and then we could put you in some rollers and set the hair under a dryer. Should be possible in an hour.'

The girl chatted to her as she worked, asking about London, about the bombs. Romilly found herself skirting the subject of the torpedo, not feeling she wanted to devote time and energy to it again. 'A side parting.' The girl drew a comb down her scalp once she'd washed Romilly's hair. 'And then some gentle waves. If you're out for dinner or the theatre, come back and I'll do something more dressy, but for daytime and work, you need something quick to fix.'

She'd never had a shampoo and set at home. It had been something she and Mama had discussed. It took about forty minutes for the hair to dry and then all the rollers were removed to show sleek, gentle waves falling to her shoulders.

It was one of the best things she'd spent money on in New York.

Her notebook was on her bed at Mrs Macpherson's, where she'd left it. Romilly took it and her pencil down to the library. The desk had gone now, but she sat, back to a wall, legs folded up to make a desk, writing more on the ivory pages with their crisp scent. Words fell out onto the paper – the beautiful, smooth unrationed paper of America. Bombs, shelters, the glory of the liner, the shock of the explosion. The way the ship had tilted and filled with water. Smoky running off down the stairs and Freddie pursuing him. The library with its tilted parquet and rising water level below them. The smell: in turn sulphurous, metallic, then oily. Then the sea itself. The plunge into what seemed like infinity: seeing the light above them and wondering if they could hold on until they reached it. The cold. She tried to conjure up the way it had clamped her chest, how it consumed her body, pressing out all ability to think. The raft and Edward sliding off it because he thought he was endangering them. She'd never thanked him for that. Then the lifeboat. Mrs Dekker, standing in front of her as they swapped places, looking directly at her, then dashed away to her death. Jennifer Smith and the rabbi. Pulling labels off the cans of condensed milk to signal with them.

I was just a girl in lifeboat six and I wasn't strong or good at navigation or first aid . . . I was only in the boat because someone sacrificed their place, their safety, for me. But once I was in that lifeboat, I wasn't going to let myself or Freddie die. We'd struggled so hard to reach safety. Exposure wasn't going to take us. But eventually the urge to shiver passed. I simply wanted to be allowed to sleep.

She realised she hadn't written about what had driven her to take the passage in the first place. It was hard to write about her mother, but not as hard as it would have been before she'd lit the candle in the cathedral. It was tempting to skirt the events, but then it wouldn't be a true account, would it? And the strange dreams or hallucinations in the lifeboat had brought both her parents back to her. She'd loved seeing them again.

My mother died in pain and I wasn't with her. I left for work in the morning not knowing it would be the last time we'd see one another . . .

You make choices and they seem insignificant. You wish you could undo them, but you can't. What would I choose? Not to accept a job as a companion taking me on

a liner across the Atlantic? But the liner was fascinating.
The people travelling with us were so different from those
I'd known in London. And I loved the comfort: the soft
carpets, the meals, the library.

Someone was pounding on the front door. Romilly looked up, pencil in hand, almost blunt now. She had no way of knowing the time and the clock had gone from the library. The shadows had moved across the parquet floor. *I left a battered old city fighting a war it appeared we couldn't win alone, and it seemed like a very good choice.* She finished the sentence and went to open the door.

Edward was standing at the top of the steps. She blinked at him, the blood in her veins pulsing. She felt like a schoolgirl, wondering if it showed on her face.

'I wasn't expecting you until later.'

'Plans have changed.' He was examining her more closely.
'Oh.'

'Do you like it?' She put a hand to her hair, embarrassed at how much she wanted him to approve.

'I certainly do.' He seemed almost embarrassed. 'Been here long?'

'I've just been . . .' She didn't want to tell him what she'd been writing, it was so self-indulgent. 'I was busy, finishing up things in the library.'

He raised an eyebrow. 'May I come inside?'

'Yes, sorry, come on in.'

'This place grows ever less cheerful,' he remarked as they went up to the library.

'There was no message for me, from the Belmans?'

'I don't think they'd ring my office. They wouldn't know the number.'

She flushed. 'Of course, sorry. They'd send Alfonso with a message.'

He looked at her with intent. 'Of course you're concerned about Freddie, but I need you to concentrate. Lindberg's rally has been pushed forward twenty-four hours. It's going to be tomorrow evening rather than Thursday, at the Manhattan Center.'

'So soon?' She felt a rush of adrenaline. They didn't have long to prepare. She wasn't ready. And yet perhaps this was the answer to her dilemma, events themselves propelling her forward.

'America First want him to stir up the masses in Chicago on Friday so they need to do New York earlier.'

'He must be popular.'

'He is.'

Romilly thought of what Leon Belman had said about the crowds on Fifth Avenue cheering Lindbergh on his return to New York from his transatlantic flight. How could they counter the appeal of a man like him? They'd have to try.

'Will there be time for Raoul to perfect my performance?'

'Raoul's tied up on Broadway with rehearsals all day today and tomorrow. We'll have to run through it again without him.'

She swallowed hard.

'Put on your best spring-time outfit, Romilly. Set off that glamorous hair style. You and I are going to take a stroll over to the Manhattan Center now and play the part of a couple out for a stroll on a beautiful spring day. Then we'll come back and Danny will meet us here for a run-through. I left a message for him at a bar he frequents.'

Her heart was flipping as she ran upstairs. But he'd only said they were going to play the part of a couple; foolish to read anything more into it, especially when Danny had ignited that suspicion about Catherine in her mind.

She changed into Ruth Belman's silk dress, which went well with the new jacket, although the comfortable brogues were perhaps not what Ruth would wear with the dress. Still, they were probably smarter than the white tennis shoes. When she came down to the library, Edward pointed at her notebook. 'Something you need to take with us?' Had he read what she'd written? Perhaps he despised her for making such a lot out of the experience.

She tucked the notebook into her bag.

Out in the street, he offered her his arm and she took it, feeling shy, almost tongue-tied. She noticed his slight limp again: not enough to slow him down much, but sufficient to make his gait slightly lop-sided. They crossed the now-familiar avenues to the western side of Midtown. Romilly hadn't spent much time here and remarked on this. 'How could you have seen all of Manhattan? You've haven't been in America a week,' Edward said.

She almost came to a halt, about to dispute the point. But it was true. The days had passed in a blur of activity. It was only just over two weeks since she'd left Liverpool.

The Manhattan Center on 34th Street looked like an opera house or theatre, which was what it had been, Edward told her. 'Auditorium, ballrooms, studios, it's all in there. Now given over to less innocent pursuits as well.' AMERICA FIRST COMMIT-TEE: COL. CHAS. LINDBERGH, lights on the awning proclaimed, along with two other names.

'Kathleen Norris and Senator Walsh are also big figures in the movement,' Edward told her.

'She's a novelist, too, isn't she? I'm sure I remember her books in the shop I worked in.'

'That's right.' He took her slowly past the main entrance under the awning. They pretended to examine a poster giving details of future events at the Center, standing at a slight angle to the building so they could look up the street. 'We can't linger here too long,' Edward said. 'I don't want people to notice us before tomorrow night. I've got it on good authority the press usually stand where that old lady with the pink hat is right now.'

'So Danny and I need to be somewhere near the man with the briefcase hailing the taxi, me facing towards the old lady and Danny coming in from briefcase man's side? What does Danny do before then? Is he eyeing me up with venom?'

A group of women was approaching. Edward shook his head. 'Too busy to hang around here now. Let's head back the way we came and find somewhere to eat.'

He took her back along the street and turned into Eighth Avenue where there was a diner that wasn't too crowded. They ordered toasted Swiss cheese sandwiches and coffee. 'I never get used to this.' Romilly sat back in her stool.

He was fiddling with a paper napkin, taking a fountain pen from his top pocket and drawing a diagram of the Manhattan Center and the blocks surrounding it on 34th Street. 'You'll have a placard. I've got the girls producing them. Before then, I've got to speak to the photographer. If the papers don't pick up the shot, it will have to be disseminated by another method.'

She frowned at him. 'What do you mean?'

He looked around the diner. 'We send the photograph and an apparent press mention in a newspaper to a news agency in Sweden.'

'Apparent? You mean something you've created yourselves?'

'No comment. It's picked up by the Swedish press. With luck, the British press then cover it too. That gives the story a respectability—'

'You mean an appearance of truth?'

He grinned. 'Which means that the story and photograph reappear here, in America, looking entirely above reproach. A young woman struck by a pro-fascist thug in the heart of civilised Manhattan.' He stopped as the waitress brought over their orders. 'Take that, Colonel Lindbergh,' he said, when she'd gone.

Romilly was thinking about Lindbergh. 'Why's such a brave man against fighting?'

'He's a curious case. Five or ten years ago he was this cosmopolitan figure, travelling the world, friends with plenty of Jewish people, collaborating with them on various projects. Goes to Germany, gets some kind of medal from the Nazis. Starts saying that America shouldn't fight them, it's not their war and there's nothing to be gained from interfering.' Edward took a swig of coffee. 'Not unreasonably, he has a fear of doing anything that makes the Soviet Union more powerful and thinks Hitler is a useful lock on Stalin.'

'Not fighting Hitler is a price worth paying?'

'To keep the communists at bay. And he has the kind of charisma that just works on a crowd.'

'Leon Belman was telling me about the big welcome back rally after he crossed the Atlantic.'

'Americans adored him for his flight. When his baby was killed, they were appalled. They're generous in their sympathy.'

'That's what we have to appeal to,' Romilly said. 'The death of children. Jennifer . . .'

'Jennifer?'

'A girl in our lifeboat, one of Louise's group. About Freddie's age.' She told him about Freddie passing her his toy rabbit to be wrapped up with the girl as they floated her body away. Edward listened, nodding. 'I've been making notes. It seems to help, writing it down.'

'The things we saw.' He looked down briefly, flicking invisible crumbs off the table. 'Not just in the water, but when the ship was sinking.'

'The boys who couldn't escape from the lower deck?'

He flinched.

'I'm sorry.' It must be awful for him to remember the scene in the flooded passageway.

'Don't be. It's fuel for our fire, Romilly. We do our work here because we care about what happened that night in the Atlantic. And on all the other terrible nights since September 1939. Keep writing.' He was speaking with a passion she hadn't heard before. They were silent for a while.

'You've adapted very quickly,' he said.

She thought of herself embarking on the voyage to America, overwhelmed, dizzy with shock and grief. She'd woken up on *The Lucknow*, become more curious about people and life in general, less passive.

'You can handle almost anything thrown at you.'

'Did you think that about me before the torpedo hit? Or was I still the little mouse?'

He pushed his plate away. 'I could see you were tougher than you knew. You were typical of a girl of your background: perhaps a little protected. But something had happened to you, something had jolted you out of your normal life. I don't know what? Did you lose someone in an air-raid?'

'Not quite,' she said. 'But my mother died suddenly.' She could say it almost neutrally now. She'd never told him what had happened to her to make her take the job with Mrs Dekker and start life again across the Atlantic. Perhaps she would, but not today.

'Despite all that shock, I sensed you were up to the job of making a life for yourself here.'

'I must have sounded incredibly naïve.'

He beckoned the waitress and waited for her to bring over the bill and leave again before continuing. 'Keen, rather than naïve, I'd say. Understandably.' He put coins on the table to cover the bill. 'I don't want to be responsible for you being packed up home on another convoy across the Atlantic. Not when it cost you so much to get here.' He was speaking quietly, intently.

'Would they really do that?'

'They're very, very suspicious of British propaganda influencing decisions. There are still mutterings about us deceiving them with dirty tricks into joining in the last war.'

'So you need me not to get myself arrested? What would they even charge me with? Pretending to have been hit by Danny? Is that even a crime here?'

'We'll do all we can to make sure that doesn't happen. Let's walk back to Mrs Macpherson's now. Danny will be there shortly for a last debrief.'

Edward offered her his arm and again it seemed the most natural thing in the world to take it. His grip was warm and strong, but once again there was no attempt to pull her closer into him. Perhaps he simply didn't feel what he had felt for her on the deck of the ship. Or acting as her boss, asking her to do things he thought were risky, constrained him to keep their relationship on a professional level.

He walked her south again before turning east past two huge and imposing buildings, one on each side of the street. 'Penn Station and the Post Office,' Edward said. 'Emblems of America opening up its interior. People and information moving around the continent. Americans are natural communicators. They like big, bold ideas.'

'You said you worked here before the war?' She knew so little about him.

'In an advertising agency on Madison Avenue for a year or so.'

Having walked up and down Madison Avenue she could picture him here, heading out for meetings, greeting newspaper sellers and shoe-shine boys. She'd still have been at school, wearing the drab gym tunic and Panama. She didn't belong to the same world as he did. But she wasn't that schoolgirl now, was she?

'Before that, I'd worked in an agency just off Piccadilly,' he continued. 'They set up a partnership with a business over here and wanted me to transfer for a year or two. When the war started, I came back to Britain.'

'To join up?'

'Sadly, I only had very brief service: I was waiting on the beach at Dunkirk to be loaded onto a boat after the retreat. A Messerschmidt strafed us. Luckily for me, it only caught my leg, but it took a few days before the medics could sort me out.' The last words were clipped. She wondered whether the others waiting with him had been killed.

'Cocktails and nightclubs when you worked here?' she asked, to give him a moment.

'Parties and sailing weekends on Long Island.'

'Does that still go on?'

'Not for me. But I've made some good friends with New Yorkers.'

She wanted to ask him if any of these friends had been female.

'A number of them aren't isolationists and think American should join the war. That actually makes it harder for me to see them now I'm back.' She looked at him, puzzled. 'I can't drop my guard with them. I might let something slip. So I keep myself to myself. Or I spend time with the Canadians.'

The secretary girls at the Rockefeller Center. Did he take them to the night spots she'd dreamed about? She cast a discreet look at him. He was wearing a light spring suit. It looked like one from Savile Row, as did his shoes. His hat had New York written all over it, though, in a way she couldn't explain. The Canadian girls would like having Edward to escort them around Manhattan. They'd be dressed up in the smart clothes they'd brought on their wages, keen to have a good time. Perhaps he had struck a relationship with one of them. Her mind went back to Catherine, how long had the spark that Danny had observed between them burned? Just for the duration of their stay here in January? Had it really been over between them when she'd stumbled upon the two of them together that night on *The Lucknow*? She couldn't think of a way to ask him.

Edward stopped. 'Look.'

A group of men and women were walking along the street towards them, handing out handbills. Some of those offered them shook their heads or threw them angrily to the ground, but others read the words, slowing down as they did, looking interested. 'Is that more of your work?' Romilly asked, under her breath.

'I couldn't possibly say.' He looked pleased though.

'You managed to get someone to print the flyers here?' He didn't answer the question. 'I know there was a problem finding a London printer.'

He gave a quick, tight grin. 'I forgot your sharp ears on the ship. We shouldn't get too close to them. I don't want any connection between us and them to be made. Let's cross over and push on a bit—we need all the time we've got to plan with Danny.'

As they reached the house, a car drew up. Romilly recognised it.

Alfonso got out of the driver door. 'Miss Romilly, I have news.'

She stepped towards him. 'Freddie?'

'He's home. Mrs Belman thinks he should go to bed and rest but he refuses. He's getting upset and says he wants to see you.'

Romilly let go of Edward's arm. 'There's not much time left,' he said quietly. 'We need to run through the plans with Danny. He'll be here any moment.'

'Freddie's waiting for you,' Alfonso said.

She was trying to work the timings out. She could read

Freddie a story in less than half an hour. Surely she could be there and back within the hour if Alfonso would drive her home again? 'I'll be back as quickly as I can,' she told Edward. 'There's still hours to go.'

He looked at her, clearly wanting to tell her she couldn't go to Central Park West.

'I owe it to him. I promise I won't be long.' Alfonso opened the rear door and she slipped into the car.

TWENTY-THREE

As they drove, Alfonso told Romilly that the doctors had apparently been pleased with Freddie's recovery.

'But he is pale, very pale. Nina is cooking him convalescent food. He needs plenty of rest. In bed.'

'He won't like that.'

'He will have short walks in the park twice a day when he's stronger, with the dog. Smoky made a huge fuss over Freddie when he came into the apartment. It was the only time I saw Freddie smile since he came back home.'

'It's that bad?'

'He just keeps saying he has to see Romilly.' They were driving the now-familiar route north. Traffic seemed reasonable. All the same, she'd made herself look less than one hundred percent dedicated to the work by dashing off just before the last rehearsal. Perhaps Edward would take her off the operation. No doubt Catherine would have been more devoted to work at any cost. She felt a curdling mixture of jealousy and self-reproach.

'Alfonso . . .'

'Miss?'

She was going to ask him to stop and let her out of the car.

She'd come and see Freddie at breakfast time. He'd be all right, he was surrounded with family, right where Mrs Dekker had intended him to be.

The image of his pale face with the blue lips flashed over her mind.

'Nothing.' She couldn't let Freddie down. They'd huddled together in lifeboat six and that trumped everything. Everyone else had gone from his life: his parents, Mrs Cohen, his grandmother. She and Smoky were the only constants. It had to matter more than any cause, no matter how pressing. But then again, perhaps Freddie and other children like him *were* the cause.

Freddie was sitting on the sofa, Smoky curled up beside him on a little rug. He looked up as she came in and smiled.

'This is quite a good book' He patted it. 'Better than that New Forest one you were reading on *The Lucknow*.' She'd been expecting to find him still upset, but perhaps knowing she was on her way had calmed him. She wanted to laugh at the thought of Romilly Brooks having the power to soothe anyone.

The book was *Tom Sawyer*. 'I was thinking of *Huckleberry Finn*. But Tom's the best one to start with. How do you feel now, Freddie?'

He didn't answer, bending down to fiddle with Smoky's collar. 'We didn't get Smoky checked over, did we?'

'No. I didn't think of that.'

'Suppose the sea got inside him too?'

'We'd know by now. Look at him, he's fine. You kept him warm on the lifeboat and gave him water.'

He coughed. 'Don't worry,' he said, catching the expression on her face. 'The doctor says it's still a bit sore down there.'

'They said you were upset?'

Freddie shrugged. 'I was just expecting you to be here when I got back.'

'I'm here now.'

'You changed your hair.' He sounded accusatory.

'Freddie, I have to come and go. And my hair needed attention. But your aunt can find me if you need me.'

'She wanted me to go to bed but . . .'

'What?'

He seemed preoccupied with the dog's collar. 'Sometimes people die in their sleep. Like Jennifer.'

'Listen to me, Freddie, you're not going to die.'

'Nobody thinks they're going to die. Jennifer didn't.'

'Jennifer didn't have a hospital and doctors. It's not the same.' She was keeping her voice very neutral and calm.

'Do you think she'd have lived if she had?'

'I honestly can't tell you.'

He was silent.

'You looked as though someone had wiped your mouth with pale-blue ink when you were in the hospital.' She was trying to distract him. 'You were in an oxygen tent. Do you remember?'

He brightened. 'I wish I'd been awake to see that.' He yawned. 'They say I can go to school in a week's time.'

'How'd you feel about that?'

He shrugged. 'It'd be good to spend time with other people. Lewis and Clara are OK, but they're cousins, so they have to be.'

'And your aunt and uncle? They seem kind?'

'Uncle Leon's going to take me to a baseball game. I have to choose which team to support.' He frowned. 'I need to think it over.'

'And Aunt Ruth?'

'She showed me some photographs of her and my mother when they were my age.' He gulped and folded his arms around himself. 'I'd forgotten what Mama looked like. And my father, too.'

'I find it harder and harder to remember what my parents look like.' He didn't say anything, but his face seemed to relax. 'I have a photo, but it's very smudged since the ship went down. Perhaps I can ask someone to send me another one from home.' She hadn't thought of doing this before. 'It's all right to need photographs to nudge our memories, Freddie. It doesn't mean we love people any less.' She struggled to find a way to explain it to him. 'I may not remember every feature of my father's face, but I can remember how he made me feel. I bet you can remember how you felt with your mother and father.'

He was unfolding his arms. 'Suppose I don't recognise them if they come back?'

'You mightn't recognise them immediately. But if they started talking about things that happened when you were small, you'd remember, wouldn't you?' Romilly stood up. 'You really do need to rest.'

'You're going?' His eyes widened. 'You can't, you have to stay with me.'

'I'll be back soon.' She took her arm from his shoulders.

'No,' he said, replacing it. 'You can't go, Romilly. You have to stay.' His voice had risen. Ruth came into the room.

'Freddie?'

'Tell her she has to stay.'

'Freddie, I can't, Romilly needs —'

'She has to stay. Please.' A paroxysm of coughing overcame Freddie. He doubled up. Ruth rushed up to him.

'The doctors said I had to keep him calm. Freddie, let's get you into bed.'

He waved a hand, trying to speak, drawing breaths. Finally, he lifted his head. 'Everyone leaves. They say it will be fine, they'll see me again. They don't.'

'Nothing's going to happen to Romilly, Freddie. She'll be back to see you.'

'I can come back again tonight. Or tomorrow morning, if it's late when I've . . . finished.' She could bear another night alone in that house in Murray Hill if necessary.

He seemed to fall back into the sofa, shaking his head. Ruth put a hand on his brow. 'He's even paler than he was before. Perhaps I should ring the hospital, see if I should have him seen again?'

'I'll stay.' The words fell out of Romilly's mouth. She knelt before Freddie. 'I'm not leaving you.' He summoned up the energy to push himself into her arms.

'Thank you,' he whispered.

'I'll have to get a message to . . . someone,' Romilly told Ruth.

'At the Macpherson's?'

Romilly nodded. 'I'm just going to write a quick note,' she told Freddie. 'I'm not leaving.' She untangled herself. Ruth brought her a correspondence card, beautiful ivory stationery of a thickness Romilly hadn't seen for a few years. *Have to stay here tonight. Sorry, Romilly.*

She addressed it to Edward.

TWENTY-FOUR

Freddie appeared in Romilly's bedroom just before seven, according to the little clock on the bedside table. 'Do you think it's time for breakfast yet?'

She looked at her watch. 'Maybe. Go and look and see if Nina's set the table yet.' Someone was obviously serving Freddie breakfast in the dining-room as he didn't reappear. Romilly got up and washed and dressed. She was waiting for something, and she knew it – he – would be turning up soon.

Over the breakfast table, Freddie ate a second helping of fried eggs. He still looked frail beside his cousins but less white. After he'd finished, Ruth insisted that he went back to bed for a few hours. 'I'm still not convinced he's as well as he seems to be. The doctor really was very insistent that he rest. But you, Romilly, you've acted like a tonic. Can you stay another night?'

Thursday today. The Lindbergh Rally was tonight. She needed to be there, she decided. The choice had been made. How to explain to Ruth and Freddie?

'He's slept through, no bad dreams,' Ruth said. 'We had a plan. Leon and I thought perhaps you and I could take Freddie down to Long Island. There's a good hotel we know. He can run around on the beach for a few days – if he feels safe close to the water, that is. The others can join us at the weekend. It would give him some sea air.'

The sea. She felt herself stiffen. Even now the thought of that blue-grey mass could do that to her. And if she went down there, there was no way she could do what Edward wanted her to do at the rally.

'Have a think, Romilly,' Ruth told her. 'You're under no obligation, of course. But we love having you here. Perhaps you could stay here until Freddie's out of bed and we can see how he's doing?'

Freddie dozed for a few hours and was then persuaded to bathe. While Nina was sorting out towels and clean clothes, Romilly sat with the newspaper. The Lindbergh rally tonight was mentioned on the front page. She read it carefully then went to the guest room, where she pulled out her notepad and pencil.

People think that once you're out of the sea the sea's out of you. But not necessarily. You can carry it inside your lungs, and it can try to choke the air out of you. Sometimes, the doctors only find out what's happening when it's almost too late. If you're a small child there may be warning signs that come and go and then a sudden crisis. The war doesn't leave you alone even when you arrive somewhere safe.

Ruth knocked on the door. 'While Freddie's resting, I'm going to start sorting out my mother's apartment.'

'Would you like me to help?' Romilly asked.

'I think I need to do it by myself.' Ruth sighed. 'But thank you.'

Romilly returned to the newspaper, rereading the article about the rally, then flicking through the pages to see if there was any other war news. The war correspondent seemed to think that nothing could stop the Germans marching down on Greece. Alfonso came in. 'Mr Witney for you, miss.'

She knew he'd come. Her note last night, saying so little. He came in with her shopping parcels and bags. She felt her cheeks flush. 'I wasn't sure if you needed these. It didn't seem right to put them in a taxi.' He placed the bags on the floor and removed his hat. 'I wanted to see how you were.'

'I'm sorry.' She could barely look him in the eye. 'Yesterday evening, dashing off like that, sending the note.'

'You were worried, of course you were.' A hint of the non-establishment accent she'd noticed before. 'I understand that.'

'Do you? I'm not sure I understand myself.'

He looked at her intently.

Romilly sat down and beckoned him to sit, too. 'Before I met you yesterday, I went to St Patrick's Cathedral to light a candle.'

'I didn't know you were Catholic.'

'I'm not, but it felt appropriate. My mother, just before she died, she went into a church. I didn't know why, at the time. She wasn't religious.' Romilly took a moment. 'I stayed out late, in an air-raid, the night she died.' She couldn't tell him why she'd stayed out late. Perhaps he guessed. 'I might have been able to get her into the hospital sooner, saved her life. Then, Mrs Dekker died, giving up a space in the lifeboat for me. All she asked was that I make sure Freddie got here safely.'

'And you did. So few of those children survived, but you made sure Freddie did.'

'But he nearly died in the hospital here. It seems that when I'm with him, he's more settled. The doctors say he needs to be kept calm.' She forced herself to meet his blue-grey gaze. 'I promised his grandmother.'

On the subject of saving lives, there was something else she needed to say, too. 'You let yourself slip off the raft into the sea, because you thought you'd be a dead weight if you lost consciousness. You could have stayed with us, but you chose to give us the best chance.'

He was starting to say something, but she shook her head. 'Don't say it didn't matter. You risked freezing in that sea for us. And I never thanked you.'

'You don't need to thank me. You and Freddie had already pulled me out of the sea, remember?'

'We both saved one another then. But . . .' Before that, on the deck of the ship, she wanted to say, was that just nothing? Surely she hadn't been mistaken, there'd been something between them. And yet since she'd come to New York he'd pulled back from her. Danny's account of what he'd seen with him and Catherine couldn't be forgotten, either.

His face was tight. 'You feel you owe me something because of what happened on the life-raft?'

'No.'

'That's why you agreed to work for us?'

'No, not at all, that isn't it. I thought you and I, that . . .' It was humiliating, seeing that she'd mistaken the moment on *The Lucknow* for something it wasn't. Two people who'd eaten and drunk well and had stood on a ship's deck and been carried away. You saw it in films all the time. She couldn't mention the kiss. 'I misunderstood.' She wanted to bury herself somewhere out of sight.

'No, Miss Brooks, I was the one who misunderstood.' His voice was soft. 'We don't want people working for us because they feel indebted to us.'

To *us*. Not to him, personally.

'They have to feel a stronger commitment than that to be convincing.'

'No, that's not what I mean.'

'Then what do you mean?'

She would humiliate herself if she said anything more, if she told him she'd thought there was something going on between them.

'You were probably suffering from delayed shock.' He spoke gently. 'Still running on adrenaline when you and I met again. And I pushed you into committing to something that's dangerous.'

'No, you didn't, you didn't push me into anything.' She was making such a mess of explaining. 'I'm not scared.'

'Then perhaps you should be.' He picked up his hat. 'Being arrested would not be an experience you'd enjoy. I can only risk it happening to you if I know you're completely committed, for the right reasons. When Freddie doesn't need you anymore, I can find you a different job. No rallies, no fighting. You haven't signed anything, but I'm relying on you to keep your lips sealed about what you know.'

'I wouldn't—'

'I heard Ruth Belman talking about a jaunt to Long Island. You should do that. Get out of town for a few days.' For a moment, the flintiness in his eyes was back. 'I'll have someone make contact with you in due course.' He sounded as if he was talking to a junior in his office. That was all she was to him: a former colleague.

'So I won't see you again?'

'Best not. It may be that the best place for you is Washington, anyway. It's a bit more above board there and as you can imagine our diplomats down there are working overtime and need all the administrative help they can get.'

She didn't want to go to Washington. She started to say more but he held out a hand. 'Romilly, I really hope that Freddie continues his recovery. Enjoy Long Island. You have so much to offer – I know you'll be happy in America.' The last words were said in the rougher accent, but they sounded gentle.

How could she be happy when he was walking away? She took the hand, emotion bubbling away inside her. But what was she going to say now: *Sorry, I thought you'd fallen for me because I've fallen for you?* Was that the only reason she'd agreed to work for him? No. She felt a burning anger at what had happened to the ship and a determination to do anything that would make the Germans less likely to fire on another passenger ship. But he now knew there was something else, some other factor in her decision to join in. He wouldn't want her working for him if he knew she had a silly crush on him. Even if he felt something for her, it could just be a passing spark.

Her life felt as though all the pages of a Jane Austen novel and a John Buchan thriller had fallen out and someone had tried to assemble a single mismatched book out of them.

This was ridiculous. A war was killing people and she was acting like a schoolgirl. She drew herself up to tell him that he didn't have to worry, she was committed, there was no false sense of obligation. 'Edward.' Her voice was decisive. He blinked with surprise. She stepped towards him. He came closer, they were nearly touching, his hand was reaching for hers, in a moment they'd be—

'Rom,' Freddie appeared in the doorway. 'I'm really bored just lying in bed. Will you come in and read to me? Oh, Mr Witney.'

'I'm delighted to see you again, Freddie.' Edward stepped back from Romilly. 'And glad that you're recovering. Do you like New York more than you thought you would?'

'The food's OK. Aunt Ruth says I can have ice-cream at lunch.'

'Ice-cream is always important, and we didn't have much of that in London, did we?'

'Go back to bed,' she told Freddie. 'I'll be there in a moment.'

Freddie vanished.

'Staying here for Freddie's sake is perfectly understandable.' Edward was trying to make it easier for her.

'He really does seem a lot better.' The lift doors clinked outside. Ruth would be returning from Mrs Dekker's apartment, time was running out. She moved towards him, taking his hand. 'Edward, let me explain what I was trying to say—'

'Do you think a refugee relief charity would want these coats of Mama's?' Ruth came into the room, coats piled up in her arms. 'Oh, excuse me, Mr Witney. I didn't know you were here.'

'Good morning, Mrs Belman.' Edward nodded politely at her.

'I'll be with Freddie.' Ruth left the room.

'I really must go now.' He let go of Romilly's hand. She wanted to pull him back, but he moved decisively towards the door.

She heard the elevator doors close and walked over to the window, needing to see one last glimpse of him. A minute or so later she watched Edward come out of the building and cross to the park. His limp seemed more pronounced this morning, but he walked briskly and was lost to her view.

Romilly stood at the window. She could run after him, catch him before he exited the park at the southern end.

'Do you have pullovers, Romilly?' Ruth came back into the room. 'It can be chilly on the coast. I found some beautiful cashmere in Mama's closet. One has the dearest little collar that would set off your new hairstyle.'

TWENTY-FIVE

They were only supposed to be visiting Long Island for the rest of the week and the weekend, but Ruth Belman's luggage was piling up. Romilly thought of Mrs Dekker's suitcases on *The Lucknow*. Neither mother nor daughter believed in travelling lightly. Remembering Mrs Dekker made her feel on edge, almost as she had on *The Lucknow* when Mrs Dekker had seemed exasperated by her passivity.

Ruth had lent her a small suitcase for her purchases from Macy's. She probably owed Edward's organisation money for some of these clothes, which he'd paid for, thinking she'd be working for him. Her cheeks pinkened. She could repay him. Surely cash sent to that International Building at the Rockefeller would find him?

Freddie had been wearing Lewis's cast-offs, but Ruth didn't believe that this would do for the Long Island hotel. 'I'll pick up some clothes for you. I'll only be gone an hour or so.' She rolled up her measuring-tape. Freddie stood in front of her. 'If there are any games or toys you want to take from the nursery, Freddie, help yourself.'

Lewis and Clara were still at school. Ruth was waiting for

them to return before they set off for Long Island, brushing off Romilly's query about them objecting to being left behind. 'It's only a few days until they can join us for the weekend. Freddie needs my attention more than they do just now.'

'They mightn't like me taking their things.' Freddie sounded unusually hesitant when they went into the nursery.

'Anything that really means a lot to them will be in their bedrooms, won't it?'

Freddie went over to a shelf of stuffed toys, taking them off one by one and examining them. 'Look.' He held up a toy rabbit. 'It's a bit like the one I had.'

'And you gave it to Jennifer. Do you miss your rabbit?' She remembered how they'd tucked it in beside Jennifer before she'd been lifted into the water.

He looked thoughtful. 'I do miss it, but Jennifer looked lonely, didn't she?'

'I'm sure your cousins wouldn't mind if you borrowed the rabbit.'

He put it back. 'My mother gave it to me so mine was a Czech rabbit. This one's American. And I'm getting too old for that kind of thing.' He moved on to a shelf of construction toys and board games. 'We could take some of these.'

Romilly was still looking at the rabbit.

'Rom?' He tilted his head. 'What're you thinking?'

She gave herself a mental shake.

'Bubbe would have told you off for daydreaming.'

She laughed. 'Yes, she would.'

'She told us off a lot on the ship, but I think it's because she knew we had to be tough.'

'Like tigers.' Yet here she was, slipping into this comfortable world of trips away and cashmere jumpers.

'I like my Aunt Ruth.' Freddie roused her from her thoughts. 'I think she likes me, too.'

'I'm sure she does.'

'And I think I'll be all right with Lewis and Clara.'

'You got along with Mrs Cohen's boys, didn't you?' She didn't know much about the household he'd left behind in London, just that there had been boys.

He nodded.

'Last night you didn't want me to leave you,' she said slowly, carefully.

'And you didn't.' He selected a wind-up train engine and sat down on the rug with it. 'I wanted you to stay. I felt . . .' he pointed to his head. 'As if I was back there again, on the ship. And you did stay.'

Romilly knelt down too. 'Freddie, what are you saying?'

'Last night, I needed you. Tonight will be different. And my aunt will be there. She sat next to me in the hospital. She thought I was asleep all the time, but I wasn't. She looks a bit like my mother.'

'I'd come back when you're home from Long Island.'

He looked at her. 'Yes, I know you would.'

Freddie trusted her. She felt something huge shift inside her. He'd given her permission to go. She heard Ruth coming back in, laughing with Nina at the amount of shopping she'd managed to do. 'You have a good time at the seaside.' She hugged him and jumped up to her feet, meeting Ruth in the lobby.

'Getting ready to go?' Ruth looked at her watch. 'We should have lunch first.' She put down her bags, frowning. 'Romilly? Are you all right?'

'I can't go with you to Long Island, I'm sorry. In fact, I have to leave now.'

'Has something happened?'

Romilly shook her head. 'I can't explain. I'm so sorry for changing my mind. Thank you for having me. I'd love to come and visit Freddie when you're back.'

'She has to do something.' Freddie spoke from behind her.

'She can't tell you what it is, but she needs to do it, Aunt Ruth.' Freddie was more perceptive than she'd realised.

Ruth was looking from one of them to the other, still frowning. 'I'll be all right,' Freddie said. 'It won't be like last night was. All the water's out of me now. Even from here.' He tapped his forehead.

'But . . .' Ruth took off her hat and fiddled with the feather on it. 'I don't understand. Did we do something, Romilly? Did I say something?'

'It's Mr Witney,' Freddie said. 'But she won't say more.'

'Freddie.' She turned to him.

He put a finger to his lips. 'Don't forget to take that.' He pointed to her suitcase. He'd been into the guest room to fetch it.

'I'm sorry,' Romilly said again. It seemed to have been all she'd said to various people for the last twenty-four hours. But she really did feel regret for leaving like this.

Her new jacket and beret had been neatly hung up by the door. She put them on, looking at the suitcase. 'May I borrow that?' Ruth nodded.

'Thank you,' she said, who raised a hand, stopping her.

'No, we made you stay yesterday. You must do what you need to do, but Romilly . . .'

Romilly paused at the lift door.

'I don't know what you're involved in, but your Mr Witney working for some kind of agency in the International Building and the fact it involves Mrs Macpherson gives me a clue. She's been hosting lunches and doing her best to persuade people we had to join in the war. Some of the things I've heard about her makes me believe her friends . . . Well, they'll do whatever it takes. They're desperate.'

'It feels desperate.' As she said it, the enormity of what they were attempting struck her. More children like Freddie were going to die and the longer America stayed out, the longer it would go on. Ruth stepped forward and Romilly found herself in an embrace. She smelled something familiar.

'Your mother's scent?' she asked. 'Mitsouko, isn't it?'

'I found a bottle in her apartment when I was clearing it out. It makes me feel close to her when I put it on.' She released her. 'I think she would trust you to make the right choices, Romilly. I don't know what you and Mr Witney are involved in, but be careful.'

'I will.' Their eyes met for a last time and then Romilly was in the lift, going down to the ground floor, waving at the doorman and dashing across the street to the park.

TWENTY-SIX

As she ran out of the park, Romilly spotted a group with placards heading west, towards the Manhattan Center. She couldn't see what the signs said but passers-by were responding with a mixture of jeers and shouts of encouragement.

Edward must surely be heading back for the office, probably already there by now. On she ran towards the Rockefeller Center.

She had no idea which floor of the International Building his office was on. The concierge on the ground floor nodded towards the man at the elevator, who pushed buttons and gestured her to go in. She hadn't ascended a building this height before and even now Romilly felt a rush of excitement as she was borne upwards. The bell pinged. The doors opened. A young woman a little older than her sat at a desk opposite. 'How may I help you?' A Canadian accent, Romilly thought.

'This is the British Press Service?'

'That is correct.'

'I'm looking for Mr Witney.'

The receptionist kept her steady blue-eyed gaze on Romilly. 'I'm very sorry, miss, Mr Witney isn't here.'

'Is he expected shortly?'

The receptionist shook her head. 'I'm not sure.'

Of course, the Press Service was a cover for his real work, but this woman wasn't going to tell her anything more. It was pointless asking if he was in another office in this huge building, she wouldn't tell her. 'If Mr Witney should come in for a meeting, please could you tell him that Romilly Brooks was just here and I'm going to the usual place?'

The woman made no attempt to write this down, her eyes stayed on Romilly. Romilly remembered the card Edward had given her. She'd put it in her new jacket pocket. She pulled it out. The card was now very wrinkled, the print faded. 'I had this telephone number to ring.' She slipped it across the desk.

The woman read the number and shook her head. 'Did you drop it in the bath?'

Romilly glared at her. 'If I called that number from a public box, none of the telephones on the desks up here would ring, is that what you're saying?'

'I couldn't say.'

'Because I don't think that's true.'

The receptionist turned away. 'You'll have to excuse me now.'

Romilly dropped her suitcase, reached across and grabbed the receiver of the telephone, pulling it across the desk. 'Excuse me,' the receptionist snatched it back. 'You should leave now.' Little patches of colour had appeared on each of her cheeks. 'Before I fetch help.'

'I'm sorry.' She pulled her notepad and a pencil out of her satchel. *Will go to MHM's. R.* 'I'm not usually . . . I don't . . .' But she was tired of apologising, of yielding. 'Please give Mr Witney this note.'

The receptionist was already looking down at the papers on her desk and made no move to take the note.

'It's me instead of Catherine.' She could barely even hear

her own words. The receptionist didn't speak, didn't lift her head, but her shoulders tensed.

No more time could be wasted here, she'd head straight for Murray Hill. Perhaps Edward was already there. She drew deep breaths in the escalator as it carried her down to the ground floor. Back on the street she walked as fast as she could, sometimes breaking into a trot if the sidewalk was clear, even though people tutted at the sight of a young woman with a suitcase hurling herself along at such a speed. Aunt Ursula would be very disapproving of her showing herself red-faced and breathless in public like this.

Grand Central seemed so familiar now that she barely noted she was passing it. Romilly hadn't realised before that the streets sloped up towards Murray Hill until her heartbeat raced even more. She pressed on and found herself outside Mrs Macpherson's, realising she didn't have the key in her satchel: she'd left it in the bedroom at Ruth's, not wishing to take it to Long Island. Romilly rapped on the door. Nobody answered. She didn't like to call out and draw attention to the house. Two o'clock now. Perhaps Edward didn't need a practice anymore if she wasn't going to be there. She'd been the newcomer, after all, the novice, the one who'd needed extra training. Without Romilly, the others could simply proceed to the rally this evening. Edward could try for a photograph of violence that hadn't been staged. Or perhaps he was finding someone else: one of those girls up there in the Rockefeller Center, one of the blue-eyed receptionist's colleagues, perhaps.

She sat down on the step and thought it over. Perhaps the best thing was to make her way towards the Manhattan Center, hole up for the day in the diner Edward had taken her to. She could keep an eye open for them. She eyed the suitcase. She'd arrived in New York with nothing to carry apart from the dog and now she was encumbered with possessions. The basement. Had Mrs Macpherson's staff locked it all up securely or were

New York houses perhaps like London houses: less secure at basement level? If she could get inside, she could drop the case and another note for Edward that was cryptic yet made it clear she was going to be at the rally. She was taking a lot for granted, she knew. He might have decided she wasn't worth bothering with.

Romilly took the steps down the basement and rattled the door. Locked, and a padlock on it as well. The window was barred. This was going to be a day when every desire was thwarted. She went back up to street level.

'Romilly?'

He was standing halfway up the stoop.

'I thought you might be here,' she said lamely.

'I'd have been here before, but I was detained at the office by an account of an agitated young Englishwoman assaulting reception.'

She had lost the power of speech.

'What do you want, Romilly?'

She tried to read his face, but it was inscrutable. 'I want to do what I was supposed to be doing this evening.'

'You're no longer involved in this project. You're needed elsewhere.'

'Not any longer. Freddie told me he can manage without me.'

'He's a child. And you're not much more than one, either.'

It felt like a slap to the face. 'Don't patronise me. I'm twenty in a month. I've been blitzed and torpedoed.'

'All the more reason why it was sensible for you to stay in that comfortable apartment with a family who seem genuinely pleased to have you there.'

'I've had enough of this.' Her voice had risen: a woman walking on the other side of the street turned to look. 'Everyone is always telling me what's right for me. I know what's right for me, what's important. In Europe people my age are being rounded up and forced to work as slaves or shot.'

'Keep your voice down.' His words were clipped, almost furious, but in his face she saw something else she couldn't decipher: a sadness?

'Let me come inside then.'

A sigh of exasperation. 'Come on. But don't expect you can change my mind.'

A cab pulled up. Edward sprang towards the passenger door and removed two long paper packages before paying the driver. 'Make yourself useful and open the door.' He handed her a copy of the key she had. She took it with her spare hand.

It was still light enough indoors not to need the lights, which was as well, as the electricity had now been switched off. 'Leave your case there. Go down to the basement,' Edward said. 'You'll find a shortbread tin on the table in the old kitchen. Bring it up.' He was issuing orders as though she was some kind of underling, making her work for his approval. She did what he asked and found a biscuit tin with Highland cattle on the lid. Edward was in the dining-room, unwrapping the parcels. He took the tin from her and took out a photograph, frowning at it.

It was a picture of a row of people hanging from a gallows. Priests. Romilly looked away.

'The Nazis are fighting a war against the Catholic church in Poland,' Edward said. 'But photographs like this are dynamite. Used the wrong way they can seem like dirty tricks.'

'Fakes?' Romilly looked away from the image.

'Indeed. But not this one. This is unfortunately real.'

'How'd it get into Mrs Macpherson's tin?' she asked.

'Her maid has contacts in the Polish community here. Some of them have relatives who've managed, God knows how, to smuggle material out of Poland. Sometimes it ends up in New York, which is useful.'

'What will you do with it?'

Edward turned it over. 'Good.' There was writing on the
back in a foreign language that could have been Polish, with
dates and names. 'We can trace the contact through the maid.
Our American friends here can talk to the newspapers and see
if they'll use it.'

Edward turned the photograph over again. Romilly saw that
one of the executed was a woman – young, by the look of it.
Edward saw her looking at the girl. 'She's just a schoolgirl,' she
said.

'Far too young.' He looked moved. 'I must admit I wasn't
sure Mrs Macpherson and her maid could organise this before
they left New York.' How many women, of all ages and nation-
alities, did Edward actually have working in his web? He was
still looking at the photograph. 'This is what we're really
fighting for.' He'd lost the polished accent now and sounded
younger. 'This is why . . .' He stopped.

'Why what, Edward?' She sat down on a dust-covered
chair.

His mouth opened. 'This isn't the time.'

'For what?'

'My personal history.' His sigh was long and deep.

'You know quite a bit about mine. Or is it only the underling has to tell all but not you?' She smiled at him to soften the
words.

'I don't think anyone would call you an underling. I was
talking about my sister.'

'The one who was much more organised than you in the
mornings when you were going to school?'

He nodded. 'She carried on being very organised. She was
in Berlin right up until the time war was declared, helping
Jewish children leave on the last train. That was September the
first, 1939. Then she vanished.'

'You haven't heard from her since then?'

'Not until January this year. My mother received a telegram

via the Swiss Red Cross.' He pulled out a chair too. 'Death from pneumonia in a camp south of Berlin. She'd been arrested for spying just after war was declared. I had never heard anything that made me think she was doing anything other than helping those children. She might have died from pneumonia. If they'd mistreated her badly enough, it's a possibility.'

'You think . . .?'

'We haven't seen the death certificate and I imagine it could be a piece of fiction. She could have died from being abused, tortured. Or perhaps they executed her.'

'I'm so sorry.'

'Emily's the reason I'm involved in this work. At first I was angry. If she had been working undercover, I thought she'd been exploited, persuaded to do it by people who can be unscrupulous. They'd seen her working with the Jewish children and knew how much she hated the Nazis.'

Had he worried he was exploiting Romilly in New York?

'But she made her own choices. Emily was in the same college as Catherine at Oxford, a few years ahead of her on a modern languages degree course. Two bright young women from the same Manchester school who wanted to fight for what they thought was right.' He looked at her. 'Emily was so young when she died.'

'It must have been a dreadful time when you found out.'

'I was here in New York. My mother telegrammed me via the Consulate. Catherine, or Louise as she was then, and I were both here, recruiting Danny and Raoul. She'd brought over another group of children. The rage we felt about Emily was certainly a spur to our efforts.'

Had the sparks Danny seen between the two of them simply been rage and grief?

'Catherine must have understood how you felt,' she said slowly.

'She'd just got engaged before we came out. I was going to

take her out that night for dinner to celebrate when I received the telegram. We turned the celebration into a kind of wake for Emily.'

Romilly's breathing quickened. 'Danny said he'd seen you that night.'

'I don't know which one of us was supporting which one into the cab.' For a moment, his face lightened. 'I came to the next morning lying on the floor of her hotel room, still wearing my overcoat and hat, suffering the biggest hangover I've ever known. I checked she was still alive and made her drink a pint of water and take some aspirin.'

'Then you lost Catherine too.'

'And now there's you.' He swallowed. 'And I don't want to lose you as well.'

'I want to do what I can. I know I'm not a bright academic. I just worked in a bookshop.' How could she compare with the likes of Edward's sister and Catherine?

'But it all starts with books, doesn't it?' he looked up, still seeming younger, more vulnerable. 'For people like you and me, at least. We read. We dream. We see a wider world, full of better possibilities. I didn't go to Oxford like my sister. I went to Manchester University. Nobody took me seriously after Dunkirk when I offered my brains instead of my physical fitness. I had to modify the way I dressed and spoke and even so there were questions about my schooling, my family.' He gave a wry smile. 'Eventually, I found an agency who were interested in what I could offer. I'd worked in advertising. I knew how to make images and words grab people's attention, how to manipulate emotions. I didn't see anything ungentlemanly in doing it, either.' She knew not to ask him who exactly these people were who'd recruited him. She thought of something else, something from the very first night on *The Lucknow*.

'Who taught you to be a puppeteer? On the ship you seemed to pick it up very quickly. Had you done it before?'

He looked surprised and laughed. 'You don't miss much, do you?'

'I was a mouse, we get everywhere, see and hear all kinds of things.'

'Our grandfather came from Austria as a young man. His family had made puppets for generations.'

'Oh, you're not . . .'

'Not completely English? No.' He looked thoughtful. 'That was another thing that bothered the people who recruited me, my Austrian antecedents.'

'Puppetry sounds harmless, though.'

'In my grandfather's village, puppets were almost sacred. He used to set up little shows for us to perform.'

'That's why you're so good pulling strings.'

'If only human beings could be as easily managed as marionettes.' He looked at her ruefully.

She reached for his hand. Now was the time to be brave. 'Our strings do get twisted up, don't they?' He didn't move the hand away.

'They certainly did. From the very beginning. You saw me with a mysterious dark-haired woman and thought I was behaving inappropriately.' His lips twitched as he placed his free hand, sandwiching hers between them, his eyes still on hers.

'At one stage I thought you were a Nazi spy.'

'Now you're just being outright offensive.'

'And then we were rudely interrupted.' They'd slanted forwards towards one another on their chairs, so their faces were almost touching.

'That bloody torpedo chose its moment.' He stood up abruptly and pulled her to her feet and towards him. The meeting of their lips felt like it had on the deck of the ship, but with a twist of urgency to it. That night on *The Lucknow* they'd still believed they had half the voyage ahead of them. They'd been in a world apart. In Mrs Macpherson's dusty dining-room, the world was very much just outside, waiting for them. The kiss pushed Romilly back so that she was almost bowed over the table. She opened her eyes and found his were still closed. Then the blue-grey irises opened and fixed on her, no longer sharp and appraising, but tender. They parted.

He let out a breath. 'I didn't expect that to happen.'

'Don't you dare apologise.' She might actually bludgeon him if he did.

He gave a low laugh. 'For a moment I was.' She batted him gently with the back of her hand. He pulled her closer to him, gently tilting her face up so that he could kiss her again.

'We have work to do.' He let her go. 'We can't be distracted, Romilly. There are men already on the street we know are paid thugs. They'll be looking for trouble, wanting trouble. We need to prepare.'

'A shame you can't line up the cameras to catch them in action.' She put a hand on his face and traced a pattern around his mouth, up his cheek to his eyebrows and down again to his chin. Very cleanly shaven, the skin as soft as hers. She pushed back the hair on his brow. 'Your head is healing. Do you get headaches?'

'Sometimes. What about your bashes and bruises?'

'I've pretty well forgotten about them.' It seemed her body had shrugged off the trauma before her mind had been able to shed it all.

'I really do not want anyone on my side hurt. Not even Danny, though anyone who'd take that maniac on would have to have a death wish.' He let her go and looked at his wristwatch. 'He'll be here shortly.'

Romilly brushed the creases out of the front of her blouse and checked the pins in her new hair style were still in place. 'We can get on with these placards.' He nodded at the unwrapped parcels on the table, which she'd barely looked at.

'We need to glue the cardboard posters to the wooden sticks. I couldn't bring them in the taxi made up. There's a tin of adhesive and a brush here somewhere.' He found them both. Romilly examined the posters. *FIGHT FOR EUROPE'S JEWS . . . EUROPE YESTERDAY, BRITAIN TODAY, AMERICA TOMORROW . . . EUROPE'S CHILDREN FIRST THEN AMERICAN KIDS.*

For the next half an hour they assembled the placards, placing them on the table once they'd been glued so they would set firm. Edward opened his cigarette case and lit one for her. It felt almost relaxing, working on the project together, almost like it had when she and Mama had first moved into the mews house and had wallpapered the small sitting room one Sunday. But then recollection of what was to happen this evening swept through Romilly and she drew hard on her cigarette.

Danny knocked on the front door and she went to let him in. His face showed amazement. 'Thought you'd still be with the little guy, Romilly?'

'It was Freddie who sent me off, told me I had to do this.'

'Out of the mouths of babes and infants, eh.' He followed them into the dining-room. 'Very neat.' He nodded at the banners. 'You even managed to make the lettering look angry.'

'Raoul's set designer friend helped,' Edward said. 'He hates Nazis too.'

'The streets around the Manhattan Center are already filling with people,' Danny said. 'Some of them have got placards like these. Others have very angry objections to any involvement with the war. I saw a few fisticuffs. And the police were looking grim, batons out, several on horseback.'

He turned to Romilly. 'Sure you're still on for this, kid?'

She felt herself stiffen. 'Never more sure of anything. We should practise our moves. Do your worst with me.'

'You sound very confident.' He grinned at her.

'I am.' She moved into position in the space between the table and door.

'I'm no Raoul,' Edward said, 'But I'll stand behind Romilly's left shoulder, see how it looks when Danny puts that left palm to her face.' She found herself between the two men. Each time Danny struck the hand he'd placed on her cheek she seemed to respond more accurately, gasping as she fell back, as much at the expression of hatred on his face.

'It's as though you really hate me,' she told him.

'Nah, you're not so bad, kid. Despite your unfortunate nationality. Come on, try from the other side, in case that's where the best camera angle is.'

She responded better when he came in from her right. 'It's not uncommon to feel sharper on one side. Luckily for you I'm equally gifted from each angle,' he told her.

'And modest with it.'

He winked at her. 'From the left again.'

She groaned.

'Don't forget to keep shouting at me,' he said. 'Right until the moment I hit you.'

Danny was able to throw his blows on both sides more aggressively as her reflexes improved.

'Not bad,' Danny said. 'Not good enough for Broadway but fine for some press photographer.'

'Even when I'm right behind Romilly's shoulder I couldn't catch you doing it, Danny.' Edward nodded. 'Well done, both of you. But the hard part will be knowing you have the right moment. Or moments, if we have to do it again. I'll guide you as much as I can.'

'It'll all be grand.' Danny sounded so confident. As soon as he wasn't staging a blow his body had returned to its relaxed yet alert stance. Years of stage and studio training, she supposed, which she hadn't had. Catherine had been a professional too.

Losing her nerve or fluffing the move could let everyone down. Romilly set her jaw.

'We just need to fix the accent.' Danny looked serious again. 'Call out the slogans again?'

'Fight for freedom. Stop the fascists. Stop the murder and persecution in Europe. America for liberty!' She knew she sounded like what she was: a young woman from London. Catherine, no doubt, would have sounded like an authentic American.

He made her repeat all the slogans, correcting the way she shouted them, insisting that vowels and consonants sounded as though they were emanating from someone who'd been born between the Pacific and Atlantic rather than in Surrey. 'Not bad.' He nodded. 'You'll be carrying the placard and you'll need to drop it as I come towards you. Directly after the blow, put your hands up to your face, so nobody can see it wasn't what it seemed.' He handed her one of the glued placards and they practised again from each side, with her dropping the placard as he approached and covering her cheek immediately after the feigned blow.

'Once you've managed the blow, Danny needs to fade away quickly.' Edward looked at her, frowning. 'Romilly, get out of there swiftly too. Without anyone following you.'

'Following me?'

'Curious journalists. Or others.'

She didn't want to ask who the others might be.

'Find a cab, then come back and wait for me here. We'll leave the key on the basement
windowsill so you can get in.'

The thought of waiting alone in the house made her remember the terrible night when she'd fallen asleep in the bath and dashed out into the streets alone in a panic. Romilly shook herself, remembering that girl hanging from the gallows in Poland. And Edward's sister: probably killed in a German

camp. All she had to do was keep her nerve in a city that wasn't
at war and where people didn't want to kill her.

'Just keep your wits about you,' Edward said. 'Some of the
people on the other side are little more than gangsters.'

'I'll be keeping an eye out,' Danny said. 'I know some of
these people, from the docks. Sure, they'll be looking for a scrap,
but they aren't all bad people.'

While Edward checked the placards for a last time Danny
and Romilly waited at the front door. 'Something about you is
different today.' Danny frowned at her. 'Something's changed,
Romilly.'

He was very perceptive, but of course he was trained to
understand body language. Had he guessed that she and
Edward, well, that they were no longer simply colleagues? Or
perhaps he meant that some of the weight she'd been carrying
since the ship went down, no, from the time of Mama's death,
had slipped off her?

'Oh, I'm probably just more confident,' she told him.

'Good.' Danny pulled his cap down over his brow and she
felt her own hands go to her beret, mirroring him, as though
they were both pulling on helmets. 'I'll hand these out when
we're nearer,' Edward said, looking down at the rolled-up placards. 'Don't get caught up in confrontations until we need to.'

As they headed west, the groups of protestors grew more
concentrated. Romilly glanced at their placards. *DON'T
FOLLOW THE HEADLINES INTO THE FRONTLINE . . .
LET GOD, NOT AMERICA, SAVE THE KING. NOT OUR
FIGHT. . . NEVER AGAIN. . .* 'Show us your signs,' a young
man shouted at Edward. 'Come on, whatever you've got there,
you're either on our side or the other.'

'Later,' Edward called back.

'So you're a warmonger?' a women in a smart buttercup-coloured hat and coat spat at them. *I DID NOT RAISE MY BOY TO FIGHT FOR BRITAIN,* her placard said. Her face was contorted into hatred. 'You want to shed American blood again?'

They walked on. Something landed on Romilly's shoulder, she let out a gasp and looked around. A small stone lay on the sidewalk behind her. 'Hey, honey, whose son or sweetheart you going to send to die?' the woman in the buttercup-coloured hat shouted at her, her face contorted into a sneer.

'You hurt?' Danny asked. She shook her head. 'Good, I won't go back and show that . . . person . . . what I think of her.'

'Just keep walking,' Edward told them. But the fact that they weren't responding to the missile seemed only to inflame the group. They followed, coming closer, the woman's shouts becoming angrier, a rumble of accompanying male voices becoming louder. Romilly didn't look over her shoulder.

Danny took her arm. 'We'll lose them when we cross.' She felt reassured by his presence. The early dislike they'd felt for one another seemed so distant. He was like an old friend now.

They'd reached Sixth Avenue. Edward muttered a quick instruction to cross right in front of a large delivery vehicle, which slammed on its brakes and hooted at them, moving on in time to block their pursuers from crossing with them. Edward took them off down a street whose sign Romilly was too rushed to note, hurrying them on into a recessed shop entrance.

'They mean business.' Danny pointed across the street. 'Look, more of them.' Heading west in front of them was another group of anti-war protestors: men of all ages carrying placards that looked as if they'd been mass-produced.

'Where are those damn photographers?' Edward was looking around. 'Come on, let's walk on quietly behind those men.' They followed the group as they turned left into Seventh Avenue, sticking to it when the men turned off to the right again. Edward was trying to circle round to the Manhattan Center from the south, Romilly realised. But if he'd hoped approaching this way would be quieter, he'd miscalculated. A scuffle broke out in front of them. Two groups confronted one another: anti-fascists and what looked like some kind of young men from a religious organisation, with a priest. Romilly thought of the photograph of the priests on the gallows. If she snatched it from Edward's pocket and marched up to those men, would they even look at it? Perhaps they'd think it was forged.

What they were attempting to do was a kind of forgery too. Danny wasn't really going to hit her, it was pretence. The photograph, if they could pull it off, would show something that hadn't really happened. She felt her footsteps slow. Danny, still holding her arm, looked at her. 'You all right, kid?'

'I'm fine.'

'Nervous?'

She shook her head. It wasn't nerves, just a sick feeling that they were being pulled into a vortex, sucked into something they couldn't control. The sensation was like falling into the Atlantic, the darkness intensifying, impossible to release herself from. The rest of the walk passed in a blur. Ahead of her she saw the illuminated name of Lindbergh on the Center's awning. People were shouting and cheering, the police had arrived and were trying to clear the road, blowing whistles. She could feel something in the atmosphere that was similar to what she'd experienced in the Blitz – that split second just before a large bomb crashed down close by when the air pressure seemed to change. A car was driving behind them. 'It's him.' Edward's voice tight. 'It's Lindbergh.'

Romilly stopped, pulling her arm out of Danny's. As the black sedan drove past – slowly, because of the crowd milling in the street – she turned to look at the passenger.

'That's not one of Lindbergh's own cars. He's got quite a fleet of beauties.' Danny sounded disappointed, but she wasn't listening.

She stared at Charles Lindbergh, famous aviator, father of a tragic little boy who'd died in a botched kidnapping, traveller, diplomat. Hitler appeaser. The man Edward and Leon Belman said had turned a blind eye to the fate of Jewish people like Irma. Irma, who'd sent Freddie to a different country, perhaps never to see him again, because it was the only way to protect him. Lindbergh knew the fate of the children on *The Lucknow*, of the civilians in British cities who'd been bombed, of the families in Poland, France and Belgium. She stared at him, expecting to see something in his features that explained why he felt as he did. All she saw was a pleasant, mild-appearing middle-aged man, who looked like a prosperous farmer, fond of sport. The kind of man Uncle Simon would have played a round of golf with and called a good fellow. Lindbergh seemed to turn and look her in the eye. For less than a second, they gazed at one another. He frowned, not looking angry, but as though wondering what had brought a girl like her out onto the streets to shout and wave a placard.

The car sounded its horn and the crowd let it through.

Edward was handing her a placard. 'We've got to do it now,' he said quickly and quietly. 'The angle's good.' He nodded at a photographer standing just where he'd predicted. So this was it. No backing out now. The cold numbness she'd felt in the Atlantic seemed to sweep her.

Danny moved into position. 'Hold the placard up. Start shouting, Romilly,' he murmured. 'I'm about to lamp you.'

Romilly waved her placard. 'Fight for freedom,' she shouted, surprised at the power in her voice, pleased with her accent. The response was a volley of shouts that she wanted to betray American lives to pay for a European war.

Edward was moving towards her, saying something, a look of urgency in his face. Did he think she wasn't convincing enough? 'Stop the fascists. Stop the murder and persecution in Europe. America for liberty!' She was glowing with passion now, there was nothing acted in her delivery. This moment was what had brought her here, to this street in New York. The people here had to believe in what she was saying, surely they could see the truth in the argument?

'Romilly—' Edward was frowning at something behind her and Danny. 'Come away now.' His arm was reaching for her. 'It's getting too rough, we don't need to do this anymore.'

Did he think she couldn't do this work? Was he still doubting her commitment? Damn him. She'd show him. She raised the placard again. Danny had been grabbed by a man in a leather jacket, he was tussling with him.

'America for liberty. Fight for free—'

'Move out of the way,' Edward shouted at her. 'Now!'

At the same time, Danny freed himself and plunged towards her, fist clenched, a look of hatred on his face. Romilly caught another glimpse of Edward, not watching Danny, but looking at something behind them, raising an arm, trying to stop something. As Danny's fist reached the palm he'd placed on her cheek, she staggered back, the camera flashed. Her look of shock wasn't put on. It hadn't hurt at all, but it would have looked perfect. A good shot for the newspapers. They'd done it. It had all gone as planned.

There was just time to see that Edward was running closer, hand raised, shouting at someone behind her.

Something hit the back of her head, the force sharp enough make her gasp. The camera flashed again.

This hadn't been part of the plan, had it? Shouts rose from the crowd. Danny roared at someone. A female voice yelled back. Romilly's legs had lost their strength. She was falling forwards onto the sidewalk, the placard toppling into the road. *They hadn't needed the stunt after all.*

Everything dimmed. She could just about make out the police horses' hooves coming fast along the road. Edward was kneeling over her, saying something in an urgent tone and someone was blowing a whistle. Was she back in the lifeboat with Freddie whistling for help? But that wasn't right: she was on land, not sea. The sharp pain in the back of her head was turning to a throbbing numbness. She was going to be sick . . . Her mother stood in front of her, telling her something she couldn't quite hear.

Then nothing.

TWENTY-SEVEN

She was somewhere quiet with white walls and people who spoke in urgent tones. Someone shone a torch into her eyes and the light made her head feel as though it was going to split. She must have called out because a hand rested on her shoulder and a needle went into her arm.

Edward said something to her, but she couldn't quite make out what it was. There was something she needed to tell him in turn, but her tongue couldn't seem to form the words. His voice dimmed. She was back in the lifeboat, no longer frightened of the sea, bobbing on the waves. Mrs Dekker rose from the sea. She looked younger, as she must have done at the time of her marriage to Jackson, face smoother. 'You don't belong here.'

Romilly tried to tell her that she wanted to stay in the lifeboat, but Mrs Dekker shook her head.

She was in a hospital bed, curtains pulled around the cubicle. She lifted her left arm to look at her watch. But of course, she wasn't wearing it because it wasn't working. Was it morning?

Afternoon? Evening? Which day? Was this the hospital Mama had died in? She knew this was a wrong supposition, but she needed a moment to work out why. New York. 'I'm in New York, aren't I?' she asked the nurse who came into the cubicle and pulled back the curtains.

'That's right, honey.' The nurse shone the torch into her pupils and put a thermometer under her tongue, looking pleased as she pulled it out. 'How's the head now?' She put her fingers over Romilly's inner wrist, checking her pulse against her watch.

'It hurts.'

'We can give you something for that, once the doctor's been to see you.' The nurse put her arm down gently on the sheet. 'In the meantime, let's sit you up and you can have a sip of water now.'

Romilly drank greedily. The nurse was looking at her curiously. 'What was a nice girl like you doing messed up with something like that rally?'

'America has to come into the war.' Romilly was speaking automatically. 'We can't do it by ourselves.'

'You were prepared to get yourself knocked out, possibly brain-damaged? Possibly even worse?'

'I didn't expect that. Nobody ever does. We just think we can live ordinary, safe lives. Until we can't. Until a torpedo hits us.' It was too much effort. She signed and closed her eyes again.

'That was no torpedo that hit you. It was a brick.'

Romilly opened her mouth to explain but the nurse put a finger up.

'Rest. I'll bring the doctor over shortly.'

Flowers arrived. A bunch of violets with a small white card with a single shamrock drawn on it. 'You've an Irish admirer.' The nurse sounded impressed. Perhaps she was of Irish descent, too. 'Will he visit you when you're allowed people in?'

'He's not my admirer, just someone I worked with.' She blushed, thinking about the man she really did want to visit her. No flowers, no card. Would he come to her?

Romilly lay back on the pillow and closed her eyes. Her brain still felt as though it was in fragments. The air-raid siren, her mother's funeral, *The Lucknow*, the lifeboat, the train to New York with Freddie and the dog: those she could place in the correct position. But everything after that was fragmented. The only thread she could pull through everything was him: Edward. If it had been anyone other than him on *The Lucknow*, would she have been sucked into this kind of work? He'd puzzled her, got under her skin. She'd even felt jealous of Catherine. Then the flicker of something between them had ignited. The intense minutes on the life-raft had pulled them closer together and the sparks had reignited just before the rally, in Mrs Macpherson's dining-room.

But perhaps it was the circumstances they worked in rather than anything deeper. She still didn't know much about him. And in wartime, people were shuffled around. Words of Catherine's echoed in her mind: *There's no point hanging around for them, it could be years they're away. If you're not really serious about someone, it's best to make your own plans.* She'd been talking about men serving in the forces, but the same was true of men who served secretly. And there was no reason to believe Edward regarded her in terms of an ongoing relationship. What had happened could just have been a release of tension before the rally.

He came the next day, preceded by a bunch of roses so large the nurse had to scour the ward for extra vases. 'Danny threw a perfect fake blow.' Edward kissed her gently on the cheek, as he would have done a female colleague. 'So convincing he had some problems explaining to the police that it was, in fact, not him who caused you to drop to the ground and lose consciousness. It was only when the hospital confirmed that the wound to the back of your head was the real damage that they let him go. It made a lot of headlines. I'll show you the newspaper pictures when you're up to it.'

Romilly laughed, wincing at the way her head throbbed if she moved any of its muscles, and resolved to remain very serious. At least for a while. Edward looked serious enough for both of them. 'Where is Danny now? Is he all right?'

'We decided it would be a good plan for him to move back west for a few weeks. There was rather more of his face in the photo than we anticipated. It mightn't be a good career move for him if things turn against Lindbergh and Danny's labelled as one of his supporters.'

'Isolationism might even become unfashionable?'

'Very much so. We've been looking at the opinion polls and there's a swing towards intervening. Americans don't like bullies. Roosevelt is starting to convince them that Hitler will carry on bullying.'

'And the person who threw the brick at me?'

'He'll be charged with assault or whatever the New York version is. I don't think he'll find much public support. The headlines sum it up: *Young Woman Still Unconscious in Hospital after Attack by Isolationist at America First Rally*.' He took her hand. It felt warm in hers. She wanted to cling to it. 'It was a miracle that thug didn't actually kill you. Even the pro-Lindbergh heavies were shocked. They melted away from the scene, muttering about never meaning to take things that far.'

'The authorities must know I'm British though?' They'd have looked in her satchel, found her passport. 'Are they talking about dirty tricks by a foreign power?'

'So far, your nationality hasn't been mentioned. The

general outrage means they aren't motivated to ask too many questions of an unarmed young female.' Edward paused and looked at Romilly, a serious expression on his face. 'I've arranged for your passport to be stamped with a new visa. You now work for the British Press Service, if that's okay with you? Your task is to monitor public opinion polls.'

Romilly sniffed. 'The British Press Service? The place that didn't seem to know who you were?'

'They certainly know who *you* are now.'

She smiled. 'What about you? Did you get away afterwards?'

He shuffled on the chair.

'The police arrested you?'

'That wasn't what they called it, but I had the feeling they weren't going to let me leave the interview until they were happy.'

'You should have left me. Nobody would have known you were involved.'

He looked at her indignantly. 'Of course I wouldn't leave you. Anyway, the situation was resolved.'

'Really?'

'Eventually, the American intelligence people we know here put in a good word for me. The photograph was cleared as authentic.'

'So we can carry on?'

He shook his head. 'Any involvement by me or you in any similar operations in New York or elsewhere is over. If they catch either of us within a mile of a Lindbergh rally, things will get unpleasant. And they mean it.'

She felt as though all the energy she'd regained in the last few days had puffed away, leaving her flattened. So that was that.

He let go of her hand and patted her bag where it hung on

the back of his chair. 'They found this and gave it to me, asked me to check that everything in it belonged to you.' He paused. 'Romilly . . . that written account of yours.'

'What about it?' She could feel her cheeks burning with mortification.

'I don't even know why we asked you to pull a stunt like this when all the time you were writing something like that.'

'You read it?

'I shouldn't have, I know I shouldn't have.' He groaned. 'I couldn't stop.'

'Is that good?'

'It's not good, Romilly, it's fantastic. And I have to ask you something.'

She looked at him.

'Would you consider letting me find a home for it in one of the papers here? Or possibly even turn it into a radio piece?'

'It's not very heroic.' She was thinking about how they'd floated Jennifer and the rabbi off the lifeboat. How she'd described what Aunt Ursula would call the lavatory arrangements. How she'd dried her sodden underwear in the lieutenant's cabin. 'I'd be a bit embarrassed.'

'Of course.' He nodded. 'I hope you don't mind me asking.'

'I never thought anyone apart from me would read it.' She wasn't sure about other people looking at her work. The old Romilly fretted that the words wouldn't be good enough. She thought of school essays marked up with teachers' ink. But damn it, she was the one who'd been on *The Lucknow*, not old schoolteachers. She'd smelled the burning metal and oil, the urine in the lifeboat, the stink of her own body when they were finally taken onboard. Those families in this city, this country planning their evenings, their weekends, their spring outfits, they should know about it all, even if it shocked – appalled – them. 'Let me think about it.'

She and Edward sat in silence for a while. He stood up, picking his trilby off his lap.

'As soon as you're fully recovered, your new job at the Rockefeller is waiting for you,' he said. 'Interesting work, analytical, charting how public opinion changes and what influences it. Decent salary. You can live at the Belmans' and have that delightful walk to work each morning.'

She was shaking her head.

'Romilly?'

'I'm not staying in New York.' Her own words surprised her. She hadn't realised she'd come to a decision yet, but as soon as they were spoken, they became so obviously the truth.

'You want to move on?' Hard to interpret his expression. 'There's Washington, that's probably still open to you? I can understand why something like this would put you off. But violence like you experienced is very rare in most of this country.'

'I can't be here any longer. I'm going home.' As she spoke the words, she realised how true they were.

'But I thought you were desperate to get out of England?'

'I was sick of London. I hated it. I hated . . . well, you've read the journal so you know what happened.' How much had she written about Mama? Or Philip? She tried to remember. She hadn't written anything about Edward in it, had she? About what that had passed between them on the deck just before the torpedo struck?

'I skipped over the personal bits,' he said softly. 'I shouldn't have read any of it, I know. But not those parts. I could see that they weren't for anyone else's eyes.'

'You can publish it.'

He frowned at her. 'But—'

'I'll write a version that doesn't have those . . . parts in it. But the rest is yours.'

He was still looking puzzled.

'I wrote it and I don't need it anymore.'

'You're a very talented writer, Romilly. Stay here and produce articles we can place in the papers?'

She looked down at the white sheet beneath her hands. 'I'm going home. You probably think I'm still concussed. But I'm not. I came here to New York, running away, thinking it would be an easier life.'

He started apologising again for what had happened outside the Manhattan Center. She put up a hand and stopped him. 'First the torpedo and then . . . But I managed. I survived. Those were both tough things, but here I am.'

'But why go back to London, Romilly? There's plenty more that's useful you could do here. More than useful – vital.'

Only a few days before she'd have stayed in Manhattan if he'd asked. Stayed, and felt overjoyed that he wanted her to remain.

'I'm not even sure I know completely why myself. When that man threw the brick at me and I fell down, perhaps it knocked something loose in here.' She put a hand gingerly to her head. Edward winced, watching her. 'But I think it was something I'd already worked out. While I was lighting a candle in the cathedral or writing in my notepad, maybe.'

'What did you work out?'

'My head's still too woolly to say it very elegantly. I love New York. But I don't think it's where I should be.'

'Everything you wanted to leave is still there at home, though, isn't it?'

She nodded slowly. 'The bombs. The dirt. The shortages and rations. My mother being . . . gone. I was so, so relieved to run away from it all. But now I want to go back. I might even join up.' She laughed. 'Who'd have thought it? Perhaps I could train to drive ambulances or become a despatch rider for the Wrens. I'd be doing something practical. Directly helping people.'

'They have particularly smart uniforms, the Wrens.' He smiled, but it was a rueful smile. 'Do you have friends, other family who can help you?'

'An unenthusiastic uncle. A former employer. But I'll get by.' She met his probing look. 'I'll miss people here, of course I will.' She waited for him to tell her how much he'd miss her. His lips were opening but he didn't say anything for a moment.

'Young Freddie will be very sorry to lose you.'

The thought of telling Freddie made her feel tired. Edward was a good listener, though something in his expression still made her think that he was holding back. They sat silently for a while.

'What about you?' she asked him. 'Will you stay in New York?'

He sat down again, lowering his voice. 'The original plan was for me to follow Lindbergh around, one rally to another. Stirring things up, ensuring there were good pictures for the press showing what we wanted them to see. But as I said, I've been warned off now. Perhaps there's enough happening organically anyway to make good newspaper headlines and photographs.'

'Reality is more convincing than pretence?'

He nodded.

'There's real momentum now.' The tone of his voice changed. 'And I've been asked to go back to England too.'

She sat straighter. 'Just for a trip? Or permanently?'

'What does permanent even mean in wartime, Romilly? First, I'm heading south on a jaunt across the southern border. For a month or so before I head back to London. Hopefully on a voyage where the most exciting thing that happens is fresh vegetables served at dinner.'

So they'd both be back in England. He'd waited until he was sure of her motives in returning before dropping in that information. Why? To make it clear he had no interest in pursuing a relationship? There was so much unsaid, and time was running out. Any moment now the nurse would come in and declare visiting time over.

'You're going to Mexico?'

'Further south.' He lowered his voice. 'Argentina. There's German activity down there we need to monitor. America's a big country, but it's not as cut off from the Nazis as some think.'

The war, it was sometimes hard to grasp how wide its tentacles spread. She wondered whether she'd ever see Edward again even if he did come to London. The thought made her feel heavy inside, but she wasn't going to tell him that. Again, Catherine's words flitted through her mind. She couldn't base her decisions around someone else.

She released her hand gently and smiled at him. 'So it all worked out as we wanted. Just not in the way we planned.'

'Perhaps there really is such a thing as destiny. We're going to write you a cracking reference.'

She noted the use of the plural. He stood up again. 'I'll deliver it to the hotel we've arranged, along with your wages and Danny's address. I'll speak to the Consulate and see if I can hurry along your passage home. May not be a *Lucknow* experience, just to warn you.'

'Nothing would make me happier than it not being like *The Lucknow*.'

'It was good, though, wasn't it? The meals, the library, that wonderful staircase and gallery. The whole voyage – right until the moment the torpedo struck.'

She looked him directly in the eye. 'I thought the very last minutes before the torpedo was the best bit.'

He held the eye contact. 'So did I, until the minutes in Mrs Macpherson's dusty old dining-room.' His voice sounded as though he had something stuck in his throat. He bent forward towards her, close enough for her to make out the scent of his freshly laundered shirt. 'They were definitely the best minutes.'

His mouth moved onto hers and they kissed, long, slow and deep. She held onto the lapels of his jacket for a moment. 'When I get to England, I'll find you, Romilly,' he said. 'I'll give you my cousin's address, the one with the children. Write to me there with your address and where you're working. I'll find you.'

'I don't know where I'll be.' She ought to feel daunted, but she didn't.

'Wherever you go, I'll come to you. Even if it's only for a few days' leave—' he looked at her with intent—'Days and nights.' The rougher yet more caressing regional accent had taken over again. She felt the nerves in her body come to life with the thrill of imagining the two of them, alone, unencumbered by other responsibilities, perhaps sneaking away to a country inn with a tolerant landlord, somewhere where the food might be a little more generous and there'd be no questions asked. 'I'll find you, Romilly. This isn't over.' She reached up and touched his head, very gently, on the temple that had been bloodied. The scar was healing well. So was her own head.

His face lowered towards hers again, his eyes half-closed and she moved her hand away from his forehead to brush her fingers through the hair at the back of his head. This kiss, urgent, almost rough, more matched the tone of his real accent, the person Edward really was. It felt as though they were finally meeting on equal terms, no longer puppet master and ingenue. The nurse clearing her throat made them separate. 'That's one way to manage a head injury,' she said, 'but not what the doctor prescribed, Miss Brooks.'

She probably wouldn't be staying in a room like this again for a long, long time, so she let herself sink back into the comfortable desk chair and enjoy the scent of the roses on the desk. Beneath her, New York's vehicles and pedestrians emitted a distant hum. It was restful to be sitting back while the city busied itself, but she needed to get going, she had people to see.

The hotel was only two blocks from Central Park. For what would be the last time, she walked up towards the Belmans', stopping to admire the mansions and the fresh green on the trees across in the park, lapping up the women in their spring outfits.

The doorman was standing just outside the apartment entrance. He nodded at her. 'Good to see you again, Miss Brooks.' She had the slippers he'd lent her in her bag and took them out, with a thank you. 'Just in case you need to rescue any other barefoot visitors.' This morning she was wearing her new shoes – with stockings – and all was well with her feet.

When Nina took her through, Freddie was lying on the floor, both his cousins piled on top of him in some kind of tick-ling contest, with Smoky running around, tail wagging. 'It's a madhouse in here,' Ruth said, coming in. 'We're off to the Park later on. Everyone needs to burn off their spring madness.' She said something to her own two in a low voice and they stood up, smiling politely at Romilly and leaving the room. Ruth made an excuse too. It was just Romilly, Freddie and Smoky again. She sat down on the rug next to them.

On her way here she'd thought about how to tell him. Perhaps start by asking him whether he'd made the decision about which baseball team he was going to support, concentrate attention on how well things were going for him now. But she couldn't bring herself to stall or tell him how he ought to feel about her departure. After all they'd been through together, he deserved directness. 'I'm going back to London, Freddie.' As she said it, she felt a pang.

He looked down at Smoky. 'Why? I thought you liked it here.'

'I want to join up. Do something for the war. Fight the Nazis.'

'How?'

'I fancy myself as a despatch rider.'

He looked up, interested. 'One of those girls on the big motorcycles? A proper tiger.'

She smiled, raising her palms and curling her fingers like claws. 'So I have to go back.'

He was silent. Romilly wanted to say more, but instinct told her to keep quiet. Forcing words out of him wouldn't help. Smoky yawned and stretched out on the carpet between them. She stroked his back. The dog's coat was glossy and he looked as if he'd put on weight. He mightn't fit inside a lifejacket these days.

Freddie got up and ran out of the room. 'Freddie . . .' She stood up too, not sure what to do: find Ruth, confess that she'd handled this terribly. But he was already coming back, holding something in his hands. A parcel.

'We were going to mail this to Mrs Cohen. But you could take it?'

He handed it to her.

'It's toys for the boys and food for Mrs Cohen. Things she can't get easily. Coffee. A bag of sugar. Chocolate. I chose it all myself because I know what they like. And a postcard.'

'I'll go down to Whitechapel myself and deliver it to them.' She swallowed hard. This boy had made such an adjustment to his new life. Again. He'd nearly died and yet he'd been able to think of the family he'd left in London.

Ruth returned. 'I overheard – you're leaving New York for London?' She looked thoughtful. 'Don't you want to stay where it's safe, though, Romilly? Our offer to put you up stands. And Leon and I will do all we can to help you settle in, introduce you to people.'

Romilly put a hand to the back of her head, as though the bump there would remind her of what had happened to her here. 'Thank you.' She really meant it and hoped Ruth could hear the gratitude in her voice. Half of her still very much wanted to stay in New York. 'But sometimes you're better off in the place you ran away from.'

Ruth stood behind Freddie, placing her arms tight around him as she stepped into the escalator.

TWENTY-EIGHT

One of them. That's what she was: one of those who were returning to a battered country still fighting on alone. Standing out on deck with the other returners and watching New York drop away made Romilly feel a kinship with her fellow passengers she hadn't expected. They exchanged half-grins. *What on earth are we doing – heading back home?* Romilly felt her stomach lurch. Even as she'd walked up the gangway, she'd had to restrain herself from turning around.

No painted and moulded plaster domes on *The Calypso*. No galleries opening to a better class of cabin at the ship's fore. No lilies wafting perfume around the passengers. What scent Romilly could smell was a mixture of fuel and grease. They were on an old liner that had been converted into a troopship and now transported cargo and civilians foolish enough to be returning to their homeland. Romilly was sharing a tiny cabin with an English girl returning from New York to take up a job as a secretary somewhere in the War Office. 'At least we're going directly and not having to go all the way up to Montreal or Halifax for embarkation,' her cabin mate told her, standing beside her on the deck. 'Longer at sea, though.'

Longer at sea. More chance of a German patrol intercepting them. Romilly could have waited for a berth in an American ship, sailed under what was still a neutral flag, but *The Calypso* was sailing earlier. Once she'd made her mind up, she hadn't wanted to delay her departure.

She'd hung on in New York only until she could produce a clean copy of what she'd written in her journal, taking out the bits about her mother. Edward had already left town, but a courier had been sent to the hotel to collect Romilly's hand-written pages. Romilly didn't know where the account would be placed, once typed up. She might never know, she realised.

The Statue of Liberty was falling back. Romilly watched her until her eyes grew dry. Her cabin mate sniffed. 'I know I'm doing the patriotic thing, but I loved New York.'

'So did I. Although I was only there for a very short time.'

'I tell myself I'll be fine once I've seen my people again. The voyage will be the worst thing. Even if we don't come across the Germans, this isn't exactly a luxury cruise, is it?'

Comfort and brightness was not what this voyage promised. Nor was it likely to be offered at their destination.

Romilly had telegraphed Uncle Simon to tell him she was coming back to England. Perhaps he'd be at Liverpool or Euston to greet her. Probably not. Travel by train for non-essential reasons was not encouraged in Britain. She had enough money to put herself up in a women's hostel in London until she could join up. Once you were serving, there was no need to worry about accommodation. And there'd be new friends to make, too. She gave a wry grin at herself: Romilly Brooks – putting on uniform, looking forward to companionship, facing the future squarely.

Emergency drill was about to commence. Romilly took the card she was handed and studied it carefully, her attention focused completely on the location of lifeboats and rafts. She glanced down at the sea and felt none of the pressing terror she'd experienced standing on the bridge. Had the fear been exorcised? Too early to tell, but she could live with it even if she couldn't defeat it.

Edward had sent her a small jeweller's box before he'd left New York. It contained a gold brooch in the shape of a clover leaf. The brooch was now pinned to her jacket lapel. She placed a finger on it and felt the luck. And the promise of future meetings still to come.

When she looked up again, the Statue of Liberty had almost vanished. She said a silent farewell to the city, promising to return one day.

A LETTER FROM THE AUTHOR

Dear Reader,

Huge thanks for reading *The Girl in Lifeboat Six*, I hope you enjoyed Romilly's voyage and adventures in New York. If you want to join other readers in hearing all about my new releases and bonus content, you can sign up here:

www.stormpublishing.co/eliza-graham

And if you would like to sign up for my regular newsletter, please click here:

www.elizagrahamauthor.com/newsletter

If you enjoyed this book and could spare a few moments to leave a review that would be hugely appreciated. Even a short review can make all the difference in encouraging a reader to discover my books for the first time. Thank you so much!

I think it was watching one of the many *Titanic* films or TV series that first made me ponder why disasters at sea make such compelling if tragic viewing. Frail human bodies in a metal structure that's collapsing under the weight of water rushing in? Knowing that even if they escape the doomed ship, they're faced with lifeboats (at best) in inhospitable waters? Trying to predict which of the characters will rise to the challenge and help their fellow passengers? Which of them will think only of themselves?

Visiting the wonderful Maritime Museum in Liverpool made me aware of the fate of the passengers on the liner *City of Benares*, which was torpedoed and sunk in September 1940, with the loss of many children's lives. There's a horrible irony in evacuee children going to America to escape the bombs but dying in their attempt. Two books were useful here for researching the Benares story: *Children of the Benares* by Ralph Barker, and *Miracles on the Water* by Tom Nagorski. I tweaked the timing of my book slightly as most of the more official child evacuations to the US happened earlier in the war. The voyage of *The Lucknow* takes place when it does, in the spring of 1941, because I wanted Romilly to be caught up in the Lindbergh rallies in America.

Agents of Influence was my source for a lot of the background to British 'persuasion' campaigns in America in the early years of the war. I wrote an earlier novel (*The Truth in Our Lies*) about propaganda during the Second World War and mentally tucked away the information concerning British efforts to influence American attitudes to joining the fight.

Philip Roth's *The Plot Against America* and the TV miniseries also gave colour to the period: fictionalised, of course, but with a starting point that was historically accurate, even if Lindbergh never became president. *Lindbergh* by A. Scott Berg was a book I started reading just to get a feel for Lindbergh's activities after 1939, the rallies in particular. I found myself going right the way through to his death in 1974 so gripped was I by the account of this controversial yet mesmerising and gifted figure.

When I was researching the New York scenes and who lived where, *City of Dreams* by Tyler Anbinder was very useful in explaining how waves of immigration rippled through boroughs and districts.

The story of Romilly's mother's death from an infection following a back-street abortion was a sadly not-uncommon one in the 1940s. Her aunt's fear that Romilly's reputation would be harmed as much by the evidence of her mother's adulterous pregnancy as by the illegal termination itself was also based on what I read about social attitudes then.

Thanks again for being part of this amazing journey with me and I hope you'll stay in touch – I have so many more stories and ideas to entertain you with!

ELIZA

 facebook.com/ElizaGrahamUK

 instagram.com/elizagraham1

ACKNOWLEDGMENTS

Huge thanks to Kathryn Taussig, my acquiring editor at Storm Publishing, for all her enthusiasm for The Girl in Lifeboat Six and for signing me up to Storm. And to Melissa Boyce-Hurd, Alexandra Holmes, Emily Gowers and Anna McKerrow for all their help and work on the book. It's been a very exciting time for me.

Thanks also to Liz Hurst for her catches on the manuscript. I love my cover art, the work of the talented Sarah Whittaker.

And as ever, I couldn't have written the book without the loyal support of Johnnie, my husband, and of Kristina Riggle, my critique partner, with whom I've been exchanging works-in-progress for what must be at least 18 years, during which time our children have almost all grown up and we have welcomed a series of dogs into our lives.

Printed in Great Britain
by Amazon

27705226R00200